Refashioned by Love

LOVE BY DESIGN
BOOK ONE

TARA L. ROÍ

BEE BOOKS
NEW HAVEN

Refashioned By Love

Love By Design series book 1

Tara L. Roí

As always, for MacKenzie

Acknowledgments

This book was my thesis at Seton Hill University's MFA in Writing Popular Fiction program. I'm indebted to program director Nicole Peeler, Professor Lee Tobin McClain, and mentor Heidi Ruby Miller for persuading me to start a new project for the program and for their expert guidance as I selected between the two ideas that intrigued me. Mentor and friend Priscilla Oliveras read multiple drafts and offered crucial notes to help me improve both the manuscript and my skills as a writer.

Special thanks to my Seton Hill critique partners: Meghan Spelbrink, Iris Matthews, Debbie Reynolds, Laura Marr, and Jen Gibson.

I'm also indebted to my beta readers Corrina Lawson and Bethany J. Miller, as well as to the members of New Haven Writers Group: Greg Greenberg, Sarah Harris Wallman, Susan Nathiel, Ken Levine, and Matthew F. Light.

Deep gratitude to Jess Pryde for copyediting.

Finally, if Thalia's dialogue has any sense of Gen-Z realism, it is thanks to input from my daughter and her friends, aka. "The Insult Assembly," who provided numerous helpful responses to my random text messages asking things like, "How would you describe someone who's...?"

Chapter One

JOSEPHINE

THE CLUB MUSIC filling the gallery boosts my pre-show adrenaline and guides my pace as I stride past each mannequin. Everything looks perfect. Except the sheath under this window-screen ballgown. How did that get askew?

I crouch, slip my hands under the satin-edged hem, and tug the linen into place. Now I can breathe. In theory. Before I'm fully standing, my mind hits overdrive. Again. One side of my brain whispers tales of disaster. The other weaves stories of hope: great press, big sales, enough money to launch my fashion house. A house that pays artisans well and offers a caring workplace. If I succeed tonight, that might be possible.

My phone chimes. Fifteen minutes until showtime. I need to run the models through their spiels and check in with Kath. Connecticut's top art gallerist and my BFF, Kath huddles over the sales desk with her assistant. I hurry past, resisting the temptation to pause and critique the film projected on the wall behind them. The video does its job:

showcase how I bring my designs to life. Not make me look glamorous.

Fourteen minutes, thirty seconds.

I enter the back office, gather the models in a circle, give a mini pep talk, and ask for a volunteer to start the run-through. The girl with the fish-out-of-water makeup steps to the center of the circle. God, I love that look on her. Blue lip glaze, sparkling skin, glossy black hair slicked back and gelled to look like a fin.

"The outfit I'm wearing is called *Modern Mermaid*." Her husky voice raises this outfit's sex appeal to glacier-melting. "The tuxedo board shorts and bustier feature neoprene dreadlocks."

My lungs seize. The other models stifle giggles. I raise my hand. "Deadstock," I correct.

"Huh?" she asks.

"Dreadlocks is a hairstyle. Deadstock means fabric or garments discarded by fashion houses to keep the perceived value of their clothing high."

Her eyes go wide, making the biodegradable false eyelashes pop against arcs of electric blue and teal eyeshadow. Stunning. Now, if she can get the story right. She apologizes.

I force calm into my voice. "No worries. Try again."

The model shakes her arms and re-starts, watching me. "…The board shorts and bustier feature neoprene *deadstock* with upcycled satin side panels. Ms. Stewart made the colorful buttons from bottle caps found during walks at Lighthouse Point Park here in New Haven."

I flash her a thumbs up. She continues. "It's a story about the fast fashion industry polluting our oceans and rivers with microplastics and petroleum-based dyes."

"Perfect." I lead a round of applause and gesture at another model. The scent of Kath's homemade bergamot and grapefruit body oil surrounds me. She links her arm through mine, a comfort that helps me hear the other models recite their stories.

I met Kath in drawing class twenty-five years ago. Through my struggle to pass Econ 101, my disastrous corporate wife experience, through the sublime years raising my child alone, then grieving when my daughter left home... Kath encouraged me to keep sewing, keep feeding my soul. She and her wife have bolstered me through a string of nightmare jobs at nonprofits that "improve society" while treating employees like garbage.

Speaking of which, my phone screams—another call from my boss, probably demanding I discuss the new brochures with him *now*. I already reminded him my show is tonight; that I'm contracted for three days a week and Friday isn't one of them. Still, he's texted or called nine times in two hours. How do people stand it? I need out, which makes tonight extra important. I silence the phone in my pocket and lean into Kath.

My garment stories shine thanks to her editing. Pride fills me as the woman in *Airy Fairy*, the plus-sized ballgown made from layers of upcycled tulle, shares her key fact, bringing our rehearsal to a close.

I let out a whoop and catch each model's gaze. "You look fantastic. I hope you're as excited about tonight as I am." *But way more relaxed*. "Let's have fun."

Kath adds, "Remember, once you share the story, send the person to me or Josephine for more info." As the models file out of her office, she turns to me and mouths, "Ready?"

I grin, excitement kicking in.

"I predict phenomenal success, Josie. The *Register* article was brilliant. Hopefully, the reporter from *The New Yorker* will arrive soon."

My heart stops. "*The New Yorker*," I squeak.

"He called to apologize. Apparently, 95's a mess with road construction."

"A major magazine is sending a journalist, and you're telling me *now*?"

"This…" She waves her hand in front of me. "Trembling, hyperventilating… is why I waited. Had I told you yesterday, you would've spent twenty-four hours fretting. Breathe. When he interviews you, focus on your vision and the show's theme."

"Right. Overconsumption must end. Fast fashion is killing us. I see a better way through transparency, accountability, and let's stop using the term sustainable because it's—"

"No long rants, Josie," Kath interrupts.

—*lost all meaning*. The words die on my lips. I know this. I've been discussing story and branding ad nauseam for years, thanks to my work in the nonprofit world. Yet when speaking of my passion, I can't seem to rein it in. Disaster scenarios get louder in my head.

"Why the fear in your eyes?" she asks.

"Want the whole list?"

"Top three. Time is short."

"One: What if this journalist *others* me and writes about my Biracial heritage instead of how I'm trying to model healing in an industry that's literally killing people?"

Kath growls. "You can refuse to answer questions on that topic. And if he's fool enough to focus on your heritage: fine. He's giving you international exposure. You follow?"

"Press is press. Right. Two: what if my parents show up and make a scene?"

"Oh, darling, that's more fantasy than fear, isn't it? When was the last time they showed up for you, even when they promised to?" Kath's reality check simultaneously deflates me and brings a wave of relief.

"Three: What if nothing sells?"

She scoffs. "Please. Did I build K-gallery by coddling

untalented friends? Your work sells because you're an artist with a bold message and a master at your craft."

"A master." I snort.

She points at me. "Say it."

I lengthen my spine. "I am Josephine Stewart, Multimedia Artist and Fashion Designer."

"Confident. Serene."

I lift an eyebrow. If I could absorb a teaspoon of her confidence...

Kath lowers her cat-eye glasses, gray eyes holding my gaze. "Visionary. Eloquent."

"Occasionally eloquent."

"A stubborn mule. Darling, from the moment you showed me that first trashion purse all those years ago, I thought: *Here's something fresh*. And you've grown bolder with every show. You finally ripped away that caution tape you used to wrap around your dreams."

She places her hand on my back and prods me out of her office, down the hall into the gallery. "But you still cling to the damn wad of caution tape. Can you please free yourself?" she asks, examining the refreshment table.

Free myself... I've longed to for decades, yet I always wind up tangled in other people's expectations and restrictions. With a deep breath, I cry, "Caution tape, away," and throw my arm out, air-tossing a roll of caution tape. Imagining yellow plastic landing in a tree makes me shiver with guilt. "Metaphorically," I say. "I'd never really toss plastic like that."

"You'd never forgive yourself," she deadpans, as the opening notes of "I Believe In A Thing Called Love" blast through the tinny speakers of her watch. "Here we go." Kath winks at me and strides to the door, her ballgown's stiff bustled skirt swishing behind her.

Looking out the plate-glass windows for the first time in hours, I'm stunned by the crowd. Two scenarios rise within me again. Disaster scenes make me want to hide behind a barricade. Are people here to watch me cower? No. They want hope, fun. They're here to discover how someone can turn garbage into beautiful garments. No more smothering my dreams. I throw caution to the wind and boldly meet the future I design.

THEO

I plug the car into the charger and rush toward the gallery. I have a good feeling about this artist, and I'm eager to see her show. This could be the start of an exciting partnership. If I get there in time to meet her. Twenty minutes stuck on the highway offramp. Fuck.

And now I'm held back by a line rivaling a rock concert. Frustration churns my gut. Are this many people interested in trash fashion? I'd never heard of it until Kim handed me the article this morning with an ebullient, "Check this out, Theo." Once again, my assistant was right. Still, I never imagined there were this many die-hard fashionistas in New Haven. Who else would brave Chapel Street on an evening like this? Slate sidewalks radiate heat absorbed from the day's intense sun, magnifying the ambient ninety-degree temps. And the humidity... brutal. I pull the handkerchief from my pocket and wipe moisture off my head.

At last, the line moves, bringing me close enough to read the words emblazoned on the gallery's plate-glass window in bold script:

The End of The Catwalk. Trashion. Transparency. Truth.

Eager to know this artist's truth, I check my watch. Seven-fifteen. The reception ends at eight. Will forty-five minutes be enough to see all the work and meet Ms. Stewart?

At seven-twenty, I emerge from the bottleneck of people by the door and find a mannequin in a full-length gown made of caution tape. Interesting. The plaque on the wall by the art gives stats about construction industry waste. I snap a pic and make a note in the app Kim installed.

She was a smart hire. Thanks to her research report and clever idea to upload it so I could listen en route from my meeting, I understand the trashion movement. Trashion differentiates itself from sustainable clothing manufacturers like Patagonia and Eileen Fisher, although those corporations also champion a triple bottom line mentality: people, planet, profit.

I have so many questions for Ms. Stewart, starting with: *Where do you see your work in relation to the art and corporate worlds?* If I can find her. Too bad the article didn't include a photo of the designer. In this crowd, trying to spot a woman I've never seen will make finding a *#N/A error* in a spreadsheet seem easy.

In the center of the room, a mannequin sports an elegant black mini-dress. Made of rubber? I move toward it, side-stepping to avoid bumping someone. Her white and black makeup contrasts with her colorful 1950s-style dress of... what is that? She smiles wide, an invitation.

I return the smile. "Great show. Are you Ms. Stewart?"

"I'm one of ten live models wearing her work. Would you like to hear this dress's story?"

"Please." I've never heard the word "story" used in relation to clothing. Intriguing.

"I'm wearing *Advertise Me*, a statement about waste created by consumerism. The artist made it from a billboard she found in Tokyo."

"Innovative. How did she manage that?"

"Kath has more info. See her? Steampunk gown matching mine? Sparkly cat-eye glasses?"

Steampunk? Cat-eye? The words lose me, so I follow the

model's gesture to the woman in question, then weave and dodge people until I reach her.

Kath's head-to-toe scan of me is so subtle, I almost miss her glancing at my Patek Phillipe watch. Her smile reveals she knows I can buy anything here. Good salesperson.

"Welcome to K-Gallery. I'm Kath Word, proprietress." Her appearance and strident voice bear stunning resemblance to Katharine Hepburn, my mother's favorite actress. There's something else in her voice, a slight twang from somewhere in the Midwest, covered with a northeastern affectation. She extends her hand, and I take it.

"Theo Casabella. Fantastic show. What can you tell me about these pieces?"

"Well, Theo, Josephine Stewart is making a statement about overconsumption. As a society, we fail to consider how often we buy new clothes or the true costs of production because the fast-fashion industry—"

"Fast fashion? Wait. I read about this. Companies like Shine..."

"Precisely. Even the high-end designer tee and trousers you're wearing. Your casual Friday attire is a garment worker's substandard wages and working conditions. Plus, the likelihood of their getting cancer or another killer disease caused by pollution from the factory where they work."

My stomach clenches. A thousand memories of Isabella flash through my mind. Her forgiveness. Her understanding. Most people would've reviled my family after learning our business polluted the water feeding their well. She and her parents gave me courage.

"Have I hit a nerve?" Kath cocks her head, curious.

"I can't bear that people suffer needlessly, especially when others are profiting from it."

Her voice brightens. "I appreciate your enlightened mindset."

If I hadn't met Isabella and her family, I might not be so

"enlightened," might never have felt the impact of NorEast Waste Management's practices. Would Isabella's parents feel better knowing I turned my family company around? With effort, I keep my voice even. "This show will certainly have me thinking twice about the clothes I buy."

Kath's eyes light up behind her glittery glasses. "At heart, fashion is personal. After that superstorm in 2019 turned our lives upside down, my wife and I were struggling. Josie made this to uplift me." She sweeps her hand over the dress, then turns to reveal hundreds of vinyl pieces that extend the back by at least a foot. The effect is an elegant and playful shape reminiscent of Georges Seurat's *A Sunday Afternoon on the Island of La Grand Jatte*.

"Impressive. I'd love to meet Ms. Stewart."

"She's currently beside the mannequin in the pop top shift."

"The what?"

"Oh, you New Englanders. The shift dress made from soda can tabs." Kath points.

I scan the room until I see the silver garment. "Is that what that is?"

"Mm-hmm. See Josephine in the glitzy tiara? She made it from die-cut street signs. Dark curls. Beautiful skin. She's with the reporter from *The New Yorker*. I'd give her a moment."

There's Ms. Stewart. Stunning. High cheekbones. Full lips parted slightly as she listens to the journalist. She responds with an intensity I rarely see, animating her words with graceful gestures, like a conductor in the pit at the opera. I can almost feel her voice's music from across the room. My body thrums in response.

"A pleasure to meet you, Theo. You'll excuse me, won't you?"

I bow my head to Kath, and she glides into the crowd. My eyes dart back to Josephine Stewart, which revs my engine again. Not good. I'm here to explore an investment opportunity. The last thing I need is a complication between my business and personal life. A ridiculous train of thought. So she's hot. I've never let a sexy woman distract me from my mission before.

JOSEPHINE

Well, I threw something to the wind. Caution? More like all my chances for success. I press my lips together—too late —as the reporter from *The New Yorker* slips into the crowd. Did I even give him a chance to ask questions? I close my eyes to erase the disaster and say a silent prayer that the article will put my work in a positive light, even if I come off like a self-righteous jerk.

Kath said, *"No long rants."* Yet off I went, dominating the conversation with a tangent about sustainability becoming a bullshit term. Bitching about carbon offsets being a shell game. Did I mention why we omitted a catwalk? Did I talk about how couture needs to come off the runway, to be accessible and transparent, so people can see what goes into making their clothes? Ugh. His mouth hung open. *My* mouth kept moving.

Now I fake a smile at the young couple approaching me. I pretend I didn't just blow my dream career, explain my creative process in a sentence, and encourage them to find the models.

Thankfully, someone who loves me no matter how badly I humiliate myself has arrived. The light of my life beams at me and squeezes her way through the crowd, totally rocking the 1970s Diane von Fürstenberg vibe. That's my girl.

"Hi, Mama." She giggles as she comes to my side.

"Muffin! Why are you laughing?"

"You look so happy. Show adrenaline?"

"That, and you're here."

She makes a gagging sound.

I cup her face in my palms and kiss her forehead. "Every time I see your precious face, it's like my heart has returned."

"Oh, Mama." She pulls me into a tight hug. Heaven.

She feels thin. Has she been taking care of herself? "You look wonderful, Thalia. Is this vintage DVF?"

"Yup. Fifteen bucks at the new thrift store near work."

"Nice! Hey, are you hungry?"

Ignoring the question, Thalia steps back and assesses me. "You are *having a moment*. Hand beaded, right? The drop waist is a whole ass vibe, and the sheen of silk shantung on you... It hits."

I strike a pose. "Whole ass vibe is good?"

She laughs. "Very. Also, the show is lit."

"Thanks, Muffin. How are you? How was the train? Did you eat? Kath got a wonderful selection of crudités, your favorite crackers, and that hummus you like with the beets in it."

"I'll grab something in a bit. I wanna chat with you before your fans swarm again."

"Fans." I snort. "Have you been eating?"

"All the time." Thalia takes my face in her hands, grinning as she mimics my classic move. "Stop worrying. I've got the adulting thing down. And you've got fans to satisfy." She gestures to the crowd. "You've noticed it's wall-to-wall people. Right? The line to get in goes all the way down the block, past Claire's and around the corner onto College. Once I got through the line, it took me fifteen minutes to find you."

"Seriously?"

"In fact, there's another fan. See that guy staring at you?"

"I see a bunch of guys, none of them staring."

"By the credit card dress. The old—" Thalia clamps her mouth closed as her cheeks grow pink. "Uh, I mean, the tall guy about your age. Linen tee and trousers. Expensive shoes.”

Ignoring the “old” comment, I follow her gaze. A purr escapes me. I hope Thalia didn't hear. But that man… well-built, forty-something, staring at me. My word. T-shirts were made for those pecs. He runs a hand across his shaved head, and his bicep peeks out of his sleeve. Thank God the a/c is on.

“He sees us watching him, Mama. That's my cue to get those snacks. Want anything?”

“What? No. Stay.”

“Smile,” she whisper-sings and abandons me.

I smile at the guy. He takes the cue and threads his way through the crowd, his air of confidence sparking a fire in me. I'd like to run, but the crowd is so tight that even as he moves toward me, he keeps disappearing behind people. Now, he's here, his smile revealing perfect teeth. “I hear you're the woman of the hour.”

His deep voice resonates in my chest. *Do not bite your lip, Josie!* I suck in my cheeks and try to act like a normal person whose insides aren't fluttering in his presence. Having him this near, I find it difficult to speak.

Maybe that's why he looks confused. “You're the artist, right?”

I force my chin up and down.

“I read about you in the *New Haven Register* this morning and had to see the show. It's brilliant. Did you make the shoes you're wearing, also?”

I babble something about reclaimed wood and artists' canvas.

“Fascinating. The article said you studied sustainable fashion design at Yale?”

“Fine arts and graphics. I got the certificate in sustainable fashion online last year.”

“Color me impressed.” He cringes. “That was cheesy.”

"That was nothing. You should hear me. Do social situations make you nervous?"

"Not normally." He extends his hand, revealing an intricate yellow spider-in-web tattoo on his forearm. "I'm Theo."

"Hi, Theo." It's a simple handshake. Yet his touch sends frissons of energy into my heart. "I..." *Like your strong hands.*

Babbling, fluttering. What is this man doing to me? I haven't felt this way since... well, ever. Not even Seth, except when I was pregnant with Thalia. Then, I couldn't get enough of him. But that was pregnancy hormones. This is... what is this?

"Did, uh, your certificate include business courses?"

I stare at Theo, confused by the strange question and his chocolate brown eyes. "Kind of. We learned theory of sustainable fashion, circular business models, stuff like that."

"I ask because from what I see here and what I read in the paper; you seem poised to launch a business."

"I've been envisioning my thriving upcycled fashion house, but I have more to learn about running a company. It seems I need to make a crowdfunding campaign, which kinda makes me wanna vomit, and—"

"Hmm. What would you do if you didn't have to worry about startup costs?"

"Wow. There's a fantasy. I guess I'd hire someone to help me figure out the details."

"Sounds wise." Theo looks into my eyes. "Finding the right person can be tricky."

"How so?"

"Relationships are everything. Which reminds me, I loved reading about your relationship with your late aunt and how she inspired you."

Memories of my aunt bring joy and sorrow. We'd pore over patterns, giggling, then she'd start coughing. Then she was wasting away. "We shared a love of sewing, but her illness... I wanted so much to make her feel better."

"Feeling helpless like that takes a toll." In Theo's gentle tone and expression, I sense understanding. Was he stuck watching someone suffer, too?

"Aunt Mary lived decades longer than most people with Cystic Fibrosis, and seeing her struggle made me obsessed with health and wellbeing. Then I learned about pollution causing chronic illness, and my obsession took a new direction."

"Sounds like we share a mission to make the environment safe again."

"It's the best way to help the most people thrive."

He rocks back on his heels, agreeing. "So you found a way to connect your love of fashion with your passion for health. Powerful. I'm blown away by the wealth of creativity here, and the article said something about additional designs. You're still generating ideas?"

"It's how I think. Everywhere I go, I see designs and fabric patterns."

"Even now?"

"Mm-hmm." In my mind, I'm transforming his long lashes and almond-shaped eyes into the lines of a delicate bracelet with brown jewels.

"You'll have to explain that to me some time, Ms. Stewart."

A date? My heart pounds. "Josephine. Please."

"I'd love to learn more about your work, Josephine. Maybe help plan your business."

"Yeah?" I bite my lip, confused. Okay, disappointed. I thought he was flirting. "What do you do, Theo?"

"I help people start the businesses they dream about."

"You're kidding." Disappointment turns to a surge of energy. This is what I need to start Josephine Stewart Designs and never work an awful day job again. Except consultants charge fees. Big fees. Reality sets in, dissolving my excitement. "I'm sorry. I don't have money to pay a consultant."

Theo tilts his head, like he's puzzled. "Pay? Oh, no. I don't charge. Listen, if you don't want to meet, no big deal, but—" He hands me a business card.

Theodore Casabella. Local phone number. *Theo@TCVC.com.* I'll look it up when I get home.

"If you want a little free advice, please get in touch. I'd love to help."

"Absolutely. I'd love to stay and touch you, Theo." *Stay and touch you?* I gasp.

Theo bursts out laughing. "That wasn't how I saw this conversation going."

I cover my mouth and speak through my hand. "I'd love to stay *in* touch *with* you."

THEO

Damn it. She's more than stunning. She's brilliant, creative, socially conscious, and adorably awkward. It would be ungentlemanly to walk away now, with this disarming goddess in such clear emotional distress after her little Freudian slip. Besides, her fragrance—light and fresh like ocean waves—it's intoxicating. I couldn't move if I tried.

Someone calls her name, and Josephine turns toward a couple in their early forties emerging from the crowd. Both man and woman hunch over a toddler, who holds their hands. The baby, an adorable blend of both parents, has her dad's sea-blue eyes and mom's creamy olive skin and curls. The woman exudes joy, though she appears exhausted in a rumpled sundress and hiking sandals. I know them from somewhere.

"Did we interrupt something?" She looks from Josephine to me.

Josephine flashes an embarrassed smile. "You rescued me before I could make more of an ass of myself."

My heart puddles in my chest. Another bad sign. First, the electric shock I got when we shook hands, then the zing to my lower half when we talked about her work. I need to get my head in the game. I'm scoping out Josephine Stewart for a business investment, not a romance.

The woman hugs her. "Oh, Josie, what did you say this time?" Now, she directs her attention to me and we exchange introductions. Sage and Wesley. Where have I met them? His solid, businesslike handshake helps me get my mind in the right place again.

Wesley gestures to the dress on a nearby pedestal. "Did you drink all these sodas, Josie?"

"Always the doctor first, huh?" She giggles. Cute. Musical. Fuck.

"Busted." Wesley smirks. "Truly, though, I'm impressed with how you integrated the public health hazards caused by the fashion industry."

"That means a lot coming from you. And don't worry. I bought a bin of soda can tabs at EcoWorks." Josephine kneels by the child, stirring something long dormant in me. The toddler points to Josephine's earrings and says something unintelligible.

"They sparkle, don't they?" Josephine coos. "Soon, you'll be making art like your mommy."

I return my attention to Wesley. "What do you do?"

"Epidemiological research on the health impacts of agricultural chemicals. Though recently, I formed a collaboration to explore issues affecting New Haven residents."

"Wait. Are you Wesley Williams?" I ask.

He blushes.

"And you're Sage DesChamps." I motion toward the woman beside him.

She nods.

Oversized photos augmented with natural elements like algae and soil flip through my mind. "I attended your stunning exhibition in California two years ago. When's the next one?"

"I've been focusing on the responsibilities that come with the Brilliance Award and adjusting to parenting." She and Wesley exchange adoring looks. "Josie, I love what you're doing. Have you considered selling your art to a fashion house?"

"Funny." Josephine rises with the child in her arms. "Theo and I were discussing starting my own house."

Sage scans my face, assessing. "If you do it, Josie, I wanna photograph you for an exhibition."

Josephine's mouth drops open. "You're kidding."

"You know I'm all about featuring environmental heroes."

"I know. But me? You'd put me in a national show?"

"Why not you? We have extra footage from the video Kath commissioned. Thanks to the Brilliance Award, I have funds to create what I want. Ooh! What if we collaborate on an installation piece?"

"That's a great idea, hon," Wesley says. "I could get public health stats for you guys."

"Yes." Sage's enthusiasm is palpable. "Data plus fashion?" She beams at Josephine, who freezes like a deer caught in headlights.

Is that because she's stunned and excited, or because she feels her friends are co-opting her work? I wish I could ask, but now's not the time. I can offer helpful info, though. "A collaboration like that could give your new fashion house important media exposure, Josephine. Plus, startups have greater success rates when their founders have solid partnerships."

"See?" Sage says, taking the toddler from Josephine's arms. "Let's catch up later. Felicia, say bye-bye."

"Bye-bye," little Felicia squeaks, opening and closing her fist.

"Bye-bye, Felicia," Josephine and I say in unison, mimicking her wave.

Did Josephine catch that? Felicia's father did. Embarrassing. Wesley grins, throws an upward nod my way. "Nice to meet you, Theo." He places a hand on his wife's back and they disappear into the crowd.

I turn to Josephine. "Josephine, a pleasure. Get in touch."

She blushes. "Oh, I will get *in* touch."

I resist the urge to look back as I walk away. True. She's spectacular. Hot as hell, in fact. But I'm not walking away from a date, or even a flirtation. We discussed business, though my body seems to think we were conversing on another topic.

Is it foolish to offer capital and business-planning assistance to a woman I find so alluring? More important, is it right to withhold an investment from a potentially impactful company because I think the founder's hot? The truth is, I came here with no idea I'd find Josephine Stewart captivating. Is she a wise investment? Her relationship with two national Brilliance Award winners is a point in her favor. A partnership with Sage and Wesley would boost the viability of my investment and attract more backers.

I check my watch. Fifteen minutes before the reception ends. New strategy. This show will be on display for a while. I can return to see the mannequins, but the models won't be here to answer questions and provide the full experience.

I go in search of a model and find one wearing a wild dress called *Airy Fairy*. She's mid-pitch about fast fashion's contribution to global warming when Drew interrupts. "Hey."

"You made it." I turn to my friend, but gesture to the model. "Listen to this."

She continues her spiel, holding me sway. But when she walks away, Drew's narrow shoulders bounce with his silent laughter. "You're not *actually* considering a fashion company."

"Why not?"

Drew groans. "It's fun for an evening, but come on, Casabella."

My neck stiffens. "I don't think you're giving it a chance."

"You called me. Right? You said you needed advice. Right? You said—"

I hate it when Drew takes on the patronizing voice. "Yes, professor, I did. And I wanna meet at least one more model before we roll."

Drew laughs. "Uh, huh. Meeting models. Sounds like a real investment opportunity."

Irritated, I press my lips together and walk away. *Be patient, Theo. Drew is still grieving. In time, he'll be his old self again.*

In the back of the room, I find a large screen displaying a silent video of Josephine arranging plastic netting on a dress form. It's hard to tear myself away. The way she moves as she works. So graceful.

A soft voice catches my attention, asks if I'm enjoying the show and whether I'd like to know about her outfit. I turn from the screen and see a ghost.

Her mocha skin glows against the leather jumper. She says it's called *Drive* and talks about upcycling upholstery from cars. I swallow.

Isabella…

Chapter Two

THEO

The setting sun casts a romantic glow on New Haven's skyline. Josephine would shine in this light, but I'm not with her. I'm strolling toward a restaurant with my lifelong friend, who should realize it's unnecessary to act strong for my sake.

"Did you see that woman in the leather outfit?" I ask.

"No."

I'd swear it was Isabella. Isabella, before she became gaunt, too tired to walk, too light in my arms when I carried her to bed. Before she tied a new scarf around her head each day, flashing an appreciative smile at me for the gift, as if it wasn't evidence of my failure to take care of her.

I put a hand on Drew's shoulder, both to ground myself in reality and to offer comfort. "How are you, really? You okay? The boys?"

"Owen seems to have regressed a couple of years."

"How so?"

"Six months and three days ago, he was a smart-mouthed pre-teen. Ever since—" Drew clears his throat. "It's like he's ten again, eager to please. Never thought I'd miss the too-cool-for-school attitude, but it worries me. Like he thinks she... *it* happened because he was being a brat, like fawning all over me will keep me around."

"Maybe he's worried about you. You haven't been yourself." I scan Drew's profile. Grief has added lines to his face and gray to his temples. He looks at me from the corner of his eye, keeps walking in silence. The pain radiating off him is almost tangible.

Isabella tried to hide her pain, even while she lay dying. I couldn't ease her suffering, so I promised her I'd ensure anyone made ill by my company's mistakes would get healthcare, that I'd be damned if anyone else got sick. I changed our operations, changed the bylaws, left NorEast Waste Management in capable hands. If Isabella could see the start-ups I've funded, she'd be thrilled. As long as I'm breathing, I'll support companies who share my mission. Nothing and no one will stop me.

Drew says, "I think Quinn started drinking."

"Shit."

"It's normal for fifteen-year-olds, but it's not like when we were kids. We know the risks now. I felt shitty leaving them tonight."

"Man, why didn't you tell me?" We weave through a crowd outside the modern steel and stone building housing Atticus Cafe Bookstore. "I could've come over instead of dragging you out."

"Nah, getting out helps me feel normal for a bit."

"Understood. Be patient with yourself. It's only been six months."

"Thanks, man," Drew says, and we mount the granite steps into the restaurant.

Ten minutes later, meals ordered and drinks in hand, Drew describes six different start-ups helmed by Yale alumni. One is in New York; three in Connecticut; one in New Jersey, and one in Vermont.

"I'm seeking hyper-local right now," I respond. "Say more about the start-ups in Connecticut. Can any move to New Haven?"

"Why limit yourself?" He sounds annoyed, as if it's his money and business on the line.

I take a deep breath, remind myself—again—to be patient. "I've funded companies all over the country while New Haven struggles. I have to change that."

"Bridgeport Food Forest might open a satellite here. Restore CT Coast intends to work on the entire coastline by 2030, including New Haven."

"Hmm." I'm not thrilled with any of Drew's suggestions. Normally, I wouldn't balk at telling a buddy what I think. But in his current state, Drew might take me rejecting his ideas personally. Thankfully, our salads arrive, giving me an excuse to be silent for a few minutes.

"Oh, my goodness." A luscious voice shoots up my spine, like the opening notes of an aria. Josephine strides toward me, her smile bright, hips swaying, long shapely legs bringing her closer with each step. My heart drums a crazy rhythm. Just when I was regaining my equilibrium. *She's not here for you, fool. She's here for dinner.* Alone? No. Now I register the women at her side—her look-alike and Kath.

I stand and we exchange introductions. "I thought you were sisters," I tell Josephine and her daughter Thalia. Josephine rewards me with a megawatt smile, but in her eyes, I see exhaustion. "Congratulations on a fantastic opening reception, ladies! You must be ready to drop."

"Does it show?" Josephine asks.

"Not at all. But I know how much work goes into putting on an event. Please don't let us hold up your quiet dinner."

The relief on her face is evident, and that makes me feel good. Too good. Good in ways that have nothing to do with business. How can I work with her when she has this effect on me? *Because you're a professional, asshole.* She smiles and makes a cute little wave. Luckily, the hostess leads Josephine and company to the other side of the room, where she can't distract me. From this distance, I only see her back, which isn't at all distracting. The way light coming through the window highlights her graceful shoulders... The way her dark curls land at her mid-back...

"Theo."

"Did you say something, Drew?"

JOSEPHINE

"You can always tell a gentleman by the way he fibs," Kath says, as we settle into a table in the corner where the cement wall meets the window.

"Seriously, Aunt Kath?" Thalia rolls her eyes, playfully.

"We look exhausted. Who wouldn't after the day we've had? But he was kind to say otherwise."

"How'd we do?" I ask.

"We met the goal," Kath says, like it's no big deal.

My eyes widen in disbelief.

"You didn't see all the red dots? There were private collectors, fashionistas wanting a statement piece, and the buyer from the DeCordova."

"No way." A thrill shoots through me. *The DeCordova.*

"They bought four pieces. The museum is collecting trashion from around the world."

"Oh, my God. What did they buy?"

"*Airy Fairy. Drive. Advertise Me. Cycle.* They tried to buy my dress. Of course, I declined."

"Mama, your work will be in a museum!"

I shake my head, stunned. "This is way better than I hoped. All I wanted was to sell sixty percent of the work. But to sell to a museum."

"One of the most highly regarded small museums on the East Coast, darling," Kath reminds me, quirking an eyebrow above her glasses.

I do a happy dance in my seat. "Between this and meeting Theo... You know, he's some sort of business consultant? He offered to advise me." I pull out his card and lay it on the table.

Kath and Thalia lean over to read it. "Funny," Thalia says. "I thought he was hitting on you."

"Me, too." Disappointment at realizing he wasn't flirting fills me all over again. Silly. "Do you mind if I look him up? I hate to be rude, but—"

"Do it," Kath says. "Let's see what he's all about."

I open my browser and navigate to TCVC.com, positioning my phone on the table so we can all see.

Theo's image pops up. My heart races looking at him, recalling his warm hand and resonant voice, his unique spider-in-web tattoo. Wow. Even in a photo, his warm, mischievous eyes draw me in. Why am I nervous? Why am I fantasizing? He offered to give me business advice, not go on a date.

"Oooh, Josie," Kath purrs. "He's not a consultant. He's an angel investor focused on eco-friendly startups. That's exactly what you need."

Thalia reads aloud. "*Current and previous investments include an environmentally sustainable heating and cooling company in Brooklyn, a cryptocurrency designed to support transparency in the organic food distribution chain, and a biomimetic engineering firm working in hazardous waste cleanup.* Cool."

"He said he shared my mission. I wish the site named the companies."

I read the rest to myself: *Prior to investing in startups, Theo worked in waste management and as a hedge fund manager. He grew up in Vermont and Connecticut, earned his undergraduate degree from Middlebury College and his MBA from Harvard.*

Color me impressed. I laugh silently until I scan his bio again. "That's concerning."

"What?" Thalia asks.

"The waste management industry has a track record of environmental violations."

"The bio says he *did* that. Past tense, Mama. Now, he invests in companies that create wellbeing."

"I wonder how many of the startups he invested in failed," Kath says.

"Good question. Since the site doesn't name the companies, the only way to find out is to ask him when we meet again. *If* we meet again."

"Well, darling, he's put the ball in your hands, so it's up to you."

Thinking about that makes my heart pound, which stresses me out. "Maybe Theo can help me take all this sustainable business theory I learned and make it practical. I keep trying to read these business books, and they put me to sleep. And so many say crowdfund, but... ick!"

"I'd love to see you out of that awful day job, but you need a good six months' living expenses to quit and search for another," Kath says. "To start your own business, you need eighteen months to two years of expenses."

"Why so much?" Thalia asks.

"Starting a business costs money," Kath says. "Marketing, websites..."

I think about what's in my bank account and cringe. Eighteen months of savings? Nope.

Kath continues. "Space, licenses, employees, legal fees..."

Six months if I live lean. If I stretch every penny, only buy absolute necessities, and give up social outings that cost money.

Kath interrupts my thoughts. "Of course, if Theo

invests, you could have the money you need to move forward without savings."

I imagine having what I need to bring my vision to life. A storefront with fitting rooms and a sewing floor in the back. A team. Money to pay people a fair wage. An assistant to help me stay organized. My exhaustion morphs into empowerment. "And if that happens, I will launch this business, stride into Mark's office, lay the key on his desk and leave without a word."

"That's how you'll quit?" Thalia asks.

"I want him to know in no uncertain terms, I don't consider him worth the words *I quit*."

"I love it!" Kath says.

Excited, I can't help releasing a tiny squeal as Thalia squeezes my hand under the table.

Kath looks wistful. "I knew as soon as I saw Theo, he was there for a purpose, and it wasn't to shop or entertain himself."

The sound of two men in strained conversation wafts across the restaurant, putting me on alert. Thalia has always hated arguing. Seeing her clench and unclench her hands worries me more. "You okay?" I rub her back.

She closes her eyes, withdrawing. "It makes me feel trapped, but I'll be fine."

"Should we go?" I ask, as the waiter brings our food. My stomach grumbles.

"This is your evening, Mama." Thalia drops her arms by her sides and rolls her shoulders, then forces a quick smile. "I'm gonna take some deep calming breaths, then dive into my fries and salad."

"Okay, Muffin." Thalia felt thin when we hugged earlier. I'm probably being overprotective again, but I can't help it. I eye her. "Let me know if you need to go."

"I've got this."

I watch the slow rise and fall of Thalia's chest as she

inhales, holds her breath, and exhales, as we learned in yoga class when she was struggling with dyslexia. I join her in the calming exercise. It only takes a minute to quiet my nerves. When I open my eyes and look at her, she sends a more relaxed smile my way, then reaches for her food. Relieved to see my daughter eating, I savor the first bite of crisp lettuce with champagne vinaigrette. Delicious.

"Theo," the man's voice says sternly. "Of all things—"

"Is that Theo and his friend?" Thalia asks. "How are we hearing them over here?"

My mouth goes dry. "This place has weird acoustics. I've overheard so many private conversations from across the room."

Theo's friend continues. "Why waste your money and time on something as frivolous as *trashion*?"

The words stab me, sucking the air from my lungs. It's not the first time people have dismissed the relevance of my work. But usually, people are gentler with their criticism.

Kath reaches across the table. "Don't listen to it, darling. Don't take it in," she whispers, her light touch on my hand reassuring.

"I'm not an idiot, Drew. For Christ's sake, I ran a Fortune 500 company for years. You wanna tell me after only five minutes in that gallery, you understand the work?"

"I've seen the work. I've seen the artist. It's clear you're not using your MBA to make this decision."

Kath's eyes widen and her mouth sets in a hard line.

Theo's strained voice reverberates. "Usually, I appreciate your input, but I'm not gonna listen to you attack me and a woman you don't even know. It's not helpful."

"All I'm saying is, if you invest in this, you'll be throwing money away. Why not support the startups I recommended?"

"They don't meet my criteria."

"These are projects *my PhD students* ideated at Yale

School *of the Environment*. They *all* meet your criteria. But don't listen to me. Talk to Eric. He'll agree."

Theo growls low, as if he's speaking through gritted teeth. "I can't drive through this town and keep ignoring the suffering while I help an entrepreneur in fucking Brooklyn. I need someone *local* and innovative."

Drew laughs. "Or local and hot?"

"That's it." Kath slams down her napkin and fork and stands.

"Oh, Kath." I know what's coming. Equal parts excitement and dread flood me.

"I am so tired of these entitled white men dictating what women can do in the world."

"I'm not sure it's about that." I try to sound soothing.

"Of course it is. Most men dismiss fashion because women care about it."

"You have a point there, Aunt Kath," Thalia notes.

Theo growls. "Man, knock it off. This isn't you."

"Go ahead. Invest in the fashion designer. I'm sure all New Haven's problems will dissolve while you screw her in the boardroom."

"I will not tolerate this." Kath turns on her heel, knocking her chair off balance with the stiff skirt of her dress.

Excitement overtakes my worry. "I'm flashing back to Sophomore year when you gave those Whiffenpoofs a piece of your mind in the dining hall."

Kath flashes her warrior grin at me, bared teeth, narrowed eyes, head held high. "Damn right."

Heads turn as Kath marches across the restaurant in her steampunk, billboard ballgown, oblivious to the stiff vinyl knocking purses off of chairs and a tray of dirty dishes off its pedestal. A busboy scrambles to clean up the mess. But most of the waitstaff stare in stunned silence.

"Oh, snap!" Thalia grins, eyes wide. We rise to watch the disaster unfold.

THEO

Drew is pissing me the hell off. In fact, my heart is thudding so loudly, the sound of stomping feet and clattering dishes doesn't register until the noise stops and I feel a presence looming. Kath. Standing by our table, hands on her trashion-covered hips, glowering.

"Gentlemen, sound carries in this restaurant. We can hear you at our table."

Mortifying. "Oh, my God, Kath, I'm so sorry." Josephine heard Drew? I look past Kath and see Josephine and her daughter standing by their table, watching. "Is Josephine okay?"

"She's strong," Kath says, then focuses, laser-like, on my companion, as if waiting.

Drew meets her silent gaze. Are they just going to stare at each other? I clear my throat, glare at Drew, willing him to apologize. Normally, he would. No. Normally, Drew would never be such a dick. *Come on, buddy. Snap out of it.* Another excruciating ten seconds pass while my friend and Josephine's stare at each other. I glance from one to the other. Dread churns my stomach as the fury intensifies in Kath's eyes.

At last, she says, "Drew, is it? How on earth can you teach environmentalism when you are ignorant about the relevance of fashion in the world?"

"Relevance?" Drew snorts.

I wince. He's gonna make this worse.

Kath's strident voice takes an even harsher tone. "You think you're above understanding fashion, Mister Environment?"

"It's *Doctor* Environment, actually," Drew mutters.

Way to miss the point, man.

"You think fashion doesn't matter?" Kath looks down

her nose at Drew, blatantly scanning him from head to toe. "It's plain to see you don't begin to comprehend it! Apparently, you don't even recognize you're wearing... Well, *fashion* is a bit of a stretch. I mean, honestly. White tube socks? With sandals?" She waves a finger in front of him. "Clearly, you have no visual sense whatsoever, but you are still wearing clothes."

I bite my lip to avoid laughing out loud.

"News flash, Professor Environmentalism." Kath weaves her head side to side. "Clothes are the fashion industry, and to ignore the industry's major contribution to *climate change* is simply asinine. Your pathetic outfit is partly responsible for the deaths and suffering of countless people around the world."

"So I'm a murderer?" Drew asks.

If looks could kill. Kath rolls her head as if to say *Oh, no you didn't*. I swallow hard.

Kath growls low, enunciating every word. "When anyone. Has the verve. To stand up and do what Josephine Stewart is doing. You should applaud that. Celebrate it. And proclaim her brilliance from the rooftops. If you can't grasp the impact that the fashion industry has on the environment, then you, Sir, have no business teaching at Yale, or even in kindergarten."

"You're delusional if you think one little *trashion* company can stop climate change."

"As opposed to watching from the sidelines and criticizing? Please. You of all people should know it's collective effort that matters."

"Collective useful effort."

"Exactly. But *you're* stagnant, Professor." Kath points at Drew. I look at Josephine again. She's still watching this train wreck. I wish I could read her facial expression better. Is she cringing? Laughing silently? Crying? No. She and her daughter are walking. Toward us. And the way they both cross their arms over their chest tells me they are not happy. *Fuuuuuuck.*

I slip out of my seat to meet them, as Kath continues. "While *you* avoid taking *productive* action and debate theory in your ivory tower, *I* will deliver the pieces that Josephine sold to *the DeCordova.*"

"I don't know what that is."

Their arguing voices fade to the back of my awareness as I approach Josephine and her daughter, my heart pounding. The women hold their heads high, but Thalia is shaking. *Poor thing.* "Are you two okay?"

"Fine," Josephine forces a half-smile. "Thanks for standing up for my work."

"Of course. I'm so sorry."

"What's happening?" Kath asks. When did she sneak up on us?

"We're just going to the restroom." Josephine flashes a genuine smile at her friend. "Wanna join us?"

"I need a moment outside to cool down," Kath says. "You know how I get after a good fight."

"Oh, I know." Josephine smirks, amused. "The Whiffenpoofs, the football team, the Chi Beta whatever fraternity, the city council meeting when you told the president of Yale where to stick the University's tax-exempt status and forty-three-billion-dollar endowment."

I grin at the images that flash through my mind, but now I need to get this situation back under control. "Ladies." I try to keep my voice extra quiet. "I'm sorry about Drew. He's not... in a good space right now. He's really a kind person."

All three women lift their eyebrows in a show of unanimous disbelief. My neck stiffens.

A server approaches. "Everything okay here, Ms. Word?"

"I made a mess, I'm afraid." Kath says, frowning an apology.

"No worries. We're already cleaning it. Just making sure everyone's alright."

We four respond at once, assuring the waiter we're fine. Inwardly, I flinch at Kath's tone and intense focus.

I apologize to the server and watch him leave before continuing. "Drew is someone I've always been able to count on for advice."

"That's nice," Josephine says, her voice laden with skepticism.

How can I make this right? "We've been friends since birth. Drew was the kid who stopped our backyard soccer game to move a frog out of harm's way."

"So he's not a people person," Kath says.

"Drew was the guy at prom, comforting that girl whose date went off with someone else. That girl became his wife."

"Lucky woman," Kath deadpans.

"But she died in an accident in January, and grief has turned my friend into someone unrecognizable."

The triumph fades from Kath's expression. "Oh, dear. I'm sorry."

Josephine and Thalia make matching sympathetic sounds.

"I know he's being a dick. And the only reason I didn't shut him down completely is because I'm afraid... well, that's not your problem. The point is—"

"Hurt people hurt people." Josephine's voice exudes compassion.

An arrow to my heart. The woman understands. If only she would look at me. "Still, I'm deeply sorry, and when Drew's in a better space, I'm sure he will be too."

"Thank you, Theo." Josephine's eyes soften, yet remain fixed on the exit.

"Josephine, I see you making a difference, and I want to help. Not sure *how* yet, but I see the value in your work." I extend my hand to her. "Please get in touch."

She shakes my hand, more businesslike than earlier, meets my eyes for the first time during this conversation, and sidesteps around me. Ouch.

While Josephine, her daughter, and their Warrior Queen stride away, I find the waiter. I hand him my credit card to cover the ladies' food and drinks, plus the cost of any dishes broken when Kath swept through the restaurant. "Also, please charge the meals of everyone here now, including staff, to my card with my apologies for the disruption."

The waiter swallows, stunned. "Yes, sir."

I hope that's enough to make up for this embarrassing debacle. I hope Josephine isn't the type to judge a man by his friends' behavior. I'm not thinking with my cock. I'm assessing the situation and the work with complete rationality. Sure, I'm attracted to her, but so what? I'm a man, and she's gorgeous. That doesn't make her endeavor a poor investment.

But I'm done trying to explain that to Drew. To salvage this dinner, I'll steer the conversation to other topics. I return to the fashion-challenged hot mess that is my best friend, chuckling as Kath's words repeat in my mind. "Seriously, dude. She's right about the socks and sandals."

Chapter Three

JOSEPHINE

STILL GIGGLING, I pour our green smoothies and settle
into my favorite kitchen chair. This is the antique I rescued
from the sidewalk, then had three-year-old Thalia paint
before I upholstered the seat with faded denim and skirted it
with white eyelet to bring cohesion to the mismatched
dining set. "News flash, Professor Environmentalism—"

"Clearly, you have no visual sense, but you are still
wearing clothes," Thalia finishes. She sips her green
smoothie, recoiling. "My God, hearing Theo and his friend
argue was rough, but once Kath stepped in, it was like
watching a bizarre comedy."

"You were shaking, though." Now, I'm worried again.

"And I breathed through it and got to enjoy some of
Kath's precious gems, like 'Your *pathetic outfit* is partly
responsible'—" Thalia catches my eye, and we double over
laughing.

"Kath is the best. She fights so I don't have to." I get up
and wash the blender as the time on my phone changes from
9:59 AM to ten o'clock. At last. I lean against the laminated

counter and open the texting app. **Nothing says I'm sorry like paying someone's dinner tab. Thanks, Theo. Great meeting you!**

Is the exclamation point too much? I change it to a period, then add: **My daughter and I will be in my studio from about 11 AM until 3 PM, if you want to drop by.** I hold my finger over the little arrow that will send the text. Is this how I should reach out? Would he prefer I call? It's Saturday after ten AM. He said contact anytime. He didn't specify call or text. Did he? God, I hope I'm not screwing this up. I take a deep breath and send the message. "It's done."

Thalia flashes a thumbs up, takes another sip of smoothie and scrunches her nose.

"Still don't like blue-green algae, huh? You don't have to drink it."

She grins. "I know, but I probably eat healthier here than anywhere. It'll make up for all the junk food I eat at home."

Junk food? I hope Thalia isn't malnourished from eating too many empty calories.

The video call app rings, startling me. My parents' smiling faces appear. Morning sunlight glows on Mom's pale cheeks and highlights the gray streaks in Dad's dark afro. My heart drops, then floods with guilt for being disappointed by a call from my parents. "Hi," I chirp.

"Sweetheart," Mom says. "We are so proud of you! Read the article for us? It's hard to see the text on this small screen."

"Can't reach your glasses, huh?" I pull yesterday's paper off the table and read the most important paragraph. "Stewart wowed us in 2019 with traditional Japanese art forms—fake bonsai, fans, tea service items—crafted from up-cycled materials found on location during an artist residency in Tokyo. Now, she enlivens our senses and brings hope for a brighter tomorrow. In Josephine Stewart's world, we learn from our societal history of overconsumption and wasteful-ness, and treat every material with reverence as a precious resource."

"Phenomenal, Sugar," Dad says, his voice gravelly. "Sorry we missed your opening reception. We were chained to the door of the Salvation Army in Hadley."

"For three full hours." Mom sighs. "It was exhilarating!"

My eyes widen. "You prevented people from entering and exiting Sal's?"

Mom laughs. "Oh, no. We would've been arrested, and we're too old for that now. People used the other door."

"Then what good did that do?" Thalia asks.

I turn the phone so my parents and daughter can see each other. They wave.

Dad sucks in his cheeks as he always does to indicate an issue's importance. "We demonstrated the need to remove brand labels from clothing sold at second-hand stores. And today, we'll hit the statehouse." He puts special emphasis on the word *statehouse*.

"Ten of us are going to Boston," Mom explains. "To hold signs and dump baskets of labels that we personally cut out of our clothes onto the statehouse steps."

"The optics will be phenomenal," Dad says.

"But what you're doing is important, too," Mom sings. "We tear down the system; you build a new one in your own small way."

Their patronization and one-upmanship make me cringe inside, but I keep my face placid. "Sounds like quite an effort, and the goal is?"

"To stop the perpetuation of fast fashion." Mom's pre-school teacher voice. Ugh. "Right in line with what you're doing, sweetheart."

"Is it, though?"

"Sugar, the connection is obvious," Dad says. "When a teenager buys a shirt at a thrift store and it's got a name brand inside, it glorifies the brand and brainwashes that child. We have to stop *brand brainwashing*."

"Brand brainwashing," Mom whispers, turning to stare at him. "That's brilliant, Frederick!"

Why did I share the article? Did I expect them to be supportive this time? Eager to end the call, I say, "Okay, guys, thanks for checking in. Have fun storming the castle."

We make kissy faces and hang up. I drop the phone onto the table and groan, heart pounding. *We tear down the system; you build a new one in your own small way.*

"Brand brainwashing at thrift stores?" Thalia rolls her eyes. "What world are they in?"

"Their own special one, loosely connected to reality."

"Didn't they used to protest real issues?"

"Yup. Now, they'll probably say I'm brainwashing people if I sew tags into my clothes."

Thalia giggles. "Maybe they'll protest your fashion house."

I laugh hollowly and hug myself, directing my thoughts to something more pleasant. If, *when*, I turn my art into a business, what will the labels look like? I could sew my initials into the garment. Or design a logo and have tags custom made. Should I make them myself?

I'm not sure when Thalia crossed the room, but now I savor the warmth of my daughter's tight side-embrace. "At least you turned out normal, Mama."

I rest my head on her shoulder. "Oh, honey, I didn't. Therapy and self-help books saved me."

"Well, thank God. I don't know how insane I'd feel if I had those two as parents, but I love that you're my mom."

"Maybe I brand brainwashed you," I joke, trying to lighten my mood.

"Nah. You just loved me like parents are supposed to."

Chapter Four

JOSEPHINE

THIS IS MY HAPPY PLACE. It costs a bit to rent the extra space across town, but after the success of my last show, I decided the benefit of having room to keep all my equipment ready for use was worth the price. My studio feels even more cheery when Thalia's here, smiling down at me from the fitting platform like she is now. "Has he texted you back yet?"

I shake my head. Maybe he changed his mind. Maybe he thought about what Drew said and decided, like my parents, that trash fashion is frivolous. Through the pins I hold between my lips, I ask Thalia what kind of neckline she wants. Someone else might struggle to interpret my words, but my daughter is used to it.

"Maybe a high neck. Or, ooh. Deep halter. A trashion Marilyn moment."

"Trashion Marilyn moment? I love it." I pin the double-faced fabric I made from purple linen and flexible window screening tight around my daughter's waist. "But not for clubbing. You'll pop out of the dress." I spit out the last pin.

"The girls love their freedom," she jokes.

"Fun on the dance floor. A little porn star moment."

"Bow chick-a wow, wow," Thalia sings. "Do you have any lace?"

"Black, white, and food wrapper." With white chalk, I mark the area where the zipper will go.

"Food wrapper? Lace?"

I pull a sample of hand-cut plastic lace from the corkboard above my worktable and give it to Thalia. Her eyes widen as she runs her finger over the cutout lines. "Whoa, Mom, this snaps! How did you do this?"

"Like this." I hold up the mylar stencil I created, then demonstrate, laying it on a food wrapper and cutting the pattern with an X-Acto knife. "It's painstaking, but I think it's worth it."

"And the mesh between the cutouts..." Thalia holds the food-wrapper-lace up to the light. "From a bag of oranges or something?"

"Yup."

"Can I post this on Snaptalk?" she asks.

"Not until it's in a garment. I think I'll be first out with food-wrapper-lace."

"Cool. Will it work for this dress?"

"If you're going dancing, the lace will stick to your skin when you get hot."

"Eew." She grimaces. "It would be amazing in a jacket, though, or pants. Haute couture rain gear."

"Sure you don't want a job in fashion? You have such great ideas."

"I learned from the best, but you've seen my drawing and sewing."

"You're too hard on yourself, Muffin."

"So... black lace for this dress?"

"Great choice." I pull a length of lace from the bin and drape it around Thalia's neck, bringing the ends to meet at the back. In my mind's eye, I envision different options for the lay of the fabric: a soft draping neckline, a stiff high collar, a ruched high neck. "By the way, since I sold so much last night, I can help you pay for your LSATs and another prep course."

Thalia shifts, uncomfortable.

"Don't move," I remind her, as I pin the lace to the window screening at her shoulders and across her décolleté. "You're still taking the LSATs again, right? You said you wanted to improve your score and your chance of getting into law school."

"I've been thinking about that," she says, careful. "Maybe my awful scores were a sign."

I stop the dressmaking and catch her gaze. "You mean a sign that it's a grueling test for everybody, with and without learning disabilities?"

She flinches, and it breaks my heart. Is there anything I can say to help my daughter stop judging herself for having dyslexia?

A knock startles me.

"It's probably Theo," Thalia whispers.

"I know." I sigh. "What terrible timing." I look from her to the door. Torn. Thalia needs me now. "Maybe I can text him later? This conversation is important."

"Mama, answer it," she whispers, her face incredulous.

I hesitate, shifting my gaze between my child and the door.

Wide eyed, she yells, "One sec."

"I'm sorry, Muffin." I squeeze her hand and stride toward the door, guilt consuming me.

THEO

A shaft of light illuminates Josephine from behind, as if

an angel or a goddess were opening the door, rather than a woman with pins sticking out of the colorful apron she wears over her clothes. I catch my breath and bask in Josephine's warmth.

"You're here," she says.

Her smile welcomes me, but there's something else in her eyes. Stress, maybe. Over what? Last night. Is she still upset? *Damn it, Drew.* "Hope I'm not disturbing you. Your text said to drop by, and I was having lunch down the street, so—"

"Wonderful." She opens the door wide and steps back to let me enter.

Corkboards on every wall catch my eye first, each spilling over with sketches, fabric swatches, scrawled notes. A long worktable spans most of the far wall. Two windows flank the corkboard above the table. Rolling high stools stand in the corners. A sewing table takes up half of another wall.

"Hi, Theo." Josephine's daughter waves from a round wooden platform that gives her about an inch on me.

They both seem friendly. Josephine sent that gracious text, leading me to believe Drew's words had faded from her mind. But if they're not still upset about what went down last night, then why is she tense?

There's a minefield of materials between us and Thalia, so I follow Josephine's tiptoed path to avoid stepping on anything and extend my hand. "Pleasure to see you again, Thalia. Listen." I meet her gaze before resting my eyes on Josephine. "I'm so, so sorry about last night. Drew is—"

"A total ass," Josephine says, then gasps and claps her hand over her mouth.

I wince. "An ass. Yes. Lately, but—"

"I shouldn't have said that. You already explained and apologized. We're good if you are."

"I'm good, too," I say and gesture to Thalia. "What did I interrupt?"

"Trashion in progress," she says.

"And why are you elevated?"

"It's easier for Mom to see how the fabric drapes. This way she can get up under the hemline. Right, Mom?"

"Mm-hmm." Josephine sweeps her hand rapidly across the back of her daughter's neck.

"What're you doing?" I ask.

"Marking the spots for button holes with chalk."

"I see. The chalk won't rub off?"

"Nope." She turns her daughter to face a full-length mirror attached to the wall behind the door. "What do you think?"

Thalia scans her reflection, turning side-to-side. "That *hemline*."

"Is it supposed to fall at her knee in front and lower in back?"

"It's called a hi-lo hemline," Josephine explains. "I use it to give a dress an extra playful, sexy feel."

"I see. At your show, it seemed like you used materials to create different effects."

Josephine looks from Thalia's reflection to mine. "In fashion, we tell a story using both materials and design. And when I'm co-creating a piece with a client, or in this case my daughter, they help inform the story and how I tell it."

"What story are you telling, Thalia?" I ask.

"This is about what we reveal and hide. Hence the lace neckline, the window screen overlay and bustle, and the hi-low hemline. This dress says 'peek-a-boo.'" Thalia brightens as she explains, and I find it delightful to see a young woman so excited about her mother's work. These two are quite the dynamic duo.

Josephine fluffs the bustle, a term I learned from Kath last night. "Want me to adorn this with found objects?"

"Yeah," Thalia says. "Tiny ones, though, not chunky things. Glittery bits."

"Metallic credit card confetti? Maybe earring onesies?"

"All of it. See what a genius she is, Theo?"

I laugh. "I see her daughter should be in sales. Have you written that into your business plan, Josephine? Thalia as Chief Sales Officer?"

Josephine smiles, but her body stiffens for a moment, and she moves closer to Thalia.

My arms tighten. Did I say something wrong?

Josephine inhales deliberately, looks from me to her kid. "Let me double check I marked each stitch point with chalk and pinned everything, then I'll help you out of the dress."

"Do you have a fitting room, or should I step out?" I ask.

"I usually work one-on-one with clients, so I've never needed a fitting room." She visibly relaxes as she circles her daughter and scans the garment.

As Josephine unwinds, my tension eases. I enjoy watching her work. Her focus and graceful movements captivate me. *Not thinking with your MBA,* Drew repeats in my head. Shit. *Focus, Theo.* "To answer your question, Thalia. I see what a genius your mother is. This dress... the way the purple color glows through the screen... what do you call that?"

"An overlay," Thalia says.

"She makes trash look like haute couture for a fraction of the cost."

"And a fraction of the environmental impact," Josephine says.

"That's the best part," I say. "I can't wait to see this dress when it's done."

"You have to come when she's starting a piece, Theo. That's the magic time, when ideas flow through her from some other place, and her whole being glows like—"

"My whole being glows?" Josephine lifts an eyebrow.

"Like you're on fire," Thalia stage whispers, gesturing to the heavens.

"This young woman definitely has a calling in sales. What stage of the business plan are you in, Josephine?"

She shrugs and purses her lips, again seeming to go from being at ease to being tense in the space of a few words. Her voice sounds slightly strained now, too. "I know less about business than you seem to know about fashion, so—"

"Have you written a business plan?"

"Um…" She meets my eyes with a sheepish expression. "I didn't expect to need one so soon. I have notebooks filled with ideas, and you can see my mood boards and swatches all over the studio." She swoops her arm to gesture at the walls. "I'm sorry. I feel woefully unprepared."

"Okay, let me step out so Thalia can change. Then we can talk. Sound good?"

"Perfect."

"I can go for a walk if you two need privacy," Thalia says.

That worried look crosses Josephine's face again, but she hitches a shoulder. Forcing casualness? "Whatever you prefer, hon. I always love having you around."

"Whatever makes you two comfortable works for me," I say, hoping to reassure them.

Thalia steps off the platform. "Let me get dressed."

I duck into the hallway and scan the announcement board without seeing it. The sound of mother and daughter speaking in low tones comes through the door, but I can't hear what they're saying. Not that I'm eavesdropping.

The door opens, and Thalia emerges. "I'm grabbing a couple salads from down the street. Want anything, Theo?"

"Thanks. I'm good." As I re-enter the studio, I notice details I missed earlier. Bolts of colorful fabric stand in a corner. A black metal flat file cabinet spans the wall under one table. Although the room looks empty without Thalia standing on the raised platform, her presence fills the space. Photos of mother and daughter adorn a corkboard by the door. At the top of the corkboard is a five-by-seven of

Josephine sitting on a hospital bed, arms around a small pale woman wearing an oxygen mask. "Is that your Aunt Mary?"

Josephine glances at the photo, smiles sadly. "Yeah."

"You have the same eyes." Inexplicably, I'm touched by the image. Near it, a photo of Josephine with an older couple —her parents?—hangs in a frame. The woman resembles Aunt Mary but mostly looks like a white-haired, short, round version of Josephine. The man, about an inch taller than Josephine, has her striking build—thin with broad shoulders and long fingers—but his skin is several shades darker. Although the elders flank Josephine and bear wide grins, they look at each other out of the corners of their eyes rather than at their daughter. That's telling.

Josephine retrieves a stack of colorful notebooks from another table. "It's not a business plan, but—"

"Let's see your ideas."

She wheels an extra chair to the table. "Have a seat. Can I offer you a seltzer? It's awfully hot out." She squats by a mini fridge under her drafting table and retrieves two bottles.

It's boiling inside, too, even with the ceiling fan. I'm tempted to rub the cool glass bottle over my face and neck, but that would send the wrong signals. God, what did Drew do to me? Planting ideas in my head. I've never felt so self-conscious during a business meeting.

Josephine sits next to me. Her phone vibrates on the table, and the name Mark pops up on the screen. She purses her lips, shakes her head and leaves the phone where it is. Whoever Mark is, he's clearly not someone Josephine feels very good about. An ex? Not my business.

I return my attention to the charming woman by my side. "So, whatcha got?" I hold out my hands.

She cradles the orange notebook, as one might a small pet or an infant. "Do you mind if I read it to you?"

I shake my head and take a long pull of the seltzer, refreshed by the cold liquid gliding down my throat.

"Okay." Josephine inhales deeply, exhales slowly, then reads an incredibly detailed list of the materials she'll use and where she plans to get them. She pauses, watching me for a reaction.

I'm not surprised by her attention to detail, given what I witnessed as she assembled that dress. And it's an excellent skill for an entrepreneur. There's a point in her favor. "Interesting. Tell me more."

"A small house with—"

"You mean fashion house?"

She nods. "—with a storefront and on-site fabrication, like Neville Wisdom."

"Great. Do you have a relationship with him?"

"Um... We're friendly when we see each other, but we don't, like, hang out, if that's what you mean. Should I keep reading?"

"Mm-hmm."

"Ultra-custom pieces made from fabric scraps, found objects and up-cycled materials brought in by the client."

"Great differentiator."

"Differentiator?"

"Sets you apart from other fashion houses."

Dimples reveal her relief. "No shipping. Local fashion by and for local people."

"No shipping—"

"Right. I envision a hyper-local business. How else can I be truly sustainable and eco-friendly?"

I knit my eyebrows, reflecting. She admitted she has no business experience. Having a product line without shipping seems like a significant handicap. I'll address that later. "How do you define local?"

"Driving distance. The Tri-state area, New England, and down to Pennsylvania. If people are visiting New Haven from somewhere else, I'm happy to serve them. But no shipping."

I press my lips together and clear my throat. "Is there more?"

"Yes. Seek experienced sewists first, but be willing to train ready learners." She turns the page. "These are drawings. Wanna see?"

"Absolutely."

She lays the notebook on the table.

"You're glowing, just like Thalia said."

"Am I?" The outer edges of Josephine's eyes crinkle as she smiles.

Fuck, that's distracting. "I guess I'm about to witness some magic."

"No pressure, though," she deadpans. Interesting how she can be so serious one minute and so light the next.

I lean closer. She flips page after page. Her light, clean fragrance is slightly muskier than moments ago, incredibly sexy. The heat must be affecting her, or maybe she's nervous.

Damn it, Theo. Focus on the notebook. Each sheet has at least one drawing, labeled with a style name and marked with ideas for materials. She leafs through sketches of dresses, pantsuits, jackets, outfits, and wearable art I'm at a loss to describe. "You're designing for women with all body types?"

"Real people come in all shapes and sizes."

A wise strategy on many fronts. "Have you thought about costs?"

Josephine reaches for the green notebook and flips it open to reveal pages filled with tiny doodles and big numbers. "Not sure what it costs to rent a space, maybe $2,000 a month? The cost to make each garment depends on materials and ranges from $10 to $100."

"Is that materials only, or does it include labor?"

"Right now, I'm the labor."

"You need to charge for your time designing, sewing, managing administrative tasks."

She wrinkles her nose. "That seems sleazy."

"Isn't one problem with fast fashion the substandard pay for garment workers? Why do that to yourself?"

"Whoa! I never thought of it like that."

Truly, I'm stunned. The connection is so obvious. How could Josephine not see it? I stare at her a moment, dumbfounded, then ask, "Why not?"

"I'm an artist in the United States. Society tells us we're lucky to earn anything."

"Damn."

"Which is ridiculous when you consider France spent almost three times what the US spent to support artists during the pandemic."

"Eye-opening. So how did you price the pieces in your show?"

"Kath did it. I gave her the cost of materials. She suggested prices for the stuff in the gallery because she wants to make money, too."

"Right. You'll need to add the costs for licensing the business, filing trademarks, legal fees, hiring, advertising and marketing."

She turns to an empty page and jots notes. Her handwriting is lovely, and why I have feelings about that is beyond me.

"I have questions," she says.

Of course she has questions. She's learning. "Please. Fire away."

"I looked at your website. How many of your startups actually succeeded?"

"Depends what you mean by succeeded."

She narrows her eyes. "Are they still in business?"

"Half of them are."

"Half?" She frowns.

"In the startup world, a fifty percent success rate is an accomplishment. Ninety percent of startups fail. Twenty-one percent fail in the first year."

"Yikes."

"And seventy-five percent of venture funded startups fail."

Josephine meets my gaze with vulnerability. "So, the odds are stacked against me."

The earnestness in her words and her demeanor quiet the critical voice in my head. "I wish I had better news. But I hope to tip the scales in your favor, so…" I spread my palms open. "Any more questions? Anything else you'd like to show me?"

"I thought venture funding was the golden ticket to success. Why is the failure rate still so high?"

"Lack of money, not enough market research, targeting the wrong demographic for the product or service, choosing the wrong business partner or having no partner."

"That's why you encouraged me to partner with Sage last night?"

"Exactly. If you join forces, that'll boost your marketing. And poor marketing is another business killer. Whether or not you pair up with Sage, you need expert marketing."

"Isn't it enough to post things on my Instapix page?"

"That depends. Are you boosting your posts? Do they link to a landing page where people can place orders? Are you analyzing the data, comparing post views to sales?"

Josephine bites her lip. *Too damn sexy. But kinda clueless.*

"Look, I've seen your Instagram. It's gorgeous, but do you know how many people came to your show because of your posts? If you're not using social media strategically, you're missing a key aspect of marketing."

"That sounds more like advertising, though. It costs money to boost posts."

"Advertising is part of marketing. The paid part."

"Advertising," she repeats, as if the word bothers her.

My arms and chest tighten in concern, but I think I understand why she's frosty. A lot of early-stage entrepreneurs want to consider money in the most general terms. Once real numbers pop up, people get nervous. This isn't a good sign, but it isn't necessarily a bad sign.

Please, God, let her show me something to justify investing in her. Right now, it's looking like Josephine Stewart has brilliant ideas and too much to learn about business. I hate to think Drew was right about her. But this fashion house may not be the wisest use of my resources.

JOSEPHINE

The sense of confidence that had been building inside me evaporates as Theo explains the costs of running a business and the failure rates of startups. This makes me realize why I've struggled to survive without a day job. It's not only that maintaining an artistic practice is hard in a country that tells artists their work doesn't matter, and they have no right to earn a living making art. It's that thinking about money gives me a violent stomachache. And advertising? Blech. That's the real brand brainwasher, not clothing labels.

Now, I press my hands into my navel to stop the gripping pain.

"Are you alright?" Theo asks.

I nod, flattening my lips. How am I supposed to respond to his questions? "I don't know how to figure out how many people came to my show after seeing my posts, unless someone volunteers it."

"Maybe Kath is already tracking that info."

"That would be nice."

My phone vibrates with another text from Mark: **NEED YOU HERE TODAY.**

I need this stomach pain to stop. Which word in part-time job confuses Mark? No way will I dignify his attempts to engage me and drag me into the office on Saturday. Maybe if Mark ever paid more for extra hours or made good on his promises to let employees exchange extra hours for time off, I'd respond.

Another message flashes on the screen: **YOUR BROCHURES = DISASTER.**

Did Theo see that text? I flip the phone face down to avoid further distraction and humiliation. Will Mark ruin this chance for me? My stomach cramps morph into violent shaking.

I take a deep breath, try to quell my trembling, and refocus on Theo. What's that expression in his eyes? Pity? Concern? Goodness. What were we talking about? I can do this. I must do this. I stroke the back of my hand to calm myself. *Orders.* "You asked about orders. I'm not set up for people to place orders. Anyway, isn't that what happens when I launch my fashion house?"

"Until now, you've only been showing in galleries?"

"Exactly."

"Why start a fashion house? If the gallery route is working for you—"

"Because I want to help people thrive by providing stable jobs in a supportive environment. Because I'm not just passionate about making clothes from up-cycled materials; I'm obsessed. And because freelancing and gallery sales are too unstable. And I've worked for a string of local nonprofits with abusive bosses and colleagues, and I can't take it anymore." Even my voice is trembling. Nervous. Embarrassed. This meeting is not going as planned.

"Sorry." Theo gentles his voice. "I couldn't help noticing the call and texts. Is Mark your boss?"

I nod, smooth my skirt and continue, afraid to look at Theo. "I *need* to quit my job. That place is not good for my wellbeing, but I'm afraid if I leave, I'll end up at another toxic organization." I take a calming breath and sneak a look at his face. "I'm sorry. That's TMI."

Theo leans in and catches my gaze. "Please don't apologize. I'm sorry you went through that, that you're still going through it."

Soothed by his nearness and his cedar scent, my heart rate slows. "Thank you."

"And it's not too much info. I appreciate your openness." He lifts his hand toward my shoulder, as if to comfort me, but pulls back.

His gesture helps. Already, I find it easier to breathe.

"It's hard to talk about abusive workplace situations," he says. "It sounds like your boss is a bully."

Heat rises in my cheeks as I fight tears, try to stop my lips trembling. His touch would calm me. *Bad idea, Josephine. Very bad idea.*

The door opens and Thalia strides in, a takeout bag in hand. "I've got—Mama, are you okay?" She glares at Theo.

I sniff. "Fine, Muffin. Mark keeps texting."

Thalia sets the bag of takeout on the table and wraps me in a tight embrace. "He's such an ass. He wouldn't even leave her alone during her show last night, Theo."

"I wish I could say I'm shocked. But I've heard horror stories about some of the nonprofits in this state. I hope you know you shouldn't tolerate bullying from your boss or anyone else."

"It's hard to stand up to them when I need the job, though." My voice comes out in a whisper.

Theo knits his eyebrows, rises. "A valid concern. Listen, I'll let you two enjoy the rest of your Saturday. Great seeing you both again."

"You too," Thalia says, digging into the takeout bag.

"I'll walk you out." I open the door and follow him into the hall and down the wide stairs that lead to the street. I wish we'd had more time to talk, that my assclown boss hadn't interrupted our meeting.

When we get to the outer door, Theo turns to me. "I love what you're about, Josephine, and I'd like to help you."

"Really?" The pain in my stomach finally releases its grip along with the shame and frustration I felt a moment ago. I clap softly. "Does this mean you'll invest?"

"To be determined."

"Fair." Not the answer I hoped for, but reasonable. "How do you decide?"

"What you're doing is amazing. I'm totally impressed, but—"

But? Excitement turns to fear, which tightens my throat.

"I need something to share. You understand, right?"

"Of course." Kind of.

"Your notebooks, studio, your ideas are cool, but they're not a business plan. I can't make projections by looking at your mood boards; I can't show sketches to investors. I'm happy to keep talking to you about this process, to give you advice. And once I see a solid plan, then we can talk about money."

"That makes sense." I extend my hand. He takes it in both of his, meets my gaze. We inhale simultaneously, smile and let out the breath together, then laugh, though I'm not sure why we're laughing. I'm nervous. But what's up with him? His eyes sparkle, which causes my body to soften and warm. Except two distinct parts that stiffen in response to his gaze and handshake. Embarrassment surges through me. *Thank goodness the apron covers my chest.*

"Along with your business plan, I'll need to see a proper budget spreadsheet by the end of next week."

Crap. Business plan and budget spreadsheet? That's only thirteen days. The business plan is no problem. I have that book. But a spreadsheet?

"You've got that look on your face again." His tone conveys both amusement and sympathy.

"What look?"

"Like you are stressed as hell."

Stressed and now embarrassed. "I'm sorry. I didn't mean to make you feel uncomfortable. Clearly, you came to help. And—"

"No worries. What's got you tense?"

I groan. "I've never made a spreadsheet."

"The library's entrepreneur-in-residence can help. If you can't get an appointment in the next couple days, hit me up. Okay?" He smiles and opens the door, letting in a wave of intense heat.

"Sure." I'm fluttering inside again.

"You know how to make a business plan. Right?"

"I've been reading about it." *The Creative Business Plan* may be my best Mini Free Library find ever.

"Great," Theo says. "I look forward to hearing from you again soon."

"Thanks for your time, Theo."

"Of course." He strides down the busy sidewalk, exuding confidence.

The view of Theo's backside in linen pants is sublime. I can't help imagining him in a swimsuit, then without one. Lovely. I shake the vision from my mind. What am I thinking? He's a colleague. Almost. Maybe. Hopefully. And I have work to do. Lots of work. A business plan to write. Thank goodness for that book. When I open it tonight, I will take notes and get to work. I will absolutely not fall asleep while reading it.

Chapter Five

JOSEPHINE

I STRETCH and push the sheets back, knocking *The Creative Business Plan* to the floor. I fell asleep reading again. Shoot. The clock on my nightstand reads eleven-thirty. Already? Now I'm awake, and my mind is racing. What time is Thalia's train? Will we get to finish our important conversation? I roll out of bed, tiptoe down the hall and peek in on Thalia—sound asleep. Hopefully, she'll open up today. Seeing the tension in her face yesterday tore at me. I have to help Thalia resolve this before she goes home, so we can both be at peace.

I'm in the middle of Chapter Three, Vision, when Thalia pads into the kitchen, hair in a messy halo.

"Good morning, Mama. Doing your homework?"

"Homework." I giggle. As if Theo's a college professor. A fun fantasy flashes through my mind, which I nip in the bud. I will not develop a crush on a colleague. "I was, but now that you're awake, I'm putting it down."

"You don't need to." Thalia leans over and hugs me.

I stroke her back, loving the contact. "I want to, though. What would you like for breakfast? Waffles? Eggs?"

"I'll have last night's leftovers." Thalia opens the fridge and pulls out a pizza box, brews herself a cup of tea and slumps into a chair next to me.

"Wanna talk about the LSATs?"

She sighs, stares into her cup of tea.

"We don't have to, but I can see it's stressing you out. Maybe talking will help."

"Do you think I really need to go to law school?"

"I don't know as much about media literacy education as you. But you've been talking about changing national education policy for a couple years. And I think—" My phone screams the annoying text tone reserved for Mark, making me growl. "Unbelievable."

"It's Sunday morning." Thalia's eyes widen.

"Actually, it's almost two o'clock, but still."

"Shit, is it that late? I have to go in like forty minutes."

"I know, so let me ignore the—" Another text message. I will not look at it. I absolutely will not. "What was I saying?"

"How I've been wanting to change policy." She takes another bite of pizza.

"Right, I think... where was I going with this?" I race backward through my train of thought. "That's right. If you want to change policy, you might need a law degree."

"Yeah," she draws out the word, "but I'm doing great at my job. And I love the kids. Maybe I shouldn't make policy. Maybe I should—" My phone interrupts her, and Mark's angry face lights the screen. Thalia looks at me, exasperated, then finishes over the irritating ring tone. "—teach media literacy."

I put the phone on vibrate. "You should do what lights up your heart. You'd be a wonderful teacher, too. What feels right to you?"

"In my heart?"

The doorbell rings. "Are you expecting one of your high school friends?"

"No."

I push myself away from the kitchen table, step onto the sun porch, and peek down at the doorway. My heart stops, then pounds wildly. Mark paces on the stoop. What the hell is wrong with him? He rings the bell again in rapid succession, fans himself with an envelope, then slips it into the mail slot in the door and leaves. Stunned, angry, I walk back into the kitchen.

"Why are you shaking, Mama?" Thalia looks alarmed.

"That was Mark. He just…"

"Your boss came here? On a Sunday?"

I nod. I try to sit but can't. I need to move, do yoga, something. I drop into a forward fold. "I don't know what this means. Is he firing me? Is this about those goddamn brochures?"

"Your boss is stalking you."

God, I hope that's not true. I roll up to standing, bring one foot to the inside of the opposite thigh in Tree Pose. "Maybe it's an invitation. A company picnic?"

Thalia raises an eyebrow, looks at her phone. "Shit, I need to get dressed and pack. There's only one train after this and it gets in late. Mama, go see what he dropped off. Then we can talk about whether you need to call the police."

"Right," I say, numb. I open the apartment door and run down the stairs, grab the thin envelope from the basket under the mail slot and rip it open. It's the brochure with a sticky note: *Board breathing down my neck. Need this fixed ASAP. I expect you in the office tomorrow.* The first sentence almost makes me feel bad for him. But the last sentence strikes my core like lightning. He expects? Not: "*Can you please call? Can you please help? I know you don't normally work Mondays. I'm sorry to bother you on a weekend.*" But "*I expect.*" I storm up the stairs and into the apartment.

"It's about the brochure," I say, walking into Thalia's room.

"So, no threats or anything?" She pulls her hair into a messy bun.

"No, but he *expects* me in the office tomorrow to fix this." I hold up the brochure.

Thalia takes it, scans it quickly. "This is beautiful. What's his problem? I mean, I see he's marked the photos, but I don't get it. They look great."

I breathe a sigh of relief, as much responding to my daughter's praise as to the realization that the envelope didn't contain something worse, like a dismissal letter. "Thanks, hon. God, I feel horrible. We were finally working through your decision."

She shoves her iPad and toiletries into her backpack and zips it closed, sighing. "You can't control what that asshole does. Anyway, the Uber should be here in two minutes. I'll call you when I get home. Okay?"

I squeeze her. "Love you so much, Muffin. It meant a lot to have you there for my reception."

"Love you, too." Thalia kisses me and slips on her shoes. "After watching you put off your dreams to raise me, I'd love to see you go for it. Get away from this Mark asshole." She runs out the door. I follow her down the stairs and wave goodbye as she gets into the Uber.

"Breathe, Mama!" Thalia yells out the window as the car drives away. My heart drops. There I was trying to take care of my daughter, and instead my child ended up taking care of me. If I had my life together, that never would have happened. I bet Thalia never needs to worry about how Seth's doing. But then, he's always had his shit together. Even in college, when I was studying graphic design and media instead of fashion, he knew he wanted to go into finance, work on Wall Street, wear a suit every day and roll in the corporate world. Then, while I focused on raising our child, he kept building his career. Why couldn't I have had a linear path? Was Theo's path linear? It wasn't clear from the bio on his website.

Well, I can stand here with the sun beating down on me and feel sorry for myself, or I can go inside and read another chapter of *The Creative Business Plan*, or say fuck-it-all and go to the beach. What I will not do is work on that damn brochure for Social Good Conn. I hear Thalia in my head: *After watching you put off your dreams for me, I'd love to see you go for it.* Before anything else, I'm booking an appointment with the library's entrepreneur-in-residence so I can learn about spreadsheets. Maybe by the time Thalia calls, I'll have part of my plan written.

It took a while to get back into it. Washing the floors and folding laundry, even cleaning the toilet seemed way more appealing than usual. But now that I'm focused on the book, I'm having fun doing the exercises to build my plan. So far, I've drafted my vision, mission, and values statement and created a marketing plan. That'll impress Theo. I'll still go to my meeting at the library tomorrow, but, honestly, the chapter that has me making a financial plan with flair seems way more useful than a boring spreadsheet. Stumbling upon *The Creative Business Plan* at the Mini Free Library truly was a stroke of luck.

As I get out my craft supplies, I consider how I'll present my vision. I'm eager to start the plan, but I really should finish reading the book first. If I finish within the hour, I'll have time to take a walk in the cool night air before bed. The phone vibrates with a video call and Thalia's sweet face lights the screen.

"Hi! How was the train?"

"Good. I'm home safe, as you can see." She sweeps her

phone around her studio apartment. "How was your afternoon?"

"Very productive. I'm really cruising through this business plan."

"Awesome! Am I interrupting?"

"Not at all. Wanna chat?"

"Yeah. I looked at the website. Registration for the next LSAT prep course closes Tuesday."

I push myself away from the table, pour a tall glass of iced hibiscus tea and step onto the sun porch. Golden evening light glows on the pavement and illuminates the trees.

"Ooh, gorgeous light," Thalia says. "Makes me wanna go out and shoot."

"Do you get to use your photo and video skills at the summer program?"

"More than I would in policy. I talked to Daddy, and he thinks I can't go wrong with a law degree."

Tension grips me. "For certain jobs. But if you wanna teach kids, it won't help. And you'll be racking up lots of student debt."

"Dad says I'll do more good in policy or teaching media law and literacy in college."

Does he? I try not to feel annoyed with Seth. He's trying to help. "Well, Muffin, the great thing about your dad and me is we can give you very different perspectives. I guess you have to ask yourself: *what kind of good do I want to do?*"

"What kind of good?"

"In policy, you'll affect children nationwide, but you'll work with adults," I explain. "As a teacher, you'll affect students one-on-one and, depending on the age, in groups as small as six or as large as two hundred. What feels right to you: writing policy, teaching college, or working with tweens?"

"In my heart?"

"Exactly. Not in your head. Not from a place of fear. You definitely have the foresight and innovative mindset for policy. But you're also compassionate and inspiring, which makes you a wonderful teacher. You'll be doing good either way. The question is: what makes you feel most alive? The possibility of working in Washington and changing the system? Or working boots on the ground, directly affecting young minds and hearts?"

Thalia works her jaw. Her shoulders rise toward her ears.

"Breathe into it." I model the technique.

Thalia follows, inhaling deeply and letting the words fall with her exhale. "Changing the system in Washington." She closes her eyes, inhales and exhales the words. "Affecting students one-on-one." She opens her eyes and says, "I think teaching."

"Yay! Adults or kids?"

"Eight-to-twelve-year-olds. They're cute and they haven't been ruined yet. Plus, helping them understand the barrage of messages coming at them online, TV and radio, in magazines and ads... That feels really meaningful to me."

"These kids won't be so easily manipulated by media thanks to you."

Pride brightens my daughter's face. Seeing her relax lifts a weight from my shoulders. "You look lighter already, like a weight has been lifted."

"I do kind of feel that way."

"And, in case it wasn't clear, I fully support that decision."

Thalia groans. "Mom, you would have fully supported any decision."

"What's wrong with that? I'm your mother. Shouldn't I support your choices?"

"I guess. But I really wanna know what you think."

"I think the best advice I could give you is to follow your heart."

"Oh, God."

"I can't make your major life decisions for you, Muffin. I don't have to live with them."

"You'll have to support me if I fail. You and Dad."

"Obviously. And your dad is comfortable enough that he can help financially. I may not have much money, but I always have a room for you."

"Thanks, Mama."

At last, my heart feels light. "My pleasure. What are you up to now?"

"Dinner, shower, bed. I have to be at work at eight-thirty. And you?"

"I'm gonna take a quick walk now that the sun has set, then see how much more I can do on this business plan."

"Wait. You didn't let me interrupt you while you were working, did you?"

I smile sheepishly. "You needed me."

"Mama! You have to stop doing that."

"Why? I love that you come to me for advice. Not everyone has that kind of relationship with their children."

She sighs. "I know. But I'm an adult. I *could* have figured this out on my own."

"You did. I only guided you a little."

"But you were *working on your dream* and you interrupted it for me. Again."

"Just say thank you and go eat your dinner."

"Thank you. I love you."

We end the call as I slip into my hiking sandals and skip down the stairs. I'm making progress on my business plan. Thalia made an important life decision with my help. And now, I get to enjoy the cool evening air on my skin, a relief after the infernal heat.

I'm stepping into the moonlight when Dad texts a link with the message: **We made the news, Sugar! Not sure**

what WTF means, but proud we're making a difference.

Hopefully, reading this won't take long. I click the link to MASSLIVE.news. A photo fills the screen—my parents and a handful of others emptying small baskets onto the granite steps, the statehouse dome looming behind them. The caption says it all: *WTF? "Activists" Dump Clothing Labels Onto Statehouse Steps.* Oh, my God. Thankfully, there's no article accompanying the photo.

Congrats! I text because what else can I say? **Love you.**

Of course, I send the link to Thalia, who responds with a laughing face emoji.

I'm still giggling when I slide into bed an hour later, *The Creative Business Plan* in hand, journal by my side. Four chapters left. I read: *"Chapter 8 - Goals, Strategies, and..."*

/ Chapter Six /

JOSEPHINE

Unfortunately, I fell asleep before I finished reading the chapter heading. At least I made progress yesterday, and in less than an hour I'll understand spreadsheets thanks to the library's Entrepreneur-in-Residence.

The sounds of children playing and the breeze riffling through the leaves overhead soften the anxiety building in me as I walk downtown. I try to focus on the flowers in the curb strips. But mental visions of columns, numbers, and dollar signs gnaw at my stomach. How did I rope myself into making spreadsheets?

Theo. His warm eyes, sexy shaved head, the way he held my gaze as we said goodbye Saturday. Swoonworthy. Did he show up in my dreams last night? OMG, he did, and he played a rather scandalous role. I'm giggling as I mount the wide marble steps of the New Haven Free Public Library. Heat rises in my thighs, and it's not from the exercise. When I pull the heavy door open, though, a blast of cold air douses my arousal. My heart thuds in fear.

This is ridiculous. It's a spreadsheet, not a firing squad. I force a laugh—a tactic that sometimes helps me relax. A vision of Theo propping himself up above me flashes through my mind, making my stomach tingle pleasantly. Not good.

Also not good: the entrepreneur-in-residence desk is empty. I check my phone—11:27, three minutes early. I peruse the library's designated room for entrepreneurs and open a book with a derogatory title about idiots learning to use spreadsheets. Maybe all I need is this book.

I struggle through the first paragraph. The condescending tone of the writing puts me off immediately. Worse, I don't comprehend a damn thing the author's saying. I skip to a later chapter with a friendlier heading and dive in. Nope. Still mystified. Third time's the charm. I flip to a chapter with an innocuous title. Again, nothing makes sense. Well, so much for spreadsheets being for idiots, too. I didn't feel like an idiot before I tried to read the book.

At 11:34, my boss texts: **Where are you? We're talking about the brochure.**

Mark, it's Monday. My schedule is Tuesday and Wednesday 9 to 6.

No one likes the new brochure design. You'll have to fix it ASAP.

Tension fills me. *No one* likes it? Maybe that explains Mark's extra obnoxious behavior over the weekend. *No one* likes it? Mark tends to exaggerate, to say shitty things and then rally support from his minions. Maybe the board doesn't like it. Mark seemed to like it fine when he approved it. Jerk. I fantasize about texting clever ideas about where to stick the new brochure. Instead, I sigh and fire back: **Would you like to discuss changing the days I work, or shall I plan to see you tomorrow?**

At 11:53, the person manning the customer service desk informs me that the entrepreneur-in-residence called out sick this morning. Had I checked my email, I would've seen the message. Great. Can't say I didn't try. Now I have no choice but to call Theo for help. What a shame. Okay, that's total BS. I have other resources, and if I don't use them, Theo will think I'm incapable.

I text Seth as I push the heavy door open and step into the sunlight. If anyone understands budgets, it's my ex-husband. But he responds that he's out of the country on business for the month. Crap. Thalia would tell me to Google it or watch a YouTube video. That never works for me. I always have more questions than those how-to videos answer. What I need is the personal touch. *Theo's personal touch.* A tingling sensation fills my chest, and I can't stop the joy from spreading across my face as I dial his number.

THEO

My speech, "Finding Your Niche: Entrepreneurial Tribalism," is going well. Unusual choice to hold an event like this on a rooftop bar, but the staff made it work somehow using technology and bamboo. I don't get it, but I don't have to. I'm educating an engaged group of entrepreneurs and sneaking in a message about mission-driven entrepreneurism. I'm in a groove now, getting to the key point. And the sound system is going haywire. Fuck. My phone vibrates on the podium. Is that the issue? I thought silencing the device would be sufficient. Apparently not. My neck tightens as I stare at the infernal thing. It'll stop vibrating in a minute.

It doesn't.

"Excuse me." I smile to hide my irritation. "I'm very popular."

The joke garners a few laughs. The phone vibrates for the fourth time making that awful feedback sound come through the speakers. "Guess that's what I get for keeping my speech notes on my phone. If I turn it off, you'll be staring at a man with no idea what he came to say." More laughter from the audience. What could be so urgent? It could be Deborah calling about Mom, a thought that makes my muscles clench. "Excuse me a moment. I'd better make sure my house isn't on fire or something."

I open my phone app: one missed call from Josephine. No voice message. Three texts. Thank God. My muscles shift from clenching in fear and aggravation to relaxing in joy.

I turn off my phone and resume my speech, gratified by how quickly I'm able to regain the audience's attention. When I finish my presentation, hands shoot up all over the rooftop. I answer questions for twenty minutes, then wrap things up. At last, I can sneak off to a private corner of the rooftop and see what's on Josephine's mind.

Hi Theo. Tried to see entrepreneur at library. Out sick. [Sneezing face emoji.]

Her second text says: **Thought I'd learn everything from friends or the excel book for idiots.** [Thumbs down emoji.]

Her last message spurs me to action: **Developing intense spreadsheet phobia.** [Screaming face emoji.] **Help?**

My fingers fly over the phone screen in response. **At your service! Friday at 11:30, okay? My office?**

I'm about to hit send when Drew's voice fills my mind again. *Not thinking with your MBA. Damn it, Drew.* That throbbing between my brows reminds me, Josephine must prove herself to earn my investment. I delete the message and instead tell her to look at the ExcelDemy website. **Call when you have something to show me. I look forward to our next meeting.**

Now, *that* is professional. So what if I'm envisioning Josephine sitting on my lap in my home office. Completely irrelevant. I'm a forty-nine-year-old man. I have needs. She has pheromones. It's a mere fantasy. Nothing more.

Chapter Seven

JOSEPHINE

EXCELDEMY EXPLAINS everything so clearly and
concisely. I take the template Theo sent and adjust it to the
fashion world, setting the formulas and adding line items.
Now, all that's missing is the numbers. How important is it
to have amounts now? It seems silly, even disingenuous to
put figures in the income column. I don't know how to find
some of the expenses. Plus, costs vary. Obviously, that information will come later.

I text Theo on my walk to work, happy to have something to think about besides what I'll tell Mark when he gets
on my case for not showing up on my days off.

ExcelDemy = Awesome [fire emoji] **Finished the
budget. Biz plan done Thursday.**

Theo responds immediately. **Wow. Impressive! Meet
Fri? My place?**

Perfect!

He texts me his address. My core buzzes with excitement
over the possibilities. In three days, I'm going to show Theo
Casabella, an angel investor, my business plan. Having an

honest-to-goodness investor could speed my timeline exponentially, get me out of my shit job sooner. Freedom. I look at the clear sky, revel in the slight humidity caressing my skin and the scent of coffee wafting from the nearby cafe. But as the cinder block building where I work comes into view, the Tuesday morning stomach cramps arrive right on schedule.

If I felt good about this place, I'd be proud of the banner above the door and the new visual identity I created for the organization. As I reach the building, I inhale, imagine golden light softening the tension in my stomach, and exhale slowly. *Release. Release. Release.* Smiling at my reflection in the glass door, I whisper, "Today will be better." I walk through the entrance and into the main office, where my boss hunches his six-foot-four frame over the bookkeeper's desk. The bookkeeper, Sara, looks up at me, her face revealing exasperation. My stomach tightens, but I force myself to smile and adopt a cheerful tone. "Good morning, Mark. Good morning, Sara."

Mark ignores me. Sara responds, "How was your show?"

"Awesome. Did you see the piece in the *New Haven Register*?"

"I loved—"

Mark interrupts with a question about payroll figures. *Shocker.* Sara slumps in defeat. I fill out my timesheet, stick it into the slot, then reach into my backpack for the key to my office. Oops. I forgot it at home, so I open the closet where all the office keys hang inside the door.

"What the hell are you doing?" Mark yells. "You have no right to be in there, Josephine."

I jump, and the key slips from my hand to the floor. "Excuse me?" I ask, shaking as I bend down to retrieve it. "I forgot my key at home."

"Then go get it," Mark says. "I'll dock your pay for the time you're gone."

Incredulous, I put the key back, close the closet, turn on

my heel, and stride outside without a word. I have creative ideas for where Mark can put the key, but I keep those to myself. Does the man respect anyone?

My freelance clients love me, appreciate my work, never balk at paying me appropriately for my expertise. Not so with employers. I had hoped it would be different here when I started. Everyone had been so pleasant during my interviews.

If I didn't need stable income, I'd quit this damn job and never work for anyone again. I miss the days when I worked for clients while Thalia was at school. But then she went to college, and the child support stopped, and the financial instability of freelancing became glaringly obvious.

I walk into my apartment. I'm home? Already? That man aggravates me so much that I just walked a mile without even noticing where I was. Something has got to change. I pull the key to my office from the hook by the door and turn around, wishing I didn't have to return.

When I arrive at Social Good Conn thirty minutes later, I go directly upstairs to my closet-sized office, unlock the door, and find Mark waiting in my chair. I jump. "What are you doing here?"

Mark levels me with a steady gaze and eerily quiet voice. "We're fixing this brochure. I logged you in."

I take a deep breath and let it out slowly, trying to quell the shaking in my hands as I hang my backpack on the door. Mark stands and gestures to my seat.

"Excuse me." I inch past him, sit, pull the chair as far under the desk as it can go. "Could you back up please, Mark?"

"I need to see."

I shiver. It's not sexual. He's making a power move.

"Let's get to work, Josephine."

Theo's words echo in my mind. *You shouldn't tolerate bullying.* "I can feel your breath on my neck."

Mark inches back.

Wow. It works. "Further," I command.

"Open the file, Josephine."

"Not until you move back or sit on the side of my desk. I'll turn the screen so we can both see."

Mark throws me a fake smile as he moves the stool across from me to the short side of my desk. I turn the monitor, open the file, put my hands in my lap so he can't see me shaking.

"What's the problem, Mark? This is exactly what you told me to do two weeks ago." I point behind me. "You stood there, literally breathing down my neck and dictated the design and placement of everything."

"The board wants the old photos."

Sure. Images of white people in power suits and non-white people holding their hands out for spare change. No stereotypes there. "Aren't we trying to promote race equity? That's why I chose photos of happy interracial families."

He snaps, "They don't like what you chose. Fix it."

"Do they have any other issues with the brochure?"

"Offensive writing. Garish color scheme."

My eyebrows go up. "What about the writing is offensive?"

"I've already told you what needs fixing. Why aren't you doing it?"

"Because these comments don't clarify what you or they actually want. And because each element of the design interacts with the others. The amount of text determines the size of the images. The images need to represent our message and play well with the brand colors. I'm gathering information, so I don't waste more energy and time."

Mark's face reddens. Sweat blooms along his thinning white hairline. "You're being insubordinate."

I speak softly but firmly, struggling to keep the tremor out of my voice. "I'm sorry you see it that way. I'm trying to give you the best of my professional knowledge, so everyone will be happy with the brochure. And I'm wondering: if they hate the color scheme, does that mean we need to redesign all the business cards, the donation cards, the thank-you notes, the banner outside, and the website?"

"I don't KNOW," he yells at the top of his lungs.

"I wonder if the board would make such a big deal about the brochure if they knew that we'll have to change everything else to match."

"Only in your mind, Josephine. Most people don't care about this matchy-matchy crap."

"You mean the branding you paid me to do? The branding the board said they wanted? What's really going on here, Mark?"

"Just *fix* the goddamn brochure."

"Okay. What color scheme do you want?"

He flares his nostrils, and I swear steam comes out. "Bridget," Mark barks at the door.

Oh, great. The ice queen cometh.

Bridget appears in the threshold, poses, and flashes a plastic smile. "Yes, Mark?"

"Josephine needs your help with this goddamn brochure."

She emits a dramatic sigh. "What a debacle! How can I help, Josephine?" she asks, piercing me with her black-eyed glare.

I throw her an equally fake smile. "I know you're the queen of fundraising, but unless you have intel on what the board wants the brochure to convey, I'm not sure you can help. Thanks, though." I open the color palette for the new brand, copy it, and bring up the gray twenty percent in each color swatch. "Now, what about this, Mark? I toned down our existing palette. What do you think?"

He examines it, nods slowly, looks over his shoulder. "Bridget?"

She drums the door with fire red nails. "Hmm. I don't know. Let's get Douglas and Xavier in here." Bridget taps her phone screen. "They're coming up."

"Who's Xavier?"

"The new intern Douglas hired to do graphic design for workforce development, since you don't grasp his vision."

Do. Not. React. I struggle to keep my expression placid. Douglas's voice booms in the hall. Bridget inches into the tiny office next to Mark, followed by an ethnically ambiguous twenty-something with black hair pulled into a man bun.

"You must be Xavier." I extend my hand, meeting his warm gaze. "Welcome!"

"Josephine, Xavier is a recent grad from Southern Connecticut State University," Douglas says, loud enough to compensate for what he lacks in height. I can barely see his blond hair over Bridget and Xavier. Douglas continues, "You'll be running all societal media twitters past him, since he's a digital native and understands the Facebooks."

The young man throws a sidelong glance at his boss. "I think you mean *social* media, Douglas," he says, turning back to me with a genuine smile. "Anyway, I plan to learn from you, Josephine. The portfolio on your site is lit. And your show? I was there Friday." He whistles. "Blessed to work with you."

I smile. "I look forward to working with you as well." *You don't know what you've gotten yourself into.*

Mark scowls. "Folks, we're trying to fix this god-awful brochure, and Josephine needs your ideas."

Xavier widens his eyes in horror and sympathy as Bridget, Douglas, and Mark lob opinions around the room like weapons, voices getting louder. No one offers constructive critique or explains exactly what is offensive about the wording. When Xavier dares to speak, they talk over him. Why am I surprised? It's not like this behavior is new. Mark looks at me, a smirk on his face that defies me to challenge him.

You missed your calling in the military, Mark. You lead quite an attack. I'd love to stand up to him again. But I don't dare with everyone in the room. That could send him over the edge. Freelancing may pay better, but I need stability more.

My phone vibrates in my lap, a text message from Sara: **I hear yelling. Everything OK?**

General VanAss leading another attack. With his eyes glued on me, I won't risk texting you back.

I force a smile at Mark and refocus on my computer. Now, I tone down the color in all the brochure's graphics. Replace the cover photo with an old one. Ignore the sick feeling in my stomach. There's always retail. But working over forty-five hours a week in retail to match fifteen hours' earnings at Social Good Conn? *Ridiculous.* With that extra time, I sewed the pieces for my show, started brainstorming the fashion house. Now, I'll use those free hours to bring my business plan to life. When Theo sees my plan, he'll invest, and I'll have my freedom.

And I won't give six weeks' notice here, like I did at the last awful nonprofit. No, I will "accidentally" delete every file I created for this organization, then "clumsily" drop my office key in the storm drain outside the building, and smile sweetly at the staff meeting as I inform them I'm not returning. Ever. Then I'll leave with no notice. They can fend for themselves. The vision sends a delightful surge of energy through my body that makes me smile.

But now, a tiny army waits to slash my brochure copy. Irritating. In my job interview, I said, *I'm not a writer.* Still, Mark expects me to pull perfect words from thin air. I replace soft verbs with power verbs, remove references to race equity, weaken the brand promise until it's almost meaningless. "Is this better?" I ask and point to the monitor.

Xavier flashes a thumbs up. "I loved what you did before, but this works. Don't you think, Douglas?" He plasters himself against the wall, making way for Douglas.

Without acknowledging me, Douglas pushes forward, glances at the screen, then looks at Mark, waiting for the appropriate response.

"Print it. I need to see it in better light," Mark orders, then scowls at his vibrating phone and skulks out. "Don't go anywhere. We're not done."

I click print and look at my colleagues. "Would one of you please go downstairs and grab it?"

Bridget follows Douglas out, as Xavier asks. "How'd you tone down the colors?"

"Easy. I brought up the key twenty percent."

"Key?"

"Fancy graphic design term for black. You know CMYK? Most printing companies still use that color format, though some take RGB files."

"I've only used hex codes."

"I see. You design for web only?"

Xavier nods.

"You know, we use Illustrator and InDesign here, right? Did you study Adobe programs in school?"

He shakes his head. "I majored in Advertising and Promotion with a minor in Social Media."

"So you are an expert." Thank goodness, Douglas hired someone skilled.

"In analysis and theory. I never took a design class. Picked up Canva on my own."

I bite my lip, worried for him. *They're going to eat you alive.*

"Like I said, I plan to learn from you," he says. "I wanna take what I learned in school and put it to good use helping nonprofits, but I'm not a designer. We could make a good team."

I see sincerity and warmth in his dark eyes. Theo's comments about advertising's importance run through my mind. Maybe Douglas just gave me a fantastic gift, unwittingly. Maybe I'll learn as much from Xavier as he will from me, and when I start my fashion house, I can hire him. Of course, that's assuming he's as kindhearted as he appears. I completely misjudged my colleagues here and at the last three jobs, but then I was desperate for stable income. It's easy to overlook red flags when you're scared.

The army storms in, bringing another one of my vitriolic colleagues—Fay, the epitome of dumpy and resentful. She waves the printout at me. "You sent this to my printer. I was in the middle of the grant proposal for the new housing initiative. You broke my flow."

"I'm sorry, Fay," I say. "I know how frustrating it is when someone interrupts."

"Thanks." Fay drops it on the desk and storms out. "It still needs work," she yells from the hallway.

"I think," Douglas booms, "that Xavier should take over the brochure project."

Bridget taps her manicured nails together. "Yes."

Luckily, Mark won't be so stupid.

"I agree," Mark says. "He's got the chops for it. And this just isn't working."

My stomach drops.

Xavier's eyes bulge. "Actually, I don't. I—"

"Don't be so modest, Xavier," Bridget purrs. "Your degree speaks for itself."

"It's settled." Mark claps Xavier on the back. "You'll fix the brochure. Josephine, you can handle the annual gala invitations, can't you? It's simple enough. Logo, fancy things around the edges. Time. Date."

"I'm on it." I close the brochure file. "I'll email this to you, Xavier. Let me know if you have questions." *Which you will. In fact, I'll probably end up designing this anyway, so you don't get in trouble and they get their damn brochure.*

Alone in my office at last, I press the heels of my hands into my eyes to stop the oncoming headache. It doesn't work. It felt so good to stand up to Mark earlier, to watch him back down. But he got his revenge. And now that he's given one of my projects to the intern, how long will it be before he tells me I'm not needed at all?

Chapter Eight

JOSEPHINE

I'm still imagining my revenge on Social Good Conn
when I arrive at Kath and Lauren's high-rise condo downtown. I love this building, with its classic brick façade and
carved stone lintels and columns. Inside, the foyer's white
marble floors gleam, and the doorman leads me to the spot-
less brass-doored elevator.

Like K-Gallery, my friends' home smells of herbal tea.
They welcome me with hugs and kisses, soothing my frazzled
nerves. A relaxing evening with friends is exactly what I need.

Lauren's blonde spiral curls are piled atop her head in a
messy ponytail that reminds me of a Greek goddess. But her
attire is all business, and she wears it well, as if she enjoys
donning a suit each day. Kath's bright orange boho linen
dress provides a sharp contrast to Lauren's buttoned-down
appearance. The fuchsia cat eye glasses she's wearing match
Kath's wedge heels and pick up the color of the embroidered
flowers that ring the bottom of the dress.

"Darling." She takes my elbow and leads me inside.

"Your face tells me everything I need to know about the day you've had."

"Which I left at the door. Let's chill out!" I hand Kath a bottle of rum. "I'm ready for your famous mojitos."

"Hear, hear," Lauren says.

As we amble through their plush living room, an augmented photograph above the mantle catches my eye. "Is that new?"

"From Sage's big exhibition," Kath says. "It's been here a year-and-a-half. You haven't noticed?"

"Guess my mind was elsewhere." I move closer and examine the image. "This is her studio after the tornado hit?"

"*Studio As Self-Portrait of the Artist Affected by Climate Change*," Lauren says. "We couldn't bear to part with it, so I bought it as an anniversary present for Kath. I'm going to finish dinner prep."

Lauren's husky voice resonates in my chest, as usual. If I were into women, I'd be incredibly jealous of Kath.

I follow them into the kitchen. It's huge, with a prep sink and a dish sink, professional-grade appliances, and wooden cabinets painted cornflower blue. "Have I ever admitted I have very intense kitchen envy?"

Lauren purrs, "You should. We have a *lot* of fun in this kitchen."

"And she's not just talking about the cooking." Kath winks and runs a finger down her wife's spine, then across the granite countertop.

Lauren makes a sexy humming sound in response. "Tonight, I'm making a vegan pasta alla carbonara with cashew creme and shiitake bacon."

"My mouth is watering." And being around these two lovebirds, I can't help lapsing into fantasy. What would it be like to have a happy relationship?

My phone dings.

"Wait 'til you taste it, darling," Kath says, opening the

liquor cabinet above the bar. "You know, my wife is the world's best vegan chef not working in the restaurant industry."

"I know. Every time she feeds me..." I sigh. "Brilliant, sexy, talented. Curse the Gods! Why am I so damn heterosexual? I want your life."

"Her milkshake brings all the girls to the yard," Kath raps. "My wife is better than yours. Damn right, she's—"

I laugh. "Keep that up, and I'ma start twerking! Now, tell me what to do."

"We're also having a radicchio and fennel salad with pine nuts and blood orange dressing." Lauren slides a wooden cutting board across the dark granite counter and plops a head of purple radicchio onto it. "Julienne this, please."

"Yum." My phone dings again. I wash my hands. With the third ding, I sigh and look at my messages. Unknown number. All too familiar message. The word "brochure" flashes on the screen, making my muscles clench.

"What's up?" Lauren asks.

Shoot. I've done nothing but wash and dry my hands. "Sorry. It's the intern. He needs help."

"At seven PM? I don't think so, darling. This job asks too much."

"You're right. It's just..." As I slice the vegetable into thin strips, I share the events of the workday and my concern for Xavier. "He's a kid, and they've put him in a terrible bind."

"Isn't he Thalia's age?" Kath asks.

"Mm-hmm." Imagining his anxiety distresses me.

"Sounds like he could've been more vocal about his skill set," Lauren says.

"I know, but—" I didn't mean to cry, but my tears drip onto the cutting board. And now, damn it, I'm sniffling audibly. "If I don't help him, and they don't get this damn brochure, Mark will blame me. And I need this job."

"You need a job," Kath says. "But this one?"

Lauren resumes slicing shiitake mushrooms and coats them with olive oil and salt, shaking her head the whole time. Finally, she says, "Josie, I'd like nothing better than to help you sue the pants off this organization. They have no right to claim they're creating *systems change* when their M.O. is intimidate, use, abuse."

"Thank you for that validation, but thinking about a lawsuit makes me so nauseous, I'm afraid I wouldn't be able to do any of the work that really matters to me. I'd be sick with nerves all the time."

Lauren sighs as she puts the mushrooms into the oven. "Good because I don't think you have a case. Their actions aren't overtly racist or sexist."

"I've half a mind to go into that toxic waste dump and tell Mark a thing or two," Kath says, handing me a mojito.

The memory of Kath putting Drew in his place makes me smile. "That would be fun."

"My warrior goddess." Lauren winks at her wife, takes a slow pull of her drink and turns serious, her husky voice strong and sad. "Josephine, I want you out of there. And don't be surprised when they hand you a nondisclosure agreement. The last thing they want is someone with a voice in this town airing their dirty laundry."

"Should I sign it?"

"Hell no! Walk away, and don't look back."

When I have enough money saved, I will. "I don't know when Theo will decide about funding my fashion house. But if he does, that might carry me a while."

"Did he say how much he'll offer?" Lauren asks.

"He's waiting to see my business plan."

"You have a business plan?" Kath asks, impressed.

"I'll finish it by Friday, when I meet with Theo."

"Excellent." Kath sips her mojito.

"The only thing I'm iffy on is the budget, but I think it's

fine to have some blank spots. It doesn't make sense to put in random numbers or estimates."

Kath's eyebrows go up in alarm. "You're wrong there. I can tell you from experience, investors expect numbers."

"How am I supposed to get numbers when I haven't started the business yet?"

Lauren clears her throat. She and Kath seem to be having a silent conversation, which makes me wistful. To be so connected to someone. They finish the silent chat with a nod at each other. Lauren turns back to food prep, and Kath points at me. "You. Come with me."

I follow her through the living room into her beautiful home office. So perfectly Kath—dark wood wainscoting topped with William Morris wallpaper, a stained-glass Tiffany lamp. The setting sun shines through the large window, illuminating her as she bends over the desk, turns on her laptop, and opens a spreadsheet.

I groan inwardly. I need to unwind with friends, but workaholic Kath... I'm being unfair. Kath loves to relax and celebrate as much as anyone. And her strong midwestern work ethic has served her well. It's not like she came from money. She had scholarships at Yale just like me.

She points to the screen. "These are numbers from your current show, the one in 2019, and your first in 2016."

"Thalia had just left for college."

"And you were finally letting yourself explore. You have this info in your taxes, by the way. I always send my artists their numbers at the close of each show."

"Oh, yeah."

She shakes her head with a sigh. "Dear Josie. Now, can you access your current budget on your phone and email it to me?"

I guess we're really doing this. I pull up the file and airdrop it, proud I remembered how.

A notification pings on the monitor. "Excellent," she

says, sitting and opening the documents side-by-side. "Come here, darling. We're going to fix this as much as we can, and then you're going to find the rest of the info after dinner."

"But where?"

"At home. I can't hold your hand the whole—"

"I mean, where will I find the info?"

"We'll figure that out." She pats a spot on the cherry wood writing table behind her.

I sit and peer over her shoulder. I wasn't envisioning a business meeting tonight, but the heaviness of disappointment lifts as I realize the importance of what my friend is doing. Kath had also planned to spend the evening chilling out. The puffiness under her eyes reminds me how little she sleeps. Instead of taking much needed down time, she's stepping up to help me, so I don't blow my first chance at getting an investor. Thanks to Kath, I'll be prepared for my meeting with Theo on Friday.

Chapter Nine

JOSEPHINE

I wasn't prepared for this. When I mapped Theo's address and saw its proximity to the coast, I imagined something enviable. But this (as Thalia would say) is a whole ass vibe. If environmental bloggers don't stop in Theo's driveway to take photos, they should. In the center of a circular drive, native plants surround a flowering tree. Under it, a sweet granite bench invites me to still my nerves before approaching Theo's house.

Shaded by the tree, the cool seat underneath me brings relief from sweltering temps. I place my palms on its rough surface and envision calming energy rising from Earth into my body. If Theo likes my plan, I will leave here a free woman. He'll like it. *Please like it, Theo!* I exhale, imagining my tension dissolving into the stone.

"That's one of my favorite spots." His voice fills my chest with excitement and embarrassment. Busted.

I squeak and turn toward the sound.

Theo strides across the driveway in bare feet and sits

beside me. He's so close, his energy both calms me and makes me tingle.

Heat rises to my face. "I hope you don't mind, I—"

He waves away my concern. "I often sit right here when I need to center myself. Sometimes, after a long meeting offsite, I use this spot to release the day before I go inside."

"That's kinda what I was doing."

"Transition spaces are important, I think. Don't you?"

"I never thought about it that way, but now that you mention it..." I nod agreement. "What kind of tree is this?"

"An olive."

"In Connecticut?"

"My grandfather brought it over from Italy. Every fall, we harvest the fruit and cure it. Fresh cured olives make wonderful gifts."

"You're kidding."

"I never joke about olives." He winks. My thighs warm. "Or business plans. Shall we?"

I follow him up a slate walkway into the foyer. "Isn't this lovely."

The ocean view through the French doors on the far wall catches my attention. I always dreamed of living by the water. High fantasy for a girl who spent winter nights shivering in a shitty New England mill town apartment with no heater in the bedroom. Going to Yale was a shock at first. Many of my friends came from wealthy families. I met famous artists, heads of state, Nobel prize winners, business leaders. Those experiences taught me at the end of the day, we're all just people.

"It's been in my mother's family since 1897. When my grandfather wanted to propose to my grandmother, he brought the olive tree as a gift for her parents."

"How sweet, and apparently a smart strategy."

"Planning was his forte, which he also used to start

NorEast Waste Management and build it into the multi-billion-dollar enterprise it is."

Waste management. The bio on Theo's website said he *worked* in waste management, not that it's his family business. Suddenly, my dress feels tight. I try to adjust it, to no avail. It's squeezing my stomach. Can I take money from someone whose family contaminates aquifers throughout the country? That pollution causes horrible chronic illnesses, mostly for people living in poverty. If Theo made one thing clear in our previous meeting, it's that his investment is more than capital; it's a collaboration. If our values aren't aligned, I can't work with him.

I massage my throat, hoping the right words will come when I open my mouth. "I, uh... I didn't realize waste management was your family business."

Theo examines my face. The scrutiny makes me uncomfortable. Why is he staring? I'd like to look away, but something tells me to hold his gaze. He seems to be reading me. I wish I had that skill. His expression is a mix of warmth and... what is that? He takes a deep breath and lets it out slowly. His gaze travels to my mouth, then back to my eyes. Is he expecting me to say more?

"Your website says you invest in companies working toward environmental justice."

"Correct."

"Waste management?"

He sighs. "The industry has a poor reputation."

"For good reason," I interrupt, ready to launch into a rant. He stops me with a look.

"And..." Theo pauses, slows his breathing, brings a hand to his chest. "I'll be honest, Josephine. I don't like it when people make snap judgments."

I look out the French doors. It must be low tide because the water is calm. Judgment. In the restaurant, when he and Drew argued, Theo defended me. Now, he's closing his hands into fists, flexing them open, closing them again. Long, thick fingers. *Not now, Josie.* "Forgive me. You invited me into your home. It's not my business how your family paid for it."

He crosses his arms over his chest. "I have no control over what my grandfather did before I was born."

"Funny. It never occurred to me; someone who inherits wealth didn't choose how they acquired it."

"The media likes to portray people with means as corrupt and self-serving."

My brows lift involuntarily. *Please don't tell me you're about to defend—*

"Some are, but my family isn't. My grandfather and my dad... It was a different time... No one knew about toxins and leaching and the connections between pollution and health."

That's no excuse to keep polluting, but I'm not telling him that.

"...provided a service people wanted. Before that, everyone burned their trash or buried it in their yards. Great for food waste. Not so great for plastic forks and diapers."

He has a point there. I bite the inside of my cheek. "I'm sorry if I offended you. I completely understand your point, and—"

"To be fair, though, the source of my family money kind of *is* your business. Systems change can't happen without transparency."

"Interesting. I never thought of systems change that way."

"Isn't that what your show is about? Transparency and truth? If I want all people to live in safe spaces, it's not cool to hide behind my privilege or pretend the service my company offers justifies polluting well water of someone living in poverty." He flinches.

"I appreciate that you're lifting the veil." My stomach

rebels at the words I have to say next. "Trying to offset the ills from your family business by funding startups like mine, but—"

He lifts his palms, defending himself. "Wait a sec, Josephine. Our polluting days ended years ago. Before I left the company, I personally ensured NorEast Waste Management is no longer a trash hauler people need to protest."

"You did."

"In college, I discovered we were harming," he swallows, "even killing people. I spiraled into shame, then spent a fortune on alcohol and therapy. But in business school, I learned I could turn the company around, make it an example of environmental stewardship. So, with my dad's help and grandpa's blessing, I did."

Maybe he did. "How?"

"Way too much to get into now. It took over a decade. But I want you to know, even though I'm a white guy with a ton of money, I want change. That's why I only invest in startups I believe will facilitate environmental justice, and it's why I wanna help you."

"You still might invest in me? After this talk?"

"I can't promise money, but I'll help however I can."

I smile, grateful. "I look forward to hearing that story sometime."

"And I'm eager to learn more about you, but let's see this business plan of yours."

"It's a work of art!" I wish I hadn't giggled when I said that, but I'm excited.

Theo leads me through a gorgeous sunken living room with blonde wood floors, coffered ceilings, and crown molding. Lights on the far wall illuminate what looks like a Chagall.

Is it real? Here's a chance to talk about something light, non-controversial. "Beautiful painting." I keep my tone even, pretending it's in a museum, not Theo's living room. I sure as hell won't let myself swoon over the art in his house. "Chagall's my favorite. His whimsical style, use of color, the way he celebrated love in so many of his works."

"Great story how we ended up with this piece."

My jaw clenches with envy. To live with a real painting, not a poster or even a lithograph, but a painting by one of the world's most celebrated artists... I can't imagine. "How did you?"

"It all started with a trip to Paris."

"Hi, there!" A petite redhead with her hair swept into a top knot emerges from a room on the ocean side of the hallway. "You must be Josephine." She smiles brightly. The glow of the tablet she holds makes her teeth look blue.

"Josephine, meet Kim Benefiel, my partner in crime."

My heart sinks, then irritation floods me. His girlfriend cannot be older than twenty-seven. What's he doing with someone half his age? Judgment. Anyway, why should I care? His love life isn't my business. I extend my hand. Kim meets it with a firm grip that conveys complete confidence. Of course, the girl exudes confidence. She's with this gorgeous, socially conscious man who lives with an actual Chagall.

I want to ask what Kim does for a living. Does she work? Perhaps she invests along with Theo, though it's odd that his website didn't mention an investment partner. Besides, unless Kim also comes from wealth, she couldn't possibly have enough to invest at such a young age, unless she's one of those phenoms. Maybe Theo's age-inappropriate girlfriend started her own nonprofit while still in high school. Maybe sh—

"I've got the dictation app all ready for you, Theo."

"You're the best."

Maybe she's a tech genius, developing software for giants in the industry. Maybe she's—

"... to drink?" Kim stares at me, awaiting a response.

"I'm sorry. Did you say something?"

"Would you like a drink? Theo's having a latte with fresh cashew milk and raw honey from our bees."

Our bees. "Sounds delicious." I force a smile.

She smiles and continues down the hallway.

I follow Theo into a large office with floor-to-ceiling windows facing the water. "My God, how do you get work done with these incredible views?"

He laughs. "It's a real first-world problem."

I gaze at the rowboat beckoning from a narrow rocky beach. Every part of this home reminds me of a fantasy I've had at some point.

Kim returns with our special coffees. But I barely register its presence in my hand because I'm watching the dynamic between this couple. Kim jiggles the mouse to awaken double computer monitors, then asks Theo if he needs anything else. He asks if the bags are packed and car is washed. She smiles, assures him everything's all set, then leaves. Young, pretty, and subservient. Men still want that in this century? No wonder I'm alone.

I sigh.

"Aw, don't be nervous," Theo says. "I'm sure your business plan is great."

THEO

The first thing I notice when Josephine opens her upcycled seatbelt messenger bag and pulls out the folder is its size. She shakes it side-to-side in front of her face, so all I can see of her cute little smile is the sparkle in her eyes. The dossier seems thicker than one might usually be, with a colorful cover and artsy font that heralds "Josephine Stewart Artisanal Fashion." I can't wait to read it and later to tell

Drew what a frigging brilliant businesswoman Josephine Stewart is, that my investment is a no-brainer. Together, we will revolutionize the fashion world and make a shit ton of money. She'll be free of her awful job, and the transformation of New Haven will begin.

Josephine hands me the folder. Why is this heavy? Alarm bells ring in my head, but she's beaming. I pull a chair out for her on one side of the desk, then settle into my grandfather's old oak swivel chair.

My chest tightening, I look from her to the dossier in my lap. "Unusual cover."

"I told you it's a work of art." She's practically dancing in her seat.

I open it. The paper has an unusual texture, which, admittedly, feels better to the touch than standard printer paper. Another artsy font lists the Table of Contents. I turn to the Executive Summary. The photo of Josephine takes my breath away, but that's the least important part. In fact, most business plans don't include photos in the Executive Summary. I scan the text and reassure her. "Nice bio. Clear, concise. Showcases your expertise and education."

"Thanks!"

I turn to the Mission, Vision, and Values section. My heart stops. What the fuck is this? The text is fine. The fashion sketches add a certain... something, but why are pieces of produce netting, fabric squares, and buttons pasted on the pages? I find more of the same in the Marketing and Positioning sections. Anxious now, I turn to the Financial section. *Thank God!* A solid excel spreadsheet demonstrates she did her research and learned how to use formulas to create a realistic budget. Of course, the projections only go out three years, and it seems she hand-sewed the spreadsheet to the page. Why? And what are the stylized designs and plastic circles surrounding the spreadsheet? Holding the book up so she can see, I point to the page.

Not even the Cheshire cat's smile could rival Josephine's in this moment. "Isn't that great? I used confetti made from credit cards! I thought it was perfect for the finance page."

"Uhhh…"

"You seem confused. Is there anything you'd like me to clarify?"

I take a deep breath, pray for courage, and feel it dissolve with a sigh.

"Do you love it? It's cool, right?" She bites her lip, looking vulnerable, sweet, and so damn sexy.

Oh, hell. I can't just break her heart. "Uhhh, Josephine." My heart hurts. "This is vibrant. Unique. I feel you in every page."

She claps. "Yay!"

I clear my throat, excruciatingly uncomfortable. Everything feels tight. "But this is not a business plan."

"What do you mean? I followed all the steps in the book."

"What book?"

"THE CREATIVE BUSINESS PLAN."

Of course. A title like that could mean anything. "I can see this as a fun exercise to get ideas down," *kind of like foreplay,* "but this is a craft project. If I took this to another investor, they would laugh me out of the room."

Josephine's face falls. "But it's creative. A creative plan for a creative business."

I groan inside, feeling like a jerk. Maybe if I speak slowly, I'll manage not to offend her. Maybe she'll see the problem. "Either to start or later to expand the business, you'll probably need a bank loan. If you take this to a bank—"

"I only use credit unions."

"Fine. Take it to any credit union or bank. They will deny your loan application."

"But why? Doesn't it have all the right information?"

"Mostly, but this is what they want to see." I pull an old

business plan from the filing cabinet behind me. "I can't give you this because I'd be violating my confidentiality agreement with these people. But see how, as I flip the pages, the only thing on each one is text, maybe a spreadsheet, maybe a colorful graphic shape?"

She sighs. Shit. Are those tears in her eyes? "But that isn't a design house plan, right? Not a creative business?"

"Listen, if you don't trust me, research creative business plans that worked. Talk to Kath, or Neville. This company," I point to the simple document I hold, "is thriving. Their text is similar to yours, but presented simply, cleanly. No texture or adornment—"

"I was trying to bring the mood board to you."

I sigh. She listened the other day. She really did, but she heard the wrong message. "You succeeded. It feels like a mood board, but it's also distracting. And here's the biggie. This is time-consuming to create."

"But you would share it."

"By email or maybe printout. You'll need several copies to take to banks, investors, potential partners. And we talked about the value of your time the other day. If you want to succeed in business, you need to put a premium on your time. Don't waste it sewing a printed spreadsheet onto a page."

Josephine looks down, smooths her skirt, looking dejected and vulnerable. "I was really hoping—"

Damn. I wish I could comfort her right now. "Hey, there's good news here, too."

She tilts her chin to meet my gaze. The hope in her eyes slays me.

"You actually have a business plan. It probably needs some editing, but first things first. Take all the words in this creative book and put them into a plain, boring Word document. Include your spreadsheets, and you'll be good to go."

"Yeah?"

"Are you open to coaching?"

Her shoulders rise. It's cute how she wrinkles her brow and scrunches up her nose.

"If I suggest specific commitments for you, will you follow through on them?"

She narrows her eyes. "What commitments?"

"For example, I'd love you to read this book about planning and running a business." I write the title on a sticky note and hand it to her.

Josephine taps her phone screen. "I'm ordering it as we speak."

"I'm sure you'll find it more helpful than whatever book inspired you to create that." I point at the craft project.

She looks down again, clearly embarrassed. I feel bad for making her uncomfortable, but sometimes a little discomfort is necessary to get people to stretch themselves. "I'd like to see a complete plan, in Word, by our next meeting that incorporates what we discussed today. Next Friday at ten?"

She drops her shoulders in relief. "Sure. Thank you."

By the time I escort Josephine to the door, she seems a tad stiff. We got off to a rough start with the talk about my family business, but we sorted that out. She must feel embarrassed about the craft project. I hope that doesn't stop her from making progress. I'm giving her another chance. Is there another VC who would be so patient, who would suggest a personal plan review meeting when email and zoom work fine? Maybe I'm *not* thinking with my MBA. Fuck. Maybe she's picking up on my attraction. Maybe it makes her uncomfortable. Then again, she thanked me about ten times for reading the whole "plan" and giving her another chance. Her face lit up when I suggested we meet next week. I watch Josephine get into her bright blue Honda and buckle her seatbelt. A fun fantasy involving seatbelts rises in my mind. She waves and zips away. My pants feel tight. *Damn it.*

Chapter Ten

THEO

WHAT IF SHE doesn't pull a proper business plan together? I fret as I stroll the aisles of Brattleboro Food Co-op looking for my mother's special vitamins. Moments later, I thank the friendly cashier and imagine telling Josephine I don't believe her fashion house is a solid investment. Envisioning the disappointment that will bloom on her face makes my stomach clench. Is there another way to let her down? Maybe I'm being pessimistic. Maybe I'm letting Drew's disapproval cloud my judgement. If I decide not to invest, why should I care about Josephine's reaction? I have to let people down when their business plan isn't solid or doesn't meet my criteria. No big deal. Except Josephine isn't "people." She's someone I care about.

Care about? I barely know the woman. Yet she's apparently gotten so deep in my head that I drove ten miles from the grocery store to the parking lot of Lexi's bakery without noticing. Drew may be right.

Lexi can help me sort this out. With our thirty-year

friendship and seven-year business collaboration, she can give me perspective.

The smell of fresh baked goods fills my nostrils as I enter the nineteenth-century Victorian home-turned-business. Lexi and I stood right here by the door and reviewed the build-out sketches. Later, we discussed her choice of white subway wall tiles, tin ceiling, and classic black-and-white floor tiles laid out in a honeycomb pattern. As I look for Lexi in the front parlor-turned-cozy seating area, I remember when I first entered Earth's Crust beside her and she showed off every feature of the space. Task lighting reflected off stainless steel countertops, illuminating a drunken "celebration" for two.

At the counter, I ask for her and order two loaves of bread and two blueberry pies. As the young man hands me my bag and credit card slip, Lexi emerges from the kitchen, pulling her hair net off to free her long bleach-blonde waves.

An image of Josephine greeting me at her studio replaces the present. Josephine's colorful apron, her sheer linen t-shirt, that sweet smile. A sense-memory of her light, clean fragrance replaces the bakery smell. Seconds ago, scents of sugar and yeast in the room overwhelmed me. Now, all I can smell is Josephine.

"Hi, handsome," Lexi says, breaking my reverie. Her cheeks flush with excitement as she comes around the counter and stands on tiptoe to kiss my cheek. Something's off.

All I can feel is Josephine's embrace, a fantasy so real it makes my heart race. What the fuck?

I take Lexi's shoulders in hand, step back, and assess my old friend. "How are you?"

"Wonderful, now that you're here. How long are you in town?"

"Just the weekend."

"Will you have time for me?"

"I'd love to hang out, Lexi, but I'm worried about my mom. I think I need to focus on her."

"Let me be your stress reliever."

Why the seductive tone?

And why am I face-to-face with Lexi but hearing, seeing, and smelling Josephine? Maybe this weird encounter is telling me it's unwise to invest in her fashion house. *Sorry, Josephine. I can't help you launch your business because my libido goes haywire whenever I think about you.* Now, she's beneath me, lush brown curls framing her face, brown eyes radiating warmth and excitement, sultry lips parting in ecstasy. My body warms.

Lexi hugs me, snuffing the excitement, thank God. "I've got a treat for your mom."

"No need."

"I want to. She's always so gracious when we run into each other at the library." Her voice takes on a melancholy tone. "Remember senior year of college, how your family would invite me to dinner?"

And you helped distract me from my grief. "Listen, I need to ask you something. Can we go outside?"

"Or to my office." She winks.

Being in tight quarters with her seems like an especially bad idea right now. "Walk me to my car." I exit, reveling in the scent of pine trees—freedom. I set the bakery bag on the floor of the car and turn to find Lexi mere centimeters from me. She runs a finger down my chest.

"Lexi, what the hell?" I sidle out of her grasp and stride across the gravel parking lot to the back of her building.

"Theo," she complains, jogging after me. "What's up with you?"

What's up with you? She's usually only this forward when she's drunk, which is why I stopped drinking with her a while back. "I need to ask you something important." I sit at a picnic table.

Hope lights her face as she straddles the bench facing me. "Yes?" A coy smile plays on her lips, not having its intended effect.

"Do you think our friendship has been affected by my investment in your bakery?"

She cocks her head. "Duh."

"What do you mean, duh?" A rock settles in my stomach.

"Maybe it was the sugar high, but Scott and I fell hard and fast."

"I remember. You married before you even graduated culinary school. I never got why you divorced him." Nervous anticipation rises into my neck.

"He said I dreamed too big. Eight years ago, when I told you about my idea to create Vermont's first eco-friendly bakery, you were super supportive. You said you were thinking about investing in startups, and maybe you'd help me." Her voice seems far away, liquid. "You and I always had this spark, and I got totally turned on by the idea of you investing, of us being in business together. I loved Scott, but I never really got over you."

"What?" I shake my head in disbelief. "You left the husband you loved, who loved you because of me? My investment?"

"After my divorce, when I was trying to get back on my feet, you came through with money for Earth's Crust."

Wasn't that a good thing?

"I knew if we could build this together," she waves her hand at the building, "we could build anything. We could build a life."

"We never even dated."

"I knew in my heart you'd come around, eventually."

Come around to what? "Lexi, when was the last time we hooked up?"

"Thirteen months and six days ago."

Her precision stops my heart. "That's a long time to hold out hope on a hookup."

"Silly, I'm totally in love with you."

"Oh, God."

"But I enjoy our casual relationship. It's fun playing around, especially knowing you'll be mine soon enough."

"What are you talking about? A business investment is not a marriage proposal."

"It could be." She winks.

"Lexi, damn it, are you drunk? Pull yourself together."

"Don't be ridiculous." She laughs. "I'm simply clear about our future."

"Our future."

"You'll have to move up here someday, and when you do, we'll be one. It's in the tarot. I've had a closet cleared out for you ever since I moved into my new house. Of course, if you'd rather we live in your parents' place, I'm fine with that."

"I've gotta go." I want to vomit. Nothing about this situation is what I believed. How could I have been so blind? "Please, please fill your closet, Lexi."

She follows me to my car and kisses my cheek, sending unpleasant chills up my spine, then purrs in my ear, "I'll be in New York mid-August. Let's go dancing or something."

If I hang out with her now, will it fuel her confusion? "Maybe coffee."

Sadness darkens her face, but she quickly replaces it with a smile. "Whatever works for you." She blows me a kiss and sashays inside.

What have I done? I start the engine and speed away. What kind of meltdown will Lexi have when she realizes the truth? How did she get the impression I wanted to be with her? *"Just a hook up, Theo? No big deal because we've known each other forever?"* Fuck. At least I have an answer. If I sent mixed signals to someone I never wanted romantically, it is way too risky to invest in a woman who I dream about constantly.

Chapter Eleven

THEO

Soothed by the piano sonata blaring throughout my parents' house, I shake off the frustration of my conversation with Lexi and emerge from the hallway onto the brick patio. My mother rests in her favorite high-backed teak chair, eyes closed, short white hair blowing around her face in the breeze. She's thinner than last month. Not good.

Whatever else is bothering me, I will not let it affect our weekend together. This is our special time, and I refuse to burden Ma with my mistakes. Besides, we need to discuss hiring a live-in nurse or overnight caregiver.

"Hi, Ma." I kneel and embrace her, mindful of her frailty. "How're you feeling?"

"Dearest." Her gentle laugh almost masks her obvious pain. She beams as she reads my face. "I've been hearing murmurings about you."

"Where? On the wind? I brought treats from Earth's Crust."

"So you're finally giving Lexi a chance! That explains the local chatter."

"Local chatter." How is Ma in tune with town gossip? I'd ask, but I'm not sure I want the answer.

"You look surprised. It's a small town, Theo. Vermonters are tight-knit. Is it true?"

"That I'm getting closer to Lexi? No." What is Lexi telling people? The tarot told her to clean out a closet for me?

Ma gives me her famous stare. "Then why go there?"

"I needed her perspective on an investment prospect. Stopping there was a mistake."

"Because the pie's not good?" she asks.

I sag. It isn't my favorite, either. I prefer Ma's pie, but she stopped baking years ago. "I thought you liked it."

"Earth's Crust was your first investment. I wanted to encourage you, and you two made our community a model of sustainability."

A model, like Josephine wants to provide in New Haven.

"Lexi's compost-for-ingredients deal with local farmers... You made it possible by taking a bold step away from your legacy. But she no longer needs your help." Ma wags a gnarled finger at me. "And you're making it difficult for her to move on."

"Move on?"

"I'm a woman. When she gives me that look at the library, I know what she's thinking."

Shit. Wish I'd paid attention to her signals years ago. "I just talked with her. Okay?"

"Good. Theo, I may not be on this earth much longer, and if I die knowing you're still dallying with Lexi—"

"I invested in her business. We were friends. Nothing more."

She lifts an eyebrow. "Then why the faraway look in your eye?"

I close my eyes, trying to center myself, and, okay, shut down the conversation. Faraway look. God almighty.

"Speaking of your remaining time on Earth." I cringe, glance at Ma. "That came out wrong. Sorry. What I'm trying to say is—"

"What I wish..." She pats my shoulder. "...is for you to find your soulmate, like your father and I found each other." She sighs.

I hate it when she sighs. Disappointing my mother makes me queasy, like I feel thinking about disappointing Josephine. *Stop thinking about her, Casabella.*

I stand and stretch. "What were you doing before I showed up?"

"Appreciating the birdsongs and the soft breeze against my skin. If you're very still, you can almost hear the butterfly wings. It's quite magical."

"You're magical."

She laughs, then takes my hand, suddenly serious. "I don't know which saddens me more—thinking you've wasted time with someone you don't cherish, or fearing you've avoided love out of misplaced duty to poor Isabella."

Even delivered with empathy, Ma's words land like a sucker punch. "I... wow... uh... Can I bring you a snack?"

"It'll spoil my dinner. And don't change the subject. You fulfilled your duty to her ages ago."

"It's only four o'clock."

"And dinner's at six-thirty. Why don't you try a dating app?"

What do you know about apps? "You heard the doctor say keep your blood sugar up."

She pats my hand. "Alright, you win. This time."

A small triumph, but as I open the door, my mother prays. "Angelo, help Theo find his soulmate before I die."

"You know I heard that, right?" I throw her a side glance and go inside. If Ma wasn't so adorable, I'd be really damn annoyed.

With the tea water boiling, I prepare two cups of

chamomile and butter thick slices of bread. Maybe next month, Josephine will stand beside me at this soapstone counter, help me arrange my grandparents' china onto the golden tray, like I am now. I'll add the ice cube to Ma's teacup so the liquid won't scald. Josephine will add an artful touch. A trashion flower?

I growl. "Stop it, Theo. Josephine will do no such thing." Because after what Lexi said, I won't risk mixing business and pleasure again. I, and apparently all women, fare better when I'm too busy to let anyone in. I've pushed other women away easily. Brains. Beauty. Humor. They had those traits, but...

Josephine is different.

That's the problem. Without trying, she penetrates my heart, mind, and body like no one else. Clearly, I can't get closer to her. I have responsibilities: investments to make, a board to chair to ensure NEWM stays on track, and this night-care situation to solve for my mother. At least Ma's with Deborah during the day. But if Ma moved home to Connecticut, I could oversee her caregivers. Living with my mother, though? I carry the tray outside, lay everything on the table between our chairs, and savors Lexi's Anadama bread.

Ma's hands tremble as she brings her teacup to her lips, and it makes me nervous. Her close examination of my face isn't helping. "I haven't seen you look like that since poor Isabella."

"Have some bread, Ma."

"She'd want you to move on, dearest."

"I have, by ensuring no one else will suffer like she and her family did."

Ma softens her gaze and tone. "Shall we stroll the garden? The veggies are coming up."

Relieved to have diverted my mother from the scent of my love life, I brace my legs on either side of her chair, slip my hands under her arms and lift her onto her feet. She's lighter every time I see her. Unsettling. Rheumatoid is a bitch, and witnessing Ma succumb to it frustrates the hell out of me.

She secures her hand in the crook of my elbow and leans on me as we stroll through her garden. Corn, squash, kale, arugula—they feel like old friends from when Nonna and I tended her garden in Branford. My mother points at delicate carrot greens, reminding me their shoulders will emerge next month.

"It feels darn good to get my hands in the dirt, Theo," she says, plucking a basil leaf from a raised garden bed and holding it to me.

I taste it. "Mm. I'm glad we built these extra-high beds for you."

"Does Josephine garden?"

"I have no clue." I stop moving. "Wait. How do you know about Josephine?"

"You were muttering so loudly in the kitchen, I imagine the governor heard you in Montpelier."

I cringe. "Speaking of... travel. We need to discuss your care. I know we love Deborah, but I want someone near you at night. How about moving back to Branford with me?"

Ignoring my question, Ma bends stiffly and yanks a weed from the tomatoes. "I'd love to see you with a gardener, someone who can feed you." She waxes poetic about how she and Dad took care of each other, then circles back to fantasies about what Josephine can offer me.

I let out an exaggerated sigh. I have led hundreds of meetings, redirected literally thousands of conversations to reach a common goal. Yet my skills are useless with Ma. Once the woman gets an idea in her head, she's like a hound on the hunt. It's how she kept my father and his bold personality in line. They were well matched. "Remember how Dad wanted to move back to Connecticut, to be near Yale New Haven Hospital?"

"He needed chemo. They can't help me. Besides, my community is here now, along with memories of your father. You could create beautiful memories with someone."

I groan.

"If you give love another chance, Theo, you may gain more energy and strength to fulfill your mission."

A blue butterfly flits from a squash blossom to my mother's shoulder. Maybe she's right. Love kept me going through Isabella's endless chemo sessions, tests, and hospital stays.

Resigned to my inability to refocus Ma's dogged attention, I show her photos from Josephine's opening reception. Of course, now that Josephine is on my mind, I'm struggling to think about anything else. I look at my mother, the garden, the diverse tree-scape and river in the distance. I see Josephine everywhere, which lights me up inside. Maybe Ma's right about love giving me strength. But Drew's also right. I can't mix business and romance. If only I could have both.

Chapter Twelve

JOSEPHINE

THE PHRASE *CRAFT project* rings loud and clear in my head as I open my Kindle and read the book Theo recommended. Okay, it's dry. Dry as my gram's burnt toast, actually. The woman had many skills, but cooking was not one of them. Luckily, I can cook, and I taught Thalia. Our cooking lessons were such fun. Memories spin through my mind, lifting my mood. Now, I... am not focusing.

Back to the book. Do I need to read it word-for-word? I search online for Spark Notes. No luck. Probably my best course of action is to convert the—ugh—*craft project* into a boring Word document first. *Craft project.* Theo was trying to help me, not shame me. I will not give into humiliation, like I did at his house. I will not give into fear. I will read his recommended book and type everything from my fun business plan into a plain, bank-worthy Word document because Theo's the expert. I set the book aside, pull my laptop from the coffee table, and begin converting my business plan. It doesn't take long, and as I finish each page, I can admit: it's not a big deal. Sure, a bikini wax seems more appealing, but...

If I had a bikini wax, I'd be smooth for Theo. His eyes would seek consent. I'd moan, "yes." He'd lower his mouth to my neck, kiss his way to my breasts, suck. And just as I was getting hot, he'd caress my folds, tease me, glide his hands ever so lightly along the insides of my thighs, then back to my folds, and I'd—

What in hell am I thinking? His fingers will be nowhere near my folds. He's a potential colleague, nothing more. So he's the most beautiful man I've ever seen and seems to have a heart of gold. That does not—absolutely not—mean I can let myself lapse into sexual fantasies.

Unfortunately, now I'm throbbing, and I don't know when I tilted my head back on the couch or thrust my chest up toward his imaginary... Dear Lord.

I must focus. Will focus. I open my eyes, glare at the laptop screen. *I am working!* Sensations between my legs are super distracting. It's Friday evening, for goodness' sake. I deserve some fun.

I put my laptop aside, lie back and resume fantasizing, replacing Theo with... That hot barista? No. Ben? Ugh. I'm way past that attraction. That hiker at East Rock Park two weeks ago. What did he look like again? Firm calves and thighs. Tight back end.

The image of Theo walking away from my studio flashes through my mind. Sweet behind. Warm handshake. Muscular hands and forearms. Biceps peeking out of his t-shirt. No one fills out a t-shirt like Theo... and those eyes, liquid chocolate. I'm wet now. Soaking. I slide my hands along my skin, imagining Theo. *No, no, no. Not Theo.* My breath comes faster. *Think of someone else!* But Theo's smile and voice, and... even when he was saying I needed to redo my business plan. A moan escapes. I liked it when he told me what to do. My nipples stiffen. I really liked it. *Tell me what to do, Theo.* I shouldn't like it. I need to stop touching myself

and thinking of him, but he's right here in my brain and...
This will be the last time I envision sex with him, so I may as
well enjoy it. After this, it's all business. Theo is not a sex
object. He's a potential investor, and I need to get that
straight in my head.

<h1 style="text-align:center">Chapter Thirteen</h1>

THEO

FROM WHERE I stand on the porch, the field stretching toward the river appears covered with jewels. I hate to leave, but ending the conversation that has obsessed Ma all weekend will be nice. Now, she stops in front of the porch swing and waits. "Ignore Drew and his closed-mindedness. Josephine's fashion line is a smart investment."

"If creativity and talent were my only criteria, sure. But she needs basic business skills." I slip my hands under my mother's arms and slowly lower her onto the seat.

She lands softly with an *oomph*, an impish light in her eyes. "So help her."

Perhaps it's best Ma stays in Vermont. "Deborah agreed to move in full-time until we can find someone to be with you at night."

"I knew you'd find a solution, dearest." The landline rings inside. Ma claps. "There's your brother."

"Shall I get it?"

"Deborah will bring the cordless." Ma tilts her face up. "Ask Josephine out."

I kiss her cheek, grab my bags, and stride to the car, texting Eric on the way. **Leaving VT. Still up for that walk?**

Absolutely! my mentor responds. **Rail Trail parking lot off the highway.**

Ma's voice carries across the yard. "I can't wait to hear about your new love."

"Only because you don't understand how badly I can fuck this up, Ma," I say under my breath. At least I can count on Eric for grounded perspective. In all his years in venture capital, he must've faced something similar.

An hour later, I find Eric leaning against his electric F-150, gripping a jogging stroller with a sleeping toddler inside. The resemblance between Eric and his grandson is so striking it makes me chuckle: dark skin, short-cropped hair, thin, athletic build. Matching fisherman's sandals. "Hope I didn't keep you waiting," I say, as I approach.

"Just got here. Luckily, Chance conked out on the drive over."

"Your daughter's visiting?"

Eric's chest puffs with pride. "She and her husband are celebrating their anniversary. Kelly and I are babysitting."

We set off on the paved path at a brisk pace, passing families in all modes of transportation. Moms jogging with strollers. Dads wearing babies in front carriers. Tandem bicycles. Couples holding hands, yelling at older children to slow down, be careful. A little girl on a pink bicycle yells for her mom to watch her ride with no hands.

Eric's grandchild screams. "Shit," Eric says under his breath, stopping in his tracks. "What's wrong?" He kneels in front of the stroller.

"Out," Chance whines, reaching for him.

"You want Grampa to hold you?"

The toddler smiles.

"You mind pushing this?"

"Not at all," I say. Then in the baby-whisperer voice that always worked with my niece, "Chance, look how big you're getting."

Eric unhooks the straps and lifts Chance into his arms. "Remember Uncle Theo?"

The boy looks at me, sticks a thumb in his mouth and rests his head on Eric's shoulder.

"How old is he now?" I ask.

"Chance and Owen are seventeen months," Eric says, "into everything, not speaking much to us yet."

"Who *do* they speak to?"

"Each other. Twin language is real."

"Cool." I push the stroller, remembering my childhood with Garrett. Our only shared language was boating and building things outside. I try to imagine feeling close enough to someone to share a private language. Josephine speaks the language of fashion, describes her designs as stories. I'd love to learn her language, to—

Fuuuuuuuuck! Be here now, Theo, with Eric, in Northampton, Mass. We're on the Rail Trail, surrounded by farm fields and maple trees, path glistening with little puddles. Must have rained here last night. The air is cool for July. I am pushing a jogging stroller. We're discussing... "What was I saying?"

"You needed to talk?" Eric asks.

"An investment opportunity. Meets my core criteria, but I fear my involvement will set us both up for failure."

"How?" Eric asks.

"She's a fashion designer. She took a sustainable business course, which was heavy on theory, light on practice. She's got sound ideas, but needs a lot of help."

"What else is new? Most fledgling entrepreneurs need handholding at the start."

What would it feel like to hold Josephine's hand? Imagining it warms my core.

Eric laughs. "This isn't about her business acumen."

"Huh?" Heat rises to my cheeks.

"The look on your face says it all. She's hot."

"Down." Chance points at the ground, squirming in Eric's arms.

He looks helplessly at me. "Do you mind? This will be a slow walk."

"It's fine," I assure him, recalling numerous family outings interrupted by my niece.

Eric lowers the child. "Hold Grampa's hand."

We continue at a snail's pace. "What Josephine's doing is incredible," I say. "A trashion house is unique, well-suited to New Haven, could easily be scaled."

"Kind of fringe, though. Isn't it?"

"The Smithsonian's trashion exhibit is quite popular. Episodes of *Project Runway* are devoted to the art form."

Eric smirks. "You watch *Project Runway*?"

"Kim included that in her report. Basically, Josephine wants to create a fashion house that turns trash into treasure."

"Trash to treasure. I can see the appeal for the heir of a waste management company."

That makes me smile. "I'd be bringing my family business full circle."

"But you're attracted to her and afraid your dick will screw things up."

"The minute I saw her, I knew it would be a problem, and it's worse than I thought."

"Worse how?"

"She sneaks into my thoughts when I least expect. I see her connecting with my mom, envision her joining me in daily tasks. I stopped at Lexi's bakery and couldn't smell the bread and cookies. It was like Josephine was there, her fragrance under my nose."

Eric laughs. "Congratulations, Casabella. You're falling in love."

"Nope." The scent of fertilizer wafts across the path, making us both reel back.

"You're describing how I felt when I met my wife."

"Not possible."

"Would it be untenable to have a lasting relationship?" Eric asks.

I open my mouth and close it. How can I explain?

Eric catches my eye. "Look, over the years I've mentored you, we've become friends. You're one of the folks I trust most."

"Same here."

"I think I know you pretty well."

"You do," I admit.

"This is something missing from your life," Eric says.

"My life's mission leaves little time for romance, and—" Lexi's desperate face fills my mind. Her insane words. The Tarot? A closet for me? My stomach churns. I slow my breathing to calm the rising angst. The one time I mixed business and pleasure. "Fuck."

Eric shoots me a questioning look.

I ignore it, focusing instead on the chipmunk outpacing us. "Greater New Haven will benefit if I help her launch, not if I play with her heart."

"So don't play with her heart. Come clean. You think your feelings are mutual?"

I've definitely picked up a vibe. Haven't I? A maple seed helicopters down, and I catch it, open the seed pod and stick it to my nose, smile and squat to show Chance. He narrows his eyes, moves closer to his granddad. Not the reaction I expected. "Okay, then." I rise, pulling the thing off.

"Next year, that'll be a hit." Eric chuckles. "As for you and Josephine sharing a mutual attraction, I'm guessing the answer is yes, or you wouldn't feel so unhinged."

"It's lust. I'll get over it."

He elbows me. "Bullshit. I've seen you on the make. Throw her business plan over the wall. Until I review it, we're just talking ethics and theory. Show me what you see in her work."

"I will, as soon as I have it."

"You haven't seen her business plan yet? Theo!"

"I saw a version of it."

"Why are you making that face?"

I school my expression to neutral. "She took some bad advice, followed instructions in a book that suggested creating a plan with *flair*." In my mind, I see credit card confetti glued to the finance page. So creative, yet so misguided. "That ridiculous document I read Friday contains seeds for a solid business plan."

"I don't like where this is going."

"Business isn't her core competency."

Eric's eyebrows rise above his sunglasses. "Yeah, given everything you've said, I'm back to suggesting you date this woman. Give true love a chance."

I groan.

"What's holding you back? This is a void in your life. We all know it."

"What do you mean, 'we all know it'?"

"We see you playing around with different women. Avoiding emotional intimacy."

I grumble. I will not go down this hole with Eric, nor anyone.

"When you talk about Josephine, your expression softens. Doesn't happen when you talk about other women."

Except Isabella. "Wait. We who?"

"We: all the guys."

My stomach tightens. "Glad my private life is entertaining you assholes."

Eric puts a hand on my shoulder. "We're concerned.

You've been dicking around with Lexi longer than is healthy."

Why is everyone saying this lately? "We hooked up a few times. Nothing more." She thought it was something more. Fuck.

After the longest, shortest walk I've ever taken, we reach the parking lot. I throw an arm around Eric's shoulder. "I appreciate you."

"Same." He returns the gesture, then straps his grandson into the car seat. "Good luck. And send that business plan. I can't wait to read it."

Josephine's business plan. That's where I need to focus. Not on romance. Why can't anyone see that? Why is everyone pushing me to date her?

I walk to my car, reach for the door, suddenly stiff in my upper body from too much sitting over the weekend. Instead of driving home now, I'll take a quick walk, get my blood pumping, and work off this nervous energy. My phone dings with a text message.

Josephine: **New, improved biz plan in Word, finished. When can I show you?**

I pump my fist. She did it! In only two days. She's serious, driven. Is she a solid investment? One way to find out. I lean against the car, respond: **Can you email it now?**

Sure.

An email alert arrives. From her. Heart pounding, stomach warming, legs and arms buzzing, and... *Damn it.* I'm ignoring the other body part responding to my inbox notification. *It's an email, fool.* Not just any email. A potentially life-altering email. I open it, see her sweet—*ahem, professional*—message and download the document.

A vehicle stops in front of me.

"Man." Eric gets my attention. Why is he smirking? "You should see yourself right now."

"Josephine emailed her revised business plan." *And it's totally normal to get a hard-on when you see a document.*

"What could be more exciting than that?"

I flip him the bird, redirect my attention to my phone.

"Glad you're keeping it professional." Eric laughs and drives away.

Finally, her document is ready. I open it. *Hallelujah*, a normal font on the title page and table of contents, and... I scroll quickly—a normal font all the way through! Also, no illustrations. She listened. Really listened. Vision, mission, and values statements—excellent. Executive summary— professional. No photos. The finance section? A thing of beauty. Spreadsheets with real numbers and, *holy shit,* foot- notes citing sources. Real sources—fashion industry reports, figures from small fashion houses. Neville Wisdom came through with estimates—a good ally. Kath provided sales figures from Josephine's latest and previous shows.

My body hums. Embarrassing. Why? No need to shame myself for feeling excited about a prospective investee giving 110%. I set off at a brisk pace along the Rail Trail and dictate a message to Josephine: **Need time to read closely. But on quick review - WOW.** [thumbs up emoji]

Yay!

How about we meet to talk business and have some fun? I tap send, then regret it. Lexi refers to sex as *having some fun.* Will Josephine think I'm suggesting sex? Those three little dots flash, indicating she read my message and is typing a response. It's taking a while. She must be thinking.

I pocket my phone. *Man, control yourself.* The phone dings, and I rip it from my pocket.

Josephine: **When, what, where?**

Me: **Your call. Dinner, beach walk, sea kayaking?**

Her reply comes immediately: **Kayaking!** [smiling face with smiling eyes emoji] **When?**

My house. 5:30 tonight?

What can I bring?

Of course, I tell her to bring a swimsuit, though I'd rather see her without one. *Enough, Casabella!*

Jogging is hard with an erection. When did I start jogging? How long have I been running? After the swimsuit text, maybe. According to my watch, that was ten minutes ago. I stop, look around, getting my bearings. A cyclist yells, "on the left," and zips past.

"Okay," I say aloud to no one, catching my breath. "I know where I am." I stride toward the parking lot, eager to get home to prepare for my meeting.

Eric is wise about many things, but he's wrong about me needing to fill some hole in my life. Coming clean with Josephine is a good suggestion, though. I'll lay my attraction out in the open, and I'll make damn sure my feelings for her don't impede whatever business arrangement we come to.

Chapter Fourteen

The din of the crowd and live jazz at the farmers' market drowns out my phone's text tone, but the vibration in my pocket alerts me. I put Persian cucumbers into my basket and retrieve my phone. Theo. My heart flip-flops as I tap a response.

"How'd you do it?" Sage asks.

"Sorry. Do what? Theo says this version looks better."

"La dee da." Sage's green eyes sparkle. "Stay sane with a toddler, husband, and career."

My phone buzzes again. Another message from Theo. "He's asking if I wanna get together to talk about my business plan and have some fun."

"Yes, you do." Sage sing-squawks, her tone matching my elation.

"I'm asking for details." I type a response, then refocus on my friend. "I didn't have a career. I stayed home the first couple years, and our marriage... Seth and I never connected emotionally like you and Wes." Maybe someday I'll find my person.

"Sounds painful."

"But I read all the books by the Yale Child Study Center."

"The ones you gave me?"

"Yup. Knowing Thalia's behavior was age appropriate removed a *lot* of stress."

"I need to read the one for two-year-olds," Sage grumbles. "I think Felicia's hitting the terrible twos early."

"Uh, oh. Thank goodness we're finally going hiking. Keeping your stress in check is key to having the patience for that stage. Plus, I've missed you."

"Me, too." Sage's laugh lines deepen as she smiles. "But you know how it is with a baby in the house."

Snippets flash through my mind. Those early years, when Thalia was into everything and I felt both energized and exhausted all the time. I lay a sympathetic hand on Sage's back. "The best and worst of times. Everything is amazing with a toddler, and—"

"Dangerous, and we never sleep through the night anymore, and God, I miss sex."

"It gets better." In my case, it got better and worse. Just as Thalia was spending full nights in her own bed, Seth started working later, coming home after I had conked out. Then again, maybe he wasn't working. He moved out soon after. Now, I worry for Sage. "Is everything okay between you two, though?"

"Oh, yeah. We're usually asleep in each other's arms by eight-thirty. Like old people," she sighs. "Then Felicia toddles into our bed around midnight, and I can't go back to sleep. But Wes is an angel."

Another text from Theo offers suggestions.

"Ooh, kayaking." I reply, then look at Sage. "You think it's a good sign?"

"I love how Theo wants to know you outside the studio. Like Meg Ryan said in *You've Got Mail*. Business oughta—"

"—begin by being personal," I finish with her. "One of my favorite quotes from that movie. When I get this house started, I want to know everyone who sews with me."

"Nice."

A gang of bikers passes, forcing me to yell over their loud engines. "Maybe if any of my horrid bosses had seen me as a person and not a 'mere' employee, I could've thrived at a day job."

"Been there," Sage says, selecting tomatoes and kale from the table.

"Even in journalism?"

"Yup."

My phone screen lights up. "He says meet at 5:30 at his house." I shimmy in excitement.

"Today?"

"Mm. It's one o'clock now. Wait a sec." I work out the time to get to and from Devil's Hopyard, shower, dress, then drive to Branford. Excitement turns to guilt. "That doesn't leave much time for our hike. I'll tell him no."

"Don't you dare." Sage flares her nostrils.

"But our plans."

"This is your first potential investor, Josie. We'll do West Rock today and a longer hike another time. It's wicked hot, anyway. I don't mind keeping it short."

"You sure?"

"Let me grab some bread, then I'll be ready." She walks away.

I hover over three containers of heirloom tomatoes. Do I want the orange, zebra, or blackish red ones? They all look delicious. Does Theo like tomatoes? His subservient redhead springs to mind. Kim. An icky feeling fills my stomach. Ridiculous. Theo's love life is irrelevant to me. I refocus on the tomatoes, complete my purchase at the vegetable stall, and find Sage at the bakery stand. Cookies. I buy a selection. "A little *thank you* for Theo."

"Sweet."

"This day is sublime, Sage. Hanging with you, hiking, mixing business and kayaking."

"I have a good feeling about this, Josie."

Sage's validation brings relief. "Glad I'm not the only one."

"Theo has a nice vibe, and I like how quickly things are moving."

"His background is all business, but he seems to get what I'm about. You know?"

"That's awesome," Sage says.

We walk toward the parking lot. My phone vibrates again and two words flash across the screen. **Bring swimsuits.**

"Oh, no." Excitement dissolves into disappointment.

"What?"

I show her the text.

"No big. We'll stop by your studio and fetch your swimwear samples."

"I don't have any right now."

Her face falls. "Can you whip one up before you go?"

"Sure, but then I'd have to skip our hike. I'll reschedule with him—"

Sage stops and grips my shoulders. "You will do no such thing. We'll postpone."

I groan. "But Sage, it's so hard for you to get away."

"Not as hard as it is to get a chance like Theo's giving you." She shakes her head and resumes walking. "I am *so* happy for you, Josie. And I could never forgive myself if I let you pass up the opportunity in front of you now. This is important. You're finally getting your shot. I know how hard it is. Remember?"

We hug, and Sage gets into her bright orange hybrid. "Promise you'll call tomorrow and tell me everything."

"And you promise you'll do something just for you today. K? Self-care, Sage!" I wave and walk the block to the building that houses my studio. Emotions well up—gratitude that I have such a supportive friend, excitement about creating something new in a pinch, nervousness about seeing Theo and proving myself. As I unlock the door and climb the wide gray stairs, I envision unique swimsuit patterns. What can I create in a few hours to help persuade Theo an investment in me is worth it?

In my studio, heart thrumming, I flip through my fabric selection. He's giving me another chance to impress him, and after my "craft project" debacle, I will not mess this up.

Chapter Fifteen

THEO

I TRY AGAIN to rehearse the speech in my head, but damn it, Josephine's legs go on for days. That little bikini bottom enhances the view. Fortunately, she obeyed my request to put on the safety vest. True, the main reason to wear it is to keep her safe if we flip the boat. But the added benefit is it covers that taut stomach, sexy divot of a bellybutton, and the shape of those luscious breasts her high-necked bikini top can't hide.

Alright, what I'm going to say is... damn it. What was I planning to say? I'll come clean, say something about being attracted to her, and... I had the perfect wording in the car. I'm attracted to you, but we can't act on it. Forgive me if I... I just wanna... Damn it.

How can I say it without sounding like I assume she's attracted to me, too? Frustrating. Sure, I get a vibe from her, but that means nothing. She may not find me attractive at all. My people-reading skills may be out of whack with Josephine, blunted by my feelings for her. Maybe I should forget about a speech and simply discuss her business plan.

My eyes land on her graceful neck, peeking above the half-zipped safety vest, and I envision caressing it with my fingertips, finding the pulse point, kissing softly. *Fuck, Theo!* I shake my head to loosen my thoughts.

"You okay?" Josephine looks alarmed.

"Yup." I force a light tone. "Just, ah...." I definitely need to address this issue today, before we go any further and I screw things up.

JOSEPHINE

His smile is kind of goofy. Cute and sweet, and... not what I should be thinking about. Thankfully, Theo is on the move, which gives me something else to focus on.

His ass.

No. Not his ass, Josie. Get your mind out of bed.

What I need to watch is the rocky path between the boathouse and the shore. The last thing I need is to trip, fall, injure myself, and kill our boating excursion before it starts. If I make it to the boat without disaster, then I'll enjoy learning more about this man who's helping me get Josephine Stewart Artisanal Designs off the ground. *J.S.A.D. J-Sad.* No, that's a terrible name for a company. JoStewFash? Worse. Whatever. The point is, I'm connecting with Theo, showing him the new swimsuits, and discussing my revised business plan for JStewAD. Blech.

If it's remotely possible to leave tonight with an investment promise from Theo—my heart pounds—that would be life-changing. I'm overthinking and it's stressing me out. I inhale the salt air, let it clear my head.

What if I forget work for a bit and just have fun with this extremely interesting man? Hearing his explanation of all the vessels in his boathouse showed me a side of him I couldn't see any other way. "You could outfit an entire team with all those boats," I say to his strong, sculpted back.

He speaks over his shoulder. "My dad's old sea kayak is my favorite. I like to take her out when I'm alone."

"Is that safe?"

"Sure. We had her custom-made for Dad's 50th birthday. He took her out each summer until he passed last year."

"I'm sorry for your loss."

"Thanks. I feel his presence in that vessel, but it's been a difficult transition for all of us, especially Ma. Those two—" He whistles. "They were a romance novel come to life."

"You read romance novels?"

"Sometimes my mom ropes me into reading aloud when I visit." He laughs, a pleasant low rumble that lands in my chest. "I had to trim the sex scenes in *Outlander* substantially. There are whole sections of that book she doesn't know she missed."

I giggle. "Or she went back and read them after you left."

Theo turns around on the rocky beach, points at me. "You may be right. What do your parents read?"

"News. Nonfiction. Activist stuff. Naomi Klein. So your dad was the seafarer and your mom the romantic, reading on the shore?" I follow him onto the dock, where a long wooden double kayak is tied to a post.

"Not at all. Mom sailed, rowed, kayaked, swam. When she came down with Rheumatoid and her joints got too stiff to paddle, Dad had the Twin Star made so he could take her out." He points at the kayak, chest puffing with pride.

"This is the most beautiful boat I've ever seen! These inlays."

"The olive tree is mahogany. The stars are ash." He glides his hand along its glossy surface. "And check this out." He presses a spot on the front of the boat, and it opens to reveal a stow hatch. I know there's a nautical term for *front of the boat,* but it eludes me. Theo slips his little backpack and my bag of cookies inside. When he closes the hatch, the seam disappears.

"Cool. What's the wood?"

"Red and white cedar."

I lean over the vessel to get a closer look. "Twin star... for your parents." I sigh.

"Dad had the builder add the stars to honor my mom and him."

"Was he always so romantic?"

"Pretty much. When he got his diagnosis, and the prognosis wasn't good, he wrote a batch of love letters and gave them all to the florist. Ma received one letter with one long-stemmed white rose each day for a year."

"Aw." His parents' romantic story and the sadness in Theo's eyes melt my heart.

"I was hoping to get my mother on the water this summer, but she hasn't been well enough to come down from Vermont." He clears his throat. "This, as you can see, is an old-fashioned metal rowboat, which I use pretty much every day."

"Really? With all these fancy vessels?"

"It's a sensory thing that brings me back to my childhood, learning to row with my grandfather."

"Tell me."

"The oars in my hands, water sloshing under the boat, the sounds, scent of the sea... Plus, muscle memory in my core is strong."

"Did you row alone?" Am I seriously worrying about his safety? Clearly, he made it to adulthood just fine.

"My brother and I were never allowed to go alone until we were well into our teens."

"You have a brother."

"Garret. Two years younger. He lives in Germany with his family."

"Nice." I scan the landscape, taking in Theo's words.

The vision of a dark-haired little boy and an old man rowing away from shore together makes me smile. I imagine two teens, awkward on land, strong and graceful on the water.

"Anyway," Theo says, bringing me back to the present, "I've been looking forward to taking you out all afternoon."

I love the earnestness and excitement in Theo's voice, which, if I'm honest with myself, sounds a little more than professional and friendly. A shame because our relationship can never be more than professional or friendly. Then again, I'm probably reading into things. Who wouldn't want this gorgeous, interesting, kind man's attention? *Pull yourself together, Josie. You're not on a date.* "When do you wanna see the swimsuits?"

He opens his mouth, closes it, rubs his chin. "I, uh, did see it." He waves his hand in front of my torso. "It looks great. That's what you're wearing, right? A swimsuit?"

I point at him. "Correct. But I'm talking about the ones I made to show you. You said bring swimsuits."

"You made more? Today? You just whipped them up after I invited you out?"

"You said to bring—"

"Like some people whip up cookies, you whip up swimsuits." He shakes his head.

"Wait. Did you mean one for me to wear?"

Eyes sparkling, he leans toward me. "That is impressive!"

Impressive. His praise makes my chest tingle, but I can and will ignore that sensation. "Funny miscommunication, huh?"

"Indeed. I'm eager to discuss your revised business plan, but we need to get on the water while the tide is out."

"Got it." His proximity and masculine salt and cedar scent settle my emotions and make me feel safe. Or maybe his voice elicits that sense of security. I'm not sure what, exactly, about Theo always soothes me, but he's doing it again.

"You know how to get into a boat?"

"Stay low." I follow his gesture and slip into the opening at the front of the boat. The wooden seat is comfortable, a pleasant surprise. Theo hands me a double-bladed wooden paddle that matches the vessel, unties the boat from the dock, and puts the rope into the stow hatch. Then he slides into his seat and pushes the kayak away from the dock.

Within minutes, we're gliding along the calm sea, paddling in rhythm with each other. My worries fade with the swish of the water against the vessel and each stroke of the oar. The muscles in my core, upper back, shoulders and arms thrum pleasantly with exertion.

"Where are we going, anyway?" I look over my shoulder at him.

"It's a surprise." Theo's arm muscles ripple as he pulls the paddle through the water, first on one side, then the other, back and forth.

Watching him could be hypnotic if I let it.

"Don't worry, though. I'll have you home before dark." He winks, and my breath catches in my throat. I turn around before he can see the color rising to my cheeks.

THEO

Josephine turns to face me, her cheeks flushed from exertion and late afternoon heat, a bright smile in her eyes. How can I look away? The sight of her affects me on every level. And when she faces the bow, her back to me, I get lost in the way she pulls the paddle rhythmically from one side to another, so at ease on the water.

My yoga teacher's always talking about chakras, and suddenly the idea clicks into place. I'm feeling Josephine's "energy" from the base of my spine all the way through the crown of my head. Of course, my energy isn't the only thing rising at the moment. Not good.

I refocus on the open water and gentle waves of low tide. The timing was perfect for this excursion. We got in the water just as the tide was reaching its lowest point, so it should stay calm and easy to navigate for another two or three hours, giving us ample time to get to the island, picnic, explore, and get back.

Josephine sighs wistfully. The sound tugs at my heart. I'm pretty sure it was a satisfied, *"This is wonderful,"* kind of sigh. Then again, maybe it was a—

I shake my head to release these thoughts. *Just stroke and breathe.* A non-boating-related image pops into my head. I chortle. *Stroke and breathe?*

"What's funny?" she asks over her shoulder.

"Oh, uh... nothing. I..." *Stroke and breathe, buddy.*

She turns around, again disarming me with her fresh-faced beauty. Not an ounce of makeup on her. Hair in a messy ponytail. Crow's feet framing her eyes as she smiles. Her joy settles in my heart. What else can I do to make her happy? "Having fun?" I ask.

She nods vigorously. "It's been too long since I've been on the water. This was just what I needed."

"Good. We're almost there."

I pick up the pace, eager to get to land, to share this beautiful place with her. Totally normal for a business outing. I'm always excited to share cool spots with colleagues. Yeah, like hot new vegetarian restaurants, or eco-friendly conference centers. Who am I kidding? I'd never pack a picnic for a business associate, except Lexi, and look where that led. Shit. And I never brought Lexi here. We always hung out in Vermont, except for that one "business celebration" in New York. She initiated it, and I ignored huge red flags, thought *no big deal.* Now Eric's words come back to me. *You've been dicking around with Lexi longer than is healthy.*

I'm not dicking around with Josephine. It's a picnic, not a hookup. And once I come clean with her, let her know I feel an attraction but want to keep things professional so I can help launch her business, then I'll feel better. She probably will, too. Not that she seems confused or upset. She's radiant. Too radiant.

Maybe this is why she gets abused in the workplace. She's outrageously distracting, and for the typical uptight man in the nonprofit world, working with Josephine must be torture. A man's got to let his frustrations out somehow, and too many do it in all the wrong ways. Another reason I *have* to help. I can't let her continue to suffer under the thumb of one asshole boss after another. She has so much to offer. She simply needs support to bring her vision to the world.

When we reach the island, I slip my paddle into the hooks on the starboard side, instruct Josephine to stay in place, climb out of my spot, and walk through the knee-deep water to offer my hand. Her fingers feel warm, her grip on my hand firm, steady. My heart beats faster as I assist her out of her seat. Together, we carry the boat onto shore. Out of habit, I tie it to a tree, though the threat of the rising tide reaching this spot is minimal. I remove my life vest and place it in my seat.

When I turn around, I catch Josephine scanning my body, her lips pursed, as if she enjoys the view. My mouth goes dry. Josephine lifts her eyes to mine and smiles. She holds my gaze as she unzips her life vest and slips it off. Is she trying to seduce me?

Asked every aroused man ever. *No, Theo, she's being her vibrant self. It's not her fault you're turned on.* I try to keep my eyes on her face, but it's a losing battle. I know she's standing there in her sexy, sporty bikini. Her bright face, slender neck, décolletage and full tits covered tastefully (too tastefully) by her bikini top, her smooth, firm abs with just a hint of feminine softness above the bikini line. The gentle curve of her hips and those long, muscular legs.

As soon as she turns to throw the life vest into her seat, I adjust myself. I pull my backpack from the stow hatch, slip it over my shoulders, and walk past her onto the narrow trail, inhaling the scent of beach roses and evergreens. "Careful. All these old pine needles make the path slippery."

"Been there," she says. "Slipping on pine needles is not fun."

"Do you hike often?"

"Pretty much every week."

"Me, too. What's your favorite spot?"

"I really love Lake Wintergreen for a quick local hike. But if I feel like driving, I often go to Devil's Hopyard," she says.

"The boulder formations there are amazing!"

"Right?"

"Do you swim at Salmon River after?"

"If I'm with friends," she says. "I don't like to swim in the river alone."

"Smart."

"My other favorite spot is... Oh, my goodness, Theo, I'm forgetting the name. Are those wild blueberry bushes off to the right?"

"Indeed." I turn around and walk backward. "You a fan?" Suddenly I'm off balance, wobbling, stumbling over uneven ground, and landing on my ass. Fantastic. Heat rises to my cheeks.

She gasps. "Are you okay?"

"Still learning to walk," I deadpan. "Turns out only idiots walk backward on a trail laden with tree roots and stones." *One of which is gouging my tush.*

She extends her hand. I don't need help. My quads are solid from hours of strengthening yoga poses. But it would be insulting to refuse her aid. I take her hand and rise, keeping my gaze on her face, though her touch is sending a delightful surge of energy up my arm.

She tilts her chin up and scans my eyes. "Are you always so hard?"

"Excuse me?"

Her eyes widen, hands fly to her mouth. She chokes out, "On yourself. Hard on yourself."

"Which question would you like me to answer?"

Her blush deepens. "Goodness. You know what I mean. Are you always so hard on yourself?"

"The answer to both questions is: only when the moment calls for it."

She covers her face. "You're not gonna let me live this down."

"I'm sorry." I make a valiant effort to stop smirking. "You were trying to have a serious conversation, and I let it devolve. Now, what's your question?"

"People fall. Why chastise yourself for how you're walking?"

My breath catches in my throat. "Oh."

"Shoot. Did I just overstep a boundary? I do that sometimes."

I shake my head. "You caught me."

"Being self-critical?"

"Uh huh."

She sighs. "Theo. I recently met a lovely man who's helping me change my life in pretty amazing ways. Please don't criticize him."

My heart pounds a wild rhythm as I gaze into her eyes. So much caring. If I could pull her close and hold her tight—but I can't. "I hope you find your new friend worthy of your appreciation and kindness."

"There you go again," she says, her voice invigorating my muscles. "Worthy?"

A desire to kiss her overwhelms, but I will not succumb. It's the epitome of male privilege to think I have a right to her affection, that I can ignore the reality of this situation. If I let myself act on my feelings, I could jeopardize what Josephine needs most from me.

Chapter Sixteen

JOSEPHINE

Theo stares at me like he's trying to convey something
with his eyes and body language. He's close enough to touch.
Tempting, considering the zing of pleasure that flowed
through me when he took my hand to get up. *Do not bite
your lip, Josie.* I wish I knew what was on his mind, but I'm
afraid to ask.

"Shall we?" He gestures to the trail.

"Onward, fearless leader!"

Theo's laughter warms my insides. Most people don't
know what to do with my nerdy humor. Maybe Theo is a
nerd in disguise. Or maybe he's being polite. I turn my attention to the gorgeous view of the landscape—and Theo's
pine-needle covered derrière. Would it embarrass him if I said
something? I scan the forested path. My gaze returns to his
behind, extra appealing in those hip-hugging board shorts.
"Hey, you know you've got pine needles all over your butt?"

He shoots a playful grin over his shoulder, eyes sparkling
as he brushes the needles away and keeps walking. That smile
makes me sigh. The deep dimples framing Theo's mouth, his

nose crinkling in the most adorable—Okay, I need to stop. I'm trying to win his backing, not his love.

Kim's face flashes in my mind. I sigh again, this time in frustration. The man is taken.

"Everything okay back there?" Theo asks over his shoulder. "I hear a lot of sighing. Getting tired?"

Excellent. Even without speaking, my mouth is humiliating me. "Not at all. Um... it's really beautiful here."

"Glad you like it. I'm bringing you to my absolute favorite spot. This is pretty, but wait."

Fifteen minutes later, we arrive at a tunnel formed out of beach rose bushes. Visions of fairies dance in the hedge, filling me with delight. "You just made one of my childhood fantasies come true."

He flashes a smile over his shoulder. "It gets better."

Through the opening, a sandy beach beckons, sparking an idea for an unexpected keyhole cutout placed strategically in a floral dress.

I bend low to follow him through the short tunnel, the lush scent of beach roses surrounding me until I emerge onto the sand. Gentle waves lap against the shore, a tranquil sound. "My goodness. It's even more magical on this side! The fragrance. Look how sunlight sparkles on the water. And those boulders covered with lichen."

"See why it's my favorite?"

"Whatever happens with my business, we have to stay friends, so I can keep coming here with you." I cringe. I basically declared I'll happily use Theo for his picnic spot.

Yet his eyes twinkle. He sheds his backpack, opens it, and removes a large woven blanket. He lays it on the ground, drops to his knees, and sets out a menagerie of food. A loaf of bread, lemon soda, sparkling water. Like Mary Poppins, Theo continues to pull things from a seemingly small backpack. Mini-cheeseboard with slicer. Half-sized wheel of brie.

Something wrapped in a cloth napkin. He unwraps it to reveal a jar of cornichons. More napkin-wrapped items.

"Shoot. Are you vegan? I should've asked."

"Vegetarian. How did you fit so much into that little bag?"

"I'm a man of many talents." He winks, lighting my second chakra aflame.

He sets out a tray of tartlets and a container of reddish dip.

"Is that muhammara? Yay." The red pepper-pomegranate-walnut dip is my favorite.

Theo grins and adds a tiny jar of black olives to our feast.

"From your tree?"

"Casabella Olives." His chest swells, accentuating his muscles under his t-shirt.

"Wow." What else can I say to make him proud?

"Uh, oh. What's that look on your face? Is there something you can't eat or don't like?"

I shake my head. "This is incredible, Theo. Now I feel bad. All I brought was cookies."

"And swimsuits." He winks. "Anyway, I adore cookies. Come sit." He slips off his hiking sandals, sits cross-legged on the blanket, and pats a spot next to him.

I toe off my shoes and join him. "Have I mentioned this is amazing?"

In response, he hovers a small metal camping plate over each delicacy. "May I serve you?"

Never thought I'd hear a man utter that phrase. Too bad he's taken. "Yes, please."

Theo points to things and watches my face for reaction, then fills my plate with bread, muhammara, olives, and brie. He hands me the plate and a fork, then pours me a glass of lemon soda. After serving himself, he holds his glass aloft. "A toast. To new adventures, new endeavors, and new friends."

"Cheers!" We clink glasses and sip. Light, bright flavor sparkles on my tongue.

"Josephine." He looks at his plate. "I have something to confess."

I lift an eyebrow, and my core tightens in anticipation. "Sounds serious."

He braves a glance at my face, sips his soda, rolls an olive around his plate. "I'm..."

Not going to invest.

"I shouldn't be," he says.

Giving your ideas to a fast fashion house so they can destroy you. Right because that's the vibe I've been getting from Theo. *Way to be paranoid, Josie.*

"I mean, I can't help it."

My stomach aches. I sip my drink. He sure is taking his time spitting out this confession. "Help what?" I ask.

"I don't wanna beat myself up, but..."

You are killing me, Theo.

"I'm deeply attracted to you." He looks down with a sigh.

My being fills with light, and before I can stop it, my heart speaks. "Me, too."

He looks up from his plate. What are his eyes showing? Longing and... Oh, shit. He didn't want to tell me because he's conflicted. My heart drops. Theo's attracted to me, but he's unavailable. That could make working together a big problem. "And you're living with Kim."

He chokes. "What? She's half my age."

"I know, but—" My face is doing all sorts of contortions; I can feel it but can't seem to stop it.

Theo laughs. "My God. I don't know whether to be hurt by your assumption I'd date a child or flattered by your assumption I could if I wanted to."

"Geez. I'm sorry. I guess... This is so embarrassing. It's really not about you at all. It's just now that I'm in my forties..." I sigh. "And Kim was in your house, and she said *our honey* like she lives there, and—"

"I've gotta get her to stop doing that," he says.

"I know I'm pretty for my age, but guys like you like younger women."

"Guys like me?"

"Brilliant, successful, hot guys over forty." If only I could sink into the earth.

"Well, thank you for the compliment, but did you hear me? I'm not into Kim. I'm into you, unfortunately."

"Unfortunately."

"Because we can't act on it. But you are the most alluring woman I've ever known. The whole package. Creative, intelligent, fun. A splendor men would swim oceans for, with expressive almond-shaped eyes like lighthouses radiating your inner beauty outward."

Inner beauty. I bite my lip. How is this moving me to tears?

"Are you crying?"

I shake my head as a tear slides off my face. "It's just a physiological reaction."

"Physiological, huh?"

I nod, looking at him through my lashes. "I'm from a long line of criers."

"Not, like, town criers," he says, playful.

I groan and look skyward. "We cry at any powerful emotion—joy, sadness, even anger."

"Sounds confusing."

"It's ridiculous, actually." I wipe my cheeks and sniffle. *Town criers.* "Now, do you make cheese, as well as olives?"

"No." He sounds confused. "Why?"

"Cause that town criers joke was cheesy!"

"Aw, come on." He crosses his arms in a fake pout, making me giggle. "I do my best."

"You do, Theo," I say in mock sympathy. "Anyway, jokes

aside, I appreciate your integrity. This attraction we feel; it's good we have it out in the open."

"Agreed." A look I have no idea how to interpret crosses his face. "Like I said at our meeting last week, transparency is crucial in this process. We need to feel safe trusting each other."

Trust. Another word I've never heard in the workplace, amazingly. He's so inspiring. "I need to add that word to my business plan. I want to be someone that people I work with trust. In all directions."

"All directions?" He scans my face, his eyes threatening to draw me in. Oops. Don't go there.

I shift my gaze, lose myself in the play of light on the gentle ripples meeting the shore. "The web of my network, people I work alongside. I guess you'd call them my suppliers. And the people I hire."

"Your employees?"

"Yeah." I dare to glance at him and look away quickly. "I hate that word, though."

"Employee?"

"It implies a hierarchy, like they're below me." I shudder. "We're equals. And people who invest are also my equals. I mean, because they have more money, most people might say my investors are above me, but—"

Suddenly, I'm imagining Theo above me, hovering, biceps working, pectorals flexing as he lowers himself. His body heat closing distance before our skin... Fuck!

Yes, please. I giggle nervously. "Gosh, I'm hungry. Are you? And should we talk about my business plan now?"

THEO

Business plan. I let myself get so wrapped up in Josephine's words, tears, body. *Language.* It's her *body language* that's held me captive. *Not* her *body*. I've been so busy trying to read her signals, I forgot the picnic and that we're also meeting to discuss her revised plan. Honestly, this went worlds better than I expected. Now, we're on the same page, clear of sexual tension, ready to collaborate.

Her stomach rumbles loudly.

"I guess you are hungry," I say.

She laughs, embarrassed.

"Let's eat, get back to shore, then open your business plan on my computer and review it together. Yeah?"

"Great."

"Here. Eat." I spread brie on a bite sized chunk of bread and extend it to her. She takes it in her long, delicate fingers, puts it into her sumptuous mouth, makes an appreciative sound. I need to look away.

She offers me a bite of bread with muhammara. I lean forward, start to open my mouth, then catch myself and extend my palm instead. She places the crudité in my hand. I close my eyes to savor the tangy blend of red peppers, walnuts, and pomegranate molasses. Why are we feeding each other? We each have food on our plates.

I pop a tartlet into my mouth, gaze at the lichen-covered boulder. How does she see this play of color and texture? I see nature. If I'm being creative, maybe a painting in the style of Millet.

She moans. "This olive is incredible."

Her voice lures me from my reverie, and my body responds. Damn it. I'm not even watching her. Clearly, I can never eat with Josephine again. Observing her enjoyment puts me on sensory overload.

"Seriously, it's the best olive I've tasted."

Talk. Banter. Good idea. "No way." I tease.

"Way. How do you make them so good?"

"It's the curing process. We follow my great-grandmother's recipe: kosher salt, secret spices, a pillowcase..."

Josephine's eyebrows go up. "A pillowcase?"

"It's crucial to the process."

"Specifically, a pillowcase."

"Okay, I guess any large piece of cloth...."

I try to ignore how good having her rapt attention feels. More important now is to provide a clear description of what Nonno taught me: to harvest olives in spring, once the bitterness is gone, then toss them with kosher salt, wrap them in a pillowcase and tie it to a branch, so the black juices drip onto the ground without ruining anything.

"That sounds so simple."

"It is." I pop an olive into my mouth with a piece of bread.

"Yet they're superb."

"It's the curing. Brine-cured olives get soft, but oil-cured ones keep their texture."

Josephine sips her soda. "And the flavor seems stronger."

"Because once they've cured about six weeks, they marinate in olive oil with fresh oregano and a touch of red pepper flakes."

"I taste the oregano and pepper. It's nice. Hey, I'd love to cure olives with you next..." Her eyes widen as her voice trails off.

Hearing her mention the future, my heart leaps. Not good. *Keep it casual.* "Could be fun. Do you like to cook?"

"Absolutely!"

"Me, too. Let's make dinner some night this week, after a business planning session, okay?" No. Why did I just say that? We can't cook together.

"Definitely!" She asks about my specialties, which leads to a full conversation about food that I'm only partially aware of, though my mouth is making sounds and Josephine seems to be responding.

While we talk, I envision her chopping peppers at the kitchen island. She looks over her shoulder and smiles as I reach around her for the salt. My erection grazes her ass through the fabric of our clothes. She leans back, presses herself into me, teasing.

Cooking together would be even worse than eating together.

I try not to look at her mouth as we finish the picnic, but that's a losing battle. Have I ever been so aroused watching a woman eat? If I stand now, I'll humiliate himself. I try bringing my calendar to mind, but that doesn't work. I recall the financial page on Josephine's original business plan, with its credit card confetti and hand-sewn spreadsheet. For some reason, that makes me harder.

One thing can bring me down right now. Lexi's confusion. A punch to the gut. *"I've had a closet cleaned out for you."* The way she blew me a kiss and sashayed away, not for the first time. Yet the only time I allowed myself to see the truth: my friend and business associate fell for me. Mixing business and lust, even rarely, confused her. Because of me, Lexi gave up what may have been her one chance at true love. And I will not screw things up for Josephine, no matter what Ma and Eric say about following my damn heart. Business and sex make a bad mix.

The sound of the waves on the shore brings me out of my haze. I look at my watch. "Wow. We've been sitting here over an hour. Better pack up and go before the tide rises."

Josephine thanks me again as we drain our glasses. I've never felt so appreciated. I wish things weren't so complicated, that her business was an obvious slam dunk, or that she wasn't so alluring and intelligent. If only she was too lazy to help me pack our picnic remains. But she doesn't simply help. She helps eagerly, says, "My pleasure," to my "Thank you." And she keeps the cookies out in case we get hungry on the way home. The woman is thoughtful, kind, adorable.

"I really appreciate that I could be so open with you today, Josephine."

"And I appreciate your willingness to be vulnerable. It takes guts, especially for a man."

My chest fills with pride. "You think?"

"Society teaches men not to cry, be afraid, or even show complex emotions. Women get to explore the full range. But guys are stuck with angry, happy, sad."

"Too true."

"And here you are, sharing how you feel and holding space for my feelings. That's big."

"I'm glad we agree we can't act on our urges."

"This relationship could change my life. I can't afford to risk anything."

"God, I would feel horrible if something happened between us that confused our business relationship. But I think we have the start of a special friendship, and I'm excited to know you better, Josephine."

"Me, too, Theo."

What a relief to have had this conversation. I stand, grab two corners of the picnic blanket. She grabs the other two corners, then we walk to each other to fold it. This went well.

Our hands meet.

Heat.

Desire in Josephine's eyes matches my feelings. Need flares.

Now, our lips join, breaths mingle, tongues intertwine. Her smooth skin electrifies my fingertips. Currents fly from every point where her fingers touch my spine.

"Oh, God," we pant together, feeding on each other, hands everywhere.

Wait. I stop breathing, open my eyes, step back. "Oh, God."

Too many emotions flicker across her face for me to read at once. "Did I imagine that?" she asks.

"Uhh." I look down. Her chest heaves with her rapid breath, nipples peek through her swimsuit. Tiny hairs on her belly stand on end. My heart pounds, cock strains against my trunks. The tapestry lies in a heap on the sand. I nod, mouth agape. "I don't think so."

"That was—" She bites her lip, unsure, sexy.

"Bad. I'm sorry, Josephine."

"Very bad. I'm sorry, too."

"It will never happen again."

"Never," she repeats.

But she's in my arms again, and I don't know if she's pressing into me or I'm pulling her close. And I don't know how we got across the beach, but now I'm leaning against the boulder, grabbing her perfect ass, lifting. She's wrapping those outrageous long legs around my waist. Something's damp. Maybe her, maybe me. Maybe we're both leaking through our swimsuits. Her jawline tastes delicious, and her earlobe... She caresses the base of my skull, my shoulders, hips, and lower. I growl into her chest, bite the swimsuit between my mouth and her skin. Needing her taste, I run my tongue along the bikini's neckline. Her head lolls back, giving me access to her neck. I suck, graze my way to her breasts, nuzzle her through the fabric, bite at her hard nipples. She moans in pleasure, squeezes my waist with her thighs. I'm getting harder?

"God, I want you." I pull her closer.

"Kiss me, Theo."

I suck her nipple through the fabric once more, then obey, sweeping my lips over hers. Her sweet sounds, the smoothness of her skin, and her fresh scent put a spell on me. The center of my forehead tingles, and in my mind's eye I see our future: *a thousand images of waking beside her at different ages in rapid succession. The engagement ring I slip onto her finger, the wedding band she places onto mine.*

My breath catches in my throat. What's happening? I can't do this right now. Not here. Not with her. What is this? I stop moving, stop breathing, slip my hands off her behind.

She pulls away, looks into my eyes. Confusion. Fear. Exactly what I was trying to avoid. How could I let this happen? "I'm so sorry, Josephine." I stroke her hair, soothing us both.

She looks down. "It was me. I shouldn't have."

I place a finger under her chin, lift her face. "It was us." My cock throbs. I want her so badly. "And it won't happen again. I promise."

She nods, looking so vulnerable I can't take it.

If only I could hold her, comfort her. "I'm sorry."

"Me, too."

I caress her cheek, then realize my mistake and pull away.

Our surroundings seem to disappear as Josephine licks her lips, gazes skyward. "On the plus side, we probably got it out of our systems. I hope."

"Yes. It was probably a good thing." I stride across the sand to where the blanket lay in a heap, shove the mess into my backpack. "Tide's coming in. Ready?"

I lead the way to the opening in the hedge and gesture for her to go ahead of me. And damn if the scent of her arousal as she passes doesn't make it hard for me to crouch and get through the tunnel. It's not out of my system yet. But I'll have to ignore my desires. I can't fuck up with her again.

Chapter Seventeen

JOSEPHINE

IT'S NOT out of my system. If my system was clear, I'd simply trudge toward the house behind Theo. I would *not* notice the stupid setting sun with its stupid romantic glow highlighting the muscles in Theo's shoulders. Seeing the gentleman open the door for me would spark nothing. Passing him on the way inside, catching the scent of his sweat wouldn't threaten to make me faint from desire. Nor would it spark fantasies of licking the sweat off his—

"Ready to talk about your business plan?" he asks, entering his office and stroking the trackpad to wake his computer.

"Absolutely." I stand in the doorway, wishing I didn't sound so breathy, but the way Theo's bent over his desk... "Where can I change?"

"Guest bath is that way." He points.

I stride into the bathroom, slip out of my bikini, and shrug my dress over my head. Facing my reflection in the mirror, I mouth a silent affirmation about self-control and return to Theo's office.

The man looks sexy as hell, reclining in his antique oak desk chair, ankle crossed over his knee. Calm, composed. His eyes light up when he sees me. "Hey, you're shaking. Should I turn down the a/c?"

"Just nervous, I guess." A lie. It's not nerves. I'm trembling with lust. What did I say on the beach about adding "trust" to my business plan?

He points to his monitor. "I like the changes. Times New Roman font. Great choice."

"Thanks."

"And the Executive Summary: clean, concise." He scrolls to the next section, his strong fingers sliding along the track pad. Watching the motion, I can almost feel his fingertips on my skin. "Mission, vision, and values statements—right on target. Now, I haven't had a chance to read the Differentiators section."

By mistake, I look down. Seeing he's aroused and trying to hide it puts me on sensory overload.

"What can you tell me about it?"

Good question. What are my differentiators? The words on the screen dance in front of me. No, no, no. What's happening? My brain is flooded with too many emotions, too many physical sensations. I can't think straight. I bumble words. Am I even making sense? We're supposed to be talking business, and all I want is to feel him hard against me again. What a mess. I look at him, helpless.

"Are you having as much trouble focusing as I am?"

Frustration squeezes my muscles. Sexual frustration. Financial frustration. "I should be able to explain my business plan, right? For goodness' sake, I wrote it. It's my vision."

"It's pretty late. It's been a long day. We're probably both... overwhelmed. Another time?"

"Yeah. A lot to process." *Right now, I'd like to wrap*

myself in your voice. I look at him, envisioning another day at Social God-Awful Connivers, and feel sick.

"Tomorrow is packed." He looks up, sympathy in his eyes and something else. Something I don't want to see.

All I had to do was keep my hands off him.

"Let's talk Friday? We already have a meeting on the books then, right?"

I nod, dazed. "Today was super fun, Theo. Thanks."

"I appreciate you coming all the way out here."

"Aww. It was worth it." *To spend time with you.* "I get that you're super busy."

"Not too busy for you," he says, then winces.

I stutter. "It means a lot that you made time for me." *And it's not your fault I foolishly hoped you'd read my new business plan and commit to investing today. It's also not your fault I have to spend another week at Shady Gaslighters Connecticut while I await your decision.*

Queasy. Powerless. I let the moment on the beach override my sense, and now... A horrible thought occurs to me. If Theo doesn't invest, what are my chances of attracting other backers? Who's in my network? *Breathe. Get your head together.* In a trance, I sling my bag over my shoulder, let Theo guide me across the threshold, escort me to my car, and open the driver's side door. I smile, don't I? Of course. His gallantry touches me. Now, he closes my car door, taps the hood, and strides to his house. My eyes follow him without my consent. He's watching me, too, leaning against the door-jamb, all masculinity and sex appeal. He waves. I wave, sigh, and drive away, ignoring the longing. We cannot get involved. I'm a jumbled mess after a little making out. If we were having sex? Lovely. Disastrous.

Chapter Eighteen

JOSEPHINE

Constellations filled the night sky at Theo's house. Back home, light pollution obscures my view. Only the strongest stars shine through, their pulsing mimicking, or maybe mocking, the pulsing between my legs. I try to ignore my arousal as I stride across the dark lawn to my door, but as I climb the stairs to my apartment, I wonder why I'm fighting my natural urges. Okay, it's clear I can't act on them with Theo. My future is on the line. But alone? I can do as I please.

Inside, I put on smooth jazz, brew a cup of chamomile peppermint tea, and fill my old claw-foot bathtub. I add Epsom salts and lavender oil with rose water, and light the candles on the windowsill, etagere, and sink. What I want, what I *need* right now, is to finish what we started on the beach.

In the bedroom, I strip, drop my clothes into the hamper, and retrieve my vibrating egg and the latest romance novel by local author Bethany J. Miller. I love this story, about the offbeat single mom with blue hair and the dad who's learning how to be a single parent himself. It's sweet, funny and romantic, and the sex scenes are spicy but never superfluous, just how I like them.

I slide into my steamy bath, submerging myself, and forbidden fantasies arise. Theo would be in the tub with me... *Don't go there.* I lift my head out of the water. After wetting a washcloth, I run it along my leg. If Theo was holding the washcloth, where would he explore first? Along the sole of my foot? Caressing my ankle, my calf? Tracing his fingers around my kneecaps, an area I've always found oddly stimulating, up my quadriceps, then along the inside of my thigh...

I sigh and caress the other leg with the washcloth, then move on to my hips, gripping firmly, imagining Theo's hands taking hold of me, running his thumbs along the ridge that protrudes from each hip, to my sides, up my ribcage, slipping a thumb under each breast. *Did you learn nothing from today? You can't act on this.* The nipples. I moan, beg him to touch them, to roll each one between his forefinger and thumb, to suck. Not like on the beach. This time, there's no fabric separating his tongue and my skin. I imagine him moaning with pleasure as he takes my breast into his mouth and sucks slowly. It's okay. It's not real. He'll never know. His pleasure, my ecstasy. I rise into his mouth, reach for him. He's stiff in my palm. I bring him to my opening and rub his tip in circles around me. If only... I press the button on my toy. Its low-speed vibrations make me moan. It's not Theo, but it feels damn good. Would he enjoy using this with me? There's a fun fantasy. Imaginary Theo dips the egg-shaped toy into sesame oil, then—

The phone rings from its perch on the windowsill. Theo's face lights the screen. He must have read the business plan! I grab the phone with my free hand, putting him on speaker as I try to turn off the egg. His voice fills the room, and I tingle everywhere. "Am I calling too late?"

"It's fine."

"Listen, I just wanted to say— Do you hear a buzzing on the line?"

"What?"

"A buzzing."

The vibrator. "Oh, uhhh.... I..." I try again to turn it off, but drop it into the water instead. It makes a loud splash and keeps vibrating. "Shit."

"Did I catch you in the middle of something?"

"Um... I..." Cannot get hold of this thing. Wet and coated with oil, it keeps slipping from my hands. "Dropped something."

"Okay." He sounds confused.

I take a deep breath. "Honestly, I was in the bath. *Am* in the bath."

"Oh! I should let you go."

If I could just get a grip on the damn toy, I could have a normal conversation with the man. "No. You called. It must be important."

THEO

She's in the bath. I'd love to see Josephine reclining in my soaking tub. Better: I'd join her, touch her smooth bronze skin, taut muscles, feel her incredibly firm breasts in my hands. Instant arousal. *Shit.* I'm calling to apologize for letting things get out-of-control today, not to ramp up my fantasies. "Sure you don't mind?" I ask. *Please say no.*

"Of course not." She sounds distracted.

That strange buzzing continues on her end of the line. It didn't start until she answered. A bad connection? "I just wanted to thank you again for coming. I had a really wonderful time with you."

"Me too." A splash on her end.

An erection on mine. *Fuck.* "Those swimsuits—so playful!"

"Glad you like them."

I'd love to see them on you. "And I want to apologize."

"For what?" she asks.

"I let things—You hear the buzzing, too, right?"

She coughs. "Uh, yeah." More splashing. "Damn it. Not you. I just—Why are you apologizing?"

"I let things get out of hand on the beach."

"For goodness' sake! I give up." The sound of water draining comes through the line.

"What?"

"Not you. This... thing. I. Ugh. I'm getting out of the bath."

"Don't do that on my account. God, first I ruined our picnic. Now—"

"You didn't ruin our picnic. I'm equally responsible. Honestly, I don't know how it happened. One minute we were folding the picnic blanket, the next we were—" She speaks up as the buzzing gets louder. "Oh, shit."

It's as if something is vibrating against a table, or the tub, or—Ohhhh.

"The next we were in each other's arms."

The bath. Buzzing. Vibrating. *Do not laugh.*

The sound stops. Josephine exhales audibly. "Thank God."

I burst into nervous laughter.

"What?" she asks, her rising voice turning the word into two syllables.

"Uhhh..." *Don't be a jerk, Theo.* "Nothing."

"Ugh. Can we pretend you didn't figure out what was buzzing?"

I try to stifle my giggling.

"You know, I wouldn't have answered the phone, but I thought maybe—God, this is so embarrassing."

Now, I feel bad. "I'm sorry. I shouldn't have laughed. I—Wait." Was she using her vibrator while we were talking? My sac tightens. I imagine stroking her with a toy, watching her swell.

"To be clear, I was using it *before*, not during our call. I tried to shut it off, but it was slippery and wet, and—"

A moan escapes. *Slippery and wet.*

"Damn it," she says with a sigh. "I put it in my mouth again."

I cough. *That'd be nice.*

She squeaks. "My foot. Put my foot in my mouth. Oh, God." She laughs nervously.

"Go ahead. Laugh," I say, letting her off the hook. "That's what I get for interrupting you in the middle of your bath."

"I should've turned it off before I answered. I just haven't been thinking straight since..." her voice trails off.

"Since we made out?"

"Yeah."

"Me, neither," I admit. The vision I had on the beach returns to mind: an engagement ring on her finger, wedding band on mine. "You lit something in me, Josephine, and I guess if I'm being honest, I really just wanted to hear your voice."

"Yeah?" she asks, quiet, vulnerable.

"A bad idea on my part."

"I like hearing your voice, too."

I shouldn't touch myself while we're on the phone. Then again, I shouldn't have called. Definitely not from bed. That was a bad idea. But she doesn't know I'm lying here in the dark, wishing she was beside me, wishing I could tell her about the vision on the beach. I'm getting harder. Can't help stroking myself. Is she aroused, too? She's silent. Waiting for me to reassure her? "It was lovely. You're lovely."

She sighs. "I wish this wasn't so confusing."

She's not aroused. She's confused. And it's my fault. I shouldn't have called. "Me, too. I'm sorry. Sogni d'oro, Josephine. Sweet dreams."

We hang up. My apology could've waited until tomorrow or Friday. It might've been better to drop the subject altogether. Unfortunately, when it comes to Josephine, I seem to lack all self-control.

Chapter Nineteen

THEO

Thoughts are not actions. True, I've probably charmed my snake more this week than I have since high school, but that does *not* make me an asshole. I neither called nor texted Josephine after Sunday night's embarrassing episode. I had Kim confirm today's meeting. If Josephine's face, body, voice, and scent happen to arise every time I touch myself, that doesn't mean I'm not thinking with my MBA.

How could I have known I'd get aroused reading that fantastic article about her show in *The New Yorker*? That beautiful photo of her with her models reminded me of our first meeting and made me feel good. It doesn't mean my business instincts are off. It doesn't mean I'm taking advantage of her. How would I have known this week's issue would feature her? Besides, reading the great press and her revised business plan helped me reach a decision, which I'm eager to share.

Now, I stand under the portico, sheltered from the rain, body thrumming with excitement about Josephine's arrival.

Totally fine. It's natural to feel excited about seeing someone special.

A rideshare pulls into the driveway and stops. Josephine emerges from the back seat, in a stunning rain jacket only she could've created. High-heeled sandals accentuate her cute painted toenails and shapely legs. Her face, brightened by that amazing smile, fills me with—that's not important.

I'd love to open my arms and embrace her. Instead, I stick my hands deeper into the pockets of my organic linen trousers (a purchase inspired by Josephine). Can I help if I'm mesmerized watching her step lightly around the puddles?

She joins me under the portico and I ask, "Where's your car?"

"In the shop." Nothing arousing about those words, but her voice... so sweet and bright.

I match my breathing to hers, trying to calm myself. "I have great news for you."

"Oh, yeah?"

I lead her inside, down the hall, where Kim meets us, ever-present tablet giving her face a blue glow. The difference between how Josephine responds to Kim today versus last time is night and day. Last week, Josephine was polite. Today, she's as warm and welcoming as my assistant. I chuckle inside. The idea that I would, one: attract, and two: want someone so much younger is truly comical. I've always had a thing for slightly older women. When I think about it, the four-year age gap between me and Josephine almost makes me feel like I'm robbing the cradle. Except I'm not. Because we're not going there.

"... for you," Kim finishes.

"Hmm?" I ask.

Josephine smiles up at me. "Kim said she set everything up for us."

I need to focus. "Can you brew me a latte, please? What would you like, Josephine?"

"Do you have tea?"

My assistant rattles off options. Josephine's sumptuous lips form words, a smile for Kim, a smile for me. She's looking at me expectantly again. "Theo?"

When did we sit? Damn it. Caffeine can't come quickly enough. "Did you see this?" I pull the magazine off my desk and hand it to her, opened to the page.

She cringes. "Kath shared it. Despite the great headline, I can't bring myself to read it. I babbled like an idiot during that interview."

"The journalist must like you because you come across as brilliant and insightful. I sent Drew the article. Maybe it will help him see what I see."

"His opinion really matters to you, huh?" Concern darkens her face.

"Not enough to stop me investing."

Her eyes widen. "Really? That's amazing news." She claps. Adorable.

"Let me rephrase." I hold up my hands. "I'm seriously considering backing you. Last week, seeing that craft project, I doubted I'd be able to invest. But your revisions were excellent. Our next steps are: polish this, create a pitch deck, and research other potential investors."

"Okay." She draws out the word, clearly trying to hide her disappointment.

Already disappointing her. Damn it.

"What do you need from me to make a commitment?"

Kim walks in, places our drinks in our hands, then leaves. I sip my latte, trying to think, but the word commitment put images of engagement rings in my mind. Now I'm seeing an altar. Ridiculous. I haven't been to mass in years.

"Sorry. Is it too soon to ask? I'm trying to straddle the line between assertive and chill. Maybe I'm just getting off as aggressive."

I choke. "You mean, coming off?"

She nods. "Right. That's what I said. Coming off as aggressive."

Straddle. Getting off. I'm not touching that with a ten-foot pole. A six-inch shaft, though... Images form in my mind. *Jesus Christ, Casabella.* I stare out the window, sip my latte. A perfect blend of bitter and sweet, with the raw honey adding depth to the flavor profile. Ready to get back in the game, I meet her questioning gaze. "You're not aggressive. I think what we accomplish today will give me enough info to decide."

"I already did some research into potential investors, including local-owned banks and credit unions."

"Fantastic. Of course, banks and credits unions are not investors. They're lenders."

"Right." She's not masking her embarrassment well, which makes me feel guilty.

But I'm moving past my feelings now. Josephine is not distracting. And I don't have a problem focusing. The problem is, I slept poorly last night. Dreams of lovemaking plagued me, and I kept waking to my empty bed.

She's here now. All business. Talking about lenders. I, too, get to act like a professional. "Once we get a sense of who's interested, then we can brainstorm how much to request in loans, what kind of percentage you want to offer investors."

"Percentage?" she asks.

"These are investments, not gifts. Investors want a piece of the company."

"Like shares? I don't want my company on the stock market."

I hold up my hands. "We're talking private investment, not public. Either way, investors get a stake." Yes, she needs remedial business training. *So? Help her,* Ma says in my head. "But you get to handpick your investors, unlike a publicly traded company. Understand?"

She nods. "I think so."

Four hours later, we have a polished business plan, with a few placeholders on the Vendors page and in the budget for what Josephine calls Sewists. I know she means sewing factory employees. Since I have several contacts in manufacturing, I make a note to reach out to them for detailed info regarding lead times, costs, and whether they can work with the suppliers Josephine wants. If they can't, I'll need to make sure they have alternate suppliers who offer the materials Josephine says are the backbone of her line. She's passionate about her work, focused, and it's my job to support her. Now, she's thinking, her jaw set in that sultry—

I take a long sip of water and listen to the pouring rain. Refreshing. Comforting. I'll get used to working with her. In time, I won't need to think of budget figures just to keep my dick in check. Soon, she'll be off on her own, and I'll have no reason to be near her at all, except for monthly check-ins. The idea of not seeing Josephine makes my heart drop. We work so well together.

The printer spits out the plan's last pages, and I retrieve them eagerly. "This is a thing of beauty." I riffle the document.

"You think so?"

"How do you feel about it?"

"Nervous. Excited. Proud!"

I offer my hand for a high five. She taps my palm, sending heat and light up my arm. Shit. I pull away like it's no big deal. "This plan is the bones, and your pitch deck will reflect that. As we're determining who to approach first for investment, we'll figure out details and lay out action steps. Divide and conquer may be our best approach." Not to mention a good way to work separately, so I won't be fighting to control my body for hours on end. "I can have Kim research the more difficult areas, like incorporation, and you can come up with other details. How does that sound?"

"I want to be a B-Corp."

"Fantastic, but Benefit Corporation denotes certification, not legal status. If you haven't read chapter five, business structure..."

She hasn't read it. I can tell because she's suddenly fascinated by her feet.

"I strongly encourage you to finish that book. Your plan looks great, but we both need to understand how business works. Okay?"

"Totally."

My phone pings. Lexi. Annoyed, I flip the device. It pings again. I ignore it. "So, we'll look into incorporation, B-Corp status, other sustainable fashion certifications. You won't have emissions, so I don't envision too much impeding our plan, but—"

Josephine finishes my sentence. "Better safe than sorry."

"Exactly. Hey, are you hungry?"

"Starved, actually."

"Let's celebrate over dinner. Heirloom okay?"

"I love that place, but it's out of my budget."

I wave away her concern. "My treat," I say, then yell, "Kim."

"Boss?" She joins us, the tablet's glow on her face eerie in the stormy gray light.

"Can you book a table for us at Heirloom for..." I look at my watch. "Five-thirty?"

"You're leaving now?"

I nod.

"You have the follow-up call with Crypto Earth in fifteen minutes. Remember? You wanted to see if they're going to pivot, if they can convince you to support them again."

"Move that."

Kim's eyebrows lift. "Okay," she says slowly. "It's only a fifteen-minute call."

"Theo, if you need to do that, I can wait," Josephine says. "I need to catch up on social media posts, anyway."

"No. I was being generous with Crypto Earth. At our last meeting," *hours before I met you, Josephine*, "they seemed uninterested in changing their M.O."

Kim swipes her finger up the tablet. "After that, you were going to Zoom with the agriculture consultant in Arizona."

Shit. I take a deep breath, trying to think. I've got nothing. Well, I'm always saying flexibility is crucial in business. "Plans change. I'm famished for some reason, and Josephine and I need to celebrate this beautiful business plan."

"Congratulations." Kim smiles cautiously. "So, I should move the farm consultant, too?"

Josephine gasps. "Oh, Theo, let's celebrate another time."

"See if he's available Monday evening."

"You're giving a speech in Boston Monday evening."

"Afterward. I can Zoom from my hotel room."

Kim purses her lips. "You got it, boss. And if they're not free Monday?"

I wave a hand. "Just find another time. It's an exploratory call."

"Okey, doke." She sounds confused.

"Like I always say, Kim, successful businesses are agile."

Chapter Twenty

THEO

"I LOVE it when the rain pours in sheets," Josephine says, dry under my umbrella, matching my gait as we stride down Chapel Street toward the restaurant.

I wish her every word didn't make me want to kiss her. This is a business dinner, and I must—I *will* prevent this from becoming romantic.

"This downpour feels like a healing offering, washing away all the terrible jobs and shitty experiences of my past, bringing a chance for nourishing work, a new life."

"This rain is doing a lot of work," I joke. Her laughter makes me tingle. Not good. My plan involves dinner, humor, and celebrating the start of a new endeavor. As long as I remain professional, everything will be fine. We'll celebrate, schedule our next meeting, I'll bring her home because her car is in the shop, and I'll go home. End of story.

"Have I mentioned I have a polished business plan?" Her celebratory shimmy makes her jiggle in all the right places. *Fuck, Casabella, look away.* I redirect my gaze to the wet granite stairs leading to the restaurant.

Her gasp startles me. She's falling. I put my arm out just in time, catching Josephine in a half-hug. "Steady there. You okay?" My heart pounds.

She looks over her shoulder at me, breathing hard. "Thanks."

I shouldn't have looked away. Withdrawing my arm from her almost hurts. What if she loses her balance again? I lay my hand on her mid-back, barely a touch, but enough to stop her falling until we're safe on the landing. As I open the door for her, she picks up where she left off, her scent tantalizing me as she passes. "True, it's just the first step, but I'm now one step closer to realizing my dream, thanks to you."

Our eyes meet. I'm lightheaded. Probably low blood sugar.

"And when that vision becomes real, Theo, every worker in my company will have a voice and earn a living wage. How sublime is that?"

"Pretty damn sublime."

Inside, I help Josephine shrug her adorable raincoat and hand it along with mine to the maître d. The pianist playing in the far corner sets a relaxed ambience. Exactly what I need.

At the table, I let the maître d hold Josephine's chair instead of doing it myself. We're business associates. This isn't a date. Obviously, I had to help her out of the car and open the restaurant door, but I draw the line at anything she could misconstrue as romantic. "You know what I loved about that article in *The New Yorker*?" I ask, settling into my seat. "The bit about transparency."

"Transparency is big for you, huh?"

"For you, too. Right?"

"Totally. Fast fashion companies hide violations behind style and keep people in the dark about where their clothes come from."

"Even me," I admit. "Here I've been working on the leading edge of environmentalism for twenty-five years. The connection between clothes and pollution never occurred to me until you and Kath opened my eyes."

"Trying to connect all the dots between modern life and pollution overwhelms people." Josephine scans the menu.

"Which explains how Drew could be so oblivious. He's fixated on trees, plants, and wildlife."

She laughs. "Yeah. I hate to harp on it, but Kath made a good point. If Drew never thinks about what he wears…"

I smirk, remembering Kath's rampage while Josephine continues, "It makes sense that he wouldn't think about *how* what he wears impacts the forests he cares about."

The waiter arrives to take our drink order. Josephine looks at the wine list, admits she's not very knowledgeable, and asks me to choose. Delighted that she asked, I select a Verdejo. "I've attended fashion shows before, Josephine. Usually, the models strut down a catwalk. Until I read that article, I didn't get why you sent your models mingling. Your quote about fashion being approachable makes total sense."

"Right? Walking among the models, talking to them about the clothes, is inclusive and empowering, unlike passively watching models stroll a catwalk. I'm glad we're on the same page."

Her use of the word "we" sends heat to all the wrong body parts. Maybe I can gently steer her away from that word. And partnership. The server arrives with the bottle of wine, pours a taste for me. Glad for something to do with my hands, I sniff the liquid, roll it around in the glass, take a sip. "Perfect." I smile.

The waiter pours each of us a full glass and leaves.

I hold my wine aloft, gaze into Josephine's warm, open face. "To the beginning of a beautiful business… adventure." We clink glasses. "After what we accomplished today, I feel confident investing."

"Yay! How much?" She cringes. "That was rude. I'm sorry."

"Clarity is important. You need to put numbers in your budget, after all." I wink. Friendly. Not romantic. "The initial figure will be low to encourage you to find several investors. Of course, I know some people who might be interested."

She narrows her eyes. "Could you be a little more specific? I mean, are we talking one thousand dollars? Thirty thousand?"

"Ten thousand, maybe fifteen."

Seeing the mixture of disappointment and excitement battling on her face tempts me to boost my opening amount to six figures. That'd get her out of her toxic workplace. A relief. A rescue mission. Not what investing is about. Not something I'd consider for any other startup.

"What happens when I find more investors, like you want?"

"Then I increase my investment in your fashion house substantially."

She lifts her eyebrows, waiting. "Substantially?"

"Depends how much you need to launch."

She sips her wine, appearing more relaxed. Thank God. "Theo, thanks to you, I see a possibility for my future that I dreamed of but didn't know how to bring together. To our delightful and exciting business partnership."

There's that word. And it sounds so good when she says it, so right. "To our collaboration. What do you think of the wine?"

"Great choice."

I savor its light, clean palate, loving the hints of grapefruit as the liquid glides down my throat. Our food arrives, an exquisite salad for Josephine and a vegetable tart for me. My experience eating with her on the beach springs to mind. I vowed never to eat with her again. Too late now. I focus on my plate.

"Here, try this." She spears a bite of greens, roasted

maitake mushroom, slivered zucchini and caramelized heirloom tomato, and passes me her fork.

Held sway by her gaze, I receive her offering. *Business associates don't share forks, Theo.* Thank God I caught myself. With my knife, I slide morsels onto my plate and return her fork. Flavors explode in my mouth, earthy and sweet. Is the food this good, or is being in Josephine's company enhancing my experience? A soft moan of appreciation slips from my mouth.

Her eyelids quiver as if she's feeling as turned on as I am. Not. Definitely NOT turned on right now.

"It's a good thing we're eating out," she says, "or..." Her eyes go wide, and she tilts her head, newly fascinated with her plate.

I laugh. What did she stop herself from saying? "Delicious, right?"

"Mm-hmm," she says, cheeks flushed, lips pressed together.

"Here, try mine." I cut a piece of vegetable tart and drop it onto her plate.

Josephine chews slowly, her smile lighting my heart. "Mmm."

Watching her swallow almost puts me over the edge. And her voice, sultry as she describes the texture of the crust, juiciness of the vegetables.... This time I mean it. We can never eat together again. Ever.

JOSEPHINE

My tastebuds are in heaven, but what I relish even more than this gourmet meal is the chance to learn more about Theo. His stories of childhood camping trips, gardening with his grandmother, and the way his parents connected with people from all walks of life help me understand why I find him so easy to connect with. Theo's family prizes relationships. Yet his brother isn't helping care for their mother in her elder years, which frustrates Theo and annoys me, too.

When I share my background: growing up with financial instability and chronically ill loved ones, the culture shock and challenges of studying at Yale, and why it seemed like a good idea to get married right out of college, I feel heard and valued. Theo listens. He doesn't judge me for decisions I made in my youth. He celebrates my beautiful relationship with Thalia and how Seth and I remain friendly. Everything about the way he speaks and listens, even his body language, makes me feel safe.

So safe that I dismiss our confessions of mutual longing and suggest we stroll the beach after dinner. We agreed last week not to act on our lust. We're mature adults, capable of self-restraint. The sky cleared during dinner, and after being cooped up all day, I'm excited to be outside and keep celebrating.

It *is* hard to keep my hands in my lap during the ride in his immaculate Porsche Taycan, but only because I can't resist touching everything as Theo describes it. It's really an astounding vehicle. Supple leather tanned with olive leaf extract instead of toxic chemicals feels buttery under my knees. Stereo speakers that span the width of each door surround me with opera. I lay my palm on my door speaker, letting the vibrations pulse up my arm.

I have no problem holding our personal boundaries, though. In fact, when I consider everything we've shared this past week, including the embarrassing moments, I'm super proud of how we worked together all day without so much as a Freudian slip. True, there was that near miss at dinner, but I stopped myself before blurting: *I'd like to do you right here on the table.*

We pull into the empty parking lot at the beach. Seeing

Long Island Sound in the golden light, I sigh in appreciation. "Looks like we've got the place to ourselves."

"Do you come to West Haven often?" Theo takes my hand and helps me out of his car, sending a charge up my arm.

I'll enjoy remembering this moment tonight when I'm in bed alone. "All the time. They just finished this bridge. Have you seen the wishing rocks?"

"Show me," Theo says, matching my brisk pace as we cross the bridge.

"It's past the romantic trees."

"The what?" He laughs.

"The tree couple. See?" I point to a pair of trees that seem to reach for each other, limbs meeting in an arch over a wooden bench.

Theo grins. "You have such a unique way of seeing things. Whoa. Do you see that, too?"

It would be hard to miss the vibrant rainbow forming beyond the trees.

We stare at it, silent. Finally, I whisper, "It's a sign. Our partnership will succeed."

"I like that sign." He gentles his voice, as if trying to soften the skepticism in his tone.

Not that I can blame him. I don't believe in signs, usually. But a rainbow emerging in front of our eyes must mean something. "Now, we *have* to make a wish." I lead him past the romantic trees, onto boulders, stumbling in my wedge platform sandals.

"Careful, Josephine. You okay?"

"Can I borrow your arm?" I hold his arm, pretending not to notice his strong bicep, and lift my foot to remove one shoe, then the other. I continue onto the boulder formation and point out striations of white and gray in the greenish rock.

"It looks like wood grain." His obvious awe makes me happy. "Nature's *trompe l'œil*," he says.

"Right? Now, come as far out on the point as you can. Throw your arms open wide and make a wish."

"I wish—"

I gasp. "Not out loud!"

"No?"

"Everyone knows you have to make wishes silently," I tease. "If anyone hears, your wishes won't come true."

"Oh! That's what I've been doing wrong." He grins.

"Ready?" I get into position and wait for Theo to mimic me.

"Eyes open or closed?" he asks.

"Either." I spread my arms and face the water. *I wish for my fashion house to succeed and help more people than I can imagine. And...* I close my eyes to stop the other wish from forming solidly in my mind, but it's out of my control. Visions flash through my brain in rapid succession without warning: *Theo and I in different places, at different ages, always embracing or kissing or...* Heat fills my cheeks as a gust of wind comes across the water, sprinkling my face. I bring my hands to my heart and say a silent thank you. When I open my eyes, the rainbow fades and the sun sinks below the horizon, shifting the light from golden to purple. "Wanna keep walking?"

"Sure." He follows me off the boulders, hovering until we reach even ground. Is Theo protecting me? I've often imagined how it might feel to be protected. Now, I know. I like it. He offers his arm so I can steady myself while I brush sand off my feet and don my shoes.

"That was fun. Thanks."

"Wasn't it perfect we finished just as the sun set?" A clap of thunder and sudden downpour drown out the last part of my sentence. We catch each other's eyes and laugh. "Why did we leave our raincoats in the car?" I yell.

Theo yells something unintelligible and wraps his body around mine, shielding me. Too late. We're both drenched. Rain pelts my back, but his heat warms my chest. Another part of me gets wet. Very wet. And tingly. Especially with his heartbeat vibrating in my body, the scent and heat of his neck warming my cheek, and his erection pressing against my hip. I brave a look at him through my lashes, then tilt my face up to see him better. Has he been looking at me all this time? Those warm chocolate eyes melt me.

His lips taste like chocolate, like the Torta Barozzi we shared for dessert. So good. He murmurs "no," lips grazing mine. "No," I whisper, meeting his lips. In his firm kiss I feel passion, tenderness, desire. I stroke his cheek, invigorated by the hint of stubble against rain-slick skin. Rain pounds our bodies, soaks our faces, drips into our mouths. "Just once," I murmur and lick his soft lips, let him pull my tongue into his mouth. I gasp. He moans. And we devour each other, our bodies doing things against our will. His hands graze my arms, back, waist, hips, making me crazy with desire. My hands slide down his chest, grab his hips and press our bodies together. Need him now. We rock against each other, moaning, biting, licking, tasting rain and skin.

"What did you wish for?" he asks, lips brushing mine.

"You."

"Me, too."

"Take me home, Theo."

Chapter Twenty-One

JOSEPHINE

THE DOWNPOUR SOUNDS on the roof, coats the
windows, blurs everything outside.

"Are we really doing this?" Theo looks at me for confirmation, his breathing rapid.

I try to catch my breath, a challenge with my body
aflame. "Just drive, Theo."

He starts the engine, turns the wipers on high—useless.
He turns off the car. "Damn it."

Our eyes meet. His exude lust. I prop my foot on the
dash and my dress slips above my knee. Feeling Theo's eyes
on my leg makes me throb in other places. "Is this okay? I
don't wanna get your car dirty."

"Get it dirty."

"Is that how you like it, Theo?"

"I like you however you come. Dirty, clean..." He slides a
finger from my lower lip down my neck to my abdomen,
electrifying me with need. "Wet, wetter..."

"Come here, so I can reach you better."

He licks his delicious lips, leaning toward me.

I run my hand over his cold, soaked linen shirt. The way it clings to his muscles is sexy as hell, but I want his skin. "We're taking this off, Theo."

"This, too?" He fingers my dress hem, sending heat throughout my body.

"Yes."

He slips a hand up my thigh. "You're all wet."

"You have no idea." I unbutton his shirt, the ache inside me deepening. He straddles the console to get closer. I keep unbuttoning, only to find an undershirt. Whimpering, I reach under the linen-cotton blend, and discover his chest hair. "I wanna see you." I reach for the hem of his T-shirt, tug at it.

Impatient, Theo grabs the back of his shirt, lifts it over his head and yanks, hitting his head on the rearview mirror with a loud thwack. "Ow! Fuck." He growls, arms tangled in his shirts, struggling to free himself.

Ouch. "Are you alright?" I swallow a nervous giggle, unsure what to do as Theo fights with his shirts.

"Can you help me here?"

"Aww, poor you. Lean forward. Give me your arms. Oh, I see. I forgot to undo the buttons at your cuffs." I help Theo out of his shirts and caress the back of his head. "Are you in pain? Feels like a lump is forming here."

"Nah." He winces. "But this probably wasn't the best idea. Car sex isn't for tall people."

"Or people over forty." I laugh.

"We're not teenagers." He chuckles, then turns serious. "If we're going to make love, Josephine, I'd prefer our first time be special."

His sincerity touches me. "Me, too. This is more than lust, Theo. I like you."

"And I you." He threads his fingers through mine, the small act of intimacy delicious. "I enjoy your presence, and I want to know you better." Another act of intimacy: his desire to know me matches my thirst to know him.

"Maybe the rainbow is saying there's hope. The downpour is making us wait until visibility improves. A message to take it slow? Maybe if we listen, we can have it all—a thriving business relationship and a beautiful romance."

Theo trails a strong finger up my forearm and back to my wrist. "We seem unable to resist each other. But if we rush or treat this energy between us like a cheap thrill, everything could blow up in our faces." He scans my face. "Is that what you mean?"

"Yeah."

"What if everything blows up in our faces anyway? What if...?" He inhales deeply and lets the words fall with his breath. "I mean, it's been a while since I chose to be someone's romantic partner. I can't see having a casual romance with you, Josephine. And last time I took someone seriously, I mean really seriously... One: it was decades ago. Two: it didn't end well."

A quote pops into my mind. Something about when a guy warns you about himself, you should listen. I bite the inside of my cheek, apprehension gripping my stomach. *Theo is not a stereotype, Josie. Give him a chance to explain before you react.* "What happened?"

"Long story."

"Seems like we've got time." I gesture at the windows sheeted with rain.

Theo shifts his gaze out the windshield, as if seeing his youth play out on a screen. "I met Isabella my first year in college. She was a senior with plans to become a teacher, like her dad. She was bright, thoughtful, silly. She collected bouncy balls and those ridiculous plastic rings kids get from grocery store vending machines. When I knew I couldn't live without her, I bought one of those rings, took her to the most magical spot on campus, and announced I wanted to spend my life with her but needed her parents' approval before proposing. She teased me, said it was 1990 not 1910; she was an independent woman who didn't need anyone's approval. But I'd met her parents a few times. I could tell her dad was more old-school than he let on. Plus, my parents would've been unhappy if I didn't handle things properly. So I held out the day-glow yellow spider ring and said, '*I want to spin a web with you that will hold us safe and sound for the rest of our lives.*'"

Envisioning the scene makes me smile. I reach for his left forearm and hover over the spider-in-web tattoo. "This is for Isabella."

He runs a finger along the image, speaks softly. "You can touch it."

I place my fingertips on the ink, somehow feeling as if I'm absorbing his memories with his body heat.

"That feels nice," he says.

I trace the tattoo's lines, keeping my voice low. "What happened next?"

Theo closes his eyes and leans back against the leather seat. "I told my parents. They adored Bella and were over the moon I'd found true love so early in life, like they had. Isabella's family meant everything to her, so instead of taking her somewhere wild and fancy, I planned to propose at her parents' house. That weekend, her brother ended up in the hospital. We met them there. He was thirteen but small for his age. Gaunt, dark circles under his eyes. Bruises all over his arms. I thought he was being bullied at school. Turned out he'd been battling cancer. No one had mentioned it before. I had the ring in my pocket. Suddenly, it seemed like the wrong time to ask about getting married, so I cringed when Isabella raised the subject. Her parents were unfazed, though. I later learned they spent so much time in the hospital with Jared that celebrating at his bedside was their way of not letting his disease overshadow everything."

"So her parents agreed?"

"Not at first. Her dad said we were too young. I was only nineteen. She was twenty-one. But I shared my five-year plan for both of us to finish grad school before we wed. Her parents exchanged this significant look, then her dad gave permission. I proposed to Isabella right there in the hospital room. She said yes. I slid the real engagement ring on her finger, and she slipped the spider ring onto my pinkie. We celebrated as a family.

"After she graduated, my parents took us to Europe to celebrate. In Lisbon, she struggled to walk up the steep hills. She'd always been strong. In the weeks following our trip, I started noticing similarities between her and her brother. Bruises popping up without explanation. Weakness. Nosebleeds.

"I started my sophomore year. She was at Teacher's College, floundering because of exhaustion. Every weekend I went to see her, she seemed weaker. Her parents were panicking. Medical bills were piling up. They were about to lose their home. With Isabella's illness, their expenses were increasing. I didn't want to throw my money around, but I couldn't let them end up homeless. I went to the bank that held their mortgage and made twelve months of payments from my savings."

"Wow."

"It wasn't much, but I was a kid, living off allowance. I hadn't held a real job yet, and my parents still controlled my trust fund."

"And it saved Isabella's family."

Theo cocks his head, considering the idea. "I guess so. But it couldn't save their children. We buried Jared that fall. Once Isabella was diagnosed with Leukemia, her parents and doctors started investigating."

"You mean, like, why her parents were healthy and the kids weren't, and why Jared got sick first?"

"Exactly. When Isabella was eight, her family moved to this idyllic cottage in rural Vermont. Their tap water tasted sweet sometimes. They thought it was normal for well water. It wasn't. Their well was contaminated. Her mother got pregnant with Jared. Her brother was poisoned in utero and throughout his infancy through his mother's breastmilk. It was the water they cooked with, bathed in, and drank. Jared never lived a day without being exposed to toxic chemicals. Isabella had a healthy start, wasn't exposed until she was eight. When she was in chemo, they figured out where the toxins came from. Pollutants from a nearby NorEast Waste Management landfill. My family business was killing my fiancé." He flexes and releases his fingers.

"You felt responsible." I place a hand on his back, hoping to offer comfort.

"And powerless, angry. I told my dad and grandfather, and they gave me hell for paying the mortgage. They assumed her family was looking for a payout. Mom persuaded me to show them the toxicology reports and health scans. Then they understood. Isabella's family had suffered while we lived in luxury and health, poisoning them all the while."

I swallow my reaction, so I can be present for Theo.

"Isabella was wearing scarves around her head because she hated wigs. Instead of taking a semester in Italy like I'd planned, I took a semester off and devoted myself to her care. We tried alternative medicines, the most expensive treatments. Sometimes, it brought her relief, but Bella didn't live to graduate."

"Oh, Theo."

He shakes his head, stares out the windshield. "After her funeral, I tried to stay in touch with her parents. I drove up to visit them once before I started back at school. They welcomed me warmly, but her dad..."

He meets my gaze with blank eyes and continues,

sounding further away with each word. "It was the first time I'd seen a man look broken. And while I craved reminders of Isabella, I got the sense that for them, I represented what killed their children more than anything else. I couldn't bear to cause them more pain. I never saw them again."

"I'm so sorry, Theo." I lean toward him. "It wasn't your fault. It's *not* your fault."

"I know." He braves a glance at me. The vulnerability in his expression sparks my protectiveness. I stroke his arm.

"I threw myself into business school, then work. My obsession was changing NorEast Waste Management's M.O. With every fiber of my being, I needed to turn that company around, so no one else would ever suffer like Isabella had."

I search his face. "Did you make time for a personal life?"

He shakes his head. "I had girlfriends, but even in long-term relationships, I stayed detached, made it clear I wasn't offering much. But now... well, Josephine, it's been thirty years since I've had a serious relationship. I'm afraid I don't know how to do this, afraid I'll hurt or disappoint you. If I screw up the personal part, it'll affect your business, and if I screw up the business relationship, it'll affect our romantic connection."

"Thank you, Theo." I squeeze his hands, listen to the rain as I process his words. "Your concern makes sense. And I'm no relationship expert. We'll risk a lot if we try this."

The same man who, mere hours ago, appeared strong and protective just revealed deep-rooted pain and fear. Theo's trust and vulnerability are sending electric currents from my heart down my core. I shift in my seat, wishing I could scratch that itch. "Your willingness to be real with me... it means a lot."

"You made it safe for me to open up."

How could we possibly fail? I've been searching for this level of honesty, transparency, trust, and kindness in a partner, and I found it in a man who wants to romance me and make my career dream a reality.

I caress his cheek, loving how he leans into my touch. "If we try this relationship thing, we'll disappoint and hurt each other occasionally because that happens in close relationships. And you know what?"

"What?"

"I can handle it if you can. After all that's happened since we met, I believe we're destined to succeed in business *and* romance."

Theo brings my palm to his lips. "I believe you're right."

I lean back dramatically, pretending to swoon. "As long as you remember those magic words, we'll never even argue."

He winks. "You're right, Josephine."

Chapter Twenty-Two

THEO

How DID I manage to bring her home, kiss her goodnight at the door, and leave? Because after that intense evening, we each needed time alone to process our decision. And we agreed to take the physical side of our relationship slowly. Holding Josephine on the beach last night felt so right, so exciting. And there's no other word for the talk in the car — beautiful.

"Theo?" My yoga teacher's soft voice interrupts my thoughts.

"Huh?"

"You've been in Down Dog for quite some time. Do you want to slow the vinyasa this morning?" she asks.

Heat floods my cheeks. "Sorry, Annie. I'm, uh, in my head, I guess." I press my hands and feet into the yoga mat, shift my weight forward to bring my shoulders over my hands, allowing my hips to drop and legs to extend into plank pose.

Josephine. On the mat. Lips parted. I lower myself onto her. Not now. *Focus, Theo.*

Despite constant distraction by fantasies about spending a night under the stars with Josephine, I get through yoga class, escort Annie out, then immediately text Josephine:
Feel like camping next weekend?

Sure. I don't have gear, though.

I'll take care of everything.

Sounds great! [smiling face emoji]

My heart lifts. I can't wait to enjoy the wilderness with her. **Can you leave Friday morning? Talk business in the car?**

What time do you want me?

Ten-thirty?

She sends a heart eyes emoji. Yes!

Chapter Twenty-Three

JOSEPHINE

At ten-twenty-five, Theo's message flashes across my screen: **I'm here.**

Be right there.

I'm on the toilet. I won't be right there, but from my current position, I cannot let him into the apartment. I groan. Caught with my pants down. Not a romantic start to our first night together.

Moments later, I'm grabbing my bag, slipping into hiking shoes. Are we taking things too fast? It's only been a week since that conversation in the car. We're going camping, not having sex. Getting tested for STI's on Wednesday after work was a precaution, reassuring for us both. I lock the door and step lightly down the stairs into the sunshine to meet my beau.

Theo stands by the car, looking relaxed and amazing. Should I have packed condoms? Shit.

"Good morning, Beautiful!"

"Hi, there." I beam at the compliment. "Sorry to keep

you waiting." When we got tested, we agreed to take things slowly.

"I was early." He takes my bags and puts them in the backseat, then opens the passenger door for me, waits until I'm settled, kisses my cheek and closes the door.

I need to calm down, so I can enjoy the weekend. Otherwise, I'll ruminate. Nothing ruins a romantic moment like overthinking, and I want our first night together to be romantic and memorable. "I love how chivalrous you are."

Theo smiles as he pulls out of the driveway.

"Where are we going?"

"To a campsite on a private lake in Litchfield County."

An hour later, we pull into a dirt parking lot surrounded by birch trees and evergreens. "It's about a mile to the site," he says. "If you handle your bag and the jug of water, I'll carry the rest. Wait right there." He jumps out, jogs to my side, opens my door, and extends his hand. I take it and let him pull me into his arms. His shoulder is solid against my cheek, and I savor the fresh air mingling with his scent.

THEO

We hike in silence, slowed by rugged terrain and the heft of our backpacks. I don't mind the extra travel time. The relaxed pace, absence of city sounds, and the adorable way Josephine's bun bounces on her head brings me into a state of deep contentment. I'm eager to share this place with her and enjoy a romantic night under the stars. Unfortunately, I also need to sort out this shipping issue with her, so I can feel confident sharing her business plan with my friends in the angel community. But that's no big deal. Once I explain my concerns, she'll come around to my way of thinking.

Lexi's text tone breaks the quiet. Annoying.

Hey, Sexy! What are you up to this weekend?

Camping with the woman I'm dating.

[kiss mark emoji]

What is up with her? I slip my phone back into my pocket.

"Wow, I didn't think our phones would work out here," Josephine pulls her phone from her back pocket. "But I have four bars."

"Me, too." How frigging irritating. Apparently, telling Lexi I don't want a future with her wasn't clear enough. Ignoring her new sexting habit these past few weeks also hasn't deterred her. Dating another woman, though? That's clear as a bell.

Josephine looks back. "Everything okay?"

"Yeah." I'd like to turn off my phone and disconnect from the outside world. But with Ma's health so iffy lately, I can't risk missing an important call from Deborah.

"Beautiful trail," Josephine says. Have I ever known anyone so appreciative? Every time she thanks me or compliments something I'm sharing, I feel closer to her.

Meanwhile, pretty much every message Lexi sends makes me feel like distancing myself. I've got to stop ruminating on Lexi's aggravating behavior, though. It was she who put me back together after I lost Isabella. Friends like that don't come around every day.

Nor do women like Josephine, and right now I'd rather focus on her and the amazing weekend we're about to share in this lovely place. Birdsongs ground me, so I lose myself in the symphony of wrens and cardinals until we reach the campsite. Whoever was here before us left the site in great condition. Clean tent platform, meticulous fire pit, no trace of their presence anywhere. Nice to see they followed camping etiquette. Not everyone is so conscientious.

"Look at that view," Josephine says.

"Spectacular, isn't it? Of course, I have the best vista."

"Really?"

I hold my hands up like a frame around her with the lake in the background. "A gorgeous setting and a radiant woman."

She groans, playfully. "That was suave, man."

"Can I help myself? If you could see what I'm seeing."

"What do I do with that?" She drops her bags on the platform. "Besides, my view is better than yours. Hot guy surrounded by lush trees."

I set the gear down, wrap my arms around her, and kiss her cheeks and neck until she giggles. "You know what else is great about this spot?" I ask.

"What?"

"It's secluded."

She leans into me. "Can anyone see us from across the lake?"

"I don't think so, though I shall honor our agreement to take it slow on the sexual front."

Her musical voice rises and falls flirtatiously. "Good to know. Serene, beautiful…" She inhales deeply. "And the fragrance."

"Wintergreen, balsam fir, and a few things I can't identify. Maybe sassafras."

"How do you know so much about trees?"

"My parents took me and my brother camping every year. Dad showed us basic plants to forage. Sadly, the only one I remember is wintergreen."

"Where is it? What does it look like?"

"See this ground cover with the glossy dark green leaves?" I pluck a leaf and smell it to make sure it's the right plant. I nibble an edge, and a pungent toothpaste flavor explodes in my mouth. "Ugh. Why did I do that to myself? Wanna try it?"

"After that sales pitch?" She smells the leaf, makes a face.

"Can't blame you. So… picnic first, or set up the tent?"

"You're the expert. You know how long it's been since I've camped?"

"Tell me." I pull the picnic blanket from my pack and lay it on the platform.

"Since before Thalia was born, and on that trip we had cabins and running water."

In other words, not camping. "What you're saying is I have a chance to impress you with my manly skills."

She snorts. "Manly skills. What's in that cooler, anyway?"

"Hey." I feign offense. "I've got manly skills."

She scans my body, bites her lip. "I'm sure you do."

I gasp. "How dare you objectify me?" As if her teasing didn't send lightning straight to my tent pole.

"Oh, Theo," she says, breathy, bringing the back of her hand to her forehead. "I'm faint with hunger. Could you use your rock-hard muscles to open the cooler? I can't manage it with my womanly weakness."

I growl, make a show of opening the cooler, and retrieve two tinfoil packages. "For you, roasted veggie sandwiches with avocado and that red pepper walnut spread you love."

"Yum!" She reaches for a sandwich, but I stop her with a look.

Using the food like weights, I strike a series of body-builder poses, flexing my biceps and pecs, growling more, and making sure to catch her eye. She rewards me with an exaggerated sigh, fanning herself until I hand her the sandwich.

"Manly enough?" I kiss her cheek.

"Silly. You showed your manly skills when we went kayaking, and worked on my business plan, and..." she caresses my shoulder, "...when you opened up to me last Friday. It takes a strong man to show his vulnerability."

The words send a surge of emotions through my body that I don't know what to do with, so I stare into the cooler and remove the natural sodas and oatmeal cookies. With nothing else to distract me, I brave a look at her. Josephine's warm smile makes me feel safe. "Thank you."

She bites the sandwich, rolls her eyes back, and moans with delight, instantly lightening the moment.

I grin. "Now that I know I've pleased you…"

"Mm-hmm."

"Shall we talk business?"

"Sure."

I've been avoiding this topic since my first visit to her studio weeks ago, trusting it would resolve itself as we created the pitch deck. It didn't. "You mentioned something during our first meeting that stuck with me. I think we need to discuss it before reaching out to other investors."

"Okay." She smooths her shorts.

Damn it; she's nervous. My neck tightens. Ridiculous. Sure, I've been avoiding the subject. Even in the car, when it would have been easy to address, I chose to woo Josephine with opera instead. But the issue is not a big deal. I haven't raised it before now because it's so minor. We're both anxious over nothing. In about two minutes, we'll have clarity and be ready for fun. First, I need to eat, though. I make a good sandwich. I take another bite, savoring the tang of red pepper spread and creamy avocado texture. *Stop procrastinating, Theo.* The back of my neck prickles. "It's this idea of not shipping."

"What about it?"

"It's very limiting."

Josephine winks. "That's the point. It makes the line exclusive, heightens demand."

"Won't the prices make it exclusive?"

"I don't wanna overcharge people."

"Sure, but once we factor in all costs, you'll have to charge more than people typically pay."

"I want my clothing to be accessible."

"To whom?"

"Everybody."

"Then you should ship."

She shakes her head. "Everybody local."

I take a long swig of water, scan her face. What am I reading in her placid expression? "I think we might have different ideas about what accessible means in this context."

"I want people to be able to buy a Josephine Stewart original, no matter what their economic situation is."

"So, we're talking about mass production."

"What? No!"

I need to move to stave off building frustration. "Don't mind me, I'm gonna set up the tent while we talk." I remove the tent and folded poles from their case, clear my throat. "In your mind, accessibility means anyone can afford the clothes, no matter their financial situation. Am I getting you?"

"Yeah."

"Great. How does that work?" I unfold the tent poles and click them into their full length. "And if you don't ship, how can customers without cars buy from you?"

"New Haveners can walk, take the bus, ride bicycles."

"With a garment bag strapped to their back? What if they have mobility issues?" I spread the tent out on the platform.

"You're really giving me a hard time here."

"Am I? Sorry. I'm just trying to help you think through some issues because—"

"You don't think I've thought through things enough?" Her pitch rises. Why is she being so defensive?

I inhale intentionally and let the words fall out with my breath as I connect a pole to the tent's outer corner. "That's not what I'm saying, Josephine."

"Then what are you saying? Could you please stop that and look at me for a second?"

Shit. I meet her gaze. "I'm afraid some of your ideals may

conflict with each other and make it difficult for your business to thrive."

"Like what?"

"Accessibility of price. I mean, if you wanna sell things cheaply—"

"What if I have a tiered payment system?"

"I don't know if that's legal for a retail—" I stop myself. "Sorry. Tell me more."

"Coaches, doctors, even therapists offer services on a sliding fee scale. I could offer my clothes that way."

Normally, I'd find the eager way she's leaning forward alluring. But right now, all I see is a spreadsheet with red numbers getting bigger, as surpluses turn into debts.

I resume clicking tent pole pieces into place.

"I've seen painters do it. And recording artists sell CDs that way. What's her name?"

I connect the remaining poles into the tent corners, joining them at the roof's center. "Voilà!"

"Impressive!"

I grin, flex my bicep.

"Amanda Palmer is a musician. She sells her albums for *Pay What You Can*."

God, I wish this conversation was over already. "Interesting. My concern is that people will pay the minimum."

"I'm pretty sure studies have shown that to be a false assumption."

"Then you need to research because *pretty sure* is not enough to hedge hundreds of thousands of dollars on. Make sense?"

"Okay."

"So, getting back to shipping."

"This tiered payment plan will make my clothes affordable to more local people, so we don't need to worry about shipping."

I stifle a groan. Deep down, I suspected this conversation would be challenging. Still, her level of resistance to this basic business practice floors me. "Have you seen any other eco-friendly fashion designers who are only selling locally, refusing to ship?"

"No, and I think that will really differentiate me." She beams.

"It'll differentiate you, alright." I communicate successfully with people from all walks of life. Yet, I'm struggling to help the woman I adore comprehend this simple concept. "Are you done with that?" I collect the empty cans and foil, put them in a trash bag, tie it to the cooler, then throw the rope over a high branch.

"What are you doing?" she asks.

"Keeping our food away from bears."

Her eyes go wide, and she swallows nervously.

"Don't worry, we're unlikely to see any, especially if we keep our food well sealed and way out of reach." I grab the dangling rope, hoist the food up, and secure it with a knot.

"Theo, if I get enough investors, that will help me keep my prices low."

I choke, stunned. "We're talking about investments, not subsidies. Remember, angels and VCs want an ROI."

She sighs. "Return on Investment." She smooths her shirt, signaling her discomfort. "Can I ask you something without offending you?"

This conversation is getting worse and worse. I sit beside her. "Sure." *Do. Not. React.*

"I super appreciate your initial investment, but you've seen my budget. I kinda thought... Well, why aren't you investing more?"

I envision the tension in my body dissipating. *She is grateful, Casabella. It's a logical question, takes courage to ask. She's probably been agonizing over it for the past week.* I take her hand and carefully measure my tone. "I would love to cover one hundred percent of your startup costs. There are a couple reasons that's unwise. One, the shift in our relationship means you'd be putting all your personal and career eggs in one basket. That's a risk I can't let you take. Two, the more investors you get, the more wind you'll have beneath your sails. Angels help with startup costs *and* become your biggest cheerleaders. We throw our time, money, and connections into the mix to help you succeed. That's a huge reason I recommend seeking angels before bank loans."

She nods, slowly. "That makes sense."

"You can approach any VCs, angels, or banks anytime. But before I contact people in my circle, I need to see you take charge and use sound business practices."

"Well, if I don't ship, I can honestly say my company has a lower carbon footprint. Why are you frowning? I think we're coming to some great understandings here."

My neck hurts. "I'm glad you feel that way. I'd like us to get onto the same page."

"Did you hurt yourself putting up the tent? Here." She moves behind me and presses her fingertips into my neck. "Wow, your muscles are tight. Inhale."

I do, then exhale as instructed, and she kneads the base of my skull. Normally, I'd love it. "Mm. Thanks, Hon." I turn and blow an air-kiss.

She smiles. "I think your question about defining accessibility was useful. I hadn't considered all the barriers someone may face."

"So, you'll try shipping locally?"

"No, but I might set up a delivery program."

It's all I can do not to palm my forehead in frustration. I love her creativity. I wish she could realize some standard business practices work; she doesn't need to reinvent every wheel. But pushing this issue will ruin our romantic weekend. She'll soften. I rub my neck. What if she doesn't?

Chapter Twenty-Four

JOSEPHINE

WATCHING Theo erect the tent and hoist the food into the tree to keep it from bears impressed the hell out of me. Although he seemed tense during our business chat, I learned something, and that's the goal. Now we can get back to the romantic part of the weekend. As soon as I get into my bikini, which is hard to do inside a tent. Theo waits outside because I want his first view of my naked body to be enticing, not me struggling to dress myself. I emerge, feeling shy. He whistles, tells me I'm gorgeous, then slips into the tent.

When he comes out shirtless, swim trunks draping softly from his hips, a low moan of desire escapes me. I'd love to wrap my arms around him, maybe crawl back into the tent together, but his face is all business. "Ready for a swim?" he asks, handing me a towel. Following his lead, I drape it around my neck, take his hand, and stride down the rugged path.

An hour later, sweaty from hiking in ninety-degree temps, we reach the lake. "At last!" I fold my towel and lay it on a rock, slip off my hiking sandals, narrow my gaze, and sprint into the water. By the time I register the temperature, it's too late. I'm already belly flopping with a splash, submerging myself in an ice bath. I pop up, shrieking.

Theo laughs, safe and warm, as he removes his hiking boots at the water's edge.

"Thanks for the warning," I deadpan.

He strides in, casual, not a care in the world, seemingly unaffected by the arctic water temperature, grinning. "That was cute."

"Was it?" I smile innocently and extend my arms behind me with an extra loud sigh, like I'm stretching, not preparing. Step by step, he comes closer, building my anticipation. Now, he's about four feet away. Perfect. I sweep one arm along the lake's surface, making an arc of water that soaks him.

He yelps, springing into action. "Now you've done it!" He grabs my waist, and I scream in delight as he hoists me into the air and tosses me. I go under, rise, and tackle him. Together, we fall into the frigid lake and emerge, doubled over in laughter. "Wanna swim to the middle?" he asks.

"You go ahead. I'll watch, or maybe I'll let the negative space those plants on the shoreline make inspire me."

"Show me."

I hold my hands up to frame my view—low-growing plants poking through the sand. "See the outlines those oblong leaves and three-petaled white flowers make against the background?" Theo looks through my hand-frame as I explain. "If the flowers are the subject, then the space between the petals is negative space."

He traces the lines in the air with his finger. "Is this what you mean?"

"Yup. Gorgeous. Right? I'd like to embroider that onto a skirt."

"I love the way you think."

"What a wonderful compliment." Heart opening at his praise, I turn toward him. His adoring gaze makes my body thrum.

"Hey, what do you think of those?" Theo points to a few clusters of light purple flowers shaped like cones further away from the waterline.

"Lovely. I wonder what they are."

"Great Blue Lobelia. My mother's favorite native flower."

"Wow. Any woman with a favorite *native* flower is a woman I wanna meet." Oops. If only I could swallow those words. *Way to put the pressure on, Josie.* "So you're showing off your manly swimming skills now?"

He responds with a too-cool upward nod and dives into the lake. His arm muscles ripple with each stroke, intensifying the fluttering in my lower region. *Manly skills indeed.* I wish my heart didn't need me to take things slow because I'd love a demonstration of those manly skills ASAP. True, Theo seems sincere, stable, my perfect match. But I thought Ben was kind, and I thought Seth was committed. Luckily, they're in my past. Now, in the very real present, I return to shore and sun myself until I hear Theo coming. When I open my eyes, I receive a spectacular view of him striding out of the water like a god, skin glistening in the late afternoon sun.

He dries off, sits, and reaches for me. "The hot sand feels great now." His phone dings. He looks at it and frowns.

"Is something wrong?"

"Nope." He takes a long drink of water.

An unpleasant sensation forms in my stomach. "Why do you look upset?"

"An old friend is texting." He pulls a bag of trail mix from his backpack. "Hungry?"

I wave the snack away. "Why is their text bothering you?"

"Because suddenly she's acting like we're dating."

"Are you?"

"Nope." He pours a handful of trail mix into his palm. "Did you overhear what Drew said to me at the restaurant? About not thinking with—"

"Your MBA? Yeah. Jerk," I huff, then almost feel sorry for the insult.

"That's been running on repeat in my head ever since."

"He really got to you."

Theo looks into his handful of trail mix, picks out a raisin. "Drew was trying to help. I know that, but afterward, I learned I'd made a mistake. Now, his words feel relevant."

"What did you do?" Concerned, I sit up and face him.

"I mixed business with pleasure."

"With the woman who's texting you?"

He sighs. "We met senior year in college. Lexi was fun, wacky, a good friend. Looking back, I should've seen she was preoccupied with me, but I was wrapped up in my pain." He scrubs a hand down his face. "I had a therapist after Isabella died, but he only labeled my grief as survivor's guilt and listened passively. It didn't help me process anything. You know?"

"Mm-hmm." I stroke his back and try to ignore him separating the components of the trail mix in his hand.

"After graduation, Lexi and I went separate ways but kept in touch. Our paths rarely crossed." He puts all the dried fruits on his right thigh and continues sorting. "Lexi married. Good guy. I met him a few times at reunions. About eight years ago, she called to run something by me. I was in Vermont visiting my parents, so we met for a drink. Her marriage was struggling. She wanted to quit her restaurant job and start a bakery. Her husband said she was being irresponsible. I thought her idea had merit, so I encouraged her. A mistake."

"Why?"

"Inadvertently, I pitted myself against her husband. Since I was the one being supportive, I won in her mind."

I gesture to the small pile of almonds and pistachios on his left thigh. "Theo, what are you doing?"

"I only like the chocolate chips."

I clamp my lips shut.

He pops one into his mouth, extends his hand. "Want some?"

I shake my head.

"They divorced soon after. She came to me with a business plan. I helped her launch Earth's Crust, the most successful bakery in Vermont. Sure you don't want some?"

"They sell bags of chocolate chips by themselves, you know."

"Trail mix is healthier."

"Only—" I squeeze my eyes shut. *Theo is being vulnerable, Josie. Do not laugh.*

"I didn't realize she always held a torch for me, or that working together was inflaming her desire. Are you crying, Josephine?"

I clear my throat. "Continue. Inflaming her desire..."

"Why are you gripping your stomach?"

I wave my hands. "I'm fine. Your story..."

"You look like you're in pain."

I force myself to keep a straight face. "Theo, trail mix is only healthier if you eat it."

He shrugs, tosses another chocolate chip in his mouth. "The night before her grand opening, we popped a bottle of champagne. She was nervous. I offered comfort. One thing led to another. We hooked up. It was sweet, a nice moment. That was seven years ago. We've hooked up a few times since, and not for a while."

"But she's still confused?"

"She was until a couple weeks ago. I saw her when I went

home. She said something that made me realize we had different ideas about our friendship."

"Oh." My heart sinks.

"But I cleared it all up." Theo rises, letting the nuts and fruits fall onto the sand. "Can I show you something?" He extends his hand.

I take it, letting him lead me along the path. "When was the last time you two hooked up?"

He steps over a fallen log. "Over a year ago. The frustrating thing is, I've been so careful. Declined every opportunity to get involved with a colleague, except for the hookups with Lexi."

"Then why did Drew's stupid comment bring up fear about mixing business and pleasure? It sounds like he just doesn't see you."

"Maybe in the back of my mind I suspected Lexi had feelings for me. I don't know, but what Drew said made me paranoid. Then Lexi's confession..." Theo turns to me, takes my hands. "Josephine, I couldn't bear to confuse you."

The anxiety that was rising slowly from my stomach into my throat subsides. Unfortunately, new questions form in my mind as I follow Theo to a clearing with boulders as big as beds. He spreads his arms wide, as if presenting them at an exhibit. "You like?"

I climb onto one, loving the grit of lichen and stone under my fingers. "Boulders make me happy."

He follows, chuckling. "Boulders make you happy. You are adorable."

We lay our towels over the rough surface, lie back and stare at the clear sky. I hate needing to ask more questions, like I'm interviewing him. "Did you end things?"

"There's nothing to end. I told her I'm not moving up there, that we'll never be a couple."

"Um, Theo, if you were sleeping with her, there's something to end. It doesn't matter whether you had a commitment or plans for the future." No more overthinking for me. This is our romantic weekend.

Tall oaks make leaf patterns against the sky, inspiring new ideas about negative space and fabric prints. A striking blue-gray bird flies overhead. "Ooh, a heron!"

"Beautiful, huh," he murmurs, voice low and comforting. He takes my hand and brings it to his lips.

Relieved, I drift off. *But why did he...* Damn it. I have to ask. Clear the air so I can drop it. "If there's nothing to end, why did you need to tell her you're not moving there?"

Theo groans. "Because she was confused."

"That makes sense. Sorry to beat off a dead horse."

Theo chokes.

"Why are you laughing?"

He shakes his head. "It's beat a dead horse, Hon."

"Yeah, that's what I said. I'm not trying to harp on this, but—"

He clears his throat. "I get it. You need to make sure I'm not entangled with anyone else. It makes sense."

"Thank you for understanding."

"I do. Can we please drop it now? Have I alleviated your concerns?"

"Mm-hmm." I allow my eyes to close. "I appreciate your transparency."

"I'll always be open with you," he says, his gentle caress on my cheek soothing.

Something scurries past. I startle and turn. A poor little chipmunk stares at me, panting in terror. Now, something runs along the side of my face. A snake? I open my eyes with a start. Theo titters as he traces a fingertip down my cheek.

"Was I asleep?"

He plants a gentle kiss on my mouth. "For about a half hour. Ready to hike back?"

My stomach rumbles.

"I heard that." He kisses my stomach, warming other body parts.

"Keep kissing my stomach like that, we'll be here for a while."

"You're right." He winks, hops off the boulder and holds his hand out. I take it and leap to the ground. A strange popping sound shoots up my body as searing pain rips through my foot and ankle, making me double over.

"Are you okay, Hon?" Alarm fills his voice.

"Fine." I wince. "Sometimes I forget I'm not five."

"You look like you're in agony."

"Embarrassment is more like it. I'm so clumsy." I lift my leg and rub the ankle. "Go ahead. I'll follow you."

"As you wish." Theo slips the backpack over his shoulders and walks away.

I step, crumple, groan. Not fine.

"I heard that." He jogs back to me, concern in his expression.

"I need your arm."

He offers his bent arm. I grab his bicep, step, and a stabbing sensation travels from my foot into my shin, stopping me. "Fuck," I whine.

He kneels beside me. "Your ankle is swollen." He presses a finger into it. I wince. "How does that feel?"

"Pretty good."

"The edge in your voice tells a different story."

This isn't a good time for a sprain. I grumble. "Let's just take it slow."

He stands and offers his arm. I grip him, take a few faltering steps. It hurts like hell, but I will power through. "I'm good. Come on."

"You're limping."

"A little limping never hurt anyone."

"It makes things worse. Come. Sit on the ground."

"What are you doing?"

Theo pulls a pair of socks from his backpack, triumphant. "The water's frigid. I'm going to soak these and slip them over your foot, like an ice pack."

"Brilliant, but will my sandal fit over it?"

"It doesn't matter because I'm carrying you."

"What?" No. This isn't romantic. This is annoying and ridiculous. Why did I jump?

THEO

Josephine's pained expression stresses me the hell out. I've got to resolve this fast. "Be right back."

I tromp through rough brush until I reach the water's edge, crouch down among tall green cattail stems, and dunk my socks in the freezing water, then clomp back through the understory. I hope ticks aren't attaching themselves to my skin.

Josephine sits where I left her, eyes closed, breathing slowly. Poor thing. "Hey, Hon." I attempt to sound uplifting. "I've got your icy socks."

She smiles as she finishes a long exhale. "I was meditating to ease the pain."

"Did it work?"

"Not really."

"I hope it's not broken." I squat beside her, remove her hiking sandal, and pull the sock's opening wide. "When I broke my leg skiing, I heard a pop throughout my body."

She winces as I slip one sock over her foot and ankle. "Cold."

"Is it too tight?"

"Perfect. I'm sure this will help."

"Thank my parents for letting me watch *MacGuyver* growing up."

She giggles. "I loved that show."

I tie the other sock in a loose knot around her ankle. "Okay?"

"You're taking good care of me." She caresses my cheek. Her touch sends ripples of emotion straight to my core.

"Do you prefer I carry you in my arms or on piggyback?" I can almost feel myself carrying her over the threshold of my home, and my heart races. Weird.

"Piggyback is less embarrassing."

"True. Those damn chipmunks and squirrels are so judgmental. You'll be the laughingstock of the forest."

"And word gets around. By the time we get home, all of New Haven's squirrels will be laughing at me, too."

"Assholes." I slip my backpack over her shoulders, then help her onto my back, and stand. Bearing her weight evokes thoughts I feel a tad guilty for having under these circumstances. Then again, what red-blooded man wouldn't feel that way with his girlfriend's bare legs wrapped around his waist, especially if she was as sultry as Josephine?

After two hours, all the lascivious thoughts have sweated out of me. It's tough carrying a grown woman for so long. Not like the fifteen-minute piggyback rides I gave my niece when she was little. Now, I thud onto the tent platform, let Josephine slide off my sweaty, sore body and roll my shoulders to work out the knots.

She crawls around to see my face. "Poor thing. You look wiped out."

"I hate to admit it, lady, but that took all my manly strength."

"My hero." She wipes sweat off my face and kneads my neck and shoulders, bringing relief.

My heart would probably leap for joy at her words and her touch if it wasn't dead asleep inside my chest. "How's your ankle? Any chance you can walk?"

"Ummm."

Now, I'm alarmed. "You were so quiet. I hoped you were feeling better."

"Once the socks warmed, my pain returned. I'm sorry."

"You're sorry?"

"I shouldn't have jumped off the boulder."

"How could you know you'd land weird?"

She kisses my shoulder. "Thanks for not being mad."

"How could I be?" I turn toward her. "Unfortunately, we need to cut our adventure short and get you to a doctor."

"A good night's rest is all I need. Please, let's not end our lovely trip early over a silly turned ankle."

"Honey, camping and immobility don't mesh. The sun is dipping below the horizon. We need to pack and get out."

"Can we do all that before dark?"

I grunt, doing a poor job of hiding my disappointment. "Fortunately, we never set up the sleeping bags or hammock. I'll dismantle the tent and bring everything back. It'll take a couple trips. Will you be okay waiting here as night falls? Or would you feel safer in the car?"

The fear in her eyes answers my question, but she lifts her chin, revealing pride, determination, caring. "You're exhausted. Carrying me now is too much. I'll be fine until you get back."

Josephine is putting aside her fear, to help me the only way she can right now. It speaks volumes. I hug her and use the magic words she shared last week. "You're right. Thanks for taking care of me."

Her eyes sparkle in the waning light. "If only I could help more."

"Will you empty the tent while I take the food down?"

"Once I change out of this damp suit." She crawls inside the tent.

Despite my sore muscles and fatigue, we break camp and reach the car within two hours. I settle Josephine into the passenger seat, drag myself to the driver's side, and drop into the car.

She strokes my arm. "You okay?"

I shrug. "We didn't have the romantic weekend I planned, but I'm thrilled with how we pulled together under trying circumstances."

"We make a good team."

"Indeed." I smile and start the engine. Once she comes to see shipping as an essential retail practice, we'll be an even stronger team.

Chapter Twenty-Five

JOSEPHINE

"We're home, Josie. Where are your keys?" Theo caresses my cheek, his touch as gentle as his voice.

Too tired to form words, I find the house keys in my backpack and hand them over before opening the car door and stepping out. Extreme pain, then blackness.

When I wake, sun shines in my eyes, and my screaming, discolored foot and ankle are propped on a pillow. Did Theo do this? How thoughtful. And disappointing. Our first night together was supposed to be romantic and memorable: talking, cuddling, and fooling around in his tent under a starry sky. Instead, I find myself at home with a vague memory of Theo lifting me off the ground, carrying me inside, cleaning me up. Now, my foot and ankle hurt so much, I feel anti-sexy.

But Theo lies asleep on the floor beside me, breathing soft and steady, handsome in the morning light. He could have slept on the couch or in my bed. Gallant. I want to lie here and look at him, but I need painkillers. Instantly. I swing my legs over the bedside, step on my left foot, lean against the bed, slide until my butt touches the floor, then pitch myself forward onto all fours and crawl into the bathroom. Some romantic weekend. The cold bathroom tile feels extra hard against my knees. What next? I pause, sit back on my heels to think, and yelp in agony.

"Josephine?" Theo calls from the other room, alarmed. "Honey, are you okay?" Now, his warm hands caress my back, soothing. I look over my shoulder. He crouches beside me, concern creasing his face.

"I'm fine. Just getting some ibuprofen." *And figuring out how to get onto the toilet from hands and knees, but you don't need to know that.*

"Can I help? Where's the ibuprofen? In here?" He stands and opens the medicine cabinet. "Got it. Let me help you up." His hands slide under my armpits, and he lifts me to sit on the wide sink. He stands between my legs. In another situation, this would be sexy time. He opens the pill bottle, drops two into his palm. "Open up," he commands gently. I do, and he pops the medicine into my mouth, then fills the glass of water I keep in here.

I swallow, then I smile as much as possible with the gruesome throbbing in my lower extremities. "Thanks."

"Do you need to use the bathroom?" he asks, as if it's the most normal question in the world. "Oh, don't look so horrified, Josie. It's no big deal."

I grumble.

"I helped you out of your dirty clothes and wiped away the road dirt."

"I noticed. Thank you for helping me and keeping my bra and panties on."

"Of course!"

"We had an anti-romantic getaway, and I may now be your anti-sex symbol, but at least a small shred of my dignity remains intact."

"Josephine. You could never be my anti-sex symbol." He

puts a finger under my chin, tilting my face up so our eyes meet. "Silly, needing my help doesn't make you less attractive."

I raise an eyebrow. Should I call him on his BS?

"If you need proof, look down."

I slip my gaze down his beautiful torso, past the waistband of his boxers, to the mound of flesh peeking through the tent opening. An uplifting sight in more ways than one. "There you go, showing off your manly camping skills again."

"Can't help wanting to impress you."

"Even after everything? With the way I look right now?"

"You're beautiful. And the only reason I'm not seducing you this very moment is because I think it's more important to get you to Urgent Care, so a doctor can examine your swollen ankle and foot. They're turning purple."

"Oh, Theo." I wrap my arms around him tightly. For the first time in my life, I feel completely taken care of, safe, and wanted all at once. "Kiss me. Then get out, so I can pee. ALONE."

Worry wrinkles his brow. "But how will you manage?"

"I'll figure it out."

He lifts my chin and meets my lips with his, a slow, soft lingering kiss filled with caring and the promise of more to come.

Chapter Twenty-Six

THEO

Two hours later, I follow Josephine as she crutches her way up the carpeted stairs to her apartment. No matter what she says, I can't let her stay here alone with a fractured metatarsal and torn ligament. She'll be on crutches for at least three weeks. Sure, she can hobble around with the walking cast, but the doctor said, "Don't put weight on your foot for the next week."

What if she falls on the stairs? Unless other people can help, I'll stay here and keep her safe. She can't drive, either, so I'll bring her to and from work. How will she get into her office? "Josie, did you say your office at Social Good Conn is on the second floor?"

"Yeah. Why?"

"Figuring out logistics for the next couple weeks."

"Theo, you don't have to. I can—" She looks over her shoulder at me and loses her balance. Jesus.

I catch her. "I want to." What if I hadn't been here?

She continues her slow ascent toward her apartment.

"I'm glad they gave me this air cast, so I can shower and stuff."

Showering. Slipping on the wet tub. Cracking her head. "Would you rather stay here or at my house?"

"I don't want to impose, Theo. Thalia's coming tonight and taking the early train Monday morning. She'll come next weekend, too."

"Or..." I take a deep breath. It's early in our relationship, but... "You could come to Vermont with me next weekend."

"To meet your mom?" She gasps. "It's your special time together."

"Listen, no pressure. If you don't want to—"

"I wanna come! I do. I—" She lets out a sigh of relief as she reaches the landing. "That was tiring."

All the more reason for me to help you this week. "You're nervous about meeting my mom? Is that what I'm reading?"

Josephine nods and tries to unlock her apartment, but wobbles on the crutches. She braces herself against the door. "These take some getting used to."

I reach around her, turn the key, open the door and follow her into the kitchen. "She'll love meeting you."

"But will she like me?"

"You make me happy. She'll adore you. What can I get you?" I ask, helping her sit at the table. "Tea? Are you hungry? Shall I order takeout?"

She points at a basket of menus on the fridge. "What if we get into a big argument between now and Friday, and I stop making you happy?"

"What kind of thinking is that?" I laugh.

She hitches a shoulder. "Paranoid musings from a mind dulled by pain and hunger."

Hint taken, I lay the menus on the table. "So you'll come?" I kneel beside her, thread my fingers through hers.

"With pleasure." She looks at our intertwined hands and

smiles. "I'm excited you want me to meet her. But can I join you next month once I'm off these stupid things?"

"Sure. You'll definitely be able to enjoy Vermont more if you can walk." I point to the Mexican menu. "I love this place."

While Josephine calls in our order, I look at my calendar for the next two weeks. Back-to-back meetings with the farming consultant, entrepreneurs I met in Boston, and people who attended my speech at the Yale Entrepreneur Group. Check-in with FungiClean on data from their first year in hazmat cleanup. Then there are the contest creators. Can a contest lure entrepreneurs into the food waste sector? Can I take these meetings from here? It would be easier if she stayed with me.

She hangs up, and I search her gaze, hoping. "Come spend the week with me. I'll bring you home Friday before I leave for Vermont."

She pulls me close and gives me a breathtaking kiss. "Too soon."

My heart drops. "But you're injured. You're not safe here alone."

"Too soon."

"Then I'll stay with you."

"Too soon."

"We're going to meet my mom next month. That's a big step, too."

"Exactly. So, we're not going to rush into practically living together."

"Josephine." I roll my head to loosen the tension forming in my neck. "I want you safe."

"Thank you. I texted people from the car. When Thalia's not here, Kath and Lauren will check on me. Sage is swamped, so Wesley will drop by to carry my grocery delivery up and laundry to the basement."

"That leaves you alone for days. I'm calling a home health service."

"You will do no such thing. I'll practice on the crutches tonight, okay?"

I grumble.

"My downstairs neighbors are helpful in a pinch, too." She massages my neck, hitting all the right spots, but the tension remains. No doubt, Thalia will be helpful this weekend, but she won't be able to lift Josephine if she falls. Why won't she let me keep her safe?

Chapter Twenty-Seven

JOSEPHINE

"Mama," Thalia whispers. "Did you have a nice nap? Dinner's ready."

I wipe drool off my face. The closing credits of *You've Got Mail* scroll up my laptop screen. Did I conk out? The last thing I remember is Tom Hanks sliding off the treadmill.

Thalia sets two plates of kale salad and avocado toast with crispy shiitake strips and tomato on the coffee table. "How're you feeling? Time for more painkillers?"

"God yes." I groan. My daughter leaves and returns with two large glasses of water, and hands me a glass and prescription-strength Tylenol.

I down both. "The food looks delish."

"It should be. I learned from you." She strokes my hair. "What do you wanna watch now?"

"Let's talk first. Last night, I fell asleep right as you started talking about your job." I bite into the avocado toast and flash a thumbs up.

"And before you told me what chores I can help with."

"It's enough that you're here, Muffin, feeding me amazing food."

"The crispy mushrooms really make it, right?" We eat in silence, savoring the food.

Seeing her relish a healthy meal brings me relief. "Rent is high in Brooklyn. Do you have enough for groceries?"

She rolls her eyes. "Mama, where is this obsession with what I eat coming from?"

"Just making sure you're taking care of yourself."

"You can relax. I got a promotion, so starting next month, I'll have disposable income."

"You what?" I squeal.

"Summer's coming to a close. They asked me to stay on staff to help run the after-school program and plan next summer."

"Thalia, that's fantastic! I'm so proud of you."

"Me, too. Dad's ecstatic 'cause I won't need his help to pay rent anymore."

"Look at you, Miss Independent! But that means you have more responsibility and you're probably working longer hours." Now, I feel guilty. "You made time to come help me?"

"You're my mother, and you're injured. Of course, I came."

"Honey, I feel terrible—"

"Stop. You'd do the same for me."

"You're my child."

"Exactly. Say thank you and tell me how to help. I wanna set you up for next week when you're alone."

"Thank you, Muffin. The laundry next to my bed, and..." I cringe, hating to ask. "Maybe clean the bathroom?"

After dinner, I follow my child into the bathroom. She dons rubber gloves and pulls out my homemade cleaning supplies, sprinkles the baking soda/borax blend into the tub and scrubs. "What about your business, Mama? How can I help there?"

"You're already doing too much, between being here—"

"Which I *like*."

"And your new promotion."

"Don't make that a new reason to worry." Thalia yells over the running water as she rinses the tub. "Trust me. I'm fine."

"And you're not drinking too much?"

She grins. "Probably, but I look both ways when I cross the street, so it balances out."

Off my frown, she asks, "Why are you so worried about me?"

"Because you're my daughter. It's my job to take care of you."

"When you said that and I was ten, even sixteen, I bought it. But now I'm an adult. It's not your job to take care of me anymore."

"It will always be my job."

"No, it was your job to make sure I could take care of myself." She polishes the mirror. "Remember that lecture?"

"I remember."

She sprays the outside of the toilet and wipes it with a paper towel. "That's why I know how to cook healthy food, do laundry, clean a toilet."

"Do you have enough toilet paper? I could have a case delivered."

"Fully stocked, but if it makes you feel better to order me TP, go for it."

I whip out my phone, open the shopping app, order toilet paper for her, and release a satisfied sigh. "Done."

"Thank you." She turns serious. "Sometimes I wonder if you focus so much on me to put off working on your dream." She scrubs the toilet bowl, the one cleaning job that always leaves me feeling filthy.

I shudder. "You're gonna take a shower after that, right?"

"Seriously?" She flushes.

"Germs."

"Fine." The scent of vinegar, lavender, and eucalyptus fills the air as Thalia sprays the tile floor and mops it clean. "Anyway, I think you might be self-sabotaging, Mama."

"That's ridiculous."

"Really? If you never launch your fashion house because you were all about me, you get to say I needed you." She stands and stretches, puts all the cleaning supplies away, then fixes a super wide-eyed stare on me. "But if you put everything into your dream and it doesn't succeed, you can't use me as an excuse. Then what do you tell yourself?"

Ouch. "You're making the wild eyes."

"And your distraction tactics no longer work on me." Despite her harsh words, Thalia exudes love, which somehow triggers a flood of sense memories from my childhood.

Solitude. Fear. "My parents made everything about how they felt, what they needed."

"Like when they called to congratulate you about the show they didn't attend, then had you read the article to them?"

"That was minor. They've learned to back off since I started setting boundaries."

"What does that have to do with you pursuing your dream?"

"Thalia, it would kill me if you believed you're less important than my work."

"No worries. I know you're always here if I need you. Now that I'm an adult and can fend for myself because you taught me so well, I'm thrilled you're creating the life you want."

Her words land in my heart. Unexpected, yet totally Thalia. Always so caring, so supportive. Emotions swirl:

appreciation, pride, relief. My eyes fill with tears. Hers do, too. We sniffle together, flashing shaky smiles at each other. "You," I whisper, unable to finish the sentence.

"Do you need to go to your studio tonight?"

"Tomorrow. I'm tired now, and you need to take a shower."

Thalia drops her head in annoyance, turns on the water, strips her shirt, and glares at me.

"Thanks, Muffin." I crutch away. The phone announces a call from Theo, which I pause mid-hobble to answer. His warm voice melts me, but his week-long obsession with every detail about my foot and how I'm getting around is becoming a bit much. Suddenly, I understand why Thalia feels so annoyed by my constant worrying. It's like I don't trust her to take care of herself. And I do, but... Has anyone ever worried about me like this? It is annoying but also kind of nice to know someone cares.

"Aww. Truly, I'm fine, Theo. My daughter is incredibly helpful."

"Phew. Listen, my friend Raouf is in town from Los Angeles. A few of us are meeting at The Blake for drinks. You and Thalia wanna join? I'll scoop you up."

"Let me check with her. She's been cooking and cleaning for me and—"

"What a sweetheart."

"Yeah." Hearing Theo acknowledge my daughter warms my heart. "I'd love to meet Raouf though."

"Charlie, Anthony, Oliver, Eric, and Drew will also be there."

All New Haven's problems will disappear while you screw her in the boardroom. Suddenly, I'm nervous. "Drew, huh?"

"Don't worry about him. He usually lets things go pretty easily. Besides, once he gets to know you, he'll love you. Promise."

I'm unconvinced. "Can I text you back? Thalia's in the shower."

"Of course."

I return to the bathroom, crack the door open, and speak over the sound of the water. "Wanna meet Theo and his friends for drinks at The Blake?"

"Sure." The water sound stops.

"They're going now, but we could be there by seven probably, right?"

She agrees. I lean against the doorjamb and text Theo: **c u @ 7-ish** [happy face emoji]

Can't wait to see you and for the guys to meet you.

Heart dancing, I reply: **me too.**

Thalia opens the door, wrapped in a towel. "I'm looking forward to knowing Theo better. He sounds nice. But so did Ben. And he turned out to be a giant fucking dick. So I'm checking this guy out more carefully."

"Aww. There you go, flipping the script again, taking care of me like you're the mom."

"I'd better help you get in the shower."

I smell my armpits. "I'm fine."

She sniffs the air around me. "Okay. After I'm dressed, we'll wash your hair."

"I'll just put it up." I finger-comb through the knots, slip the hairband off my wrist and secure my hair into a ponytail.

"Yeah, no." She recoils, shielding her herself with her hands. "It's a mess. You absolutely can't meet them like that."

"Theo thinks I'm beautiful, no matter what."

Thalia palms her forehead. "Thank God I'm here. I mean, I'm glad Theo doesn't care how you look, but these are his friends. They'll be judging you."

"I know." My voice rises defensively. Still, I'm relieved by her presence. With Thalia beside me, I'll feel more confident meeting Theo's friends. Hopefully, they aren't all as critical as Drew.

Chapter Twenty-Eight

JOSEPHINE

THALIA HOLDS the elevator doors open. I hobble out and scan the swanky rooftop bar. It has a pleasant, if underwhelming, view of New Haven. Rooftops upon rooftops. Brick buildings with gothic stone façades. The industrial white metal roof of the gas station down the block. On the distant horizon, the sun lowers, casting a golden halo around Theo. I savor that view until I notice the five other men at his table. A lot of guys to meet at once, especially since they'll be appraising me. My stomach tightens. But Theo's warm brown eyes send comfort as he rises and threads his way through tables to meet us.

"You look amazing." He kisses my cheek, sending a pleasing current to my core. "Is this dress the same material you used in that mermaid outfit at your show?"

"Look at you learning your fabrics. Color me impressed!"

Theo winks at me and greets Thalia with an awkward wave. It's cute how he's trying to be casual with her, yet clearly feels unsure of himself. With good reason. Has he picked up that Thalia's watching?

He leads us to the table, asking people to clear space for me to hobble through.

"This is Josephine," Theo announces as he helps me sit and stows my crutches under the table, "and her daughter, Thalia."

"Ladies." Drew smiles, though the sadness in his eyes morphs into disdain. For us?

Compassion, Josie. I wrap an arm around Thalia and smile at each man as Theo introduces him. Should I mention I'm tired and won't recall these names and backgrounds in thirty minutes? The surfer dude lifts his glass. The serious man with fashionable glasses welcomes us. Lovely accent. Middle Eastern?

Theo points across the table at a heavyset bald guy in a golf shirt with a corporate logo. "Charlie and I were buddies from Boy Scout camp. Drew introduced me to Eric." A study in contrasts: white hair, dark skin, intense, yet respectful gaze. The man exudes calm amid a boisterous group.

A short guy with a young-looking face and Hawaiian shirt waves. "Anthony."

Golf shirt grabs a handful of nuts from a shared bowl. "I wanna hear about this so-called trash fashion. We're talking disposable clothing?"

I point to my dress. "Does this look disposable to you?"

He shakes his head. "You made that?"

"Yup. But I didn't come here to talk about me. I came to meet you. How do you spend your days?"

"We have boring jobs," Surfer says. "I practice law. Anthony builds restaurants. Charlie sells drugs."

"Pharmaceuticals, asshole," Golf shirt says.

"Exactly." Surfer continues, "Eric funds startups. Drew

teaches environmental shit, and Raouf makes films." Raouf. Fashion glasses.

"Anything we might know?" Thalia asks. "Or could share with tweens?"

"Thalia teaches media literacy," I boast.

"Wonderful!" Raouf smiles. His gentle voice and the kindness he exudes soften my nerves. "I make short documentaries. Perhaps not age appropriate, but they are on my website. Have a look."

He shares his web address, and Thalia calls it up on her phone. "Nice."

I smile, catching Surfer's playful gaze. "None of your jobs sound boring, except sales." Oops. Laughter peals around the table while I wince. "Sorry, Charlie."

He hitches a shoulder. "Pays the bills, and nobody complains when I take them out on my boat. Back to your dress."

"The base is neoprene deadstock. I got bags of it during a four-week artist's residency at MacDowell Plastics in Cancer Alley, Louisiana."

He chuckles. "I only understood about five words in that sentence."

"Spend more time with Josephine and you'll know the lingo soon enough." Theo fills two plates with appetizers from platters on the table and puts them in front of me and Thalia. "Artist residencies are a major coup. Josephine got one in Japan in 2019 and in Louisiana last year."

"Impressive," Raouf says.

"Also," Theo continues. "Thanks to Josephine, I now know most clothing manufacturers throw away or burn unused material. They call it deadstock. Right, Hon?"

Taking care of us and talking me up simultaneously. His reverence gives me goosebumps. "Exactly. Often, pieces are large enough to turn into another garment, or to recycle and re-fabricate into new material. MacDowell Plastics has a take-back program. To avoid waste, they encourage customers to return unused material or unsold garments for recycling."

A server arrives and takes our drink orders.

"So you only work with neoprene?" Surfer... *Oliver* asks.

"I use whatever upcycled materials I can get, as long as they help me tell a good story."

"Do you have photos?" Raouf asks.

I call up my trashion album and slide my phone to him.

He scrolls through the images. "Josephine, these garments are poetry."

"Thanks. From my latest show, *The End of the Catwalk. Trashion. Transparency. Truth.*"

"Currently at K-Gallery on Chapel," Theo says. The look that passes between his buddies strikes me, but I'm not sure what to make of it.

Charlie leans in to see. "Holy shit."

Anthony side-eyes Charlie, as if debating, then gives in to curiosity. He gets up and peers over Charlie's and Raouf's shoulders.

"Man, personal space," Charlie growls.

Anthony wedges his arm between his friends and swipes through the pictures. "Looks like real clothing."

I laugh. "It is real clothing. Made differently."

"And this is good for the environment, how?" Raouf's tone conveys interest, rather than disbelief. Refreshing.

I share the lowdown on illnesses caused by river and groundwater pollution near leather tanning and denim factories.

Thalia adds, "Plus polyesters, microfibers, and acrylics are plastic. So, when you buy a fleece made of virgin polyester, you're contributing to increased cancer rates among marginalized people of all ethnicities."

Drew looks at his thin fleece vest. "How?"

"Because," Thalia says, "plastic manufacturing causes so much pollution in areas like Cancer Alley, where most residents are non-White and living on low income, that those people get poisoned by their environment."

"You're saying fleece and polyester are plastic." Oliver swigs his lager.

"Correct," I agree, "and—"

"Let me make sure I understand," Oliver interrupts. "Making plastic pollutes the air, water, and soil. So, anyone who lives near a plastic factory gets exposed to that pollution."

"They can't avoid it unless they move," I explain. "Factory workers stay for their jobs. People stay on land inherited through generations, which is now unsaleable due to pollution. Others don't have money to leave, or they're already so sick—"

"Damn." Anthony rattles the ice in his glass.

I add, "And plastic pollution isn't only a problem for people of color or folks in Cancer Alley. If you wear plastic fibers, every time you wash that garment—"

Charlie laughs. "I have people for that—"

I interrupt. "Whenever *anyone* washes that garment, it sheds microplastics into the wastewater stream. Those microplastics end up in oceans, and if you eat fish—"

"You're eating plastic," Theo finishes. "So, if nothing else, consider what you're doing to yourself."

"Pro Publica did a brilliant series on Cancer Alley a couple years ago," Thalia says. "It turned me off polyester, acrylic, and fleece permanently."

The server delivers a round of drinks. I sip my gin and tonic, peek over the glass at my boyfriend and daughter, feeling supported. To be honest, watching Theo's friends gape in stunned silence boosts my ego. For once, I explained myself eloquently and calmly. My voice didn't even shake.

Oliver breaks the silence. "I questioned Theo's judgement about investing in your business. All things considered, it could have promise."

"Thank you."

Theo lifts his glass. "To partnership, trying something new, and the people who inspire us to do it." Our eyes meet, sending chills down my spine.

I raise my glass. "To partnership and those open-minded and open-hearted enough to support people taking a risk."

"I still say it's a poor investment," Drew grumbles.

"Not this again." Theo lowers his glass and glares at him. "Let it go, Drew."

Drew looks around the table. "Friends, what good can one little clothing company do? Theo could invest—"

"Immense good," Theo growls, "but if you refuse to hear it, lay off."

Thalia stares into her mojito, practicing calming breaths. I rub her back, as tension travels among the guys, all eyes on me. Theo's expression encourages me to rise to the challenge.

I smooth my dress, lift my chin, and meet Drew's unpleasant gaze. "I've thought a lot about my brand, what it means, what it promises anyone who will come into contact with it. My house will be one of a few fashion companies that nourishes employees, customers, and, little-by-little, the planet."

"Sounds like greenwashing." Drew's words strike my heart.

Anthony cringes. "Jesus, Drew."

Greenwashing. Brand brainwashing. Drew thinks I'm lying about the environmental benefits of slow fashion and he won't back down. I inhale, envision channeling my inner Warrior Goddess and put the force of my exhale into my words. "Why do you care about environmental issues, Drew?"

His face softens. "Back when Branford was rural, my dad would take me hunting and fishing. I felt safe, at peace in the woods. Proud when we fed our family and gave meat to people in our community who struggled to put food on the table. I want that for my sons, all kids, for seven generations. But wildlands around the world are being developed, devoured by wildfire, contaminated."

I slide my hand toward him, hoping he won't notice me shaking. "I love your vision. For me, environmental activism is about making land, air, and water safe for everyone. Right now, our environment is so toxic it's killing people." My stomach tingles. For the first time, maybe ever, I feel powerful. This must be how Kath feels when she stands up to people. "I'm starting small, and my business can't instantly do much to turn things around, but I'm not making things worse. With luck, I'll offer a healthier model for fashion companies."

Everyone is silent, like they're letting my words sink in. Finally, Oliver emits a low whistle. "Right on."

"A voice for those who do not have one." Raouf slides me a business card. "That is a documentary I need to make."

"Seriously?" He's probably being nice to make up for Drew's behavior.

"It is fascinating, visual, thematically significant. Ingredients for an engaging short film."

Eric clears his throat, drawing everyone's attention. "I read your business plan. I believe you have a good shot." The authority in his voice seems to quell the group, but I'm stunned.

I murmur to Theo, "I thought we weren't showing it to anyone yet."

"Eric's not anyone," he murmurs, soothing. "He's my mentor in the VC world. His perspective will help you."

Cautious, I refocus on Eric. "Did you see anything that needs tweaking?"

"It's unclear how you'll replicate that dress made from layers of plastic packaging and the sheer stuff."

"Tulle," I say, calling up the photo on my phone and handing it to him for confirmation.

He nods. "Is this practical to reproduce?"

"My vision is to create wearable art for the everyday, like the dress I'm wearing now. The one you're talking about, *Airy Fairy,* is a signature piece—a unique trashion couture garment priced higher than anything else in my store. I'll make one per year."

"Photos enhance a pitch deck," Eric says, returning my phone. "Make a prototype of each everyday design you plan to sell in year one. Photograph it. Include images and details about materials in the pitch deck. For instance, will it be available only in black neoprene deadstock, or in other colors and fabrics, too?"

"Like a look book." Tension and elation grip my stomach. "I can do that."

Theo squeezes my leg under the table. "Shall we try that toast again?"

A series of looks passes from man to man, and each one, including Drew, lifts his glass. Eric adds, "If you finish your pitch deck by August 21st, I'll bring it to my conference in Atlanta."

That's three weeks away. The doctor said I can't sew until September. I smile to cover my nerves. Pain surges in my foot.

Chapter Twenty-Nine

JOSEPHINE

I WANT TO SCREAM. Two garments—ruined by my inability to control the pressure I apply with my left foot. "Third time's the charm," I say aloud, praying it will be true. I load the material and lower the walking foot onto the fabric. "Ready, PIP?" Extra careful, I depress the foot pedal. "Ooh. Good start. Let's keep this nice, even pressure—"

Nope. I lose control again, making the machine sew too fast. Another seam botched. I let out a primal yell, regain my composure, and look at the photo of Aunt Mary on the wall for inspiration. *Be patient with yourself, Josie. It takes time to learn a new skill.*

"Right. Sewing with my left foot is a new skill. Okay, PIP, we're going to practice like we did when I was a teenager. Remember those days?" *You don't. That was PIP#1.*

I move the fabric under the walking foot and sew one straight stitch after another until I can maintain even foot pressure and sewing speed long enough to sew a full-length dress seam.

Slow. To maintain even pressure with my left foot, I must go slow. I sigh and repeat the process with the overlock stitch. "Hey, we're doing it."

Finally, I can breathe. Slow is better than nothing. "Think we could finish a couple pieces today?"

A horrifying clunk followed by the sound of a jammed motor stops my heart. "PIP?"

I take a deep breath. "You're fine."

Usually, I can lift the needle from the fabric with the hand crank. Stuck. I lift the walking foot and examine it. Normal. No tangle of thread on top of the fabric. I loosen the needle clamp, remove the needle from the bar, and lift it out of the fabric slowly. Thread comes with the needle. I clip it and examine the needle. "Fully intact."

I slide the fabric away from the needle plate, expecting to find a tangle of thread underneath. What's going on? Even the bobbin case seems fine.

"Work with me, PIP. This is no time to throw a tantrum." I open the bobbin case and remove it, then unscrew the needle plate and look down into the empty area around the bobbin case. Seeing nothing wrong, I try the hand crank again. Still stuck. "Fuck, PIP!"

"Mama, what's wrong?" Thalia spins my chair to face her. "Why are you yelling at PIP? I could hear you in the hallway."

I reach for a hug, confused. "When did you get here?"

"Now. You weren't home. You didn't answer your phone. You always answer my calls, unless you're so focused, you don't hear it ringing. I figured you were here."

Her concerned expression prompts me to glance at the wall clock: eight PM. Now, I notice the quality of the light has changed. Out the window, the sky is darkening rapidly. "No wonder I'm tired. I've been here for like ten hours."

"Have you even taken a break?"

I groan, sweeping my arm across the mess that is my studio. "I've done everything but sew the garments."

"I love your mood boards. The healing power of fashion —nice theme."

"Theme doesn't matter a damn if I can't make the prototypes and photograph them—"

Thalia kneels by my chair. "You're making progress, even with your injury."

"Not enough progress. Everything is so damn difficult right now. I'm not ambi-footrous, but I practiced long enough to feel confident sewing with my left foot. Now fucking PIP is jammed, and I can't figure out why. Wait. Where are you taking me?" I lift my legs to avoid getting tripped up as Thalia rolls my office chair toward the door.

"Home. You need food, rest, and perspective." She helps me stand and gives me the crutches. I hobble back to the sewing machine.

"Mama, why not wait another few weeks until you're healed?"

"Eric needs the pitch deck with images for that conference in Atlanta in two weeks. Investors will be there."

"Aren't investors everywhere?"

"No. Plus, Theo's making his initial investment *after* I get a second backer."

"No pressure," she grumbles.

"If I want this, I need to play by their rules. I can sew fast, but even if my foot's one hundred percent by next weekend, I doubt I can sew, embellish, and photograph thirty garments, then update the pitch deck in less than two weeks alone." I stroke PIP, willing the machine to speak to me. "Do you need cleaning?" With the lint brush, I dust PIP's feed dogs, walking feet, bobbin chamber, and needle bar. The crank remains stuck. I moan. "I think we need to bring her in."

"Seriously?"

Deep breath in. Deep breath out. "She's probably past due for a tune-up, anyway. Would you unplug this?"

Thalia crawls under the table. I disconnect the foot pedal from the machine, leave it on the table, and crutch to the door while Thalia heaves the sewing machine up with a grunt. "Why is PIP so heavy?"

"She's metal, not plastic," I answer, mentally reviewing the backpack process. The simple act of putting on my backpack now requires planning and machinations. I will never leap off a boulder again. If I'd wrapped a little caution tape around my exuberance, I wouldn't be in this mess.

It's pitch dark when we reach the car, both out of breath from our exertions and sweaty from the heat and humidity. It's too late to bring PIP anywhere now. We'll have to do it first thing in the morning.

Morning flew by. We arrive at the repair shop at one PM, as the guy turns the door sign to closed.

"Shit," Thalia says.

"Muffin, can you please beg him to take this?"

She jumps out and runs to the door. The guy yells and points to the sign, but Thalia gesticulates wildly, points at me, and pleads dramatically. Finally, he opens the door. My daughter sags in relief and runs back to me. "He'll call you when it's done." She grunts as she lifts the machine, then hurries back to the shop and passes it through the door.

A moment later, she collapses into the driver's seat. "Whew, I need to do more arm days at the gym. He said it sounds like a broken motor belt, which happens with wear."

I wave at the guy, sending grateful thoughts. "This sets me back a few days, but PIP will be ready to handle anything when she comes home."

Monday afternoon, I call the shop to find out what time PIP will be ready. The repairman laughs. "Ma'am, I just ordered the part this morning."

"You don't have it in stock?"

"Believe it or not, aren't too many of these heavy-duty machines in the region. I don't carry those parts."

"When will it be ready?"

"Part's on backorder, so we're looking at four to six."

"Friday?"

"Hopefully, right after Labor Day."

"What? I thought you said four to six days."

"Weeks, Ma'am. Part's on backorder. Hopefully, it arrives within a month, but with labor shortages everywhere, hard to tell."

"I need to have thirty garments ready for a photo shoot next week." I moan.

He whistles. "If it was me, I'd be looking at a new machine. You're sewing that much, can't hurt to have a backup."

"Do you sell new machines?"

"Not heavy-duty. Home use. Lightweight fabric. No denim or leather."

When we hang up, I search online for sewing shops. Every phone call leads to a dead end. I'll have to go to New York to get a new machine. Without driving. I envision struggling on and off the train on crutches, falling flat on my back, hitting my head, getting a concussion before I even get to the shop. And what would I do with the box?

Maybe I'll find a place that ships. Oh, the irony. I have to injure myself to see Theo's point about shipping. Now that I do, I'm adding it to the business plan, which means... My stomach tightens, as I write **find shipping company that**

uses electric vehicles + alternative energy on my three-page task list.

More irony: the one shop that sells the heavy-duty machine doesn't stock it. It's backordered until Friday. If they ship it here, I'll receive it Monday or Tuesday, leaving me only ten days to sew and photograph thirty garments and incorporate them into my pitch deck in time for Eric's conference. Really eight days, because I have work on Tuesday and Wednesday. Stress attacks my head like an ice pick. What am I going to do? Theo's taking a risk on me. His friend is ready to take a risk on me. I need this to work.

Chapter Thirty

THEO

MUSCLES THRUMMING, skin slick with sweat from my morning row, I lift the metal boat and carry it into the boathouse. As I walk up the stony path to the house, a memory of rowing with my grandfather flashes through my mind. The gentle, undulating waves. Nonno's soft features and mirthful eyes. If only Dad and Nonno could have met Josephine. They would've loved her.

With a glance at the cloudless sky, I step inside, shower, and turn my mind toward work. In the *Times*, an ad for a Chagall exhibit at The Metropolitan Museum of Art leaps out. This weekend. Josephine loves Chagall. Does she have plans? Our camping trip was a disaster. Maybe a weekend in New York would go better. She'll still be on crutches, but Manhattan's easy to navigate, especially if we take cabs everywhere. I dial her number, excited to hear her voice. But when she answers, her tight inflection and sniffling make me tense.

"Are you crying?"

She groans, apparently upset by someone named Pip. Is this an ex?

I rub my neck. "Who's Pip?"

"My sewing machine. P.I.P. I named her after *Pretty in Pink*."

Adorable.

"But now I'm struggling to find PIP a sister, and I don't know how I'll have the pitch deck ready for Eric."

"Shit. I'm sorry, Hon."

"On the plus side, I see your point about shipping now."

"I love how you look for the silver lining. Here's another, if you don't have plans. The Chagall exhibit is opening at the Met this weekend. What if we drive into the city Friday, pick up PIP's new sister, then spend the weekend? We'll get a room at 1 Hotel Central Park, see the exhibit Saturday afternoon, get massages, have beautiful meals."

She sniffles. "That sounds wonderful. But I need to get back to my studio and sew as soon as I get PIP's sister."

"I hate to play devil's advocate, but are you 100% confident you can sew a full wardrobe with your left foot? You really only had a few minutes of success before PIP broke. And the doctor said pressing the foot pedal could slow, even stop your healing."

"It'll be three weeks on Saturday. And I feel better already."

Stubborn woman. I tap my fingers on my thigh to release my frustration. "I hear the importance of sewing ASAP, but I recall the doc saying four weeks before you could try sewing and no driving or walking without the air-cast for six. Maybe it's time to outsource."

"To whom?"

"You need to find tailors, anyway. Use this opportunity to test some people."

"Mmm. Hire them for piecework. You may be onto something, Theo. I still need a new machine, though. If whoever I hire doesn't have a heavy-duty one with differentiated feed—"

"Differentiated feed?"

"So the feed dogs can sense the type of fabric and adjust. Without it, we won't be able to assemble the neoprene pieces. I'd better get off the phone and find people and a machine."

Sewing really is another world. "It surprises me the manufacturer doesn't accept online orders."

"Huh."

For a moment, the only sound coming through my phone is fingers tapping a keyboard. This never occurred to her? How will she run a business?

"Great idea, Theo! The last time I bought a sewing machine, I don't think Singer even had a website. I went to a sewing shop."

Relieved on a few fronts, I ask, "Does this mean I can take you out Sunday instead? Yale Opera is performing *Turandot* at seven."

"Where? Damn it, it won't get here until Saturday. Back-ordered until Wednesday, takes them another two days to process the order before they ship. I've gotta run."

"Wait. Wait. *Turandot*? Sunday? The Shubert? I know it's not the Met, but Yale Opera puts on a solid performance, and I'd love to share my favorite opera with you. Does that give you enough time to work?"

"Depends on whoever I hire."

"Yes? Come on. It's ten minutes from your place."

"I've wanted to see *Turandot* ever since you played it for me on the drive to the campsite."

"I'm ordering tickets. Okay?"

"Yes, but Theo, don't be upset if I have to cancel last minute. You'd never consider investing in someone who dropped the ball in their business to go out and play."

"Understood." *And touché, Josephine, proving your head's in the game.*

Wish mine was, but thinking about Josephine's ever-improving business skills lights a fire in me that only her presence will quench. I doubt even our nightly video chat can relieve my excitement.

Sharing *Turandot* with her will be phenomenal. And I'll do everything in my power to make the evening romantic and beautiful. Delight buzzes through me as I complete the purchase, imagining our wonderful evening. Even Lexi's name flashing on my phone can't bring me down.

Hey handsome. NYC this weekend. Meet at my hotel?

I told her I'm dating someone. I sigh. **Taking my girlfriend to Turandot.**

Fun! I'll check out tix.

My heart drops. **In New Haven?**

We'll grab dinner after. #Threesome

LOL. Clearly, she's joking. I hope. Lexi has a twisted sense of humor. **I'm planning a romantic evening with her. She's very special to me.**

[Purple Heart emoji] **Can't wait to meet her.**

Something about this doesn't sit right. But if Lexi shows up at the Shubert and we run into each other, she'll see with her own eyes that I'm unavailable.

Chapter Thirty-One

JOSEPHINE

I sweep my hair into a loose side braid, leaving a few strands free. When it dries, soft curls will frame my face. I look tense. Unsurprising. Tapping cream around my eyes can only relieve so much stress. Even as I massage vitamin C oil into my cheeks, appreciating how it makes me glow, my mind reels with concerns. The week's events, remaining tasks, the pitch deck's aesthetic, and Eric's looming deadline coil and spin.

The four PM arrival of my sewing machine still aggravates, not that I could use it anyway. Thank goodness Angelo and Marina brought their machines to the studio. Their work wasn't stellar enough to hire them full-time, but thanks to them, I have six upcycled wool-crepe dresses to photograph. The remaining eight pieces are more complex and require my heavy-duty machine. With three days to finish, I'll meet Eric's deadline. If the woman coming Monday has the skills she claims, she should be able to make four garments. A relief on so many fronts, including my ability to enjoy a beautiful evening out with

Theo tonight. Our nightly chats have been fun, but between Thalia's visits and his business and travel schedule, it's been too long since we've been alone. I'd better get dressed.

My bias-cut, upcycled raw silk shift flatters my figure, and its crimson color brightens my complexion. The white gold and pearl teardrop earrings and pendant my grandmother gave me complement the dress perfectly. Her voice fills my head. *Someday you'll find a man who understands your true worth. Wear these for him.*

"Theo might be that man, Gram," I say aloud to the mirror, seeing her soft features and white hair in place of my own.

I imagine her gentle, sweet laugh. *I sent him to you.*

"He's the first guy to suggest I value my time, and he understood when I said I might have to cancel tonight." I open my hemp-based eyeshadow palette, sweep golden taupe across my lids, rose gold in my eye-creases, and umber along my lash lines, so it looks like my eyes are naturally luminous. A stroke of collagen boosting mascara completes the look. Crimson lip stain brightens my mouth without making it look painted on.

The doorbell rings. I slip my left foot into a cork and canvas wedge decorated with raw silk leftover from the dress, grab my vintage opera purse, and hobble downstairs. Life is so much easier with the boot. I can almost ignore how it kills every outfit. Speaking of outfits. With his fine physique, black linen suit, and multi-color nubuck wingtips, Theo makes my front porch look like a set for GQ. He gazes at the sky, like a model in a clothing catalog, but he's not posing. That's Theo appreciating nature, undoing me thread by thread.

"Hi." I squeak.

He turns. I'm lost in laugh-lines and dimples, in the way Theo's collarless button-down accentuates his pecs, and how the casual drape of his pants can't hide the growing bulge beneath. My thighs tingle.

He strides to me, pulls me close and whispers, "Hello, Goddess."

"Hello, Adonis."

"I'm a mere mortal?" He pulls back, feigning offense as he offers his arm. A gentleman's move to help me down the stairs and to the car.

"Adonis is a Roman god," I explain.

"Greek mortal. Lover of Aphrodite. Hmm. Now that I think about it, I don't mind being a mere mortal, as long as I get to worship you."

I make a gagging sound.

"Was that over the top?"

"Just a tad." I grin.

What a beautiful opera. I replay the first act of *Turandot* in my mind as I wash my hands and assess my reflection, ensuring my teeth are free of salad bits.

"Gorgeous dress." The woman at the adjacent sink smiles, lipstick on her teeth. "Cavali?"

"PHINE Artisanal Fashion." Why not practice promoting myself?

"Artisanal Fashion. Sounds cool." She tosses long bleach blonde waves over her shoulder. "Where can I get one?"

"I'm still building the company," I say, reapplying lip stain.

"Wait. Did you design that?"

"Sewed it, too."

"Hashtag impressed."

"Thanks." I scan the woman's skin-tight dress and stiletto heels, looking for something to compliment. "I love your necklace," I offer on my way out.

Theo waits outside the restroom. "All set?" He slips his arm around me. Cozy.

We walk toward the theater, leaning into each other. "I can't wait to find out whether Prince Calaf wins the princess' hand."

"Theo?" A shrill voice calls behind us.

With our bodies pressed together, I feel Theo's muscles tense at the sound. He looks over his shoulder. "Lexi." His too-casual tone brings me to alert. I turn with him and see the woman in the stilettos.

"Oh, wow," Lexi says, louder than necessary, coming too close. "When you told me you were coming to *Turandot*, I hoped I'd run into you. And here you are. Hashtag synchronicity!"

"Here we are." He gazes at me adoringly.

"Here we are," I repeat, taking comfort in his warm eyes. "I think I've heard about you, Lexi. Theo invested in your business, right?"

"Vermont's first sustainable bakery," she boasts.

"And you came here hoping to see Theo."

She giggles. "I tried to lure our guy away with me this weekend." She presses her hand into his chest playfully. Hashtag WTF?

He flinches and glares at her.

"But he said his favorite opera was running, and I thought, what the heck? New Haven is on the train line. We always have fun together. Right, bad boy?" Lexi scans his body, lingering at the crotch before looking up and winking.

He looks at her like she has two heads. "We've shared some good times, and I told you I was bringing my girlfriend to see *Turandot*. Lexi, this is my partner, Josephine."

"Nice to meet you." I smile and rest my head on Theo's shoulder, telegraphing *back off, Lexi* with my eyes.

"You, as well," she says. "Theo, will I see you next time you're in town?"

"We may stop by, so I can show Josephine my first investment."

I watch Lexi's response carefully, disturbed by the way she covers her disappointment with a too bright smile and a touch on Theo's arm. At least there's still lipstick on the woman's teeth.

At our seats, when I'm satisfied Lexi is out of earshot, I ask, "This is the woman you said is over you? The one who felt confused about your relationship?"

He grumbles, strokes my palm. "That's her. I'll admit, she acted pretty forward tonight."

"Pretty forward? She couldn't keep her hands off you."

His breath is hot in my ear as he whispers, "I can't help what she does, Josie. Let's not let this ruin our beautiful night. Please?"

Maybe it's the pleading, or the lovely sensation that travels south from my inner ear, but I see his point. Besides, her advances clearly repulsed him. Focusing Theo's attention on her will distract him from our special night and what we're building. "I'd rather enjoy you anyway," I whisper, finishing the statement with a kiss on his temple.

Act Two is riveting. The music, set, costumes mimicking historic Peking. Still, I feel a distracting thrill whenever Theo's thigh touches mine. Then it takes a moment to refocus on the stage. When Act Three begins, Theo whispers, "My favorite aria is coming up."

I love hearing excitement in his voice, and when Prince Calaf sings *Nessun Dorma* and Theo whispers the English translation of each line in my ear, my body buzzes. Until something vibrates in his jacket. *His phone?* He ignores it during the song, but it keeps vibrating. With a quiet huff and an apology, he pulls it from his coat pocket, hiding the screen so its light doesn't bother anyone. His eyes widen, then narrow. He shakes his head and shoves the phone into his pocket. I tap his thigh to get his attention, mouthing, "What's wrong?"

He shakes his head and mouths, "Lexi."

"Texting you? Now?"

His frown and measured breath tell me all I need to know. Lexi wants him, and she'll fight to win. Will Theo defend our relationship from Lexi's attacks?

Chapter Thirty-Two

THEO

It's bad enough Lexi texted me during *Nessun Dorma*. I cannot tell Josephine the content of those texts: photos taken between Lexi's legs. Did she stick her phone up her dress during the opera? With people around? Or did she go to the restroom? I shouldn't be trying to figure this out.

I start the car and pull out of the parking lot. I should be —want to be—focused solely on the woman I'm falling in love with, not the one I can't shake. "What did you think of Turandot?" I ask.

"Beautiful. Amazing. This night was absolutely—"

Has Lexi completely lost her mind? Going to the bathroom would at least show she still has a modicum of class, though that outfit... I shiver.

"Are you cold?" Josephine asks, running her hand along my arm.

"Huh? No, uh..." I let my voice trail off. Josephine would never wear anything so trashy, an interesting irony.

"You seem far away," she says.

"Do I? I'm sorry, I—"

"What did she say in her text?"

"Uh... say?"

Josephine's grip tightens on my arm.

I'll hurt her if I tell her. "You don't wanna know."

She releases her hold on me. "Why not?" That hitch in her voice—already hurt. Damn.

"It was inappropriate. A photo. I deleted it."

"Oh," she whispers, smoothing her dress, tugging my heartstrings.

I have to salvage this evening. I was hoping to make love with her, but the discomfort in the air is dampening my desire.

JOSEPHINE

I fiddle with my necklace, confused, aroused, anxious. I want to take Theo while he drives, unzip his pants, bring my face to his lap. But that would cheapen the moment, and I refuse to ruin a beautiful evening by acting from this strange fear-arousal. Seeing Lexi, the lengths she took to "run into" him, how she texted during his favorite aria... I hate to admit it freaked me out. Worse, knowing the woman sent a photo. Hashtag synchronicity? How about hashtag desperation? Hashtag psycho-bitch.

"Theo, I need you to put a stop to this."

"I promise I will, but tonight is for us. Right?"

"It was supposed to be."

"It still can be. Please?"

He's right. If we spend the night dealing with the Lexi problem, she wins.

"All I wanna think about right now is you, Josie. You and me."

At least Theo deleted it without responding. Facing Hashtag Psycho-Bitch together, arm-in-arm, I'd felt protected and loved. I want to keep it that way. Things slowed between us when I broke my foot and kept Theo away. Maybe that was a mistake. Maybe I should've stayed with him and let him take care of me. But I hadn't wanted to feel physically dependent on him, along with everything else.

Now, he strokes my palm.

"Mm. That feels nice."

He brings my hand to his lips and kisses my fingers. At the stop sign, he leans over and kisses me—slow, sumptuous, delicious. Yes. This is what I need. Connection. I'm not letting that woman ruin our romantic night.

I lead him up the stairs and remove my shoe on the landing. He does the same, then follows me into the kitchen.

"Tea?" I ask, nervous, excited, unsure of myself. That damn woman and her damn text, messing with my head. I fill the kettle, set it to boil, and open the cupboard. I'm reaching for teacups when Theo comes up behind me, laying one hand on my hip, the other on the counter. His breath warms my shoulder, lips graze my skin. A thrill shoots through me.

He whispers, "There's no one more beautiful to me than you, Josephine."

My second chakra tingles, but my brain is still processing earlier events.

The water boils. "Are you sure?" I slip away from him to pour the tea.

He strokes my back. "Look at what you do to me."

I set the kettle down and turn to face him.

His hardness strains the crotch of his trousers—for me. He brushes a tendril off my face, tucks it behind my ear, massaging the edge.

"That's so relaxing," I whisper.

He slides his fingers down my neck onto my collarbone, sending a zing lower.

"Mmm." He hovers his mouth near mine, until I moan my consent, and kisses me with enough pressure to convey he's taking charge. With Theo in control, I feel safe.

"No one but you," he murmurs against my lips.

Such pretty words.

He slides his fingertip from my décolletage onto the mound of my breast, moving back and forth across the silk covering my hard nipple, stimulating me more. He glides his hand down my side, onto my hip, until he reaches my dress hem, teasing, running his finger along the inside of the hem, grazing my thigh. His touch, his words, are so arousing, but also provoke unfamiliar and confusing emotions. "Theo."

"Can I take care of you tonight? Show you how beautiful you are to me?"

"Yes," I pant, then shake my head. "No. I don't know." I hate feeling so needy and confused.

"How about I massage you? No sex."

"And hold me?"

"As you wish."

He sweeps me off my feet, stealing my breath. I rest my head on his shoulder as he carries me through the kitchen and living room, down the hall, across the threshold into my moonlit bedroom. He meets my gaze as he lays me on the bed and kisses me.

How do I feel vulnerable and safe at the same time? I bite my lip and watch Theo step back, remove his suit coat. Is he going to undress for me? He stops moving, transfixed by something above me. "Ma vid visha vahai?" he asks. "Did you paint that on the headboard?"

"Yes. It's a line from a Sanskrit prayer I love."

He smiles and sings, "Om, sahana vavatu."

I gasp and sit up.

Theo continues, his voice deep and sonorous as he

chants. "Sahanau bhunaktu. Saha viryam kara va vahai. Tejas vinam vadi tam astu. Ma vid visha vahai."

I finish the chant with him. "Om, shanti, shanti, shanti. You know it."

"Practicing yoga all these years, I picked it up." He sits beside me. "It's one of my favorites, too."

"You're kidding."

"I never thought of putting it in a bedroom, but I like the suggestion that romance is more than playing and sex. You're saying a couple can teach and learn from each other. Right?"

I nod, excited. "Exactly. Intimacy can be spiritual, as well as emotional and physical. And of course, Ma vid visha vahai."

"May no obstacle arise between us," Theo translates. "Beautiful, Josie."

"I was feeling so vulnerable, Theo, like an obstacle was arising between us that I didn't know how to handle, and now..." I sigh, happy, and take his hand.

"It's like kismet." He caresses my cheek. "Let's take our time. Shall I get the tea?"

"Yes, please." I like that Theo's slowing things down. When he leaves, I hang his suit coat in my closet so it won't wrinkle.

"I didn't see it last time. Did you just paint it?" he asks from the kitchen.

"About a year ago," I yell. I open the bed covers, pull massage oil from my nightstand, light the candles on my dressing table, and remove my jewelry.

Theo's hungry growl alerts me to his return.

THEO

Moonlight illuminates her bedroom, casting a glow

across the floor and highlighting Josephine's gentle curves and reflection in the mirror.

I set the teacups on her nightstand. "You are a goddess."

"Unzip me?" she asks, looking at my reflection.

I stride across the room. My hands want to explore every part of her landscape at once. But she asked for one thing, and one thing only. I grip the zipper and take my time sliding it down, savoring the experience. *The first time I unzipped your dress.*

As I reach her waistline, Josephine turns to face me. "Would you like to undress me or watch?"

I swallow hard. "Step back, so I can see you bathed in moonlight."

"I like it when you tell me what to do, Theo," she says, voice husky as she obeys, sending heat to my lower half. The silver moon-glow illuminates her high cheekbones, her sexy pout.

"Stop there. Take off your dress."

She slides the straps off her shoulders and lets the dress fall. A crimson lace bra covers most of her full breasts, but her areolas peek over the top. Tempting. As is her taut belly and the panties that match the bra. Her strong, lean legs. "Thank you. Are you ready for your massage?"

"Come to me." Confident and serene, even with the walking cast, Josephine exudes sex.

I step closer. I bring a finger to her swollen mouth, loving the sign of her arousal. She parts her lips and draws my finger in. She sucks gently, making me swell. "Undress me," I command.

She works my buttons, slips my shirt off, then my undershirt, runs her hands over my head, down my neck, explores my torso, purrs. She travels the trail of hair to my belt and unbuckles it. Her breath is hot on my neck. "Take off your pants."

Loving her command, I open my button-fly and let my trousers drop to the floor.

She steps back, appraising me. The fire in her gaze signals her pleasure. "Before my massage, there's something I've been wanting to do all night."

Every word makes me swell more, and when her gaze returns to my crotch, my cock bursts from the opening in my boxers. I watch her watching me push them to the floor. She licks her lips. "*That* is a work of art."

Her appreciation makes me groan. "I need you now."

Two steps and her thighs are straddling my hips, arms encircling my neck, our bodies pressing together. Our parted lips meet and she inhales my breath, until I'm empty, then exhales into my mouth as I pull her breath inside me. Incredible. She leads the cycle, and I lose myself as we repeat it over and over, the intimacy and eroticism of exchanging breath with her inducing euphoria.

When she finishes with a nip on my bottom lip, I carry her to bed, lay her down, elevate her broken foot with a pillow, and lie beside her. I trace her skin with a fingertip. Her supple, strong calf, delicious knees, thighs that make me want to cry, her hips with their sexy stretch marks. Her abdomen bears only a hint of evidence that she once carried a child. Everything about Josephine makes me want to dissolve into her. My fingertips reach her breast, and I slide my hand to her back, unhook the bra, gently set it aside. I take her nipple, sucking gently, loving her gasps of pleasure and how her hard nub presses against the roof of my mouth.

She reaches between my legs and grabs my sac, then my length. "Theo."

Her voice travels up my spine and out every nerve ending, enhancing the sensation of her stroke. I am very ready. "Josephine, I want you."

I kiss her forehead, eyelids, cheeks. Her ears, lips, chin. I suck on her neck, kiss her cleavage, find her breasts again. She moans. My lips travel to her sternum and down past her navel, landing, at last, at her delicate groomed garden. The fragrance makes me woozy with lust, but I lift my head and ask, "Do you want your massage?"

She giggles and pushes my head back down.

Thank God. I slip her panties off, spread her legs, bring my mouth to her entrance, and find the pearl. I run the tip of my tongue around it, tasting its sweetness, and suck, gently at first. Josephine's pleasure moans course through *my* body. Incredible. I increase the pressure, and finally press my tongue and fingers into her depths. Her softness around them is both everything and not enough. I need to become one with this woman.

My shaft throbs, and she's grasping for it but can't reach. Keeping my fingers inside her, I move my mouth to the insides of her thighs, her left calf. I kiss each toe. "May I touch myself?"

"No," she pants. "Let me taste you."

"After I finish worshipping at your temple."

"Ma vid visha vahai."

I want to obey, to please her. Instead of touching myself, I kneel on the bed, slip my hands under her hips, cradling them as I bring my face back to her beautiful garden and feast.

With my tongue inside her, she tenses and releases, riding wave after wave of ecstasy. Her orgasms are so intense, the sensations overtake me, too. Drinking her nectar brings me to climax, and I release onto her bed.

I lie back, spent, amazed, enjoying her heavy breathing. "Wow. Coming without anything touching me. That was a first."

She kisses down my torso to my mons, then licks my soft tip. "You came, too?"

"Isn't that wild? See what you do to me?"

She giggles as she takes me into her mouth; the vibrations

overwhelming me. I moan. "Too soon. Let me clean up my mess."

"Leave it. I'll throw it in the wash tomorrow." She returns to my lower half, kissing the insides of my thighs, running her fingers over my abs and hips. "Now?" she asks.

"Not yet."

She blows on me, her cool breath piquing my attention. One sensation after another envelops me as Josephine nibbles a circle around my belly button, giggles into my navel, pinches my tiny nipples.

"You are divine."

She hums, pressing her hands into my torso as she explores, finally sliding a hand between my legs and squeezing the sac. "Now?"

I moan.

"Tell me what to do, Theo."

"Take me in your mouth."

"Like this?" She sucks until I grow inside her mouth. "Or this?" She runs her tongue up the vein, making me gasp. "Or like this?" She licks around my tip, then flicks the groove over and over, driving me crazy. "Don't tease me, Josephine."

"You love it."

I moan.

"Tell me you love it, Theo," she says, her breath hot on my shaft, hands barely stroking my sac.

I pant, "I do. I love it, Goddess. You know what I need."

"Yes," she coos, then pulls me fully into her mouth, sucking over and over until I cry out a warning. She ignores it, holding me down and swallowing my essence as I climax.

Chapter Thirty-Three

JOSEPHINE

HE'S HERE. He's really here. Waking in each other's arms, naked together, exceeds my dreams. Theo's delicious scent, musk and cedar mixed with sex, fills my nostrils, evoking memories of last night and fantasies of what we'll do when he's wide awake.

"I thought that was a dream," he says, his voice rough.

"Me, too, but it was very real." I run my hand over his head, stroke his ear lightly. "And we can—"

His expression changes suddenly. "Shit. Is that clock on your nightstand correct?"

"Usually." I turn over to see the time. Seven-thirty AM.

He kisses me quickly, then leaps out of bed, throws on his clothes, and runs into the bathroom. "She'll be there shortly."

"Who?" I drag myself out of bed.

He runs into the kitchen and opens the door. "Annie."

I follow him. "Who's Annie?"

"My yoga teacher. She comes to the house three times a

week at eight AM sharp. She's always on time. Usually, I'm there to greet her."

"Is it too late to cancel?"

He sighs. "I'll call you, Hon. Sorry to run."

Then he's gone.

I stare at the door, stunned, feeling a void left by his whirlwind exit.

"It makes sense he would have to go," I say to the empty room. "It would be rude to leave someone hanging when they're there at his request and counting on the income."

I put the kettle on and sag against the refrigerator. In eleven days, we'll go to Vermont, fall asleep and wake together, and he won't run away. Perhaps we'll linger in bed, and I'll finally get to feel his gorgeous cock inside—

The teakettle's whistle urges me back into the present. I prepare my morning pick-me-up, drag myself to the kitchen table, prop my foot on a chair, and make my to-do list. Yoga and meditation top it, followed by exercise.

Private yoga teacher. That'd be nice, especially next to Theo.

I sigh. What else goes on my list today? One thing: finish muslins with Cora. Tomorrow, I'll photograph them and complete my pitch deck.

Before I finish my list or my tea, my phone screams with a text from Mark.

Need you to come in today. Urgent meeting. 9:30 AM

Ugh. It's not even my scheduled day.

Mark it's 8:24.

Be here.

???

Your presence is required.

Is it legal for him to do this to me? That's irrelevant. I need the job, and I'm tired of being on his shit list. **See you soon.**

My boss may be an ass, but he offers a decent hourly rate, so I can pay rent, heat, and electricity every month. Freelancing offers no stability. And retail? No. I need free time to build PHINE. Working forty-five hours a week to earn what I earn in fifteen hours at Social Good Conn would be stupid. If I work today, maybe Mark will let me skip Wednesday.

After a quick shower, I'm ready to awaken body and mind. I unfurl the yoga mat in my bedroom and do a few prone asanas that don't put pressure on my foot.

At 9:13, I get into the air-conditioned ride-share. In the car, I practice yoga breathing and repeat the *Om* mantra silently in my head, preparing mentally for another day at Social Good Conn.

Chapter Thirty-Four

JOSEPHINE

BY THE TIME I arrive at Social Good Conn at 9:21, meditation has calmed my nerves. Except for this job situation, my life is pretty perfect. I'm dating an amazing man and starting my dream business with his help. Thalia is thriving. What more could I want, aside from success? Gratitude fills my heart as I pull the steel and glass door open and enter the building.

Inside, a heavy energy descends, reminding me I need this day to go well, need Mark to appreciate me showing up. In the last two weeks, he's given three of my projects to Xavier, either not knowing or not caring the kid comes to me for help. I can't afford to piss Mark off until I'm positioned to quit.

I punch in and hobble to the conference room, where the entire staff waits.

"Hey, you've graduated from crutches to a boot," Xavier says.

I open my mouth to respond, but Mark barks, "You're late."

The clock on the wall reads nine-thirty AM precisely.

"I thought you said nine-thirty."

"Early is on time. On time is late."

"Forgive me." I sit and prop my foot on an adjacent chair. "I did my best on short notice, especially since it's not my scheduled workday."

Mark's scowl normally strikes me like a slap in the face. Today, I see it for what it is: bravado. Instead of feeling afraid, I'm mildly amused, even sorry for him. How sad his life must be that he needs to find a scapegoat in every situation, must always belittle someone.

I smile at each of my colleagues. Only Sara and Xavier smile back. Mark sneers as he explains an unexpected budget shortfall means everyone must work overtime through year-end. How will I work full-time while building a business?

My heart drops, but as numbers flash through my mind, I see a benefit. Usually, I'd work 270 hours between now and December 31. Forty hours per week over eighteen weeks equals 720 hours. The jump in income might set me up to quit this job sooner. I'll put those numbers into my personal budget tonight. "I'm happy to help, and the boost in income will be nice."

Sara speaks with closed eyes. "There will be no boost in income."

"Excuse me?"

"We're in a financial crisis." She braves a glance at me.

"Don't we have an endowment to tap in financial crises?"

Douglas scolds, "The endowment exists to keep the lights on, so we can keep serving our constituents, not ourselves." He's always so abrasive.

I stare at Sara. She looks mortified.

Mark flashes a constipated smile. "This is your chance to serve and shine, Josephine."

The numbers I envisioned in my budget disappear. "You

expect us to work extra hours for four-and-a-half months without more pay? How will you compensate—"

Mark interrupts. "First things first. After we get grants to make up for the funding the state pulled, we'll figure out back pay."

Xavier's eyes bulge in fear. His paying job has to come first. Does Mark get that?

Theo told me not to tolerate bullying. When I took his advice last time, Mark backed off. When I channeled my inner Warrior Goddess, I earned the respect of Theo's friends. I have to stand up for myself and Xavier now. Fear rushes through me, but I swallow it and speak. "I want to help, but it's unfair to expect employees to work for free, Mark."

"Get out."

"What?"

"I need team players, and I've had enough of your insubordination. You're fired. Sara, escort Josephine out."

Stunned, I struggle to my feet and follow Sara to the door. As she opens it, I stop and turn. I will not leave without speaking truth to power. I glance at each of my colleagues until my eyes meet Mark's fearful glare. "Exactly what social good can come from an organization that treats staff like property? If you only hire people who can afford to earn nothing, you'll remain out of touch with those you claim to serve."

"Out!" Mark roars, pointing at the door.

Outside, my body goes haywire: trembling, laughing, gasping for fresh air.

"Are you okay?" Sara asks, placing a hand on my shoulder. "That was outrageous, even for Mark. I'm so sorry!"

I stare at her, grateful for the apology, although it's

coming from the wrong person. "I think I'm in shock or something."

"What a shit show."

"Seriously." My throat tightens. "Extra hours without pay for months?" I rub my throat to loosen the constriction.

"I better get back before General Von Assclown thinks I've emptied the safe for you." With a little wave, Sara goes inside.

I glare at the building, then remember the office key in my backpack. I lost the satisfaction of quitting and deleting all my files, but I can still do this. I lift the key high, let it fall into the storm drain with a pleasing clunk, hobble away and don't look back. Time for a treat. It may be ten in the morning, but I'm not ashamed to be seen at Ashley's Ice Cream. It's twelve o'clock somewhere.

Mint ice cream and chocolate chips will soon dance on my tongue. Sweet revenge. Until I turn from Whitney Avenue's brick sidewalk onto Grove Street, and one painful truth stops me. Without a job, my disposable income is officially zero. I will not be treating myself to ice cream soon. Of all the things to make me cry, why being unable to buy an ice cream at ten AM on a Monday does is a mystery. Silent tears flow as I continue toward the unattainable comfort food.

"I'll be fine. It's only ice cream," I say aloud to myself. But I can't stop trembling, and now a massive headache takes hold, stabbing my head like an ice pick.

I pause by the cemetery's tall iron gates. I'm not even hungry. What I need now isn't comfort food. I need to take advantage of this free time. Mark gave me two extra days to sew and finish my pitch deck. I'm calling an Uber and going to my studio. Cora is supposed to sew with me this afternoon, an appointment I scheduled because my Mondays are usually free. Thank goodness Mark fired me. I would've been stuck at work, unable to meet Cora, failing to hit Eric's deadline.

Chapter Thirty-Five

JOSEPHINE

Thursday afternoon, I send Cora an online payment and close the door behind her. Had I known I was about to get fired, I never would've outsourced. It's nerve-racking to pay someone to sew after losing my job, but I'm thankful I found an expert tailor who's pleasant and was available on short notice. My pitch deck will reach Eric in time, giving me a better chance of attracting investors.

Refocusing on the mannequin, I snap images of the wool crepe sheath Cora finished, carefully highlighting the peekaboo cutouts and plastic lace embellishments. I change the garment, open the camera app again, and press the shutter button. The screen goes black. Weird. I charged the phone. Didn't I? I press the power button. Nothing. I plug it in, stare at the screen. No response. The little lightning-battery image that usually pops up when it's charging doesn't appear. A pit forms in my stomach.

How many times did Thalia warn me to upgrade my phone before it died? *"Five years is vintage for an iPhone, Mama,"* she kept saying. If only I had listened. This timing couldn't be worse. Not only do I need to finish the pitch deck tonight to get it to Eric while he's still at his conference, but also, a new phone will probably cost… I don't want to think about it. The revised personal budget I made after losing my job Monday gave me a stomachache. This makes matters worse. I envision numbers on my spreadsheet turning red. Last month's car repairs went on my credit card. I planned to use the balance for heating oil in September and again this winter.

Lamenting my financial situation, I throw the dead phone and charger into my backpack and open the studio door to find the building owner, hand lifted to knock. Luna's brown eyes widen. I yelp. We burst out laughing.

"Sorry." I close the door and lock it. "I'm on deadline. Hitting the Apple store ASAP to replace my damn phone, so I can finish my project. Talk later?"

Luna follows me to the stairwell. "Sure. I came to remind you rent is due tomorrow, and starting next month, it's increasing fifty dollars."

"Great." *More money leaving.*

"You look panicked."

"Do I? It's been a week, but—"

"I'm here if you wanna talk."

"Thanks. I'll have a check for you tomorrow. Okay?"

"Sure. Let's have tea."

"Maybe. Gotta run, though. Finishing this project tonight could mean the difference between needing to find another job and not."

"Find another job? What happened?"

I sigh, annoyed I let the job comment slip. Now I have to explain. "I got fired Monday." I try to say it like it's no big deal, like it isn't totally humiliating that I can't keep a stupid job, can't seem to get my life together. But I'm not going down that road now. I'm going to get a new phone with money I don't have, so I can create the life I want, or at least try.

Luna hugs me. "You always land on your feet, Josie."

I nod, trying to stop my lip quivering. "Talk tomorrow," I whisper because if I speak at normal volume, I'll flood the damn stairwell with tears and my eyes will be so puffy I'll be too embarrassed to walk into the Apple store.

While the Apple genius transfers data from my old phone to the new one, I escape next door to a fast fashion store that pretends to be woke. The plethora of sights, sounds, and scents make me shiver. PHINE Designs, or whatever I'm calling it, will be a peaceful, relaxing place to shop. None of this blaring techno pop and five different video screens, toys, clothes, books, etc. I self-soothe by zeroing in on a patterned boho top. Cheap quality. Exorbitant price. This was Thalia's favorite retailer. Thank goodness, she converted to thrifting and finding eco-friendly, fair wage alternative clothing lines.

"Finding everything you need, Ma'am? Oh, hi Josephine."

I look from the blouse's tiny flowers to the voice. "Xavier. Hi. This is your day job?"

He looks pained. "Not what I thought I'd be doing after college."

"We all start somewhere. Listen, do you have any time this evening? I'm working on a pitch deck, and I'd love your thoughts before I send it tonight."

"Tonight?" He frowns. "I'm working 'til close, but I can meet at Yorkside at nine-thirty. After all you did to cover for me at Social Good, I owe you."

"You don't, but thanks."

At the Apple store, my debit card is declined for insufficient funds. I search for the silver lining in using my credit card to pay for the phone, but it's hard to get past the realization I only have $520 in my checking account. Studio rent is

$600. I'll need heating oil soon. How much is in savings? At least now I have a phone. I open the banking app. Yikes. Trying to ignore the upcoming bills flashing in my head, I return to my studio, finish photographing the garments, and go home to put the photos into my pitch deck. Numbers scroll through my brain, a loop more obnoxious than the techno pop playing in the clothing store.

Opening the door to my side of the duplex, I find an envelope from my landlord in the basket below the mail slot. My heart thuds. Letters from the landlord are always bad; opening it, I discover this one is, too. To cover building repair costs, rent will increase by $125 in November. *Fan-fucking-tastic.* My savings will disappear in time for Christmas. I have no job, no leads, and as yet, no investors in my business. Luckily, I'll get a final paycheck from Social Gaslighting Con-artists next week, which will cover September rent and a partial tank of heating oil. After my show closes at K-Gallery in September, I'll get proceeds from sales. At the opening, we met the goal of selling sixty percent. If everything sells, I might net enough to cover living expenses for three or four months. Enough to get through winter if I'm frugal and if my car doesn't need more repairs.

Ruminating isn't helping, and it's 9:18. I put my laptop in my bag and order a rideshare to take me to Yorkside Pizza.

While Xavier reviews my pitch deck, the server brings the bill. I snatch it off the table, prompting a diatribe from my inner critic about irresponsibility. *Yes, I'm offering a gesture of appreciation that's out of my budget. Shut up, Inner Critic. I'm trying to listen to Xavier.*

He suggests a few tweaks to make the text "hit." I change it immediately. Together, we review the pitch deck again. Finally, with Xavier's encouragement, I send it to Eric along with a silent prayer that it will launch me into a better life.

Chapter Thirty-Six

THEO

ELEVEN DAYS without the woman I love is too long. So, although I'm stunned by the time and effort Josephine's putting into packing, my body thrums with excitement about our upcoming weekend together. If we can get out of her apartment.

I did not allot enough time for this process. Free of the walking cast, she buzzes around. I sit on her bed, occasionally catching the blur of her in action. "Can I help you pack?" I ask, as she whizzes past me.

"No thanks," she yells from another room. "Sorry. I guess I didn't plan appropriately. What time does your mother expect us?"

"Mid-afternoon. I like to take her for a stroll around the garden, relax before dinner. She's eating earlier these days." The stack of folded clothes next to the empty bag on Josephine's bed seems like it would outfit her for a week or more. "You know, we're only going for two days."

She rushes back into the bedroom, face flushed. "I like to be prepared for anything."

"It's August. Hot days, cool nights. Mom prefers eating at home, so you don't need fancy outfits. Honestly, Hon, I think you're making too big of a deal of this."

She glances at me. "I just wanna have the right shoes." Is that a tremor in her voice?

She turns away, but I catch her and draw her close. "Hey. What's going on? Why are you being so weird?"

"Theo, I'm meeting your mom."

"She'll love you!"

"What if she doesn't?"

"Trust me. Your shoes won't affect her opinion."

Josephine drops her shoulders with a sigh. I cup her face gently. "My mom is a woman of substance. She loves the arts and fashion, but she doesn't judge people based on looks."

"Everybody does a little," Josephine mumbles.

"Come on. Give her and yourself the benefit of the doubt. When Mom meets you, she'll see how perfect you are for me."

"You think I'm perfect for you?"

"I do."

"Me, too," she whispers.

"Really?" Happiness floods my veins.

A wealth of emotions crosses her face, settling on unease. "Why do you think I've been so nervous about meeting her?"

"Aww. Come on. Let's go." *Meet your future mother-in-law.*

"I guess I'll wear—"

"The sundress you're wearing. I love it, and with your hair swept to the side like that, it's hard to take my eyes off you."

"Aww."

"Except you're making me dizzy with the speed you're buzzing around."

She laughs, a sound I want more of, especially since she's been so stressed lately.

"Can I bring you home now?"

Her smile lights her face. This is what I want to do every day for the rest of my life—make her smile. And after this weekend, with the blessing Mom will surely offer, and the lovely visit I expect with Josephine's parents on Sunday, I'll feel confident suggesting we take our relationship to the next level.

JOSEPHINE

Dream house number two appears before my eyes as Theo pulls into a u-shaped cobblestone driveway. Past it, a wildflower field tempts me to stroll down to a riverbank. Rising from the landscape, a white Craftsman-style mansion with a wide front porch and big square columns welcomes us. Stone chimneys stand tall on the slate roof. "You grew up here?"

"In summers and on vacations. When I went to Middlebury, my parents moved up permanently, using the place in Branford for special occasions." Theo parks next to a small red car. "That's Deborah's. She's our Godsend." He leaps from the Porsche and runs around to open my door. "Let's bring everything in, then go find Ma. She's probably on her patio." He takes my hand and leads me up wide, wooden steps. "I'll give you a tour later."

"Great!" My heart pounds. Theo's about to introduce me to the most important person in his life. Mrs. Casabella's opinion of me will matter. I'd be a fool to think otherwise, even if Theo believes it will be love at first sight. *Please prevent me from saying something stupid.*

Three hours without a faux pas. Hallelujah. We made it to dinner, and I am savoring this gourmet meal. Apparently, I passed the Angela Casabella test because she just asked if my parents will like Theo as much as she likes me. *She likes me.* I sip my Pinot Grigio, giddy with relief until it registers: she expects me to answer her question. Could we discuss the elegant cream-colored wainscoting surrounding us instead?

Angela's gaze rests on me. Patient.

I attempt a neutral expression. "I don't see how they couldn't." *Except they're them.* I take another sip of wine. Dry and fruity, with notes of fear. Not fear; bitter almond.

"What kind of people are your parents?" Angela asks, before placing a bite of quiche in her mouth.

"Mom and Dad are," I swallow, "unique. High minded. Hard working. They... hold their beliefs tightly, and..." *don't make room for other opinions.* I force myself to meet Angela's eyes.

Theo squeezes my hand under the table. "They must be fantastic, Ma. Look at Josephine."

Angela presses for more. I sip my wine, feeling two sets of eyes on me. "They're... protective. I'm their only child, so... Is this William Morris wallpaper original to the house? It's stunning."

"No. It's a reproduction."

"The grapes practically leap off the walls." I take another sip and tackle the garlic-glazed green beans. Too forceful. My fork misses the food, making an awful scraping sound against the fine china and catapulting a green bean off my plate.

I cringe, stunned, as it soars through the air and lands. On Angela's plate.

She freezes like a deer in headlights. Is she mad? Amused? Embarrassed for me?

"Oh, God." My germs are on her food. I try to stand and retrieve the offending bean, but this chair is so solid, it won't slide back. Trapped, I can't rise to reach her plate. "I'm sorry," I groan.

She shakes her head, smiling.

"Hon." Theo stifles a chuckle.

I look at him over my shoulder. Laughing? Seriously?

"Your dress."

"What?"

He gestures with his eyes. I look down. Fan-fucking-tastic. The blouson top of my sundress is blousonning right into my plate, soaking up the garlic oil from the beans and the maple tahini salad dressing. Defeated by vegetables, I sag into my chair, flash a weak smile at Angela. "Would you excuse me while I clean up?"

"Of course, dear."

"This chair is heavy," I mumble to Theo.

Taking the hint, he pulls it back without even standing. Damn. He's strong.

Once I'm out of the room, I speed across the hallway, up the stairs to the master bath, strip off the coated garment and throw it into the clawfoot tub, where I douse it with water and hand soap. This may not work, but I can't worry about that now. I find a washcloth and clean the oils off my chest, then rip through my suitcase until I find another dress. See, Theo? I did NOT pack too much.

As I near the dining room, his mother's giggle rings into the hall, a sweet sound. Except, I think she might be laughing at me. Not sweet.

I straighten my spine and enter the room, as graceful as possible. "I really know how to stick my dress in it, don't I?"

Mother and son smile at me, exuding what looks like affection.

Theo winks. "Here you are, looking even more delicious than before."

"It must be the tahini dressing," I quip.

He stands, waits for me to reach my seat, then tucks it under me. "Ma was wondering how you started sewing. And I only have part of the story."

"Oh." So, I get off that easy? "My aunt and my Gram bought me a sewing machine. I took inspiration from Molly Ringwald in *Pretty in Pink.*"

"What a lovely gift," his mother says. "What's *Pretty in Pink*?"

"A movie, Ma. Did you take lessons, Hon?"

"I read the sewing machine manual. My aunt knew a few things. Mom did, too, but she said it was silly to focus on how I looked."

Angela's eyes widen. "You don't seem especially vain, but I suppose teenagers do focus on their appearance."

"I tried not to, but everyone else seemed obsessed with my looks—"

"Because you're so beautiful, no doubt," she says.

I wince. "I was the kid at school whose sleeves and pants were always too short. It made me a target. Plus, being the only biracial, ethnically ambiguous kid in town... Classmates, parents, coaches, sometimes even teachers, all needed to figure out *what* I was."

Theo tenses, then blows out a puff of air and lays a soothing hand between my shoulder blades. I meet his eyes. Should I stop? His compassionate gaze and touch encourage me to continue.

"They'd glare, finally ask *what are you?* Emphasis on the word what. Then they'd spit the options, as if they were dirty: *Black? Puerto Rican?* Like they wanted me to explain why they found me unacceptable. I came home crying a lot."

"Oh, people can be cruel." Angela reaches across the wide table. A sweet gesture that reminds me of my grandmother.

I meet Angela halfway, and her papery fingertips wrap around mine. Connection. Something I've lacked with my mother. It fills my heart with a mix of emotions. "It was painful, but this long, looping road brought me to my career and to Theo."

His eyes crinkle. "I wish you hadn't had to deal with such bullshit, Josie, but talk about resilience, creativity, and strength. Isn't she amazing, Ma?" His admiration warms me.

Angela bestows a loving smile on us.

Theo squeezes my hand. "I can't wait to meet your parents tomorrow. I bet they're as inspiring as you."

"I wish my Gram and Aunt Mary were alive to meet you." I could count on them being supportive. With my parents, all I can do is hope for the best.

THEO

In the rearview mirror, the image of Ma and Deborah standing on the porch grows distant. I turn from the driveway onto the long gravel road, and Josephine takes my hand.

"I love your mom."

"And she adores you. The visit could not have gone better."

"Aside from the green bean debacle, I agree." Her contented sigh adds to my pleasure.

Now, if I impress her parents, everything will be aligned for me to suggest we take the next step in our relationship. "Hey, what's their last name?"

"Stewart. I reverted to my maiden name when Seth and I divorced. Look, a deer!"

I slow so we can admire the doe grazing on the roadside. "Beautiful. Are you excited to see your parents?"

"I'm glad it'll be short." She makes a strangled sound, and her voice flattens as she speaks. "That sounds harsh. I enjoy them... in small doses."

I cringe. Josephine never speaks in a monotone. She sounds resigned. My heart aches in sympathy. "You've reached some hard truths. Haven't you?"

"What's that prayer? God, grant me the serenity to accept what I cannot change, the courage to change the things I can..."

"And the wisdom to know the difference."

"My parents think they're supportive but lack emotional intelligence and self-awareness."

"And yet you're so self-aware." I squeeze her hand, eliciting a pleasing coo from her. Our experiences growing up were more different than I thought, not just because of money. Josephine's relationship with her parents is night to my day. "I'm sorry, Josie. I hear the sadness in your voice when you talk about them. I wish you could've had the kind of closeness I've always shared with my parents."

"It is what it is. As an interracial couple in the seventies and eighties, Mom and Dad had to fight for their right to love each other. They extended that to fighting injustice everywhere and brought attention to important issues. It would've been great if they'd recognized I needed their protection and attention, instead of leaving me by myself, scared."

Envisioning a sweet little girl home alone wanting nothing more than her parents' care prickles the back of my neck. How could her parents be so oblivious?

I pull off the interstate, pass through a tiny village, and enter a long driveway abutting Route 91 and acres of farmland and forest. A ramshackle white farmhouse surrounded by cars stands in front of a field. I park behind an old Ford truck. "You grew up here?"

"No. The next town over." Josephine leads me up a worn wooden stairway onto a porch and knocks on one of three doors. Like she's a guest, not family. "My parents have moved a lot."

The door swings open. I recognize the man from the photo in Josephine's studio. His eyes light up, and he pulls her into a tight embrace. "Sugar!"

"Hi, Daddy."

"How nice of you to drop by. Who's this?"

"This is my boyfriend, Theo."

Her dad keeps one arm around Josephine while appraising me, like I'm sixteen. Finally, he offers a firm handshake. "Theo."

"Good to meet you, Mr. Stewart."

"You, too, son. Josephine didn't tell us she has a new beau."

Ouch.

"Yes, I did, Dad. Remember? Last month on the phone. I said I had a date with a new guy I really like, who's helping me build my fashion house."

"That's right. We were on our way out. Guess I forgot."

Josephine throws me an exasperated, wide-eyed gaze, reminding me, again, of the picture in her studio: her parents smiling at each other, ignoring her.

"Come in. My wife will be eager to meet you. Margaret! Josephine and Theo are here."

We follow her dad upstairs into an expansive room with a worn sofa, high-end dining set and hutch. A beautiful coat rack stands in the corner, surrounded by boots and shoes. I follow Josephine's lead and remove my loafers.

"Oh, my goodness." A short woman trundles down the hallway to us, opening her arms. She draws Josie close. "My beautiful girl! And Theo, we've heard so much about you."

"Not that much," her father grumbles.

"We knew they were dating. That's more than we usually get."

"I'm sure I told you more than that." Josephine sits on the worn couch and extends her hand to me. I interlace our fingers, feeling good as I sit beside her.

"A little," Margaret accedes. "Theo, it's such a pleasure to meet you. You've just come down from Vermont, where your people are?"

"My mother is the only people left in Vermont. She fell in love with Josephine."

"Of course," her parents say in unison.

"What's not to love?" her father asks.

"I have to agree with you there. I've found nothing unlovable in this woman."

Margaret pats Josephine's arm. "Because she's a perfect angel. Isn't that right, Frederick?"

"As far as we can tell."

"You guys are embarrassing me. Listen, why don't we take you to lunch?"

"Wouldn't that be lovely? Let's have tea, then stroll around the property before we go into town." Margaret fills the kettle and sets it to boil.

"Um, sure," Josephine says, looking at me for confirmation.

"Whatever you prefer. I'm eager to get to know you."

"As much as that's possible in such a brief visit." Margaret stands on her toes, reaching into the cabinet.

I join Margaret at the cabinet, wincing inside. Ma has her ways, but she'd never make a passive-aggressive dig. "Can I help you?"

"I've got it."

Later, we stroll the property, and I strain to hear her parents over the road noise. Frederick holds his hand to his ear, while I shout answers to their questions:

Where did I grow up? Where did I go to school? What's my brother like? Why aren't Garret and I close? What are my parents like? Do I have children? When did I get divorced?

Between their body language, assumptions (divorced?), and tone of voice, Margaret and Frederick convey judgement and disapproval of my answers. This may be why Josephine doesn't enjoy their visits. They grill her during the drive into town.

Now, as we settle into seats inside the small sunlit cafe,

they ask about her job. I assume she's told her parents all the horror stories before. Seeing their faces widen in shock, I realize I missed something.

"Wait. Honey, what did you say?"

She looks down, whispers, "I got fired last Monday."

"What? Why?" *And why didn't you tell me?*

"Mark called me in for an emergency meeting and announced everyone would work overtime through December for free. When I said it's unfair to make employees work without pay, he fired me."

"Josie, that's illegal," Frederick says. "You should sue them to get your job back."

"Dad, I don't want that job back."

"They're a good organization, though. Doing good work."

"At what cost?"

Frederick scans his menu. "Sugar, you're so lost in your little airy-fairy art world you don't understand how the world works."

She tenses visibly at her father's patronizing tone. Anger rises in me, too. She doesn't understand how the world works? Airy-fairy art world? With luck, a change of subject will quell my desire to whisk Josephine away. "What do you do, Frederick?"

"Retired a few years back. Now, I take the occasional woodworking job."

"Frederick is quite a cabinetmaker. Isn't he Josie?" Margaret sips her ice water.

"He made that beautiful reclaimed wood coffee table in my apartment."

I nod in respect. "Gorgeous piece."

"He also made their dining set and hutch. But now, they're full-time protesters," Josephine explains.

"If we could have devoted our lives solely to activism, we would've, wouldn't we, Frederick?"

"Indeed, but there's honor in an honest day's work for honest pay."

"Absolutely, sir. I couldn't agree with you more."

"Me, too," Josephine says. "So how can an organization create race equity when they treat employees like enslaved people and fire the sole non-white woman when she insists on compensation? They say they're promoting social justice, but they insisted I remove all photos of happy interracial families from their marketing materials."

Her parents exchange a pained glance, mirroring each other's frowns, then turn their gaze back to Josephine. Is that pity in their eyes? It doesn't look like support. I flex my fingers under the table and try to keep my jaw relaxed.

After an uncomfortable silence, Frederick says, "Josephine didn't say what you do, son."

"I fund environmental startups. That's how we met." I look at Josephine, seeking connection. She beams up at me, and I feel at home.

"Theo really gets what I'm doing with fashion, how it matters to people living in poverty, especially in regions polluted by—"

"Where do you get the money?" Margaret asks.

"Investments, earnings from years running my family business."

Josephine squeezes my thigh tightly, sends a warning gaze.

"Family business?" her mother asks.

Suddenly, I realize I'm wading into dangerous territory, but what can I do? I won't build a healthy relationship by being evasive. "NorEast Waste Management."

Her parents' mouths drop and their eyes narrow. A server approaches and requests our orders. Ignoring her, Josephine says quickly. "It's not what you think, guys. Theo turned the company around."

"I'll have a seitan sandwich," Frederick orders, then turns

to me. "We spent years protesting your family business." He spits the words *family business* like dirt from his mouth.

"The environmental violations!" Margaret shakes her head. "Pasta with artichoke sauce, please."

Josephine clutches the side of the table. "I thought that, too, at first. I almost declined Theo's generous support."

If Earth opened up to swallow me, I'd be less stunned. "You did?"

"Until you explained how you'd turned operations around, and you aren't trying to keep status quo. Then you shared details about your other investments, and—"

"The denial among the top brass." Frederick growls.

"Are you two eating?" The server looks from me to Josephine.

"House salad and ginger lemonade, please." Josephine lays a hand on my arm, looking at each parent. "I knew then, he's straight up. An environmental hero working for change."

Margaret turns to Frederick. "Tigers don't change their stripes."

"Sir?" The waitress asks.

I lost my appetite somewhere between the words "Protesting" and "Violations." I glance at the menu, at Josephine, at her parents' matching scowls, at the pen poised above the server's notepad. "Salad's fine."

I reach across the table, laying a hand in front of each parent. "Look, I didn't build the company. I took over when my dad retired."

"Apples don't fall far from the tree," Margaret mutters.

"My father was a good man, doing what he thought was right. He didn't understand."

"Or care about anything but profit." Frederick folds his arms across his chest.

Josephine puts her head in her hands. "You aren't listening. Theo's a good man, from good people. When his grandfather built the company, he didn't have research saying practices that seemed innovative would be problematic."

"Problematic!" Margaret reaches across the table toward her daughter. "Josie, tell me you don't buy this corporate garbage, no pun intended. It's a line propagated by greed."

"Colonization in organizational form." Tears spring to Frederick's eyes.

I come from a long line of criers. When Josephine said that during our romantic moment on the beach, I thought it was cute. Now, it feels awful. Apparently, her father is so repulsed by my family business that simply mentioning it provokes tears.

I've dealt with protesters before. In college, I protested other companies, but now, my stomach churns with indignation. I want to quash my ignorant opponents' dissenting voices, but these aren't opponents. Frederick and Margaret raised the woman I love. They're no worse than my father and grandfather. Like Dad and Grandpa, Josephine's parents have limited information. I take a deep breath. "I understand where you're coming from. Like you, I felt disgusted when I learned my family business had harmed people throughout New England, so I turned it around."

Josephine leans against me. "See? It's not the company you protested. It's changed."

"I made NorEast Waste Management an industry leader in environmentally responsible practices. Our landfills do not leach. We have no trash-to-energy plants releasing dioxins into the air. I hate to sound like an ad, but I led this approach. We regularly screen all employees for environmental illnesses. Since 2003, we've found no evidence of illness in any employee that could be attributed to their work environment."

"Workers aren't the only ones who suffer, Theo." Margaret's tone irks me. "Residents near your landfills and transfer stations—"

If she knew about Isabella, she wouldn't condescend to me. But I won't risk sharing my pain with these people. "Understood, Margaret. That's why we offer free health screenings to anyone living within ten miles of our properties."

"With your doctors, no doubt." Frederick snorts.

"With their chosen doctor. We encourage residents to go where they're comfortable, even Boston or New York. We only require they send us their toxicology reports. Since 2003, we've seen no new cases of environmental illness in residents under thirty. And we've paid healthcare costs for residents over thirty who lived in the area before 1997 for at least three years."

Josephine looks pointedly at her parents. "Sounds generous."

"It cost NorEast a lot up front, but I refused to worry about cost."

"Why would you sacrifice profit?" Margaret asks.

In my mind, I watch the color leave Isabella's eyes, feel her hand grow cold.

Josephine pats my hand under the table. "Theo?"

I look into Margaret's disbelieving blue-gray eyes. "I need to sleep at night."

"Interesting." She watches our meals arrive and dives into her pasta.

"My grandfather and father operated on information available then. I have better intel. That heightens my responsibility."

Frederick tucks his napkin into his collar. "But you're not running the company now?"

"I stepped down five years ago, after rewriting our corporate bylaws to ensure the company can never waver from its new mission to promote environmental justice in all activities. Now, I chair the board of directors. A friend from business school, who shares my values, is CEO."

Frederick grunts and wipes his eyes. Not the response I hoped for, but it's the best I'll get from Josephine's father today. *Grant me the serenity to accept things I cannot change.* Luckily, Josephine gets me. I failed to impress her parents. In fact, they seem to hate me. But I won't lose the second woman I've dared to love because of my family business. I can't. Not when I see a lifetime with her.

Chapter Thirty-Seven

JOSEPHINE

I stare out the window, still in shock at how the conversation between my parents and Theo devolved so quickly. The gritty rooftops of Springfield flash by as Theo rounds the bend to stay on Interstate 91.

"I hate this turn," I say. "It always comes up so fast."

Theo doesn't respond.

"I'm sorry about my parents. I tried to warn you."

"You don't have to apologize for them."

"You seem upset."

"I'm surprised by how they vilified me."

"I knew they'd overreact when you shared your background, but they exceeded my expectations." I place my hand between the seats, an invitation. Usually, he takes it. Now, he flattens his mouth in a hard line. If Theo's not mad about my parents, why is he flexing his fingers like he's tense? "How are you feeling?"

He grumbles.

I sigh. "I'm so sorry. I wish they—"

"Josephine, as long as we're together, they'll be in my life. You adjusted your expectations of them. Now, I have, too. The relationship between you and me matters."

"We had a great weekend."

"Until I heard you got fired and hid it from me."

Suddenly defensive, I cross my arms over my chest. "I didn't wanna pressure you."

"Hmm."

"You understand that. Right?"

"Being open about your life doesn't pressure me. What's this really about?"

"Are you saying I'm lying?"

"To yourself."

"Wow."

"Why didn't you tell me you lost your job? It's been thirteen days."

"I didn't want you to worry."

"Mm-hmm. And?"

"I don't know."

"I'm your boyfriend. Why didn't you tell me?"

"You keep asking me that."

"I'm not satisfied with the answer."

I huff and look out the window at the blur of trees. We pass the blue Welcome to Connecticut sign. "It seems like you're making my problem a problem for us, like somehow—"

"Josephine, we're a couple; your problem is a problem for us to handle together."

"Maybe I can solve it on my own."

"Hon, please let me take care of you. I won't let you down."

"Take care of me? Like a sugar daddy?" I shudder.

"Gross." He softens his voice, glances over. "I know it's soon, but the way I feel about you... I'd like us to be full-time partners, for you to move in with me."

"You mean live off you."

"No."

"If living together is your solution to me losing my job—"

His phone trills.

I grumble. "Perfect timing. What's that?"

"Lexi. Read it to me?"

"Do you have a special text tone for me, too?" I pull his phone from the cup holder.

"Yup. Thanks to Kim. Keeps me from checking every text instantly."

Lexi's words strike my eyes and grip my stomach. "Hey, lover," I read aloud, my voice constricting with each word. "Imagining your long, hard cock inside me."

Theo curses.

I massage my throat, but the clenching muscles won't loosen.

"I'm so sorry, Josephine. I shouldn't have had you read it."

That doesn't make me feel better. "Why is..." *hashtag psycho bitch* "she sexting you?"

"Who the hell knows? I've been ignoring her."

"How long has she been doing this?"

"A couple, few months."

"Please tell her to stop."

"She'll get the message, eventually."

"We've been dating two months. Lexi saw us together and sexts you, despite your lack of response. She's missing the message."

"She has a weird sense of humor."

"Do you find this funny? I don't."

"Look, Josie, do you trust me?"

"This makes me wonder if I should."

"Jesus Christ."

"I'll respond, tell her I read it, and—"

"Not a good idea," Theo warns.

"Lexi needs to see—"

"Josephine, don't."

"Fine." Hands shaking, I put his phone back in the cup holder. "Did you hope I'd see?"

He scoffs. "I thought meeting you last week would show her I'm taken."

"In my experience, being unavailable turns some people on."

"In your experience?"

"I've been cheated on before, Theo."

"I'd never cheat on you." He grips the steering wheel so hard his knuckles pale.

Why the death grip? Is it denial? Anger? Both?

"Some women love to screw men who are in committed relationships. Maybe it turns you on knowing two women want you."

"Trust me, Josephine, it doesn't. I don't care." His voice is so flat, I actually believe him. He continues, "If we ignore her, she'll stop. The situation will naturally resolve."

"What were you just saying about wanting to take care of me?"

"That's different. We're discussing your survival."

"I survived fine before we met."

"Let's talk about something else. I have good news for you."

"What's that?"

"I wrote to a couple buddies in textiles manufacturing. One got back to me this morning."

"About?"

"Helping produce your designs."

"Excuse me?"

"There's no way you can sew everything, and—"

"Right, and hiring local tailors will take pressure off me and provide jobs."

"But that's not enough for a real business."

"A *real business?* Theo, you read my plan, polished it with me, and sent it to Eric. You don't think it's a real business?"

"For launch, your plan works, but in a year or two, you'll need to scale up. You need a few good factories on your vendor list."

"Factories! Dear God, that's the last thing I want." Maybe he doesn't truly get me.

"Have you finished reading that book?"

"No," I confess, ashamed to have ignored his specific advice. I stare at my hands, and my mind scrolls through all the things I did instead of finishing the book.

We fall silent. He turns on the radio, filling the car with a violent symphony.

"Can you change that, please?" I ask. "It's giving me a headache."

"Go ahead. Find something you like."

I change the station to classic rock. It's not my favorite, but I know Mick is right: you can't always get what you want. And the last thing I need right now is to hear some pop star sing about a strawberry lipstick state of mind or blaming it on the juice. The Rolling Stones fade out, replaced by Phil Collins singing about not caring anymore. Maybe I should stop caring. We spend the rest of the drive listening to music, hands on our sides of the car, not touching. It seemed we were getting closer. Now, I wonder: can we even continue? At least we're seeing our incompatibilities before making a serious commitment.

Considering everything in context—Theo reached out to factories without consulting me, probably ignoring the impact of those factories on surrounding communities. He's letting his friend sext him. He asked me to live with him because he thinks I'm helpless. I want to live with him when it makes sense for our relationship, which may never happen.

I hate to admit my parents may be right. Can Theo see past his privilege to empathize with people? If he can't empathize, can he truly love someone? Or will our relationship be one-sided? I couldn't bear another one-sided love affair.

Chapter Thirty-Eight

THEO

We enter New Haven, and my heart falls. I feel hurt and angry, but I still love Josephine and the thought of being apart bothers me. "Josie," I say, as I pull into her driveway. "I'm sorry we argued, and I'm sorry about Lexi's text. I understand why you're upset about the factory thing, but for now, can we agree to disagree?"

She's silent. I reach for her. She takes my hand, a lifeline.

"Hon, I don't feel good about the conversation we just had, but it hurts to think of going home without you. I need you in my arms tonight."

Josephine keeps her gaze on her lap.

"Please look at me? Say something?"

She puts a hand over her heart and takes a deep breath, lets it out, then moves the hand to her stomach and does the same thing. Her intense eyes probe mine. "I don't think I've ever felt so hurt by a man, so angry with him, and so in love with him at the same time. That conversation brought up a lot of questions, Theo, and I don't know how to answer them."

"In love?" I ask, hopeful.

She winces. "I didn't mean to say that."

Why didn't I tell her? I planned to tell her this weekend in Vermont, hoped to make it a romantic moment, but Ma stayed up late, energized by our visit. By the time Josie and I got a moment alone, we fell asleep without even fooling around. If I don't tell her now, I may lose the chance. "Josephine, I fall more deeply in love with you every day. Even when we argue and your parents berate me. I love you."

She meets my gaze, vulnerable. "You do?"

I stroke her cheek. "This isn't how or when I wanted to tell you, but it's true. I can't deny it or let you think your feelings are one-sided."

Her smile nourishes me like ambrosia.

"That says something, that we love each other even after our first argument."

Before we left Vermont, Ma gripped my hand, commanding my attention. "*You're infatuated now, but there will be times when you hurt each other and you won't know how to come back from it. That's when you dig deeper. Find what you can offer her and your relationship. If you build a firm foundation for your love, nothing will shake you apart.*"

"Let's make up. Can we spend the night together and agree not to talk about these subjects until we've had time to think?" I ask.

"Sleeping together might cloud our judgement."

"Or connecting will help us get past our hurt, so we can discuss the tough stuff more easily."

"I can't wake up and see you rush out the door tomorrow."

"Come spend the night in Branford. We can practice yoga with Annie in the morning. She's a great teacher."

"Sounds pretty wonderful."

I lean over and kiss her. "Do you need to change out the clothes in your bag?"

"It might take a little while. Wanna come in?"

Thirty minutes later, an amount of time that confounds me... But Josephine needed to divide the clothes into laundry and dry cleaning, then repack. She had to find an outfit for tomorrow, different "appropriate" shoes, plus yoga clothes. Then there were the vitamins. This will be an adjustment.

I envision the thousand trips we'll take together and the time she'll need to pack for each adventure. Thirty-thousand minutes over a lifetime. Five hundred hours? I'd better find a hobby to occupy myself while she packs.

Chapter Thirty-Nine

THEO

Waves crash against the shore outside as I lead Josephine into my bedroom for the first time. Will she like it? See herself in it? Want to live here? Heart pounding, I look for signs of approval in her expression. "What are you thinking?"

"How masculine this room is."

"Sounds like you dislike it."

"I love it! It's a man cave. The only feminine influence is the white crown moulding."

"How would it look if you decorated it?"

"For you?"

"Or..." I clear my throat. "Us."

"Oh, Theo." She shakes her head. Not the reaction I hoped for. "I wouldn't decorate a room for us."

I step back, hurt. "Wow."

"If a couple co-creates a space, it represents what they want for their life together."

Her words bring relief. "I never thought of it that way."

"I probably think too much about these things. Mind if I look around?"

"Go ahead." I stand in the threshold, trying to calm myself while she explores. She caresses furniture, picks up the photo of my parents on the dresser, smiles at them, sets it down. Isabella's neon yellow spider ring lies beside my parents' picture. Josephine hovers her hand above it.

My lungs seize.

She looks at me for approval, bringing relief. "May I?"

"Sure."

As if she knows my need, Josephine waits for me to join her before touching this important piece of my history. Now, she lifts the ring and places it in her palm with such tenderness that I feel held.

"You would've liked each other, both so passionate and idealistic. Quirky."

"I'd love to hear more about her." She leans back against me, reassuring.

"Soon. Okay?" I say into her hair. "I wanna focus on us now."

She returns the ring to its spot and goes to my nightstand, picks up *The Recognition Sutras* and leafs through it. "I haven't read this. Is it good?"

"Mind bending for a lapsed Catholic boy from New Haven."

She reads a random passage aloud, and I stand very still, letting the rhythm of the text and the music of her voice settle into my skin. "You read beautifully, Josephine."

"It's gorgeous writing. I'd like to read the rest."

"We could read it together." *When you're living here.*

"During our nightly video chat. Great idea! Are these your grandparents?" She touches the gilded frame on the wall.

"Mm-hmm. How else does a couple co-create a space?"

"They discuss what matters to them, what they want to share."

"Like hobbies?"

"Are there parts of your life that matter so much, you'd want to share them with your…?"

"Wife?" My spine tingles when I say *wife*. She licks her lips. Her excitement fuels mine. "My spiritual growth is crucial."

"Spiritual growth matters to me, too."

Our eyes meet, and the room disappears. She blinks. Her laugh lines crinkle. Appreciation illuminates her gaze.

"Ma vid visha vahai." As if pulled by a thread, I return to her side. "Would you keep your headboard?"

"Only if my man and I have a queen bed."

I have a king. I take her hand, trace the lines in her palm. Currents zip through my body. She shivers, too. Of their own accord, my fingers slide up her bare arm onto her shoulder, over the soft fabric of her dress to the small of her back. She's closer now, caressing my shoulder, running a finger down my spine.

"How would you represent… a marriage?" Another surge of energy floods me.

Her breath warms my neck, my chin, my ear. "A special photo. A sculpture or painting from an artist they both love."

Words form in my mind, but speaking them… a struggle. "Chagall?"

"I love the romance of Chagall's work." Her smile lifts her voice, and its music floats into my skin, cradles my heart.

"My parents always said they were who they were together…" She caresses my chest, and I'm lost in her touch. "… because they loved… who they were separately."

"Beautiful."

"Hard to live up to their legacy." I lower my mouth to hers.

She parts her lips for my tongue, and I savor our mingling breath, the sensation of her whispers filling my mouth. "How would the room represent you, Theo?"

"Color." I nip her bottom lip. Delicious.

"Your walls are gray."

"Do we have to discuss this now?"

"I thought you wanted to."

"I... do," I moan, entranced. I slide my hand up the back of her neck into her hairline, massaging her. "Soft... natural... hard to think."

"Yes." She tilts her head back, giving access to her neck.

I taste her skin, nibble her jawline. "Your room has... floral stuff. Not my thing, but..." I graze her earlobe.

"But if it mattered to your wife?"

"I'd love it, like I love her and what she cares about."

"Gray reminds me of hospitals."

Her curls wrap around my fingers. Incredible.

She caresses my cheek. "Did I insult you?"

"No." My hunger inflamed by her touch, I kiss along her hairline. Her shoulder tastes delicious. "We'll find another color for this room."

Her nipples stiffen against me, making me harder. "But we don't live together."

Not yet. "Silly." I rub her tush, pull her closer. "I asked you about decor for a reason."

My shirt is on the floor, and I'm slipping the sundress over her head. Tears stream down her face. I kiss each rivulet.

"I feel so open to you, Theo."

"Josephine." I lift her onto my hips, and she wraps her legs around my waist. "Tomorrow's a light day. Let's get away to Sherwin Williams."

She giggles into my neck, vibrations of her voice thrumming through me. "You make it sound like a vacation. Get away to Sherwin Williams."

I bite her neck. "Every moment with you feels like a vacation."

"Can I have some wine with that cheese?"

"You love my cheese."

"You think so?" She squeezes me tighter, presses her chest into me.

Her little hard nubs send frissons of heat down my spine and up my shaft. "Yes, to the paint store?"

"Yes." She purrs in my ear, "If you let me play with your stir stick."

"With pleasure."

I carry her to the bed, lay her down.

Her seductive, sensual gaze stokes my fire. My eyes travel from her full mouth down her long neck to her beautiful breasts encased in a lacy white bra. Her belly quivers, and her white satin and lace panties shimmer with her dew. The signal of her arousal piques my excitement. "Wet panties are uncomfortable, aren't they?"

She tugs at them.

I slide them off, cast them aside, bring my lips to her kneecap. Her delighted sounds—I can't get enough. I switch to the other kneecap, kiss gently. "You like?"

"Yes." Her husky voice lures me closer.

I push her legs apart, making her gasp. She sighs as I run my tongue up the inside of one thigh while sliding my thumb along the other. I trace both kneecaps, glide my hands to her entrance. If Josephine could see her flower in full bloom, how would she describe it? Where is the negative space? I trace its outline lightly with my finger, then with the tip of my tongue. She moans my name. I circle her tasty pearl with my tongue and suck gently, pausing only to say, "This color's nice."

"What?"

"The pink petals of your opening. Beautiful color for walls."

She giggles and pushes my head down until I resume pleasing her.

When she pants, I slide a hand to her navel. It pulses with the rhythm of her shallow breath. Rhythm. Sound. I hum into her opening until she screams in ecstasy, arches and squirts into my mouth, melting me with her taste and fluttering lips. Wild with desire, I lick her entrance again and again while she writhes, groaning, "Theo, I need you," hands fisting the duvet.

Needing her, too, I slide my body above her, bring my tip to her entrance. "May I?"

"God yes!" Her voice, ragged with need, slays me. "Wait."

"Condom?"

"Yes."

While I reach into my nightstand drawer, body thrumming with desire, she cradles my hard shaft, strokes the sac and squeezes gently, making me moan. She presses her fingertips against my perineum, slides them firmly back around the balls and up my erection. Condom in hand, I kneel, straddled above her.

"Let me," she commands, sultry.

Powerless to deny her, I open the wrapper and offer the condom. She slips it over me, slowly, gently, making me arch back in delight. I let her pull me to her entrance, move my tip in circles around it. "Lube?"

"You made me wet." She dips a finger into herself and wipes her essence on my bottom lip. Hot as hell.

I growl, desperate to plunge, to fill her now, but her eyes say wait. I hold her gaze, lower my face to hers, deliver a slow, passionate kiss, and murmur, "Tell me how you like it."

"Start slow until we find our rhythm." She keeps a firm grip on me, stroking my sac.

"Are you ready?" I ask.

She grabs my hips and pulls me inside, and I lose myself

in the symphony of her welcome. Josephine. Warm and soft, cradling, enveloping, surrounding me. Our union is everything I ever needed and wanted; never knew I was longing for. My tears spill onto her cheeks.

JOSEPHINE

I never felt incomplete before. Yet somehow, with Theo inside me, I am more complete, and the universe makes sense. Surrendering to sensation, I lose myself. Let my body dissolve.

He's crying, laughing, kissing me, moving with me slowly. I squeeze when he pulls out, so he'll feel my desire, and open to receive every thrust. Ecstasy. I can't stop stroking his smooth skin and taut muscles, firm as the rod filling my need. He swivels his hips, circling inside me.

"Oh... my... goodness, Theo."

"You like that?"

"So right."

He fills me, exits, fills me again, stitching our bodies together. Tapestries surge through my mind: our future, our past, other lifetimes showing me our souls woven together over eons. Another image, another climax. So, why is doubt invading now? I push it away.

He kisses my eyes and wet cheeks. "Love, are these tears of joy?"

"Theo, I love you. I want..." The words die. I can't say I'm afraid. Can't say I need to know we can overcome our incompatibilities. I want to spend a lifetime making each other feel this good. Be here now.

His gentle caress on my stomach brings me into the moment. Inside and out, he strokes, faster, faster. I rock with him, reeling with waves of pleasure. I can't stop, but he does. He rolls, pulling me on top. "Take charge?"

How does he know my desires before I know? Woven souls.

I straddle him, press my hands into his firm chest, and rock, relishing the control. Feeling his shaft inside me makes me wild. I reach behind my hips to grip his sac; stones in my hand. He's close. I'm close. Slowly, I squeeze my sheath and lift off him.

He groans. "More. Come back."

I gratify him, but keep teasing; pulling away until he begs me to return, until I can't endure separation. Now, I grind into Theo, squeeze tight and ride, so his base rubs my clit and his shaft massages my g-spot. Squeezing and pressing, over and again. Holding him inside me until I feel him harden, loosen, ready to release. Trust, vulnerability, delight in his eyes. I hold his gaze, seeing eternity as we merge and rise into the euphoria of complete union.

Chapter Forty

THEO

THE FIRST TIME I woke with you in my bed. I pull
Josephine closer. Everything about this moment feels right.
My grogginess. The sound of waves on the shore mingling
with the rise and fall of her breath. Her heartbeat under my
palm. The way my growing shaft nestles between her legs. I
want to wake up like this every day. Maybe after last night,
and private yoga with Annie this morning, showering
together, breakfast... we can go to the paint store, choose a
new color for the bedroom, start planning a future together.
I nuzzle her neck, loving the scent of her hair. She rewards
me with a delicious little moan.

An unfamiliar ringtone brings me out of my reverie.
Josephine grumbles as it rings again. "Something must be
wrong for them to call this early." She grabs the device from
the nightstand. "You guys okay?"

"Sugar, we had to call. We've been terribly distracted
since you brought that man home."

I stop breathing.

"I find him quite distracting, as well." She reaches back and strokes my hip, soothing.

"We understand the appeal," Margaret says. "He has an elegance, but Josie, your father and I are of one mind."

"One mind," Frederick echoes. "That's the secret to the longevity of our marriage."

"We want that for you, too."

Josephine mutters. "I'm not sure I want that for myself."

"Oh, no, Sugar. The entire world could disappear, and your mother and I would be fine."

"The entire world, huh? Everyone?"

"Even you and Thalia."

They didn't just say that to their daughter. What is wrong with these people?

"Wow," Josephine says.

"Our union is that deep. Of course, you've always been our priority, but you're grown."

"As you know, dear, having an adult daughter, there's a time when you simply let go, let the child be themselves and do what they're going to do."

"Mm-hmm."

"So we need to warn you against getting any closer to this colonizer," Frederick says.

I choke.

"Excuse me?" Josephine bolts up and looks at me wide-eyed, apologetic.

"Sugar, look where he comes from. His family history. The rape of the land."

Josephine groans. "I'm not even awake yet, Dad. I need tea."

"You can talk and make tea at the same time."

She slips out of bed and strides into the bathroom.

JOSEPHINE

Mortified doesn't begin to describe my feelings. I can only imagine how Theo feels. No way will I subject him to more of my parents' compost. I close the bathroom door and turn on the faucet to cover their voices.

"Did you call Theo a colonizer?" I wet my toothbrush, start brushing. "Just say you don't like him. You don't have to call him names."

"We like him! We love him. He's charming," Mom insists.

Dad interrupts. "Theo's an interesting dinner companion, but that doesn't make him a suitable partner, and Sugar, you have a history of choosing men for all the wrong reasons. Men who are terrible for you. We said nothing about Seth and look what that got you."

"It got me Thalia," I say, steeling my voice through a mouthful of foam.

"We kept quiet about that fellow you dated after your divorce. And that last one... Bill."

"Ben."

"Ben. Awful. He didn't appreciate you," Dad says.

I spit and rinse, turn off the tap, hoping Theo can't hear. "You're right about Ben."

"We fear you're missing the truth in front of your eyes. Your values and Theo's... they can't be compatible because you don't come from the same people."

"Correct me if I'm wrong, Mom." I stare at the toilet. "Aren't you two from different backgrounds, what with Dad being a Black guy from Boston and you a White girl from Maine?"

"Of course!"

"You found common ground." I cross my legs.

"Because we shared values, Sugar. You don't share values with Theo."

"We're both ardent environmentalists."

"He encourages you to take part in that awful system of brand brainwashing we're working so hard to derail. The optics—"

"I hear what you're saying, and I appreciate your concern and advice."

"It's all love, Sugar."

"Mm-hmm. Listen, don't lose more sleep over this." I sit on the toilet. "I'll be fine."

"Are you peeing?" Mom asks.

"I tried to tell you I had to get off the phone."

"We'll let you go. Love you so much, Josie."

"So much, Sugar."

"Love you, too."

We end the call. What did my therapist say all those years ago about parents with narcissistic personality disorder? God, I hope Theo didn't hear them. I splash water on my face, pat it dry, and open the door to the bedroom. "Are you hungry?"

Theo sits cross-legged on the bed, glorious in the morning light. "Annie will be here in about thirty minutes. I usually have coffee before class and eat after. Cool?"

"Sure."

He quirks an eyebrow. "Colonizer?"

Shit. "They're nothing, if not dramatic." I jump onto the bed and embrace him from behind, speaking between each kiss I plant on his neck and shoulders. "Now." Kiss. "You know." Kiss. "Why." Kiss. "I don't have." Kiss. "More money. In savings."

He looks over his shoulder at me. "I don't follow."

"So much of it goes to therapy."

Chapter Forty-One

THEO

I LOCK the door behind Annie and jog to the bathroom for my first shower with Josephine. Teased by the steam on the glass shower doors, I catch mere glimpses of Josephine's sinuous curves, long legs. Inside the shower, I'm entranced by the crook of her elbows as she washes her hair, and the way water drips from her curls onto her luscious breasts. My appreciative growl makes her smile, though she keeps her eyes closed as she rinses the shampoo out. "That was the best yoga class ever."

"Annie's great." I turn on the second shower head and get down to business.

"And that serene yoga room." She sighs. "Plus, there was this hot guy next to me in class. I tried to keep my eyes on my mat, but it was hard not to be distracted by his bulging muscles."

"I've got another bulge that might compete."

She purses her lips in her sexy way and purrs, making me want to reach out and pull her close. I'd love to show her exactly what's on my brain, but it's Monday morning and my schedule's already in motion. I settle for a quick nip at one of her perky little nubs and enjoy the squeal it provokes. She wipes the water from her eyes and reaches for me.

"Uh, uh," I wag a finger at her. "If you get me going, we won't have time for breakfast."

"Breakfast," she says, incredulous. "You'd take breakfast over—"

"Meal of champions, and after the week you had, you need extra nurturing. Besides, Kim's due here in one hour."

"Oh." Her face falls. "It's Monday."

"And we move at the pace of business in this house, love. But with you here this morning, I'm thinking how beautiful it'd be to have you by my side during every yoga class."

"Om saha navavatu," she sings. *May we be protected together. May we be nourished together.* "Saha nau bhunaktu," I sing, giving myself a final rinse.

We finish the chant together. Nourished by our connection, I plant a soft kiss on Josie's mouth and drag myself out of the shower. "Clean towel on the counter. Maybe by the time you're out, I'll have a smoothie ready for you. Can you stomach spirulina?"

"I make a strawberry spirulina smoothie every morning."

"Really?"

"Strawberries, spirulina, raw honey, chia seeds, and either cashews or almonds."

"Love, we make the same smoothie every day. We may come from different worlds, but we're of one mind."

She giggles. "Like the Borg on Star Trek."

"Or a hive of drones. And because we're so in tune, I sense you need another five minutes in the shower."

"At least. Curly hair is hard to detangle."

"So I'll make breakfast."

"Leave me something to do."

"No way. I wanna nourish you."

THEO

I'm flipping the omelette when her cat-call rips through the house. "There's only one thing sexier than a man with a vacuum; a man with a spatula."

I shake my ass. "Play your cards right. This sight could be yours daily."

"Enticing," Josephine purrs and sidles up to me. "Beautiful kitchen, by the way. I love the layout and all the woodwork."

"All this could be yours," I whisper, mimicking a game show host. "Speaking of which, if you work here, we could swing by Sherwin Williams before I bring you home."

"That's a fun idea."

"Cool." I slide the omelette onto a serving dish and bring it to the breakfast nook.

"Goodness, Theo. Where did you get fresh flowers so early in the morning?"

"Outside in the garden."

She leans over the vase and inhales. "These roses smell incredible."

"*Rosa blanda* Aiton. They're native."

"Nice. Do you always set the table so beautifully for breakfast?"

"Only for you."

"And the smoothie—"

"Tastes better in a wine glass."

"Spirulina needs all the help it can get." She kisses my cheek, then slips into the window seat. "I feel so special."

"When I said I wanted to nurture you, I meant all of you, not just your stomach."

She sighs. The way she's looking at me as I slide in beside her fills my chest with light. "Today's a research day for me.

Since you're here, we can work on the phase two plan for your company."

"Phase two?"

"When you scale up."

"Scale up." Her voice takes a hard edge.

My muscles tense. I take a bite. Shiitakes hit the spot. "You like?" I gesture at the dish.

"Delicious. Thanks. And the smoothie's sweeter than mine."

"Too sweet?"

"Perfect. Must be the crystal." She winks, but then purses her lips.

Uh, oh.

"We didn't plan well last night. I should've followed you in my car."

"I'm happy to bring you home this afternoon and explore paint colors together. Or I can call a rideshare for you after breakfast. Your choice."

She gazes out the window, thinking.

"Kim should arrive in about twenty minutes. I know we tried to discuss this yesterday, but I haven't had the chance to tell you about these factories."

Josephine isn't even looking at me, but her narrowed eyes hit me in the gut.

I add quickly, "And you haven't had a moment to share about the people you hired recently."

"They were great. One woman, in particular. I could see hiring her full-time."

"Only one? Well, don't be discouraged. You did great on short notice."

Her face relaxes. "The other two were good, but I'll keep looking."

"Hiring takes time."

"Seriously, Theo, this omelette is amazing. You can nourish me any day."

"Now, I know you plan to produce 450 garments a year to start. When you scale up—"

"You keep saying scale up, but why would I?"

"Starting small makes sense to test the market. After two or three years, you'll want to expand."

"No. I'll want to maintain a small staff of fashion artists. Scaling up would put undue pressure on them. Plus, the last thing I want is to flood the market with needless stuff."

"Four or five hundred pieces of clothing a year is hardly flooding the market. The name brands produce millions of garments a year."

She scoffs. "Shine makes a million t-shirts a day. It's disgusting. They can't possibly sell them all, and instead of donating unsold clothes to people struggling financially, they burn the excess to keep the perceived value of their cheap clothing high."

I hold up my hands. "Truce. You're right."

She shoots me a look that says *I know*.

"I'm not saying you should follow their model, Hon."

"Good because I don't intend to."

"Can I show you something that may ease your mind?"

She quirks an eyebrow in disbelief.

"You have the most expressive eyes." She narrows them again. Damn. "Sorry. You're cute."

She growls.

"I can't help it. I'm in love. But if you'll bear with me, I wanna share photos and video I took at my friend's factory in China. Be right back." I run to the office and grab my iPad. Kim's due in ten minutes. Shit. We'll resolve this before she arrives. We have to. I return to find Josephine washing dishes. "Leave that. The maid's coming this afternoon."

"You have a maid?"

"Of course."

She sighs. "Well, I'm not leaving dishes with food on them. That's just gross."

"Suit yourself. Can I show you this?"

"Bring it here, along with your plate, if you're done."

I carry my empty plate to Josephine. She rinses it and puts it in the dishwasher. "Go ahead. Show me, but I can't work with a factory in China. Too many human rights violations. Plus, global shipping spews tons of CO2 into the air."

"We can plant trees to offset emissions."

Her body goes rigid. "What about the horrific treatment of workers?"

"Those stories are true. Also real are Chinese manufacturers like my friend, who value and honor workers' humanity."

"Seriously."

"I took these myself during a visit last year."

"Why were you there?"

"Lee wanted my advice, so I toured his facility, spent several days working with him. Honestly, what I saw impressed me."

"How do you know this guy?"

"Business school. He inherited the factory from his father, who had a very strong humanitarian ethic and raised his children with humanitarian values." I pull up images on my iPad. "Here's the main floor. They make garments for top couture designers."

"Aha."

"Look at the photo. What do you see?"

"A man and woman sewing. Bolts of fabric."

"What do you notice about the space?"

"It's light and bright."

"Do you see where that light is coming from?"

"You don't have to talk to me like that, Theo. I'm feeling kinda patronized."

"I'm sorry, but do you see the wall of open windows on the opposite side of the room?"

She nods.

"Doesn't that contradict everything we've heard about these factories?" I ask.

"Yes."

"Now, in this photo, notice anything about the people sewing?"

"They're smiling."

"Smiling," I repeat.

"How do you know they aren't smiling because their photo's being taken by the white male visitor while their boss stands there?"

Damn, she's shrewd. Impressive. "I don't."

"Exactly. Now, what am I looking at?"

"This is the floor, literally the floor. What do you notice?"

"It's shining."

"Do you see any debris on it?"

"Nope."

"Okay, now I took a video starting at that same spot. Ready?"

I play the video and watch her reaction to the bustling scene. Josephine is not relaxing. Does she recognize how happy and engaged these people appear?

She pats my back. "I see your point. If they aren't trying to please the white man and the boss, if this is how things usually are, it looks decent, like a pleasant workplace for sewists."

"That's why it impressed me."

"Great."

"Darling, I care about people, too. That's why I changed our company's entire M.O. Like you, I won't have my livelihood contributing to anyone's suffering. We share those values. We're *of one mind*."

She smirks. "Haha."

"And I'm here, helping you create the company of your dreams."

"Beloved, in the company of my dreams, I know everyone who brings my designs to life."

"If we traveled to China, you could meet—"

"By keeping manufacturing in my store, I'll know my fashion artists personally. Plus, my customers can meet the people who make their clothes. Imagine the transformative possibilities for our community."

I let the idea hang in the air.

She continues. "Imagine the mindset shift when someone walks into my store, chooses an outfit, and meets the person who crafted that piece from start to finish. The fashion artists I hire aren't cogs in a line. They're individuals who take pride in their creation because they make the whole garment, not just a sleeve or a collar. Plus, it limits workplace disputes. If a zipper gets messed up, there's no blaming whoever's on machine A. If Zelda made the garment, she knows she's responsible for fixing any problems."

"Your vision offers peace, connection, mutual respect. It's lovely and idealistic."

"You say that like it's bad, but isn't your sense of idealism what drives you to invest in eco-startups?"

I feel her frustration rising along with mine. I inhale and exhale slowly, hoping Josephine will also calm herself. "Let's take a breath."

She plays along, matching my breathing. It's clear she's playing along because the fire in her eyes singes me. "I want to see my colleagues in the checkout line."

"Alright. It'll probably mean higher prices, but you can make it work." She'll come around, eventually.

"Thanks for listening."

"I have great respect for you and your ideas. That's why I'm backing you, and it's one reason I love you. And you know what I learned from this conversation?"

"What?"

"We're both super nerds. You dream of seeing your colleagues in the checkout line. I dream of buying house paint with you."

"We're back to that, huh?"

I wince. Not the response I hoped for. How should I react? It almost seems like Josephine doesn't want to live with me. I thought she declined my offer last night out of pride and because we were arguing. What's up now?

The front door opens and Kim announces her presence.

I pour another cup of coffee, groaning inside. "We're in the kitchen."

"We?" Kim strides in, hair in two frizzy braids. "Oh, hi, Josephine. Did you guys see the news about Hurricane Ida?"

"No," we say together, alarmed. *Of one mind.*

Kim lays the paper across the counter. "It's heading for Cancer Alley. That's where you're from, right Josephine?"

"No. I spent a month there making art and getting to know the community."

"They're evacuating everyone because of the hurricane and damage to the factories," Kim explains, worry in her voice.

Josephine leans over the paper. "This says petrochemical plants release extra toxins into the air during hurricanes. They evacuate residents, but each factory leaves someone onsite to ensure things don't blow out of control. Can you imagine being the one to stay?"

"Horrifying." I rub Josephine's back, to comfort us both. "Their toxin exposure is increasing exponentially."

She looks over her shoulder, meeting my eyes. "I'd bet anything Helena will stay."

"Why?"

"She won't let an employee take a risk she's unwilling to. If she knows how to keep the plant from emitting more crap, she'll send everyone away."

"Damn."

Josephine grabs her phone from the counter. "Sorry. I need to text her."

"Kim and I will be in my office. Can we finish our chat in fifteen minutes?"

"Sure." Josephine nods, already absorbed in her phone. "I'll get my stuff together and make a plan."

I wrap an arm around her, kiss her head, and stride out, mind turning to tasks.

When I return, she's sitting on the couch, packed bag beside her. "Reach Helena?"

"No, and it's making me nervous. Anyway, I need to follow up with Eric and get my head together."

"So, you're going home now? I thought you brought that book, and you can send emails from your phone. Right?"

"Yes and yes, but I need a sense of direction. I think better in my own space."

"This could be your space. You could move in without interrupting your lifestyle. Morning yoga, green smoothie, beautiful home—"

"It *is* my dream home."

I kneel at her feet, murmuring, "And if last night is any indication, earth shattering sex."

"I think we rearranged the universe." She bites her lip.

I scan her face. "You're happy with the home, the sex, the food, and the yoga, and you still won't live with me. Should I be worried?"

"Why rush into it?"

"To save you money in your time of need."

"You are so thoughtful. But I'll get investors soon, and I'll be fine."

She stares out the window, unaware I'm seeking reassurance in her eyes. My throat aches. I should've kept quiet. I thought she needed me like I need her. Maybe everything Josephine endured last week threw her off. Then her parents made things worse. Colonizer? She can't take them seriously. Can she?

Chapter Forty-Two

JOSEPHINE

COLONIZER. The word has been popping up in my mind all week. Ridiculous. Completely ridiculous, like their brand brainwashing campaign. People on the Louisiana coastline are facing real danger. Meanwhile, my parents are focusing on silly issues like clothing labels, and misjudging Theo. If they saw us together in our daily lives, how he protects me, how he's hovering as I slowly and carefully climb the boulder from the bay onto the wooded path overlooking it, they'd recognize his kindness.

We arrive at the top, and he wraps an arm around my shoulders. "You okay?"

I smile, appreciating him. "Let's take a selfie."

He pulls me closer, lifts his phone, and snaps the photo as a notification pops up: *Cancer Alley Flooded. Millions in Damages.*

Our smiles drop. Theo opens the article and holds it so I can read with him. The story describes plumes of black smoke filling the air as refineries and factories burn millions of pounds of toxic gasses.

"Millions of pounds? That's insane. Why?" I ask.

Theo reads aloud, "A spokesperson for a major refinery says the factory is 'experiencing elevated flaring due to lack of steam generation.'"

"What the hell does that mean?"

Theo hitches a shoulder. The article says residents have high levels of chemicals in their bodies, causing autoimmune diseases and cancer. Nauseated, I lean into Theo, calming myself by watching the gentle ripples on the bay.

I call up the article on my phone and text it to Thalia: **See this?**

She writes back immediately: **Yeah. Notice the headline focuses on money lost, instead of PEOPLE? Totally dehumanizing.**

OMG. I didn't catch that.

Great lesson for the kids. Gotta run. [red heart emoji]

I send a red heart emoji and pink hearts emoji.

"I need to call Helena," I say, dialing. The automated message says all lines are down, and a rock settles in my stomach. I search Theo's warm eyes for comfort. "Let's keep moving?"

"Yeah, I need to burn some nervous energy, too."

We walk away from the water along the path that leads deeper into the woods. I try to focus on nature's calming sounds: the lull of the bay at low tide, bird calls, squirrels and chipmunks rustling through the understory. My mind keeps returning to the place where I did my artist residency last year, the kind people I met, how they must be suffering now. How many of the homes I visited did Ida destroy? Who escaped in time? Who stayed behind, either unwilling or unable to leave?

When the trail narrows, I follow Theo off the main path to a flat boulder overlooking a small inlet. I lean into him, safer in his presence.

THEO

Anger surged through me when we read that article. Now, three things temper it: hiking the rugged coastal trail, keeping Josephine safe, and holding her. I offer her my water bottle, and she accepts it. Amazing how a tiny gesture can make me feel useful. "I dislike feeling helpless, Josephine, and this situation in Louisiana triggers that big time."

"Same. I'm trying Helena again." She taps her phone screen, holds her breath. It dings a moment later, and she exhales. "She's safe, but—" Josephine's phone dings several times in rapid succession. "Oh, fuck. Theo, look." She holds it up.

Photos. In one, black smoke fills the daytime sky. In another, cows roam a flooded field in front of a huge leaking oil tank. My heart aches for the cows—innocent and suffering because of human greed, absorbing toxins through their skin that will poison them and anyone who eats their dairy or beef. Bile rises in my throat.

"We have to do something," Josephine says, endearing herself to me more.

"Agreed."

"I'd go down and help if I had the skills. If my company was running, I could make t-shirts or bags and sell them as a fundraiser."

"Where would the money go?"

"Helena sent me a link to a mutual aid organization down there."

"Send it to me?"

She taps her screen, and my phone vibrates as it receives the link she AirDropped. I open the website, scan the info, and click donate, making a $50,000 gift from my personal account. I forward the link to NEWM's C-suite and board members, dictating into the messaging app, "Let's contribute $100,000 to this mutual aid organization for the residents of Cancer Alley, Louisiana."

"You can just do that?"

"We have a CSR fund." A text arrives. "Unfortunately, our CFO says this year's monies are committed." I dictate: "Got it. Put 'Tap Reserves' on the next board meeting agenda."

"CSR... Corporate Social Responsibility?"

"Correct."

"Most corporations donate to a Political Action Committee and call it social responsibility." The admiration in her voice warms my heart.

"We're not most corporations. We're about direct action, real change, not lobbying congresspeople to create laws that lower our tax liability."

"Look how you use your privilege to help people in need." She nestles deeper into me, her words filling me with pride. "I love that."

"And I love how you show me more ways to help. Your t-shirt idea is great. Let's get in touch with Lee."

"Who's Lee?"

"My friend who owns the factory I showed you."

She sighs.

"What?"

"Why Lee?"

"He has infrastructure to make your t-shirts inexpensively, even with organic bamboo or something. You design the logo. I have Kim put up a landing page."

"A what?"

"A single web page where people buy the t-shirt and get on your mailing list."

"I don't have a mailing list."

"You'll start one."

She groans.

"This is business, Hon, though you can have a marketing

company do your newsletter later. Pumping out a couple thousand activist t-shirts is a pretty great soft launch activity."

"That feels icky."

"Really? Why?"

"Theo, why are you pushing this factory thing so hard?"

"Because I want your company to succeed."

"Can't you see there's another way?"

"I see that's what you believe."

She sighs and pulls away. "Let's drop this subject for now."

I follow her onto the trail. "I guess you could wait until customer demand rises before you outsource. Careful, Josie. This path is rough for speed walking."

She shakes her head, maintaining her pace. "Factories created this nightmare in Cancer Alley, and you're still pushing them. I don't get it."

"All factories aren't equal. How many t-shirts can you sew a day with PIP?"

"Probably twenty if I hustle."

"So... 120 if you work for the next six days. And how would you embellish them?"

"Maybe screen print a statement or a logo on the front. Sew a patch of plastic mesh or food packaging onto the sleeve to make a point about the cause of this nightmare."

"Do you have the fabric you need?"

"No, but I can get deadstock in the fashion district tomorrow."

"If you sell each t-shirt for $150 and donate your time, you could raise $18,000 before expenses." Outsourcing to Lee, she could sell 2,000 shirts for $20, and raise $20,000 after expenses, with far less work on her part and far greater messaging impact. "What will the fabric and screen printing cost?"

"I can get my friends to donate the screen printing."

"In business, we never assume someone will donate their time. Remember how you felt when Mark insisted you donate your time to save Social Good Conn?"

"Touché."

"If the right deadstock is unavailable, what will new fabric cost?"

She shrugs. "I never buy new cloth."

"Look, I'm not convinced this'll produce the highest ROI, but I'm willing to try."

She glances over her shoulder at me. "Try what?"

"I'll buy the materials, have Kim set up the landing page so you can sell the shirts. If you wanna do this, I'll help."

"Why do I feel placated?"

"I don't know because I think I'm being supportive. Oh, Josie! A heron!"

She stops and watches the bird glide overhead, giving me a chance to approach her. "Come here, you," I say.

"Herons mean transformation and good fortune. This is the second one to fly over us."

"Having you in my life is definitely good fortune."

"Aww, Theo." She lets me envelop her, and I bury my face in her neck, inhale her sweet fragrance, nibble her. She giggles and guides my face to hers. We kiss, slowly, then hungrily. "I missed you these last few days, Theo."

"Spend the night with me?"

"Yes, please."

I take her hand and lead her onto the narrow trail that parallels the rocky shore. Suddenly, I know how to get through to her. "I understand your concern about using a faraway factory."

"Do you?"

I wish her voice wasn't laden with skepticism. "These petrochemical companies killing Cancer Alley are based in other states or countries. When you operate far from home, you forget your work is damaging an ecosystem and community. You convince yourself it's irrelevant. But honey, NorEast Waste Management evolved. Some factories are choosing healthier methods, also."

"Like Helena's."

"Exactly. But our system is imperfect. There's no silver bullet yet, so I love backing entrepreneurs like you who are discovering how to turn this sinking Earth-ship around."

We reach the point that juts into the ocean like the bow of a magnificent yacht. The gently rolling waves remind me of making love with her. My mind veers in that pleasant direction, until Josephine says, "We do share values."

I do a double take. "Uh... yeah. That's why I went to your show. Why would you think otherwise?"

"My parents. They're worried we don't share values."

"But we're of one mind," I deadpan, eliciting a snort and eye-roll from her. "Are they concerned we don't share each other's values, or that we don't share theirs?"

Her eyes narrow. "I guess they mean *you* don't share their values."

"Right." After I explained everything, demonstrated I support their daughter and her activist company, they think I don't share their values? Maybe I don't. Maybe I value Josephine far more than they ever have. But I can't say that. Not now. Not ever. It doesn't matter, anyway, does it? "You're not worried about their opinion of me. Are you?"

"Please!" She laughs. "You've heard how illogical they are. Besides, I'm a grown woman with a child of my own. My parents stopped influencing me decades ago."

I appreciate her reassurance, but my gut's telling me something's off.

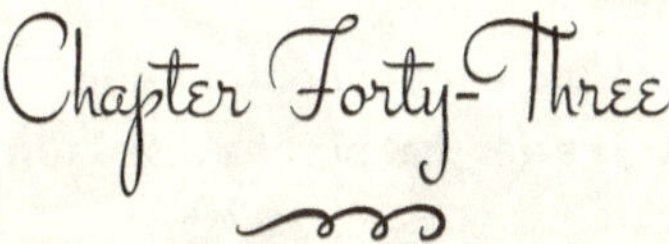

Chapter Forty-Three

JOSEPHINE

I LEAN against Theo's bedroom window, entranced by the waves rising, crashing against the shore, and subsiding. Their motion evokes a sense-memory of moving on top of Theo, rocking with him. The pulse of our breath. The energy coursing up my spine, flooding my torso.

He sneaks up behind me, slipping his arms around my waist. "Do you need to do female things to prep for bed, or can I take you here and now?"

I absorb the warmth of his touch. "I'll be quick, especially since I didn't plan to stay and don't have any of my products."

"Gotcha covered." He grins.

"Okay?" I enter the bathroom. There, on the gorgeous marble sink, are boxes of my favorite skin care products. "Theo, how did you know which ones I use?"

He stands in the doorway, sexy as hell in his boxers. "I saw what you brought to Vermont and made a mental note."

I never considered skincare products arousing, but the fluttering between my legs is real.

"That's okay, right?"

I giggle.

"I did good?"

"Believe it or not, this is a total turn-on."

"Face wash?"

"You noticed and went out of your way."

He shrugs. "It's not that big of a deal. I just ordered it online. I mean—"

I open the hot water tap. "I feel cared for. No guy has ever done that for me."

"Oh, Honey, they should have." He strides in and wraps his arms around me from behind, pressing himself against my backside. "I'm not sure I can wait for you to do all these preparations."

"You're going to have to," I tease, as the fluttering between my legs intensifies. I wiggle against him until he gasps.

"Can I help?"

"Wash my face?"

"Yeah. How do you do it?"

"I get the water hot, soak the washcloth, and press it against my skin."

He takes the cloth from my hand, soaks it in the hot water, turns off the faucet and, still standing behind me, brings the washcloth to my face. I lean back against his chest, held. "Apply gentle pressure."

"Like this?"

"Mm-hmm." Steam warms my face. Theo presses gently into my cheekbones, forehead, nose and chin, relaxing me. "Run it from my chest up my neck."

He obeys, making me moan with pleasure.

"Now what?"

"Add a drop of cleanser to the washcloth, a bit more water, then move the cloth in circular motions all over my face and neck."

"I can't do this from behind." He turns me around and pulls me close. His tent meets my silk panties. Is the dampness between my legs coming from my body or his? Maybe both. He moves the washcloth as instructed, from my forehead, down the bridge of my nose, onto each cheekbone, to my chin.

"This is Heaven."

"Good." He runs it around my mouth. "I enjoy making your lips wet."

I laugh. "Cheesy!"

"Oh, no. Not cheesy." He murmurs, then hums *Nessun Dorma* as he finishes washing my face. I sigh as he slides the washcloth along each arm, caresses every fingertip, then sweeps my hair over my shoulder and glides the wet washcloth up the back of my neck. Deeply enjoying his touch, I close my eyes.

"That's it, Josie. Relax. Raise your arms." When I obey, he slips my tank top off, unhooks my bra, and runs the washcloth down my spine, applying perfect pressure. He moves around me now, surprising me with where he places the washcloth. As he slides it around my waist, I unbutton my shorts. They fall to the floor. He slips my panties off. I hear the faucet running, then feel the cloth, hotter, wetter, on one hip, then the other, then under each butt cheek, and down the back of each thigh. When he glides it up the inside of my thigh, I gasp. "Enough. I want you."

"Are we done washing your face? What about these creams?"

"Later. I want you now." I open my eyes. He kneels, gazes up at me, those warm eyes melting my heart, and brings his face to my garden, inhaling, licking, sucking. Bliss.

A frenetic text tone sounds from the bedroom. *Hashtag PsychoBitch.*

My arousal turns to anger, gripping my stomach with

such force I could vomit. I back away from him. He drops his head to his knees.

"It's almost ten PM," I say through gritted teeth. "Why is she texting you now?"

He remains in child's pose. "I don't know."

"Shall I read this one to you?"

"Go ahead."

"Why would you agree?"

"So you can see I haven't responded to her since we went to the opera."

"Please respond now. End this."

Theo looks up. "Josephine, we've been friends for thirty years."

"Then she can handle your firm, authentic no to her sexting."

"She'll get the hint, eventually."

"I doubt it."

"Can't you ignore it?"

"Do you care how this makes me feel, or are her feelings your priority?"

"You know I love you. She's the one who's struggling."

"Theo, I need you to make this right."

"But I've done nothing."

"Exactly." I squirt face oil into my palm and rub it vigorously into my face, neck, and décolleté. "By doing nothing, you have a fallback. When things get tense between us, you've got Lexi to stroke your ego. Why else would you let her sext you?" I let that sink in while I tap eye cream into my laugh lines, watching Theo's reflection.

He shakes his head. "You're asking me to hurt a friend who was there for me during—"

"Her feelings aren't my concern, and I'm mystified why they're yours."

"You're not being reasonable."

"We disagree about what's reasonable, which makes one too many misalignments in values. I need to go."

"What? No. We can work through this." Theo looks up from his position on the floor.

I pick my clothes off the bathmat and step around him. "I'll leave the toiletries for Lexi."

"Don't be ridiculous." Theo rises and reaches for me, but I keep moving, dress in the hallway, find my phone, and hail an Uber. I retrieve my backpack from the sofa, slip into the hiking sandals I left at the front door and leave, ignoring Theo as he calls my name.

A moment later, he joins me on the stone bench under the olive tree, still in his boxers. He holds his phone out. "Please, Josephine. Look! I haven't responded to her."

I stare at the ground, so he can't see me crying, but my hoarse voice probably gives me away. "I told you to respond, to stop her. Lexi knows what she's doing, Theo. She wants me out of the picture. She knows how to make it happen, and she just did."

"Don't say that."

"Unlike you, I have no problem speaking truth when people need to hear it. So tomorrow when you're wondering why we're not a couple anymore, remember this: I'm not your side hustle. I'm not your woman of convenience."

"What are you talking about? I've never treated you that way."

"I will be your one-and-only, or nothing, which means you will never communicate with any woman like you've been communicating with Lexi."

"Josephine, she's just a friend. You're the one I love."

"And I love you, but this isn't working, and it looks like it won't."

"We can make it work."

"That takes two of us."

"You know I'm here for you, emotionally, physically, financially, whatever."

"I realize you haven't been a partner with anyone in decades and you had a short time with Isabella. But I assumed you'd learn how to be a partner. I thought you'd see you can't take your conflict-avoidant M.O. and bring it into a serious relationship."

Theo lays his hand palm up on the bench between us. I long to take his hand, and I feel sick knowing I can't.

"Josephine, I can't give up on you."

"Pretty words. Unfortunately, I must give up on you."

A car pulls into the driveway, the bright rideshare sign glowing in the windshield.

Theo steps between me and the car door. "Please, Josephine." His voice is ragged. He's struggling.

I look into his eyes, caress his cheek. "Goodbye, Theo." I reach around him for the door handle and get into the Uber's backseat. As the car reaches the end of the driveway, I try not to look back. But hearing Theo yell my name, I can't help myself.

"Should I stop, ma'am?" the driver asks.

"Keep going."

Theo runs after the car as the driver pulls onto the road. I wish I hadn't looked because now I can't look away as the car increases speed and Theo fades into the night.

THEO

I run after the Uber, calling Josephine's name until my throat is dry. She's gone. Sobs rip through my body with an intensity that makes me gag as I stand in the middle of the road, waiting for her return. Headlights approach, giving me hope.

The car passes and honks. Its teenage passengers lean out the window, yelling wiseass remarks.

Josephine isn't coming back tonight. I trudge up the driveway and wander inside, confused, distraught. Pacing around the living room, I open my messaging app and, without looking at what Lexi wrote, delete the message thread.

See how little Lexi's messages affect me, Josie? I should call and tell her I deleted them.

No. When someone leaves, it means they need space. I'll give her what she wants. A day, maybe two. She'll come to her senses. She's rational, and she loves me. You don't just throw love away.

The sun warms my face. I should be waking beside Josephine. Did she text? No. My phone dings frenetically. Lexi. I grunt and delete the message without reading it. Last night's drama replays in my mind. The hurt in Josephine's eyes. Her angry words. Did I miss something? Could I have done anything differently?

Chapter Forty-Four

I'M USED TO DISAPPOINTMENT. So Theo didn't text. It's fine. I dump frozen strawberries and chia seeds into the Vitamix, add spirulina powder, dates, and coconut water, and blend on high speed. Knowing Theo is making the same recipe, probably at this very moment, doesn't faze me. I turn off the blender and go through the rest of the motions, ignoring thoughts about him as they vie for my attention. I take my breakfast to the backyard, stare at the rose garden without seeing it, and drink the smoothie without tasting it.

As much as I hate to admit it, my parents are probably right. Theo's views on business are patriarchal and reveal a colonizing attitude. This Lexi situation... Who but a colonizer would dismiss my wishes? I'm his partner. I *was* his partner.

In my mind, I replay the fantasies I had of our future, envisioning an eraser wiping away each scene. I had to end it. Luckily, I did before we got too attached.

Without Theo in my life, I must choose my path: move forward with my business plan and approach other investors, or start smaller. Forget a team of fashion artists and a store-front. I'll start with fundraiser t-shirts and sew them myself. I can make a landing page myself, too.

I choke on my smoothie. "Who am I kidding? Thalia had to set up my Instagram."

Theo's text tone disrupts my thoughts and opens my chest in relief. I knew he'd see reason. He loves me.

If you still want to make fundraiser t-shirts, call me. I'm free all afternoon.

T-shirts? I collapse into the lawn chair. Working with him would hurt too much.

My parents' words echo in my head. *You have a history of choosing men for all the wrong reasons. Men who are terrible for you.* He seemed so right, at first. Then it became obvious he neither values slow-fashion nor respects me. Painful.

If I seek investors, I'll find people who respect me and my values. I'm tempted to go inside, crawl into bed, and spend the day bawling, eating ice cream I can't afford, and watching movies. Dating later in life sucks. Breakups suck. This one is the worst because I felt more connected to Theo than any other guy. Plus, our adventure in dating not only hurt my heart; it screwed up my dream. Mix business with pleasure? Throw caution to the wind? Never again.

A mourning dove lands on the rosebush and coos, its haunting wail matching my feelings and reminding me of an Aunt Mary-ism. *Pay attention when animals visit; they have messages.* What did she say about doves? *Freedom. Possibility.* In the negative space around the creature, I see a logo for the fundraiser. A dove represents the possibility of healing and freedom for people in Cancer Alley. It flies away.

If I launch the fundraiser, how will I support myself? Can I segue from fundraiser shirts into other pieces? Nice idea, but unlikely to pay bills anytime soon. A disturbing statistic springs to mind: it takes ten years for most fashion houses to turn a profit. Two to three years to break even. I groan, hating the truth—I must find a job. Another opportunity to be mistreated while doing work I don't care about. The smoothie settles like a rock in my stomach. Job? Business? Fundraiser? What would Theo advise? Fear and confusion paralyze me, blocking my ability to problem-solve. I can't afford to stand still. More anxiety. *Do something, Josie.*

I open a group text as I return inside: **Who knows how to make a landing page?**

Kath: **K-Gallery has people for that, darling.**

Helena: [thinking emoji]

Sage: **When do you need it?**

Me: **ASAP**

Xavier: **I can write/edit copy. Free now. Meet up?**

Sage: **I'm at Manjares for another 45 minutes.**

Me: [folded hands emoji] **See you in fifteen. My treat.**

Not that I have money to treat anyone, including myself. Hopefully, they won't order much. I throw everything I need into my backpack, strap my helmet on and run downstairs, hop onto my bicycle and speed through town. How can I buy the materials for this fundraiser when my finances are so unstable?

Fifteen minutes later, sweaty from my ride and flustered from rushing, I join Sage at an umbrella table. "Thank God for the shade."

"It's a hot one. I have a hard stop in thirty minutes. What do you know about building websites?"

"I've updated several." I pull my laptop from my backpack.

We hurriedly discuss CMS platforms and agree on the best one for my needs. Under Sage's guidance, I set up an account.

When the server comes, I hand her a mason jar to fill

with green juice. Without warning, memories of Theo surge. I close my eyes to erase them.

"What's up? You okay?" Sage puts her hand on mine.

I swallow a jumble of feelings, wishing I had called her sooner. If anyone understands how hard it is to find love after forty, it's Sage. "You're busy. You don't need my drama."

"Not too busy to help a friend who's hurting. We're heading to Boston to see Wesley's family, but—"

"Josephine." Xavier smiles as he strides to the table.

"Hey!" I clear the emotion from my throat and make introductions. Just as well. If I went down breakup road right now, there'd be no coming back, and I need a landing page more than a shoulder to cry on. "How's it going at Social Good?"

He blows out a puff of air. "As expected, after seeing how they treated you."

I cringe. "Oh, no!"

"That bad, huh?" Sage asks.

Xavier shrugs. "I'm learning about the nonprofit world, and it looks good on a resume. Right?"

Sage and I exchange sympathetic glances. "Let me catch you up to speed real quick, Xavier," Sage says.

Twenty minutes later, I wave goodbye to Sage and refocus on Xavier's writing. We work steadfastly until PHINE Artisanal Fashion has a landing page. Woohoo! It still needs photos and a logo, and the copy is rough, but we're progressing. "Ready to finesse the words?" I ask.

He's looking at his watch. "Sorry. I need to be at work in ten minutes."

"Don't apologize. You've helped so much."

"Happy to take another pass at the copy before you publish it." He flashes a kind smile. "Gotchu."

As Xavier leaves, the server brings the bill. Yikes. I could feed myself for two days. I sigh, leave cash on the table, and put the cost into perspective. It still costs way less than a marketing person. Somehow, this will all work out. I hope.

As I unlock my bike, my phone buzzes with a text from Sage: **I'm free. Wesley's driving, and Felicia's bouncing to Rafi**.

I call and share the details of my breakup. Between Sage's compassion and the kid music in the background, I feel uplifted although nothing has changed.

"God, Josie. I'm sorry. What can I do to support you?"

"You already supported me. Thanks to you, I can move forward with this fundraiser. That oughta keep my mind busy."

"Yes! Focus on next steps. What's your action plan?"

"Design the logo, then the t-shirts. Create mockups for the landing page. Thanks to Theo, I know how to price things."

Suddenly I'm queasy. There's still a ton to do, and most of it's new to me. When Theo was holding my hand, I felt safe. Now he's not, which means I might seriously screw this up.

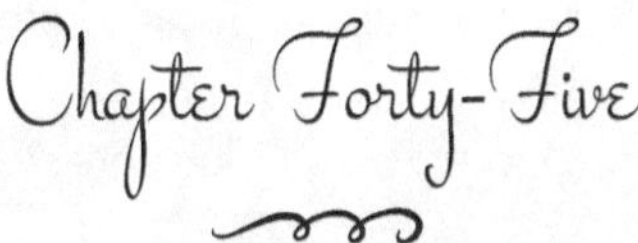

Chapter Forty-Five

THEO

FRIDAY. Saturday. Sunday. Nothing. How much space does she need? Josephine was excited about the t-shirt idea. Of course, we started arguing about factories during the fundraiser discussion. She needs more time to come around.

I move through my morning vinyasa like a slug, unmotivated, uninterested, unable to feel anything in my body. I'd better get over this fast, or this busy week will be a disaster.

Sunday night, still on the couch where I parked myself after yoga, I text her: **I miss you. Can we talk?**

She doesn't respond. Lexi, however, sends a picture of her tits. I delete it, as my soulmate's words replay in my head: *She wants me out of the picture. She knows how to make it happen, and she just did.*

Josephine has the most beautiful breasts. Smooth, firm, perfect size. I open a photo of her reclining on a boulder at Rocky Neck only three days ago. That light in her eyes undoes me. I grab a bottle of bourbon and return to my self-pity spot. Josephine's wrong about Lexi. Isn't she?

Yes, but Lexi's wrong about me. I text her: **I don't appreciate the pics and sexts. Stop.**

No response. Thank God.

Sunlight wakes me. Neck and shoulders uncharacteristically stiff, I look around. Still on the sofa. I groan and shove my face into a cushion.

Kim's text tone sounds. **You okay, boss?**

Fine.

Annie said your car is in the drive but you never came to the door. She wanted to call an ambulance.

Fuck. Get it together, Casabella. It's a breakup, not a natural disaster.

Boss?

I'm fine. Just…

Depressed about your breakup with Josephine?

How does she know? **Did I tell you we broke up?**

[eye roll emoji] **You were exuding jilted boyfriend vibes Friday.**

What?

Kim sends a grimacing emoji. **Over the line? Your personal life isn't my business. Sorry.**

I drop my head. "Fuck!" **It's fine. Thought I was covering it well. Thanks for the reality check.**

Now I notice the time. I slept through yoga. A first. Poor Annie. How long did she wait outside? I need to apologize to her and get my mojo back, but all I want is to lie on the couch nursing this bottle of bourbon.

See you in thirty, Boss. Want anything from the cafe? Croissant, quiche, latte?

Please and thank you.

I'm not hungry, but I'll force myself to eat if it will get me out of this funk. Maybe that's why I overslept. Did I eat this weekend? Did I shower?

Whatever my problems, I'm not subjecting Kim to an

assault of the senses. No need to sniff my pits to know it's time to clean up my act, literally.

After a shower, I shelve the bourbon and dial Josephine. Straight to voicemail. I struggle to sound upbeat. "Hi, Josie. I miss you so much. I know you need space, but we can work this out. We have business to discuss."

The front door opens. "Theo?" Kim calls.

"In the kitchen."

"Breakfast is here. You've got a busy day ahead. Pre-meeting research, then the biomimicry meeting, then follow-up. Plus, we're writing the Bioneers Conference presentation proposal, and your interview with Green Investing is at five."

I blow out a puff of air. All these events I booked with such excitement seem unimportant now. What does any of it matter when Josephine's not here to share it? Sure, my investments, mentoring, and chairing NorEast's board are helping bring equity and justice for all people, but.... I finally understand that Rumi poem. "Life without love isn't a life."

Chapter Forty-Six

JOSEPHINE

A WEEK of throwing myself into work has distracted me enough to dull the heartache. Whenever I catch myself lamenting or wishing Theo could respect me, I force myself to focus on the project. Now, I'm not thinking about him at all.

My new brand and logo have my attention, and I love both. The PHINE Artisanal Fashion brand (PHINE AF for short) is Playful, Heartfelt, Individualized, New, and Elegantly Earth-conscious. The logo, with its unusual font and intertwining letters, conveys it perfectly.

As for the fundraising t-shirts, I'll appliqué a unique version of the Cancer Alley awareness dove image onto each t-shirt. That way, no two shirts will be the same. It'll take more time to create, but as Theo would say—not that I'm thinking about him—the uniqueness will up the perceived value for each customer.

Ironically, since we broke up, I've had more time to read that book. In the chapter on manufacturing, once I got past all the stupid stuff about big factories, I read inspiring information about just-in-time manufacturing. Small companies can avoid large runs that force them to store hundreds or thousands of unsold items. Perfect for PHINE. Now, my only expense is the base material for the t-shirts. I'm inclined to take the pattern I cut for the embellishments and logo and start cutting as soon as the base fabric is en route. But what I read in the book convinced me not to do that. Following the book's suggestions, I'll handle tasks that lead to sales. Only once I receive customer orders will I actually make the t-shirts.

I also created mockups that show PHINE's logo on the left sleeve, and the Cancer Alley awareness dove emblazoning the front. Below the "buy now" and "give more" buttons, a statement explains how every t-shirt is unique. I email the copy to Xavier. He sends it back with tweaks.

With your purchase, you help people in dire need. You'll receive one of forty unique, handmade t-shirts, numbered like a fine-art lithograph and embellished with a dove crafted from found objects or up-cycled plastic. The dove represents the possibility of healing and freedom for people of Cancer Alley.

Much stronger.

I'm a solopreneur, so allow 4 weeks for me to hand-craft and ship...

Shipping. If Theo could see I'm offering shipping, he would choke. Or hug me. Luckily, I am not thinking about him.

I click away from the landing page and resume my online search for base material. At last, I find ninety yards of recycled linen-cotton jersey at Deadstock Heaven. I place the order, check that off my punch list, and look at the next item. Feedback, then Promotion. Is it ready? I send the landing page to Thalia, Helena, Kath, Sage, and Xavier for feedback.

The series of positive messages that flood my phone give

me courage, but I've been sitting too long. I stand, swing my arms and do side bends. If it's ready, why do I feel so nervous? I calm myself with yoga breathing, and the answer comes. Because it's a big change. It's the same feeling I get before every art show. Life will be different after this.

I do jumping-jacks, jog in place, exhale forcefully, and return to the laptop. "Here we go!" I let out a squeal and click publish. Nausea blooms in my stomach. I shake it off, stare at the landing page, check the link in another window. It works. "Oh, my goodness!"

I send the new link to the group and Thalia. My screen fills with hearts and confetti. I'd share it with my parents, too, if the mere vision of the logo wouldn't inspire lectures about brand brainwashing. Why subject myself to that? The only approval I need is for customers to order shirts, so I can make a difference.

Helena texts: **I'm back in Mass. Up for a visit? I need help brainstorming.**

You had me at visit.

A notification pops up: *Sage DesChamps and K-Gallery posted on Instagram.* I open the app and see my friends shared my landing page.

Xavier texts several lines of promotional copy to use on social media. Grateful, I create graphics to accompany his words and schedule posts on all my feeds.

Just like that, I've moved from the Feedback stage to the Promotion stage. Look at me go! Theo would be proud of me. Not that I need his approval. Wanting his approval is ridiculous. My goal is to make a difference.

Theo was helping me achieve my goal.

My heart sinks. Our sessions together and the book he insisted I buy truly shifted my perspective on business. Even our casual conversations helped. Without Theo's influence, I wouldn't have gotten this far.

My mistake was believing I was also influencing him.

Entrenched in his view, Theo couldn't see mine, or seriously consider it. These depressing thoughts have me craving ice cream again, despite my roiling stomach.

Enough, Josie. Theo helped you, but it's your vision coming to life, not his, not anyone else's. You are your own person.

"I am my own person," I say aloud.

An artist/businesswoman promoting your work like a boss.

"I am an artisan promoting my work like a rockstar. No, like a boss. Eew. Like a... oh, who cares? Look at that landing page, those social media posts."

My skin prickles. There's no going back now. I put my dream into action on my own, and what I do from here will help it soar. Or crash and burn. No wonder I feel queasy.

Chapter Forty-Seven

THEO

I'M FASTENING my seatbelt when the notification flashes across my phone: *Josephine Stewart posted for the first time in a while.*

Ignoring the heaviness in my chest, I click. Her post leads to an impressive landing page. She did it without me, without letting me know. Why'd I have to push the factory agenda? I swallow the lump in my throat. Well, good for her. She's launching her way.

As I drive away, I call Kim. "Hey, check out Josephine's latest Insta. Can you please repost it on all my feeds?"

"Of course." Her voice oozes sympathy.

Why couldn't Josephine have more sympathy for me, see how hard I've been trying, how much I love her? So, what, I encouraged her to use a factory? It's not a crime. What happened to all her appreciation?

Feeling unappreciated pisses me off. Another fucking feeling. If I could stop feeling so much, I could get my shit together. Thank God for my buddies. Camping with them is the perfect remedy for the swirling emotions making it so hard to focus recently.

As I pull into the parking lot, memories of our aborted adventure in camping overtake me, adding frustration to my damn emotional soup and tightening my throat. God, why'd I bring her here?

Several hours later, a collective groan rises around the roaring campfire into the clear night. I stare into the flames and wonder why I brought myself here. Why did I tell them Josie left me?

"Dude." Oliver gapes at me from across the fire. "What were you thinking?"

"That I care about Lexi."

"So you told your girlfriend that?" Charlie shoves a blackened marshmallow into his mouth.

"Should I have hidden it?"

Eric shakes his head. "Choosing her would've been prudent."

"I was supporting a friend."

Charlie spits out his marshmallow as he, Oliver, and Anthony double over laughing.

I expected ribbing from my buddies, maybe ass-kicking, not derision. "What's so funny?"

"Since when is letting a woman sext you supporting her?" Anthony asks.

Oliver grunts. "You basically told your girlfriend she doesn't matter as much as the woman you fucked on occasion."

"Must be some Grade-A pussy for you to throw Josephine away," Charlie says.

My stomach clenches. "What do I do?"

"Meet Josephine's needs." Drew's using that damn patronizing tone again.

"Maybe I'm not cut out for partnership."

"If you're unwilling to do the work, you're not," Oliver says.

"Girls, women, whatever you supposedly enlightened guys wanna call them, they have feelings," Charlie adds.

"I've been incredibly sensitive to her feelings."

Again, laughter peals around the campfire.

"Quit busting my balls. I've been trying." I kick an errant log into the fire pit.

"If I was sitting next to you," Raouf points with his marshmallow roasting stick, "I would give you the slap upside the head you need and deserve."

"On it." Anthony whacks the back of my head.

"Ow!" I side-eye him. "Fuck you guys."

"How would you feel if an ex-boyfriend was sexting Josephine?" Charlie asks.

I flex my fingers, in my mind flattening a faceless opponent with my fist. Not the solution. Not who I want to be. Anyway, Josephine wasn't receiving sexts. "I was gearing up to propose."

Oliver chokes on a s'more. "You're joking, right?"

"She's a kind, sensitive woman." Drew kneels by the fire, waving smoke toward himself and over his head. "You think she deserves a husband who won't stand up for her?"

Everyone stares at him, stunned.

"What?" Drew asks. "She got to me that night at the bar. In fact, I owe her an apology."

"Yeah, you do," I say. When my shock subsides, my mind returns to winning Josephine back. "How do I let her know I love her and can't see my life without her?"

Eric swigs his beer. "Why do you feel that way?"

"She's the happy ending to my opera. After Isabella, I gave up." I look around the fire. "With Josephine, I hear music again, see our future played out as if on stage."

"How does that occur?" Eric asks.

"By building on our deep connection."

"Wrong," Anthony says.

I glare at Mr. Know-it-all.

"Shared values," he explains.

"You haven't once mentioned values," Charlie says.

I scan my circle of friends, tiring of the heat coming off the campfire. "Values."

Drew looks at the sky. "Help us get through to him."

Raouf walks around the fire, I assume to offer a compassionate embrace. Instead, I find myself in a headlock, getting —of all things—a noogie and a lecture. "Theo, shared values and trust are the foundations of a healthy marriage."

"The fuck, Raouf?" I grumble and break free. "We're not in college anymore."

"True. You were smarter then."

"She's not realistic about some things. For one, she's anti-factory."

"She's right," Eric says. "You're a poor fit."

"What?"

Charlie says, "If I loved a woman who held her beliefs as strongly as Josephine, I'd at least investigate them."

"Fact is," Oliver chimes in. "Zora and I often disagree. Eastern Philosophy and Catholicism don't exactly mesh. But we work to understand each other and enjoy the common values in our spiritual practices."

"Michelle told me about Waldorf education. I thought: weird," Anthony adds. "Luckily, I listened. Wife's happy. Twins are thriving. That's what we value."

Drew's voice breaks. "Susan and I disagreed a lot, and I still fight with her ghost about why that meeting was so damn important, she had to get into the car before the roads were cleared. But we cared about each other's ideas. If you want to marry someone, Theo, you're interested in their thoughts and feelings. You don't dismiss them or try to prove you're right without considering their view."

"That's not what I did."

Silence fills the air, interrupted only by the sounds of crickets and the crackling fire.

I gaze into my open palms, recalling all the times I brought up factories despite her objections. I dismissed her.

"Look." Charlie claps me on the back. "I agree with you. I don't see how Josephine could watch that video from Lee's factory and not see positive ROI. But what'd she do?"

I close my eyes, waiting for Charlie's answer.

"She watched the video, heard your perspective. Josephine listened. You show her that much respect? You look into this... what's she call it? Slow factory?"

"Slow-fashion. In theory, it's great."

"How do designers put it in practice?"

"It's not fiscally sustainable."

"If I were her," Eric says, "I'd think you aren't interested in my world, and I'd go find a man who is."

"Fuck."

"Calling it like I see it, Theo."

"Ditto," Anthony says. "Don't seem like you respect her intelligence."

"That's one reason I'm in love with her."

"Your actions say different." Raouf pulls a beer from the cooler.

"Come on, guys."

"Why argue with us?" Oliver asks. "Accept she walked away. Move on."

"You're so into fashionistas, find a lady who works for Chanel or Dior," Charlie suggests.

"That's the complete opposite of what Josephine's about."

"Why?" Eric asks.

I'm about to school these assholes when it hits me. I don't have a clear answer.

Chapter Forty-Eight

THEO

I WAKE to a mosquito buzzing and a woodpecker rapping at
a tree. Oddly soothing, unlike my friends' words, which
hammered my heart and mind, infiltrating my dreams.
Morning dew makes the chilly air cooler, perfect for hiking,
but I won't be joining the guys today.

I hate to bail on our annual trip, but my hike will be to
the car. How can I spend another moment toasting marsh-
mallows in the forest when I should be learning about
Josephine's world? I roll up my sleeping bag and mat, get
dressed, build a fire, and set a pot of water on it. Before
travel, coffee. While it brews, I bang out a few sun salutations
and other yoga poses.

When we're having coffee by the fire, I tell the guys my
plan. Their smiles travel around the circle like a tenor's voice
in an opera hall.

I arrive home at ten AM, rush into my office, turn on the
computer, and dash into the kitchen to brew a pot of coffee.
What convinced Josephine that slow-fashion is the only way?
I need and want to understand. I've been so pigheaded, so

absolutely assured of my rightness, so confident that I refused to explore her perspective. It makes me cringe.

Then again, my role is helper and guide. Usually, I work with people who are more familiar with business principles than Josephine. It doesn't excuse my grandiosity, but I don't have to beat myself up over it either. Josephine wouldn't want that. She'd say be nice to her friend Theo.

Does she still consider me a friend? My stomach clenches.

All her attempts to explain slow-fashion, all those chances she gave me with the Lexi situation... Why didn't I consider how Josie would feel whenever the phone dinged with a message from Lexi?

As if on cue, she texts a video of herself making a kissy face. "Christ almighty," I say aloud. I told her once I don't appreciate the overtures.

Lexi, what are you doing?

Letting you know how I feel. I should've told you sooner.

I'm in love with someone else.

You'll get over it.

I growl. She doesn't have my best interests at heart. What kind of friend is she?

At last, the Moccamaster finishes brewing. Coffee in hand, I return to my office, glance out the window at the shore, and dive into research.

Lexi's text interrupts my work: **Going to NYC tomorrow. How about I stop by and we have some fun?**

Something in me snaps. I attack the phone screen. **You're disrespecting Josephine.**

So?

Shaking too violently to text, I dictate: **I won't stand for it. Stop, or I'll block you.**

You don't mean that. She sends a lewd pic.

Actually, I do. We're done, Alexandra. Goodbye.

I block her number. Instantly, I feel lighter. I should've done this months ago, like Josie requested. She deserved better from Lexi, and more importantly, from me. I take a screenshot of the final exchange to show Josephine, then delete the message thread.

Three hours later, back stiff, hips sore, I stand and stretch. I took in a lot of information, data, and ideology, and there's way more to learn. I'm beginning to understand Josephine's passion. But if I try to absorb more right now, I'll forget it. My brain and body need a break.

I head out the back door to the winding path Dad cut around the property. The full loop, with its twists and turns, is a mile. Someday, I'll show Josephine this if she'll let me.

Now, I take comfort in the beauty surrounding me. Calls of summer birds. Scents of ocean, evergreens, and wildflowers. Water lapping against the shore. The occasional whoosh of a car passing on the road not far away. Heaven.

Would Josie see me if I call again? I long to hear her voice, but it would distract me from the important work of understanding her world, hearing her needs, and figuring out how to meet them. That's the message I got from my buddies last night. Romantic gestures become meaningless without shared values behind them and a firm foundation of genuine care about each other's needs. Ma's ringtone blasts through the quiet.

"Hi, Ma. How are you feeling?"

She fills me in on the latest news from my brother, avoiding the topic of how she's feeling. "You sound dejected. How's Josephine? I never heard about the visit with her parents."

Frederick's tears fill my mind. *It was great, Ma. I repulsed them so thoroughly, her dad cried.* I take a deep breath, hoping my mother will respond with compassion and wisdom. "Josephine's upset with me. I... haven't been showing her the respect she deserves."

"Oh, Theodore."

Ugh. It's like I'm five again. My mother's disappointment levels me.

"Respect and trust are the cornerstones of a solid foundation. Didn't we talk about this when you were here?"

"Yes, Ma. I thought I knew what you meant. Apparently, I had no clue."

She sighs. *Sighs*. Even worse than using my full name.

"Based on how Lexi's kissing up to me at the library lately, I imagine the trust between you and Josephine is shaky, too."

A groan escapes my throat. "I messed up bad, Ma, but I'm trying to make amends now." I walk into the house and toe off my shoes at the door.

"How?" she asks.

"I'll tell you later. Gotta run. Love—"

"Theodore," she stops me. "You weren't unfaithful to her, were you?"

"No! Ma, how could you think that?"

"To hear Lexi—"

"You know me, right? Your son? Honest? Occasionally stupid, sure, but trustworthy? I'd never cheat on Josephine. But Lexi did create problems for us, so I cut her out of my life."

"Good. I love you." She ends the call.

More determined to keep researching and deepen my understanding, I make a green salad with marinated tofu and olives and eat while watching *The World's Most Polluted River* documentary on YouTube. Finally, I see the problem's enormity without the bottom-line clouding my view. I also see that some slow-fashion companies work with factories outside their region. I wasn't totally out of line. But I appreciate why Josephine wants to operate locally.

God, I fucked up royally. Will she let me make it up to

her? Seeing her perspective won't be enough. She deserves proof that I care. How can I earn back her trust?

I dedicated this morning's practice to deepening connection with Josephine, and I set the intention to open my mind and heart to guidance. I got into the rhythm of the vinyasa, flowing from one pose to the next before moving into a series of challenging arm balances.

Now, arms shaking, I transition from elephant pose to figure eight, wrapping my legs around one arm and extending them out to the side. The word *subsidies* flashes through my mind. Perfect.

As soon as I finish my practice, I dive into research. Zero subsidies exist for the fashion industry. No surprise. Yet government grants prop up industries serving over-privileged individuals like myself. Private jet manufacturing? Come on.

Subsidies could increase the viability of slow-fashion by supporting small manufacturers. I hate to involve Government when clothing shouldn't be a political issue. Still, policies create solutions to many problems. I'll draft a pitch deck today, have Kim look at it tomorrow. Once she's worked her editing magic, I'll send it to the statehouse.

Josephine might add something important. If she'll speak to me.

I lapse into a romantic fantasy, then shake the images from my brain.

Focus, Casabella. If I can persuade our lawmakers to act, we could create important infrastructure for Josephine's business. If she refuses to speak with me, can I be satisfied with helping her from afar?

<h1 style="text-align:center">Chapter Forty-Nine</h1>

JOSEPHINE

MY PHONE CHA-CHINGS, letting me know I received another order. That brings the three-day total to sixteen orders, plus $1,000 in donations. My body hums with pride as I refocus on the plastic food labels on my cutting table. While I wait for the base fabric to arrive, I'm creating doves to embellish the shirt fronts. After this, I'll embroider the PHINE Artisanal Fashion tags for the sleeves.

Thanks to Theo, I understand my business expenses include paying myself a living hourly wage for designing and producing every piece, plus my time creating the landing page. If I sell all forty shirts, after costs, we'll raise $5,600 for Common Ground Relief plus whatever comes in through donations.

The phone alerts me to order number seventeen, for three shirts, bringing sales to the half-way mark. I do a happy dance, then return to my task. I'm sliding the X-Acto knife along the bird outline when the phone rings. Automatically, I pause, but I'm not interrupting my work for anything, especially not for Theo's ringtone. "Deprogram that, so you don't feel excited every time you hear it," I instruct myself.

I'm not excited. I'm frustrated and anxious. Why is he calling? Not a word in two weeks, no doubt because he moved on with Lexi. Who cares? I have work to do.

I reposition the knife and move it slowly and carefully. The phone rings again, followed by his text tone. Startled, I jump and slice my finger. "Damn it, Theo!"

I run out of my studio into the bathroom, wash my finger and the knife, wrap my finger in a paper towel, dry the knife, and return to my studio, where, WTF, the phone is still ringing. Exasperated, I answer. Theo's face fills the screen, filling me with grief. "Hey. What's up?"

His smile falls. "Did I catch you at a bad time?"

"I was cutting an embellishment, and got so startled by the phone, I slipped and cut my finger."

"Shit! Are you okay?"

"Fine. Just a little agitated. So, what's up?"

"I'd like to show you something."

I sigh.

"I've been working on a presentation, and I'd appreciate your input. You have a level of expertise that I don't."

"Oh, yeah?" I stifle a laugh. Since when does he pair my name with the word expertise?

"I've, uh, been looking into slow-fashion, and I think you're right."

My eyebrows lift automatically.

"Kim thinks it's good, but before I share this proposal, I need to ensure it's not missing anything important."

"Huh. Okay. How should we do this? Orders are rolling in, including from you and Kim, so I need to make shirts. I have time for little else."

"You need food, right? Let's have dinner."

Sure. Dinner. Like talking with you doesn't hurt.
"Honestly, Theo, if you want me to have an intelligent

response to your presentation, it's better if you're not there."

"Okay." His voice catches and breaks my heart a little more. "Can I email it to you?"

"I'll try to review it over the next few days. Alright?"

"Great! Thanks, Josephine."

"Sure. By the way, in case you missed it, I'm offering shipping. You don't have to pick up your t-shirts."

"We both know driving my electric car to get the shirts is better for the environment than shipping, especially since I'm in New Haven often for errands and meetings."

"Great." My heart sinks as I imagine being near him.

"I had Kim share your Instagram post on all my social media."

"Thanks. I now have..." I look at my sales app... "twenty five orders total!"

"I always knew you could build a great brand, and—"

"Listen, I've gotta run." I need to end the call before he sees me break down.

"It was nice to see you," he says.

I press my lips together.

"Don't cry, Josie."

"Gotta go." I hang up.

My finger throbs. The paper towel is soaked through. I search my backpack for a bandage and antibiotic ointment, return to the bathroom, tend the wound, then lock my studio and leave. The temperature, sunshine, and light breeze calm me. I need to eat, pull myself together emotionally, and try to keep my hand still, so blood doesn't pump through it. The last thing I need is to bleed on my materials.

I stroll to the cafe by the park and take a seat outside. Money's tight now, but Kath will pay my cut of gallery sales next week. I order a green juice, plus my favorite comfort brunch: fried eggs, mashed plantain, and fried yucca with avocado slices and hot sauce. As I enjoy the meal under the table umbrella's shade, I open Theo's presentation on my iPad. "Subsidies for slow-fashion."

Whoa.

The first slide highlights data about US government subsidies. They exist to give different industries a chance to flourish, which ultimately should benefit all citizens. Agriculture subsidies lower prices of essential foods, so families living with meager incomes can afford basic nutrition. Thank goodness. Other funding programs make my stomach burn. How does a billionaire need taxpayer money to buy a private jet?

This is what my parents should protest, not clothing tags at second-hand stores.

The next slide talks about the fashion industry, damages fast fashion has caused the environment, ultimately sickening, disabling, or killing countless people. Theo found photos from different documentaries and websites, reputable sources like The World, PBS, and BBC. The images hurt my heart. He even found pictures of clothing being burned.

I take another bite of fried yucca and click through several slides. Now he presents the solution: *slow-fashion, an industry that's been growing with no support from government. An industry dedicated to the wellbeing of all, not just people who can afford outrageously overpriced garments made by someone who wasn't paid a fair wage.*

He talks about companies in the UK, in Portugal, the US, and Brazil—all making clothing and shoes from organically grown fibers and other natural materials. He presents a solid and clear argument for the benefit of subsidizing slow-fashion manufacturing in the United States, starting in Connecticut. He estimates the number of jobs that could be created if nascent companies like PHINE Artisanal Fashion and others were uplifted through government support.

Theo demonstrates the potential positive impact with a web graphic. He shares the meaning behind the movement:

true sustainability, community building, care for all. He shows the ripple effects from one designer in New Haven, to the locally owned and operated fabric manufacturer, to the local factory that produces designs for local designers, to the service organizations like marketing companies and shipping companies. Finally, to the pride of ownership that anyone gains as they purchase and wear a garment, knowing everyone involved in its production can afford a decent life for themselves and their loved ones. He also highlights the importance of a lasting garment, and the need for a shift in mindset from—

I can't read the last few slides; my eyes are so full of tears. This blows me away.

"He listened," I tell my iPad. "He respects me and cares about my values. And he's trying to help my business, after I ejected him from it."

We may be unsuitable life partners, but Theo's come so far my way, maybe we could work together. He didn't offer to invest though. He asked for my input. I wipe my eyes and read the final slides.

It takes only a few minutes to finish reading the deck, but a full ten minutes to pull myself together. I pop my earbuds in, open the video chatting app and dial Theo.

He answers immediately, sounding uncharacteristically anxious. "Are you crying?"

I sniffle. "I finished reading your pitch deck."

"It's that bad?"

"Theo, it's wonderful."

He visibly relaxes. "Thank God, and thank you for reading it. What do I need to change?"

"Nothing."

"Truly?"

"I'm impressed. Surprised. What changed your mind?"

"Love."

How am I supposed to take that? "You flipped your position because you missed me?"

"Nah. I thought you were wrong, and that I knew better. God, I wish I was having this conversation with you in person."

I'd be even more of a mess if he were here.

"Listen, Josie, I'm sorry I didn't take you seriously. I was condescending. I can see why you got fed up, why your parents view me so negatively. I acted like a self-important jerk."

"You did," I agree, stunned.

He flinches and continues. "The guys encouraged me to investigate your beliefs instead of dismissing you. So I left our camping trip early and spent the past two days immersing myself in all the info I could find. It's not enough. I could study a ton more. That's why I asked for your perspective. You understand this stuff. I'm just dipping my toes in."

"You found great resources, and I'm impressed with the way you put everything together. Clear. Persuasive. Of course, in my case, you're preaching to the choir."

"Kim said it's persuasive, too, and she's got strong opinions behind that friendly demeanor."

"So, what's next?"

"Well—"

My phone makes the cha-ching sound several times in rapid succession, drowning out Theo's voice. "One second. My phone pinged and I couldn't hear you." I look at it. "Oh, my goodness. I just sold the last t-shirt."

"What do you mean?"

"I sold all forty shirts."

"Congratulations!"

"Thanks." Theo witnessed my triumph. A thrill. Silly. I don't need his approval.

"Wanna celebrate tonight?"

Yes! And...? Confusing. Life without him has felt unbearable, but watching him move on with Lexi would be worse. "I'm proud of you, Theo. Proud that I had any influence at all. But tonight won't work. I need more time."

"Time for what?"

To get over these feelings so I can sit near you without longing for you. "Now that I have all these orders, I have to fill them." I force a laugh. "Don't get me wrong. I'm firmly committed to slow-fashion, but I imagine it would be a relief to have a factory handle this."

He laughs. "No worries. Although my proposal includes money for slow-fashion factories in Connecticut, I'd never assume you'd outsource production."

"This makes me more determined to get my company running, to build a small, happy team."

"We can still make that happen, you know."

"We?"

"Josephine, I want to help you, be with you."

I inhale sharply. The good feeling that had built up inside me leaks away. "Come on, Theo. You've got your thing with Lexi."

"There is *no* thing with Lexi. Literally nothing."

"You say that, but..."

"I was wrong about Lexi, too."

"You were wrong?"

"I'm sorry." Theo steeples his hands in front of his chin. "I should've stood up for you, for us. Immediately. You were right about her."

"I was what?"

"You were right, Josie. I'm sorry it took me so long to see. I guess nostalgia—Anyway, I blocked her number a few days ago."

My heart stops. "So, in two days, you did all this research, created a pitch deck, and set Lexi straight?"

"Sometimes I'm slow to catch on, but once I do…" He bows his head.

"Wow. And what are you doing with your pitch deck?"

"Bringing it to my friends in Hartford."

"Friends in Hartford."

"The only way to change policy is to reach politicians. I'm not deep in that world, but you don't grow up the way I did, go to business school, lead a Fortune 500 company without meeting people in government. Now that I know this is solid, I'll share it with friends who have power to make it reality, starting in Connecticut, then heading South."

"To D.C.?"

"Exactly. I've booked a few presentations to HBS alumni, too—Uh, oh. I didn't mean to make you cry. Are those tears of joy?"

"Mm-hmm."

"So, um, about that celebration…"

I flash my credit card at the server. "Helena's coming tomorrow, and I've got a ton of work to do."

"Later this week? Josie, I wanna support your business. You started slow, but—"

My bandage is soaked with blood. "I might need to go to Urgent Care."

"What?"

"I'm still bleeding. If I sew now, I'll leak on everything." The server brings the bill and takes my credit card.

"Shit. Why are you talking to me?"

"Waiting for the bill." I pack my stuff.

"Josie, your fundraiser impressed me. It's a perfect springboard to launch your brand."

"Thanks, Theo." The server returns my card. I sign the slip and stride briskly to my car.

"What's on the screen, Josie? Is that blood?"

"Eew. Sorry." I wipe the camera lens.

He groans. "Please let me call you a rideshare."

"I can drive." I unlock the car and get into the driver's seat. "Gotta go."

"K. Bye. I love you." He ends the call.

I stare at the black screen, stunned. He loves me? I didn't expect to hear those words from him again. Not when I was reading the pitch deck or hearing how he stood up to Lexi. Because Theo took so long to catch on. But he did what I asked. He moved past pretty words and took loving actions, like a man who wants to grow and become the partner I need. I stick the key in the ignition, confused and a little lightheaded. From blood loss, or Theo's confession? I don't know, but the sight of blood dripping onto the steering wheel is making me queasy.

Chapter Fifty

JOSEPHINE

THANK God for dissolving stitches and a good night's rest. With focus, I might finish embroidering forty logo patches before Helena arrives and make the remaining T-shirt embellishments after our visit. I get to work, thrilling every time the phone cha-chings with a new donation for residents of Cancer Alley.

I don't know when I stopped noticing my surroundings, but the knock startles me from my flow state. Hopefully, whoever is here won't distract me for long. There's so much more to do.

Helena stands at the door, hazel eyes sparkling, auburn hair cut in a flattering, asymmetrical bob, voluptuous figure masked by a black rain cape. We squeal and hug.

"Is it noon already?" I ask.

"I'm an hour early. I'm sorry. I thought traffic would be worse on 91."

"I'm thrilled to see you."

Helena surveys the room from the doorway, then tiptoes

inside. "I've been dying to see your studio since you left Louisiana."

"Please explore."

Helena moves around the space slowly. She leans toward mood boards, steps back to examine garments on dress forms, drawing my attention to different things that intrigue her. "In my alternate life, I would've been an artist. Instead, I became a yoga instructor."

"And now you run a neoprene recycling company. How on Earth?"

She frowns. "Family business. Dad insisted I replace him, and I saw a chance to change things. Hey, I'm a little antsy from the drive. Feel like walking in the rain?"

Arm-in-arm, we stride briskly past the Village of Westville's cafes and shops. Puddles dot the path into Edgewood Park, and the empty tennis courts and outdoor exercise station. As we cross the bridge under the trees, I glance at the full river below. Raindrops make ripples that form interlocking circles, an intricate pattern I'd like to replicate on a t-shirt. I could use plastic six-pack rings to signify the ripple effects of plastic manufacturing on Cancer Alley. "So, your father groomed you for the plastic business?"

"He tried. Oh, cool graffiti art." Helena says, as we amble past the community building and the quiet skate park. "He'd roll over in his grave if he saw how I've changed his company." As Helena shares more about her father, the company, and the way her colleagues on the board of directors bully her, I recognize similar dynamics in my life.

"I found my inner strength in yoga. Ironically, while Dad tried to control me, he accused my yoga teacher of brainwashing me."

Colonizer flashes before my eyes, followed by Mark's face and my previous three bosses. My parents spring to mind.

"You look like you've seen a ghost, Josephine."

"Your father wanted you to be like him, so he claimed

the people who encouraged your self-discovery were trying to control you. He was the one manipulating you."

"Sound familiar?"

"My parents…" I sigh and give Helena the lowdown on my relationship with Theo. "His mom loves me. She's totally supportive. My parents call him The Colonizer."

"The Colonizer?" Helena laughs. "Like some comic book villain?"

I giggle. "It sounds ridiculous when I say it out loud. And sad because I started to believe them. Theo never tried to manipulate me." My voice echoes as we walk under the stone bridge. "Thanks to him, I learned a lot about operating a business, like how and why to create projections, best practices in communicating with investors, and different manufacturing methods."

"Pretty basic stuff, no matter your approach."

"Right? You may have noticed I'm using just-in-time manufacturing for this fundraiser."

"Good strategy."

"Anyway, I see now that while Theo tried to help, my parents dismissed my work, made not-very-subtle suggestions that I'm a brand brainwasher."

"A what?"

My phone chirps. Theo. "Don't ask. It's their latest crusade. And they encouraged me to beg my abusive boss to rehire me, so I could have a job they approve of."

"Ouch."

Theo's text tone pings again, needling my heart. I need to deprogram his special settings. "Helena, if you hadn't shared your experience. I might not have recognized—" Two more messages come in quick succession. I stop and stare at the flooded grass by the duck pond. Is he okay? Why the urgent texting? "Would you excuse me?"

"Sure."

I read Theo's messages, blink, read them again. I text him a happy dance GIF. **Incredible! Thank you!**

"Good news?" Helena asks.

I describe Theo's proposal for slow-fashion subsidies, feeling more energized with each word. "Helena, he met with our State Rep, Senator, and Governor."

"So Theo's slow-fashion subsidies proposal could be on the docket for the next state congressional vote? Damn. What a self-serving jerk."

"Yup. My parents pegged him, alright." I roll my eyes. "Anyway, you wanted my help?"

As we turn around and retrace our steps, Helena reveals her insecurities about transitioning MacDowell Plastics' operations slowly, from making virgin neoprene to the less harmful process of recycling neoprene, and ultimately to producing bio-based neoprene. "I wish I switched gears at the outset, but I thought the board would warm up to my sustainable mindset if I eased them into it. I accomplished nothing by placating them. Now, I need your help brainstorming how to make a regenerative alternative."

I lift an eyebrow. "I'm a designer."

"Don't worry. I've got top scientists on this project, too. But they can be super myopic. You bring a creative perspective. We're moving operations to Massachusetts, near HQ, but we won't lay a single brick until we have a regenerative business plan in place."

"That's bold, Helena."

She hitches a shoulder. "Cancer Alley is too polluted for people to live. Once hurricane season ends, I'm shutting down our facilities, doing hazmat cleanup, and demolishing our buildings."

In awe, I say, "Let me know when you need me. I'm thrilled to help."

We exit the park and stride across the street into the Middle Eastern cafe. I slide into the plush booth seat, suddenly famished. The waitress comes immediately with menus and waters.

"Helena, if you like lentil soup, theirs is the best. Also, their falafel is light and fluffy."

"Sold. Are you having the same?"

"Absolutely."

The server takes the menus and leaves.

"Would you consider being on my advisory board for PHINE AF?"

"I'd be honored. Investors get a seat, anyway, right?"

"Right, but you don't have to invest to be—"

"I'd love to back PHINE."

"You would." My stomach tenses and I'm not sure why. An advisor. Additional support. Isn't that exactly what I should want? It's exactly what I need. Especially if Theo backs out of his investment. It's not like I have reserves to launch PHINE. I'm lucky I'll be able to pay my personal bills next week once I get my cut of the gallery sales.

Helena scans my face. "Did I offend you?"

"Sorry. You caught me off guard. You haven't even seen my pitch deck."

"Actually, I have."

"What? How?"

"I met a guy named Eric at a conference last month."

My mouth drops open.

Helena grins. "Small world, right?" She reaches across the table and squeezes my hand. "We're kindred spirits. We need to stick together to make the positive difference we both want."

"True and true. Thanks, Helena." Now comes the hard question. My stomach goes from tense to roiling. Why? Helena is a friend, and she raised the topic. She probably expects me to ask. "How much do you want to commit?"

"I'll know once I read your business plan. Can you send it today?"

"After I adjust the projections. This fundraiser was a test to see if I could get traction, and it seems I can. Also, I might write an alternate plan. Scaled back."

Helena cocks her head, questioning.

"Maybe I don't need a storefront or sewing floor now. I can operate from my studio, hire people for occasional piece-work until I have more capital."

"Send me your current plan. The scaled-back business could probably work, but your pitch deck inspired me with your vision for community regeneration created through fashion."

I purse my lips. Would Helena be impressed if we weren't friends?

"Don't sell yourself short. Several folks at the conference were interested."

"Alright." My skin prickles in amazement. I'm in a much different place than I was two months ago when I met Theo. Which reminds me, "My exhibit at K-Gallery is coming down this weekend. Wanna see it while you're here?"

"Totally," Helena beams, as the waitress brings steaming bowls.

The crispy, sweet fried onions and creamy soup dance in my mouth. One hour ago, I fretted over not finishing all my logo patches today. I felt guilty for taking time off to have fun. What a difference an hour can make. With Helena's backing, I can take the next step launching PHINE and attract other investors. Having a solid group of supporters will make success more likely. I need to apologize to one of those supporters ASAP. He may not be investing, but his proposal is bigger than me, bigger than New Haven, and there's no denying it will help my business.

That I allowed my parents to get into my head, to convince me that Theo, of all people, was trying to control me, is insulting. True, he was patronizing and dismissive on occasion. But from the start, he only wanted to help. But once we fell in love, I let pride and fear stop me from seeing him. While demanding transparency, I hid the truth from Theo because I feared he'd criticize me for failing. I'm in a better place now, with the soft launch of my brand complete and Helena's possible investment. Even if I were still floundering, I'd owe him an apology. I'll say sorry when I deliver his shirt. Theo deserves to hear it in person.

Chapter Fifty-One

THEO

THE LAST TIME I saw Josephine in person, she was leaving
in the backseat of an Uber, refusing to look at me. Yet I've
felt her presence these past few weeks, whether I was meeting
state officials or presenting the slow-fashion subsidy idea at
entrepreneur and VC groups.

Now, though she's surrounded by mist, Josephine illuminates the granite art gallery plaza from half a block away.
My heartbeat thrums faster with each step that closes the
distance. Can I hug her? Her smile welcomes me, but she
stays rooted, as if weighed down by the two packages in her
lap. I drove downtown under the auspices of getting my
fundraiser shirts. Really, I'd have jumped at any chance to see
her. Is it wrong that I want her to notice how I've grown,
how she inspired me to become a proper partner? Am I
wrong to want her back?

"Nice packaging." I sit at the tiny metal cafe table.

"You too." She winces. "I mean, nice package. I mean…"
She takes a breath. "Hi."

"Hi. How are you?"

"Great. So much has happened, you wouldn't believe."

"Tell me." My phone pings. I jump, then laugh at myself. A silly marketing text. I shove it in my pocket. "Sorry. I'm on edge waiting for word from the governor."

"When did you see her?"

"A week ago. The state needs funding for this program. I said I'd help." I wave a hand dismissively. "Lots of details. More than you probably want."

"I want details, but I only have a few minutes between meetings."

"Oh." My heart falls. I thought we'd get to spend at least an hour together, maybe the afternoon. A few minutes? "I hoped to take you to lunch."

"No time, but there's something I need to say to you in person. And here are your shirts. What do you want first?"

"Your call." *I'm just happy in your presence.*

She looks from the packages to my face, clearly deciding, bites her lip—sexy—and hands me a package. Brown paper wrapping tied with twine and stamped with her logo. "The other one is Kim's."

"I really love the packaging. Simple. Makes a statement."

She claps. "Open it!"

I slide the hemp twine off and unwrap the paper. The cream-colored shirt feels soft against my fingertips. "What's the fabric?"

"Unbleached organic cotton-linen deadstock from a factory in California. It has a nice hand, right?"

"Hand. That's the feel of it?"

She nods and presses her palms into her seat, gripping the front of it as I unfold the tee.

"Wow!" I feel her gaze as I touch the embroidered logo on the sleeve, the mesh embellishments that form a web—for me and Isabella?—and the brown plastic food wrapper cut into a bird shape. "I love everything about this."

"Really?"

"The details, like how you sewed the number into the hem: 8/40. That means this was the eighth shirt you made?"

"Yeah."

"If you hadn't warned me about wearing new clothing before washing it, I'd put it on."

"I washed the fabric, and I don't apply formaldehyde or anything, so go ahead."

I glance around. It's New Haven. No one will care if I'm shirtless for a minute. I remove my t-shirt and slip into Josephine's creation. "I love how this feels."

"Yay." She must enjoy seeing me wear her art because she's stroking her lips.

"How do I look?" I like making her blush. "Pretty good, huh?"

Her eyes flash, playfully. "It's a flattering t-shirt, if I say so myself."

"Aw, and here I thought you'd tell me how good I make the shirt look."

"Poor you." She teases. "Fishing for compliments and coming up dry."

I make a pouty face.

She smiles, but her eyes telegraph concern. "Listen, Theo. I talked with Helena. Hearing her story made me reflect on what happened between us. I owe you an apology."

My heartbeat speeds. "Apology for what?"

She smooths her skirt. "I should've told you I lost my job. My pride and fear kept me from opening up, and that's not what partners are supposed to do. I'm sorry."

I reach for her hand. She lets me take it but doesn't flip her palm over to meet mine. "Josephine, when you broke up with me, you said you don't want to work together. I'm not here to change your mind, but if I'm reading you right, you regret saying that."

She cringes and tears form in her eyes. "I'm not finished. More important than whether you become my angel again." She covers her face and grumbles. "My angel INVESTOR. Could I sound more awkward? Okay, take a breath." She inhales and lets the words fall with her exhale. "More important is that I own my closed-minded view of you. I felt hurt because you were defending Lexi and ignoring my concerns about factories, so I put up a wall. Once that wall was up, it was easier for my parents to influence how I saw you, even though I knew better."

I press my lips together. Josie said she was immune to their influence, but they got into her head, just like Drew got into mine.

She interrupts my thoughts. "You never tried to control me. They do, in their own weird version of love. You're not a colonizer."

"What do you mean, I'm not a colonizer?" I deadpan. "I had an avatar designed and everything. I'm getting the tattoo here tomorrow." I palm my chest.

She freezes, stares, then throws her head back in laughter.

"Come on, Josie. I had one designed for you, too. Mine says, 'The Colonizer.' Yours says, 'The Colonizer was here.' I paid good money."

"If you didn't order avatars like that, you need to." She giggles, eyes watering.

"The tattoo artist will use twenty-four-karat gold ink, mined and processed by children in war zones."

She holds her stomach. "Perfect! We can show them off next time we see my parents. I mean…" She flinches, looks down. "Shit. Is it really two o'clock? I'm supposed to be on Broadway now."

"Oh?"

"I'm looking at storefronts."

"Phenomenal. Seeing spaces, getting rent and buildout costs will enhance your—"

"Helena's covering two years' salary. And one of Eric's contacts offered free legal aid until launch, plus cash to pay one year's rent and buy four new PIPs."

My head jerks back in surprise. "Damn. You're impressive."

She beams. "I just toured that place on the corner and one further down the street. Not enough foot traffic." She stands and slings her backpack over her shoulder. "Sorry. I've really gotta run."

"May I walk you?"

"Sure." Her voice brightens, filling me with hope.

As we round the corner onto York Street, I wrap my arm around her shoulder, give a quick squeeze. "I appreciate your apology. And it seems I owe you ten thousand dollars, per my commitment to delivering once you got a second investor." I call up Venmo on my phone and send the money. "As you recall, these funds are unrestricted."

Josephine reels back. "Thank you! After I said we couldn't work together, I didn't expect you to keep your commitment."

"I always honor my commitments. That's why I'm so careful about making them. As far as collaborating—"

She interrupts. "I'm sorry I refused to work with you. At the time, it made sense, but we've both opened our minds and come toward each other's ideas. I think you've been a great influence on me."

"You've influenced me, too, to the degree that we may have slow-fashion production and employment subsidies in Connecticut come Spring."

"Sublime," Josephine says.

"Imagine environmentally safe, equitable manufacturing in Connecticut. All the speeches I had scheduled this week had a last-minute change of topic: slow-fashion subsidies. But it'll be a while before that helps you. So, if you'll let me, I'd like to invest more."

"Really?"

"You've got two investors already—"

"Plus, a possible third," she adds. "Another referral from Eric. He's reviewing my plans, and we're speaking next week."

I shouldn't be surprised. I believed in her for a reason. Still... "Josie, the momentum you've generated is blowing my mind. I'd hate to see it slowed by an ongoing search for money. I'll cover the rest."

"What do you mean, the rest?"

"If your first three investments combined cover thirty percent of your budget, I'll handle the remaining seventy percent. Whatever it takes to get you to one hundred percent investment," I explain, as we enter the crosswalk.

"Theo!" She stops, seemingly unaware we're in the middle of the street.

A car blares its horn, barrels toward us. She stares at it, frozen in place.

"Josie!" I grab her arm and pull her to the curb. "Careful, Hon." Heart thudding, I draw her close, protecting her, needing her near. "I can't lose you again," I mumble into her hair, unable to catch my breath.

She gazes up at me, panting.

A tiny moan escapes my throat.

Our lips are close. I want to kiss her so badly. But she has to come to me now. I won't take what she doesn't want to give.

JOSEPHINE

I wait for his kiss. Our lips are so close. The near miss on the street stopped my heart. Then Theo pulled me out of the speeding car's path, and his touch sent frissons of energy from my waist in all directions, reigniting the desire I spent weeks trying to quench. His heart pounds against me. We're both breathing heavily. He could lower his mouth. *Kiss me, Theo!* He doesn't.

I swallow my disappointment. How could I indulge that fantasy for one second? We met for business, not to reunite. Maybe I was holding a fairy dust speck of hope that my apology would heal our hurts, and...

Attitude adjustment. I'm getting way more than I expected. He's investing to the tune of... I recall the budget spreadsheet. I didn't realize he *had* that much cash available.

"Thank you, Theo." I pull away to prevent our lips from meeting accidentally, winking to lighten the intensity of the moment. "Partner."

What's that expression in his eyes? Have I disappointed him?

"I'm free if you'd like another set of eyes on that space."

"Great. Now that we're back in bed together." I clap my hand over my mouth. "I mean, in business together, I have so much to share with you."

I've been trying to move forward without him. But now, he's back as a business partner. (Despite it being a common expression, I will not say "in bed together" again). We can't help the chemistry, but I'll learn to ignore it. "Aren't these buildings great?" I ask. "I love how Yale designed the dorms to look like historic structures."

"Beautiful ironwork on the gates," he agrees.

"That was my dorm." Our fingertips graze, but I ignore the impulse to hold his hand. I can take a hint.

Across the busy intersection, the realtor, Yvette, stands out in a tacky red suit. As we reach the corner unit, she greets us with a super bright smile, hands me a listing sheet, unlocks the door, and begins her spiel.

The first thing I notice is the energy. The space feels vibrant. Natural light flows throughout, beaming from windows on the far walls. Two simple ADA-compliant bathrooms on the first floor. Perfect. Worn hardwood floors give the space an artsy vibe. Foot-wide chestnut columns suggest an easy way to segment the space, and I envision where I'll place the cutting tables, sewing machines, dress forms, and mirrors. I hold my hands up, creating walls and doors in my mind's eye.

"What do you see?" Theo asks.

"Fitting rooms."

Yvette points to a wood-paneled sliding door. "There's an elevator, but I think you'll love the spiral stairway. See the chestnut treads and risers? Original to the building."

"Beautiful," I say. An image of a possible future flashes before me. I send it to the back of my mind and climb the steps.

On the second story, I fall in love all over again. "I knew I liked this place when I walked in, but now?" I smile at Theo. "And it's within my budget."

"This is your favorite, huh?" he asks.

"It's got a great vibe. Sure, I'll have to build fitting rooms and a counter, but... How does that work? Do I find my own contractor, or does the owner require I use theirs?"

"They have contractors. Now, one of the great features is this back room." Yvette leads us down a hallway. "This could be a beautiful office."

Three skylights illuminate the large room, and French doors lead to a fire escape. I immediately envision where I'll put my desk, bookshelves, and cork boards. "This is the one."

"Excellent," the realtor says. "I'll get in touch with the property manager and set up a meeting."

I press my palms together, resisting the urge to clap and jump up and down.

We part with Yvette and retrace our steps, talking about the space, the future, and everything I need to do to file as an LLC and certified Benefit Corporation. When we reach the

corner of Chapel and York, I'm not ready to say goodbye.
And I've been having this nerdy fantasy. I may as well
share it.

THEO

People whiz by us, as we lean against the brick wall,
sipping green juices, and watching foot traffic across the busy
intersection. It feels like time has slowed, and I'm lost in
Josephine's effervescence. Her nerdy fantasy? Green juices
and foot traffic. I'm happy to oblige. Being in her presence is
a gift I will never take for granted or try to deny myself again.
"I'm so glad we're friends again, Josie. Thanks for letting me
back into your life."

She sips her juice. "You look sad, though."

"Nostalgic."

"Over…"

"Us," I admit, adding quickly, "but I appreciate friendship, and I'm thrilled to work with you again."

"That's funny, because for a moment on York Street, I
thought you might kiss me."

"Did you want me to?"

"Yeah." She gazes into her empty juice bottle.

"Why didn't you kiss me?"

She hitches a shoulder. "I can take a hint."

"What hint?"

"Our lips were almost touching. The chemistry was
there, but you didn't make a move."

"Because I screwed things up last time." And it still frustrates me.

"We screwed things up. Partners talk things through.
Instead, after telling you how important transparency is to
me, I kept you in the dark, then shut you out."

"True, I would've liked more openness from you." I face

her, the bustle of the city fading into white noise. "But did I create a safe space for that? Not really. I dismissed your business ideas when I disagreed. I dismissed your concern about my friendship with Lexi. I pretended the wealth and status I inherited had no effect on our dynamic but got upset when you wouldn't let me rescue you, as if your feelings and problem-solving abilities were inconsequential. And I said over and over that I didn't wanna hurt you. All while I protected myself."

She presses the bottle into my chest. "Hey, Theo?"

"What?"

In her eyes, I find safety.

She takes my hand, traces an infinity symbol into my palm with her delicate finger. "Tell me what you want."

"I want to know you see me growing, for us, if you'll have me."

"I do."

Those words send a thrill up my spine.

"I see you." She interlaces our fingers. "Tell me what you want, Theo."

"You."

She smiles, pulls me closer. Our bodies almost touch. "Tell me what you want, Theo."

I lower my face, hover a breath away. "I want you to kiss me." I feel so needy, so ready.

"Say it like you mean it."

"Don't make me beg," I murmur, totally willing to beg if that's what she wants.

"No begging. Quietly demand what you want."

I look into her eyes for confirmation, tighten my stomach like I'm in a negotiation. Ready to lead, I speak from my core. "Josephine. Kiss me now."

She raises onto her toes, closes the distance, grazes my lips once, twice, then presses her mouth onto mine, teasing my lips apart. I'm home at last.

"Theo," she murmurs into my mouth. "Are you crying?"

"I thought I lost you."

"I'm right here. We're here."

I pull her close, taking control of the kiss and reigniting our love.

Chapter Fifty-Two

JOSEPHINE

THE CHILLY OCTOBER wind sends dry leaves skittering. I nestle deeper into Theo's embrace, appreciating the buffer. "Here we are again, making out like teenagers on the corner of Broadway and York."

"A fitting way to celebrate. Don't you think?"

"Sure, and I'm excited to celebrate with you and our friends after I sign the lease. I never imagined it would take six weeks to get the paperwork." I sigh. "What was that, Theo?"

"What?"

"That look in your eye."

"No idea what you're talking about, Hon."

Something's up with him. He's been acting strange all week. Extra goofy. Mysterious. And the outfits. What could explain his insistence on wearing a suit every day this week, always with a shirt I made him? "Hey, I know you wanna be supportive, but you can wear other brands. You had a full wardrobe before we met."

"I know," he grins.

I crane my neck. "Is that Sage coming up Elm? See? With the big camera?"

"Hmmm? Oh, look, Yvette's waving from the storefront."

I wave, take Theo's arm, and stride across the street. We shake hands with the realtor and enter.

"I've been waiting for the owner," Yvette says. "We planned to meet a half-hour ago to review documents."

"I'm sorry you had to wait on my account," I say.

She shrugs. "It's the job. Although, all I planned to do was introduce you. I have another appointment in Trumbull. If you don't mind, I'll leave you to wait."

"What if he doesn't show?" I ask.

She looks from Theo to me. "I trust you folks to lock up. You may as well hold onto the key. It's gonna be yours soon, anyway."

Mine. A thrill runs through me as I take the key and watch Yvette leave. "How strange."

Theo nods, lips pressed tight, and gestures toward the back of the store. "Restroom. Meet you upstairs?"

"How'd you know I'd go there first?"

He points to his third eye, then mine and stage whispers, "One mind."

I giggle, savoring the view of his tush in his wool suit pants. Will I ever tire of that sight? I step lightly up the wide spiral staircase. The play of light and shadow on the wooden steps' rich hues is especially vibrant today. How is that possible? It's overcast.

One look at the second floor provides the answer. The room is lit with candles. Beautiful, but why? Who did this? And where did this handwoven runner come from? My body fills with anticipation as I stride down the red carpet to my future office. Classical music floats up the stairs, and I hear the elevator's hum, a clunk as it stops, its doors sliding open, footsteps. Sounds fade to the background as I enter the office. An antique coffee table stands on a stunning area rug. On the table rest two china place settings, crystal wine glasses, a silver candelabra, and a bottle of Verdejo chilling in a sterling silver bucket engraved with my logo. Delicacies on platters of varying sizes: quiche, apple tart, salad, sautéed wild mushrooms, olives, figs drizzled with honey, almonds and hazelnuts. My stomach rumbles. I've been rushing around from the moment I woke until Theo picked me up to come here.

Now, Theo's body heat warms my back and he lays a hand lightly on my hip. Comfort. And... I was duped. I don't know whether to feel charmed or annoyed. "The owner's not coming, is he."

"It looks that way." Theo guides me into the room, gestures to a huge cushion by the table. "But we're here. Have a seat."

Confused, curious, I sit cross-legged on the soft cushion facing the French doors. He sits beside me, fills each wine glass. "Josephine, ever since that first night you spent with me, I've had one special fantasy."

"Are you about to get kinky in my office before I've even signed the lease?"

"Put a pin in that idea." He winks. "I've been dreaming of going to the paint store with you and choosing a new color for my bedroom."

"Your bedroom. You've been longing to paint your bedroom?" I'm leaning toward feeling annoyed.

"I love it when you give me the evil eye. So cute. Do you remember we discussed what makes a couple's bedroom represent their union? We agreed they both should like the wall color. You don't love gray."

"Theo, are you asking what I think you're asking?"

"I'm hoping you're ready to accept now. Will you share my home with me?"

Charmed, I take his hand. "I'm ready."

He brings my hand to his lips, sending pleasant shivers up my arm.

"Also…" He reaches inside his suit jacket, pulls out a folded document. "There's a property manager who handles details, but will you take ownership of this building, so you alone are in charge of the destiny of PHINE Artisanal Fashion?"

"What?" My hands tremble as I open the document. Three words jump out: *Deed. Josephine. Stewart.* Is the room tilting? "Theo, this… the build… The whole building?"

"I wanted my investment in you to last a lifetime. Is that alright?"

"Alright." I grip his arm, elated. "It's… I can't even… Oh, my goodness. It's amazing. You are—"

"I'm glad you think so because I think you're amazing, too, and I won't be satisfied just sharing my home and my prime New Haven real estate with you."

He taps his phone and the music changes from classical to sitar. My hands fly to my heart. The Indian chant we both love fills the space as Theo drops to one knee, pulls a small velvet box from his pocket. "Josephine, your love nourishes me as I strive to nourish you. You inspire me to learn with you and for you. Please say you'll share this life with me. Since our first kiss, I've seen a future where we are husband and wife. Will you make that vision real?"

Theo opens the box, revealing a large square-cut diamond on a filigreed white-gold band. "It's conflict-free," he assures me, melting me with his earnest gaze. "Will you marry me, Josie?"

I laugh and tears spill onto my cheeks. I need to touch him, to anchor myself because this can't be real, but it is. Theo's on bended knee with a ring and the most thoughtful, amazing gifts I've ever received. "All these blessings. So much beauty and kindness, generosity, and humor."

"Is that a yes?"

"Yes! Absolutely, yes!" I take his face in both hands, nuzzle his nose, and bring my forehead to his. "Of all the incredible gifts you've offered me today, the most precious one is life at your side, the chance to hold you and rest in your arms. We may not be of one mind all the time, but we are beautiful together because of who we are individually." I kiss him passionately now, and he melts into my embrace.

From our first kiss on the beach to this one, the electricity between us has grown, the magic intensified.

"Uh, Josie?" He asks, brushing my lips.

"Mmm?"

"Would you like to wear the ring?"

I nip his bottom lip and pull away giggling. "Yes, please." He slides the engagement ring onto my finger. A perfect fit.

Epilogue

SIX MONTHS LATER

JOSEPHINE

A WARM BREEZE carries the scent of cherry blossoms and jasmine, delighting me as I cut the ribbon and pose for press photos with the Governor. Applause washes over me, its positive energy helping me push the heavy door open. After examining every detail during the build-out process, I can see each baseboard, wall sconce, and electrical outlet in my sleep. Still, entering now flanked by my fiancé and my daughter, I view PHINE Artisanal Fashion with fresh eyes. I greet my sales and production staff, accept a glass of champagne, and welcome the community into my fashion house.

My phone vibrates, and my parents' faces light the screen.

"What do you think? Lost or not showing?" I hold the phone so Theo and Thalia can read over my shoulder.

Sorry we couldn't make it today, Sugar. Urgent climate change demonstration. Dad sends photos:

He and Mom positioned too close to adjacent Monet paintings.

NO NEW OIL spray-painted on the wall between them.

Three younger people, also dangerously close to priceless paintings.

I gasp, praying they're not damaging art or risking arrest. **Where are you???**

Glued to frames in Yale Art Gallery.

"Oh, God," I say, then write: **So you tried to see me but got stuck down the street?**

"Literally." Theo rubs my back.

Thought we'd finish by 1. Security taking its sweet time getting solvent to detach us.

Thalia rolls her eyes. "Tell them this so-called climate action is irrelevant."

"Would hearing they're making environmentalists look bad wake them up?" Theo asks.

"They can't hear it. The hallmark of Narcissistic Personality Disorder is an inability to be accountable. In my entire life, I've never seen either of them acknowledge an error they made."

Join us after your shindig? Dad texts a selfie, cheeks sucked in. His self-important look. **Imagine 3 generations protesting together. The optics would be phenomenal.**

They sure would. Super busy here, though. Important day for me. I shoot a short video of myself, Thalia, Theo, and the crowd, and send it. **Good luck getting unglued.**

Proud of you, Sugar. Raised you right. Congrats to Theo on slow-fashion subsidies.

"Geez, Mama, even without coming, they tried to make your special day about them."

"Sadly, Muffin, one-upping is how people with NPD try to connect. Luckily, we're sane, and we have each other and Theo." I pull her close. "I'm savoring every minute with you."

Theo wraps us both in a bear hug. "Let's reframe Fred

and Margaret's misguided attempt to connect as one colorful thread in the fabric we began weaving today."

"I love it."

"Wholesome," Thalia says. "When do we start part two?"

Theo looks at his watch. "Half-hour."

As the ribbon cutting celebration winds to a close, I grab the mic from its stand near the threshold and thank everyone for coming. "Normal business hours start next Saturday. Now, I believe business oughta begin by being personal, so I'm inviting you to stay and watch the first PHINE AF fashion show. Trust me, this won't be business as usual."

I lead Thalia, Kath, Sage, little Felicia, and the makeup artist upstairs, past the dressing rooms, racks of ready-to-wear garments, and reclaimed wood checkout counter. Motion-sensor lights snap on, illuminating the hallway. Will I ever lose the thrill of unlocking my office door? It swings open, and I usher my loved ones inside.

Moments later, the makeup artist applies color to my lips while I savor the view of my daughter and besties.

Sage photographs the makeup artist at work. "Wait til you see yourself, Josie."

"Really?" I close my eyes and enjoy the soft eyeshadow brush caressing my lids.

"You're effervescent, darling." Kath beams.

"You've got a whole ass vibe, Mama."

"Stop smiling, Josephine," the makeup artist warns. "Mascara time. Look up."

A knock sounds and Raouf asks, "Is everyone decent?"

Staring at the ceiling with so much going on around me is unnerving. The door opens and someone whistles low. "Theo's a lucky man," Raouf says.

"And I'm a lucky woman. Raouf and Sage, let's catch up next month to talk about our collaboration."

"Absolutely," he says.

"Okay, you're done." The makeup artist turns me to face the full-length mirror propped against the wall. "Do we love it?"

I nod in stunned silence. Of all the things to make me emotional, I didn't expect seeing my reflection to do it. But I'm flooded with memories of each careful stitch, every important decision that led to this moment.

Now, Thalia, Kath, and Sage crowd around me, all facing the mirror, gazing at themselves and each other.

"You each look radiant, but this one steals the show." I gesture at Felicia, who dances in front of us, singing to her reflection and giggling at the gold-painted rubber duckies bouncing from the hem of her tiny silk and window-screen dress.

Raouf circles us slowly, then crouches to Felicia's height. "Hi, sweetheart."

Strains of sitar music come through the loudspeakers, our cue. I usher my "models" onto the sales floor. Raouf and the makeup artist disappear down the back stairway.

"Come with Mommy, Felicia." Sage lifts her up and blows a kiss. "Have fun, everyone!" She carries Felicia down the wide circular stairway as Theo speaks over the music, first introducing them, then telling the story of their dresses. The sound of Felicia crying, followed by the guests' sympathetic "Awww," floats up the stairs.

Kath winks at me and Thalia, mouths "love you," and strides down the stairs, looking regal. Applause wafts up the stairwell as Theo announces Kath and describes the materials and significance of her tea-length dress and accessories.

"You look stunning, Muffin."

Thalia sniffle-smiles. "You did it, Mama. I'm so proud of you."

"Oh." Sniffling, I grab a tissue off the checkout and run my pinkie under her wet bottom lashes. "Thank goodness for waterproof mascara."

We embrace tightly, air-kiss to avoid ruining our makeup, and Thalia saunters down the stairs. I wish I could watch my baby shine. Instead, I dab my nose, fan my face, and calm my thudding heart with yoga breaths, until Theo speaks again. He describes Thalia's dress, and my heartbeat slows.

Savoring the applause for my daughter, it takes a moment to catch the change in music to George Harrison's and Ravi Shankar's version of "Sahana Vavatu."

This is it! I descend the stairway, taking each step deliberately, slowly, head held high, eyes cast down like I practiced. Still, I see Helena beaming, Angela wiping her eyes, and Theo's brother and family smiling. Xavier gazes at Thalia, as if in awe. Interesting. Friends, colleagues, and community glow in the candlelight pouring from wall sconces.

"Our designer and fashion artist Josephine Stewart is wearing PHINE's first trashion couture bridal gown. Handcrafted by Ms. Stewart from upcycled silk velvet, vintage lace her great-grandmother knit, costume jewelry rescued from our moms, the pages of an opera program, and silk scarves I saved from another life, this gown tells a story about true love, shared values, and overcoming obstacles to union."

I pause at the bottom of the steps. Raouf moves like a panther, drawing my gaze to the camera lens, then he backs away. My focus shifts to the purple and white flower vines adorning the threshold where the bridal party waits, radiating love. Drew and Eric wink at me. Oliver stands tall, ready to officiate.

At last, I drink in the view of my man, fit in a charcoal wool suit and amethyst collarless button-down I made from raw silk deadstock. I float toward him, my hips swaying, watching his lips as he reads, "The only item not produced at PHINE Artisanal Fashion is the conflict-free diamond engagement ring by—"

Theo glances up, does a double take, and releases a slow

breath as he watches me stroll toward him. "Damn! People, I get to marry that woman!"

I giggle with the crowd. Theo winks at me and explains the Sanskrit lyrics coming through the sound system. "This song, traditionally sung by yogis before spiritual study reflects a value Josephine and I strive to bring to each day. Translated to English: May we be nourished together. May we work together with great vigor. May our studies be enlightening. May no obstacle arise between us. In everything, peace."

At last, I reach my bridal party, and Oliver opens the ceremony. When Theo speaks his vows, they fill my chest, nearly causing me to swoon. As I recite the vows I wrote for him, I appreciate how closely he listens. We speak the traditional words that accompany the ring exchange. I watch and delight in the sensation of him gliding the symbol of his commitment onto my finger. He beams as I slip the engraved white gold band onto his finger effortlessly.

"You may seal your vows with a kiss."

I tilt my face toward Theo, melting for the thousandth time in his warm chocolate eyes. He pulls me close, lowers his mouth to mine, and I am lost.

In the distance, someone clears their throat.

"Mama," Thalia whisper-sings.

"Hmm?" I open my eyes, meet Theo's mirthful gaze. "Oops."

Laughter surrounds us. The warmth in my cheeks matches the pink in Theo's face. We pull apart with sheepish grins as Oliver announces, "I now present Mrs. Josephine and Mr. Theodore Casabella-Stewart."

I bask in the words, feeling weightless as I join hands with my husband and step through the threshold into the sunshine on Broadway. We pause to savor the warmth, look at the city through new eyes, and kiss again.

Theo escorts me to the electric limo where the driver waits to open the door.

"Mama."

I turn to my daughter.

"Your bouquet!"

"Oh, right." With a last look at the yellow flowers I crafted from caution tape, I look over my shoulder, wink at our community, and throw my bouquet into the air.

Afterword

Thank you for reading *Refashioned by Love*. If you enjoyed this book, please leave an honest review on the site where you bought it or at goodreads.com, and please share it with your friends!

To learn more about the fashion industry read *Consumed* by Aja Barber. Or follow me on social media, where I often repost info about environmental issues.

https://linktr.ee/TaraLRoi will take you to my latest favorite online play spaces.

Discussion Questions

1. What did you know about trashion before reading this book?
2. What did you learn in this book that surprised you?
3. Which characters did you enjoy the most?
4. Which characters frustrated you?
5. Who would you like to read about next?
6. What did you know about the waste management industry before reading this book?
7. What do you think about making clothing from upcycled fabric and items people normally throw away? Would you wear it? Why or why not?

About the Author

Whether she's practicing yoga, weeding the community garden, or making fashion from trash, Tara L. Roí is often thinking up meet cutes for her quirky older characters. You can find her online chatting about romance novels and the writing process.

To set up a reading or other author event, reach out at TaraLRoi.com.

Get her newsletter *Love Notes from Tara* at xoxoTara.substack.com.

Also by Tara L. Roi

Haven: Love & Disaster book 1

Harbor: Love & Disaster book 2

Hope: Love & Disaster book 3

For the Birds

www.ingramcontent.com/pod-product-compliance
Lightning Source LLC
Chambersburg PA
CBHW020325010826
48973CB00005B/1136